Praise for *The Mission Song*

'Perhaps now, fans still praying for a reprise of le Carré's Cold War brilliance will finally get over it. He is the greatest spy novelist of our time...'
—*The Hamilton Spectator*

'John le Carré is a master of the dark, rich and profound espionage novel.'
—*Winnipeg Free Press*

'The failure of colonialism, the corrupt influence of foreign interests in Africa and the evils inherent in man are all on display here. Another fine work of intrigue from a skilled interpreter of all things topical.'
—*Kirkus Reviews*

'Smiles and sadness await the reader of *The Mission Song*. Smiles for the sheer brilliance of the work and sadness for the ending which comes far too soon.'

—*The Chronicle-Herald* (Thunder Bay)

'Amid the bursts of humor, le Carré convincingly conveys his empathy for the African nation and his cynicism at its would-be saviors, both home-grown patriots and global powers seeking to impose democracy on a failed state. Especially impressive is the character of Salvo, who's a far cry from the author's typical protagonist but is just as plausible.'

—*Publishers Weekly* (starred review)

'A tale that few could equal and none will surpass.'
—*The Observer* (U.K.)

'A fast-paced and entertaining book. Le Carré has constructed another one of his meticulous plots that satisfies in terms of theme, suspense and style. One is delighted by its satire, and moved by its insistence on the importance of doubt and the necessity of choosing responsibly at every moment.'
—*The Times Literary Supplement*

'Top-notch fare from a literary heavyweight.'
—*The Christian Science Monitor*

PENGUIN CANADA

THE MISSION SONG

JOHN LE CARRÉ was born in 1931. His third novel, *The Spy Who Came in from the Cold*, secured him a wide reputation, which was consolidated by the acclaim for his trilogy, *Tinker, Tailor, Soldier, Spy; The Honourable Schoolboy;* and *Smiley's People*. His recent novels include *Tailor of Panama, The Constant Gardener* and *Absolute Friends. The Mission Song* is his twentieth novel.

ALSO BY JOHN LE CARRÉ

JOHN LE CARRÉ

THE MISSION SONG

PENGUIN
CANADA

PENGUIN CANADA

Published by the Penguin Group

Penguin Group (Canada), 90 Eglinton Avenue East, Suite 700, Toronto, Ontario, Canada
M4P 2Y3 (a division of Pearson Canada Inc.)

Penguin Group (USA) Inc., 375 Hudson Street, New York, New York 10014, U.S.A.
Penguin Books Ltd, 80 Strand, London WC2R 0RL, England
Penguin Ireland, 25 St Stephen's Green, Dublin 2, Ireland (a division of Penguin Books Ltd)
Penguin Group (Australia), 250 Camberwell Road, Camberwell, Victoria 3124, Australia
(a division of Pearson Australia Group Pty Ltd)
Penguin Books India Pvt Ltd, 11 Community Centre, Panchsheel Park, New Delhi – 110 017,
India
Penguin Group (NZ), 67 Apollo Drive, Rosedale, North Shore 0632, Auckland, New Zealand
(a division of Pearson New Zealand Ltd)
Penguin Books (South Africa) (Pty) Ltd, 24 Sturdee Avenue, Rosebank, Johannesburg 2196,
South Africa

Penguin Books Ltd, Registered Offices: 80 Strand, London WC2R 0RL, England

Published in Viking Canada hardcover by Penguin Group (Canada), a division of
Pearson Canada Inc., 2006. Simultaneously published in the U.K. by Hodder & Stoughton,
a division of Hodder Headline, 338 Euston Road, London NW1 3BH.
Published in this edition, 2007

1 2 3 4 5 6 7 8 9 10 (OPM)

Copyright © David Cornwell, 2006

Manufactured in the U.S.A.

LIBRARY AND ARCHIVES CANADA CATALOGUING IN PUBLICATION

Le Carré, John, 1931–
The mission song / John le Carré.

ISBN 978-0-14-305684-3

I. Title.

PR6062.E42M58 2007   823'.914   C2007-903998-7

ISBN-13: 978-0-14-305684-3
ISBN-10: 0-14-305684-0

Visit the Penguin Group (Canada) website at **www.penguin.ca**

Special and corporate bulk purchase rates available; please see
www.penguin.ca/corporatesales or call 1-800-810-3104, ext. 477 or 474

'The conquest of the earth, which mostly means the taking it away from those who have a different complexion or slightly flatter noses than ourselves, is not a pretty thing when you look into it too much.' — Marlow.

Joseph Conrad, *Heart of Darkness*

1

My name is Bruno Salvador. My friends call me Salvo, so do my enemies. Contrary to what anybody may tell you, I am a citizen in good standing of the United Kingdom and Northern Ireland, and by profession a top interpreter of Swahili and the lesser-known but widely spoken languages of the Eastern Congo, formerly under Belgian rule, hence my mastery of French, a further arrow in my professional quiver. I am a familiar face around the London law courts both civil and criminal, and in regular demand at conferences on Third World matters, see my glowing references from many of our nation's finest corporate names. Due to my special skills I have also been called upon to do my patriotic duty on a confidential basis by a government department whose existence is routinely denied. I have never been in trouble, I pay my taxes regularly, have a healthy credit rating and am the owner of a well-conducted bank account. Those are cast-iron facts that no amount of bureaucratic manipulation can alter, however hard they try.

In six years of honest labour in the world of commerce I have applied my services—be it by way of cautiously phrased conference calls or discreet meetings in neutral cities on the European continent—to the creative adjustment of oil, gold, diamond, mineral and other commodity prices, not to mention the diversion of many millions of dollars from the prying eyes of the world's shareholders into slush funds as far removed as Panama, Budapest and Singapore. Ask me whether, in facilitating these transactions, I felt obliged to consult my conscience and you will receive the emphatic answer, 'No.' The code of your top interpreter is sacrosanct. He is not hired to indulge his scruples. He is pledged to his employer in the same manner as a soldier is pledged to the flag. In deference to the world's unfortunates, however, it is also my practice to make myself available on a *pro bono* basis to London hospitals, prisons and the immigration authorities despite the fact that the remuneration in such cases is peanuts.

I am on the voters' list at number 17, Norfolk Mansions, Prince of Wales Drive, Battersea, South London, a desirable freehold property of which I am the minority co-owner together with my legal wife Penelope—never call her Penny—an upper-echelon Oxbridge journalist four years my senior and, at the age of thirty-two, a rising star in the firmament of a massmarket British tabloid capable of swaying millions. Penelope's father is the senior partner of a blue-chip City law firm and her mother a major force in her local

Conservative Party. We married five years ago on the strength of a mutual physical attraction, plus the understanding that she would get pregnant as soon as her career permitted, owing to my desire to create a stable nuclear family complete with mother along conventional British lines. The convenient moment has not, however, presented itself, due to her rapid rise within the paper and other factors.

Our union was not in all regards orthodox. Penelope was the elder daughter of an all-white Surrey family in high professional standing, while Bruno Salvador, alias Salvo, was the natural son of a bog Irish Roman Catholic missionary and a Congolese village woman whose name has vanished for ever in the ravages of war and time. I was born, to be precise, behind the locked doors of a Carmelite convent in the town of Kisangani, or Stanleyville as was, being delivered by nuns who had vowed to keep their mouths shut, which to anybody but me sounds funny, surreal or plain invented. But to me it's a biological reality, as it would be for you if at the age of ten you had sat at your saintly father's bedside in a Mission house in the lush green highlands of South Kivu in the Eastern Congo, listening to him sobbing his heart out half in Norman French and half in Ulsterman's English, with the equatorial rain pounding like elephant feet on the green tin roof and the tears pouring down his fever-hollowed cheeks so fast you'd think the whole of Nature had come indoors to join the fun. Ask a Westerner where Kivu is, he will shake his head in ignorance and smile. Ask an African and he will tell you, 'Paradise,' for such it is: a Central African land of misted lakes and volcanic mountains, emerald pastureland, luscious fruit groves and similar.

In his seventieth and last year of life my father's principal worry was whether he had enslaved more souls than he had liberated. The Vatican's African missionaries, according to him, were caught in a perpetual cleft stick between what they owed to life and what they owed to Rome, and I was part of what he owed to life, however much his spiritual Brothers might resent me. We buried him in the Swahili language, which was what he'd asked for, but when it fell to me to read 'The Lord is my Shepherd' at his graveside, I gave him my very own rendering in Shi, his favourite among all the languages of the Eastern Congo for its vigour and flexibility.

Illegitimate sons-in-law of mixed race do not merge naturally into the social fabric of wealthy Surrey, and Penelope's parents were no exception to this time-honoured truism. In a favourable light, I used to tell myself when I was growing up, I look more suntanned Irish than mid-brown Afro, plus my hair is straight not crinkly, which goes a long way if you're assimilating. But that never fooled Penelope's mother or her fellow wives at the golf club, her worst nightmare being that her daughter would produce an all-black grandchild on her watch, which may have accounted for Penelope's reluctance to put matters to the test, although in retrospect I am not totally convinced of this, part of her motive in marrying me being to shock her mother and upstage her younger sister.

*　*　*

A word here regarding my dear late father's life struggle will not be deemed out of place. His entry into the world, he confided to me, had been no smoother than my own. Born in 1917 to a corporal in the Royal Ulster Fusiliers and a fourteen-year-old Normandy peasant girl who happened to be passing at the time, he spent his childhood on the shunt between a hovel in the Sperrin Mountains and another in northern France, until by dint of study plus his inherited bilinguality he clawed himself a place in a Junior Seminary in the wilds of County Donegal and thus set his young feet unthinkingly on the path to God.

Sent to France for the greater refinement of his faith, he endured without complaint interminable years of gruelling instruction in Catholic theology, but as soon as the Second World War broke out he grabbed the nearest bicycle, which with Irish wit he assured me was the property of a godless Protestant, and pedalled hell for leather across the Pyrenees to Lisbon. Stowing away on a tramper bound for Leopoldville as was, he evaded the attentions of a colonial government ill disposed towards stray white missionaries, and attached himself to a remote community of friars dedicated to bringing the One True Faith to the two hundred-odd tribes of the Eastern Congo, an ambitious commitment at any time. Those who now and then have accused me of impulsiveness need look no further than my dear late father on his heretic's pushbike.

Aided by native converts whose tongues the natural linguist swiftly made his own, he baked bricks and limed them with red mud trodden by his own feet, dug ditches in the hillside and installed latrines amid the banana groves. Next came the building: first the church, then the school with its twin bell tower, then the Mother Mary Clinic, then the fish-ponds and fruit and vegetable plantations to supply them, such being his true vocation as a peasant in a region lavishly endowed with Nature's riches whether you are talking cassava, papaya, maize, soya beans, quinine, or Kivu's wild strawberries which are the best in the world bar none. After all this came the Mission house itself, and behind the Mission house a low brick hostel with small windows high up for Mission servants.

In God's name he trekked hundreds of kilometres to remote *patelins* and mining settlements, never failing when opportunity arose to add another language to his ever-growing collection until a day when he returned to his Mission to find his fellow priests fled, the cows, goats and chickens stolen, the school and Mission house razed, the hospital pillaged, its nurses hamstrung, raped and slaughtered, and himself a prisoner of the last rag-tag elements of the fearsome Simba, a murderous rabble of misguided revolutionists whose sole aim, until their official extinction a few years previously, had been to visit death and mayhem on all perceived agents of colonisation, which could be anyone nominated by themselves, or by the guiding spirits of their long-deceased warrior ancestors.

As a general principle, it is true, the Simba stopped short of harming white priests, fearing that by doing so they would break the *dawa* that rendered themselves immune to flying bullets. In the case of my dear late father, however, his captors were quick to set aside their reservations, arguing that since he spoke their language as well as they did, he was plainly a black devil in disguise. Of his fortitude in captivity many inspiring anecdotes were later told. Whipped repeatedly in order to expose the true colour of his devil's skin, tortured and forced to witness the torturing of others, he proclaimed the Gospel and begged God's forgiveness for his tormentors. Whenever able, he went among his fellow prisoners, administering the Sacrament. Yet not the Holy Church in all its wisdom could have been prepared for the cumulative effect on him of these privations. Mortification of the flesh, we are taught, furthers the triumph of the spirit. Such however was not the case for my dear late father, who within months of his release had demonstrated the flaw in this convenient theory, and not merely with my dear late mother:

If there is divine purpose to your conception, son, he confided to me on his deathbed, resorting to his lovely Irish brogue lest his fellow priests should overhear him through the floorboards, *it is to be found in that stinking prison hut and at the whipping post. The thought that I might die without knowing the consolation of a woman's body was the one torture I could not bear.*

*   *   *

Her reward for producing me was as cruel as it was unjust. At my father's urging she set off for her home village with the intention of giving birth to me among her clan and tribe. But these were turbulent times for the Congo or, as General Mobutu insisted it be known, Zaire. In the name of *Authenticity*, foreign priests had been expelled for the crime of baptising babies with Western names, schools had been forbidden to teach the life of Jesus, and Christmas declared a normal working day. It was therefore not surprising that the elders of my mother's village baulked at the prospect of nurturing a white missionary's love-child whose presence among them could invite instant retribution, and accordingly sent the problem back to where it came from.

But the Mission Fathers were as reluctant as the village elders to receive us, referring my mother instead to a distant convent where she arrived with only hours to spare before my birth. Three months of tough love at the hands of the Carmelites were more than enough for her. Reasoning that they were better placed than she to provide me with a future, she consigned me to their mercy and, escaping at dead of night by way of the bath-house roof, crept back to her kin and family, who weeks afterwards were massacred in their entirety by an aberrant tribe, right down to my last grandparent, uncle, cousin, distant aunt and half-brother or sister.

A village headman's daughter, son, my father whispered through his tears, when I pressed him for details that might assist me in forming a mental picture of her to sustain me in my later years. *I had taken shelter under his roof. She cooked our food and brought me the water to wash with. It was the generosity of her that overwhelmed me.* He had eschewed the pulpit by then, and had no appetite for verbal pyrotechnics. Nevertheless the memory rekindled the Irishman's smouldering rhetorical fires: *As tall as you'll be one day, son! As beautiful as all creation! How in God's name can they tell me you were born in sin? You were born in love, my son! There is no sin but hate!*

The retribution meted out to my father by the Holy Church was less draconian than my mother's, but severe. One year in a Jesuit rehab penitentiary outside Madrid, two more as a worker-priest in a Marseilles slum, and only then back to the Congo he so unwisely loved. And how he swung it I don't know, and probably God doesn't either, but somewhere along his stony path he persuaded the Catholic orphanage that had custody of me to give me up to him. Thereafter the half-caste bastard who was Salvo trailed after him in the care of servants chosen for their age and ugliness, first in the guise of offspring of a deceased uncle, later as acolyte and server, until that fateful night of my tenth birthday when, conscious as much of his mortality as my ripening, he poured out his very human heart to me as described above, which I regarded, and still do, as the greatest compliment a father can pay to his accidental son.

*   *   *

The years following my dear late father's death did not pass smoothly for the orphaned Salvo, owing to the fact that the white missionaries viewed my continued presence among them as a festering affront, hence my Swahili nickname of *mtoto wa siri* or secret child. Africans maintain that we derive our spirit from our father and our blood from our mother, and that was my problem in a nutshell. Had my dear late father been black, I might have been tolerated as excess baggage. But he was white through and through, whatever the Simba might have thought, and Irish with it, and white missionaries, it is well known, do not engender babies on the side. The secret child might serve at priests' table and the altar, and attend their schools but, come the approach of an ecclesiastical dignitary of whatever colour, he was whisked to the Mission workers' hostel to be hidden until the threat blew over, which is neither to disparage the Brethren for their high-mindedness, nor to blame them for the occasionally excessive warmth of their regard. Unlike my dear late father, they had restricted themselves to their own gender when addressing their carnality: as witness Père André, our great Mission orator who lavished more attention on me than I could comfortably accommodate, or Père François, who liked to think of André as his chosen friend and took umbrage at this flowering of affection. In our Mission school, meanwhile, I enjoyed neither the deference shown to our smattering of white children nor the comradeship owed me by my native peers. Little wonder then if I gravitated naturally towards the Mission servants' low brick hostel which, unbeknown to the Fathers, was the true hub of our community, the natural sanctuary for any passing traveller, and the trading point of oral information for miles around.

And it was there, curled up unnoticed on a wood pallet beside the brick chimney-breast, that I listened spellbound to the tales of itinerant huntsmen, witch doctors, spell-sellers, warriors and elders, scarcely venturing a word of my own for fear of being packed off to bed. It was there also that my ever-growing love of the Eastern Congo's many languages and dialects took root. Hoarding them as my dear late father's precious legacy, I covertly polished and refined them, storing them in my head as protection from I knew not what perils, pestering native and missionary alike for a nugget of vernacular or turn of phrase. In the privacy of my tiny cell I composed my own childish dictionaries by candlelight. Soon, these magic puzzle-pieces became my identity and refuge, the private sphere that nobody could take away from me and only the few enter.

And I have often wondered, as I wonder now, what course the secret child's life might have taken, had I been permitted to continue along this solitary and ambivalent path: and whether the pull of my mother's blood might have turned out to be stronger than my father's spirit. The question remains academic, however, since my dear late father's former brethren were energetically conspiring to be rid of me. My accusing skin colour, my versatility in languages, my cocky Irish manner and worst of all the good looks that, according to the Mission servants, I owed to my mother, were a daily reminder of his erring ways.

After much intrigue, it transpired against all likelihood that my birth had been registered with the British Consul in Kampala, according to whom Bruno-Other-Names-Unknown was a foundling adopted by the Holy See. His purported father, a Northern Irish seafarer, had thrust the newborn child into the arms of the Carmelite Mother Superior with the entreaty that I be fostered in the True Faith. He had thereupon vanished without leaving a forwarding address. Or so ran the implausible handwritten account of the good Consul, who was himself a loyal son of Rome. The surname *Salvador,* he explained, had been selected by the Mother Superior herself, she being of Spanish origin.

But why quibble? I was an official dot on the world population map, ever thankful to the long left arm of Rome for coming to my aid.

* * *

Directed by the same long arm to my non-native England, I was placed under the protection of the Sanctuary of the Sacred Heart, an eternal boarding school for ambiguous Catholic orphans of the male gender set among the rolling Sussex Downs. My arrival within its prison-like gates one arctic afternoon in late November awoke a spirit of rebellion in me for which neither I nor my hosts were prepared. In the space of a few weeks I had set fire to my bed-sheets, defaced my Latin primer, absented myself from Mass without permission and been caught attempting to escape in the back of a laundry van. If the Simba had whipped my dear late father in order to prove that he was black, the Father Guardian's energies were directed to proving I was white. As an Irishman himself, he felt particularly challenged. Savages, he thundered at me as he toiled, are by nature rash. They have no middle gear. The middle gear of any man is self-discipline and by beating me, and praying for me while he was about it, he hoped to make up for my deficiency. Unknown to him, however, rescue was at hand in the person of a grizzled but energetic friar who had turned his back on birth and wealth.

Brother Michael, my new protector and appointed Confessor, was a scion of the English Catholic gentry. His lifelong wanderings had taken him to the remotest ends of the earth. Once I had grown accustomed to his fondlings we became close friends and allies, and the Father Guardian's attentions commensurately declined, though whether this was a consequence of my reformed behaviour or, as I now suspect, some pact between them, I neither knew nor cared. In a single bracing afternoon's walk across the rain-swept Downs, interrupted by demonstrations of affection, Brother Michael convinced me that my mixed race, far from being a taint to be expunged, was God's precious gift to me, a view in which I gratefully concurred. Best of all he loved my ability, which I was bold enough to demonstrate to him, to glide without hiatus from one language to another. At the Mission house I had paid dearly for showing off my talents but under Brother Michael's doting eye they acquired near-Heavenly status:

'What greater blessing, my dear Salvo,' he cried, while a wiry fist shot out of his habit to punch the air and the other foraged guiltily among my clothing, 'than to be the bridge, the indispensable link, between God's striving souls? To draw His children together in harmonious and mutual understanding?'

What Michael didn't already know of my life history I soon recounted to him in the course of our excursions. I told him of my magic nights at the fireside of the servants' hostel. I described how, in my father's last years, he and I would journey to an outlying village, and while he was conferring with the elders I would be down on the river bank with the children bartering the words and idioms that were my day-and-night preoccupation. Others might look to rough games, wild animals, plants or native dance as their path to happiness, but Salvo the secret child had opted for the lilting intimacies of the African voice in its myriad shades and variations.

And it was while I was recalling these and similar adventures that Brother Michael was granted his Damascene epiphany.

'As the Lord hath been pleased to sow in you, Salvo, so let us now together *reap*!' he cried.

And reap we did. Deploying skills better suited to a military commander than a monk, the aristocratic Michael studied prospectuses, compared fees, marched me to interviews, vetted my prospective tutors, male or female, and stood over me while I enrolled myself. His purposes, inflamed by adoration, were as implacable as his faith. I was to receive formal grounding in each and every one of my languages. I was to rediscover those that in the course of my roving childhood had fallen by the wayside.

How was all this to be paid for? By a certain angel delivered to us in the form of Michael's rich sister Imelda, whose pillared house of honey-golden sandstone, nestling in the folds of middle Somerset, became my sanctuary away from the Sanctuary. In Willowbrook, where rescued pit-ponies grazed in the paddock and each dog had its own armchair, there lived three hearty sisters of whom Imelda was the eldest. We had a private chapel and an Angelus bell, a ha-ha and an ice-house and a croquet lawn and weeping lime trees that blew down in gales. We had Uncle Henry's

Room because Aunt Imelda was the widow of a war hero named Henry who single-handed had made England safe for us, and there he was, from his first teddy-bear lying on his pillow to his Last Letter from the Front in a gold-cased lectern. But no photograph, thank you. Aunt Imelda, who was as tart in manner as she was soft in heart, remembered Henry *perfectly* well *without*, and that way she kept him to herself.

*   *   *

But Brother Michael knew my weak spots too. He knew that child prodigies—for as such he saw me—must be restrained as well as nurtured. He knew I was diligent but headlong: too eager to give myself to anyone who was kind to me, too fearful of being rejected, ignored or worst of all laughed at, too swift to embrace whatever was offered me for fear I wouldn't get another chance. He treasured as much as I did my mynah-bird ear and jackdaw memory, but insisted I practise them as diligently as a musician his instrument, or a priest his faith. He knew that every language was precious to me, not only the heavy-weights but the little ones that were condemned to die for want of written form; that the missionary's son needed to run after these erring sheep and lead them back to the fold; that I heard legend, history, fable and poetry in them and the voice of my imagined mother regaling me with spirit-tales. He knew that a young man who has his ears open to every human nuance and inflexion is the most suggestible, the most malleable, the most innocent and easily misled. Salvo, he would say, take care. There are people out there whom God alone can love.

It was Michael also who, by forcing me down the hard road of discipline, turned my unusual talents into a versatile machine. Nothing of his Salvo should go to waste, he insisted, nothing be allowed to rust for want of use. Every muscle and fibre of my divine gift must receive its daily workout in the gymnasium of the mind, first by way of private tutors, afterwards at the School of Oriental and African Studies in London, where I obtained First Class honours in African Language and Culture, specialising in Swahili with French a given. And finally in Edinburgh where I achieved the crowning glory: a Master of Science degree in Translation and Public Service Interpreting.

Thus by the close of my studies I boasted more diplomas and interpreterships than half the flyblown translation agencies hawking their grubby services up and down Chancery Lane. And Brother Michael, dying on his iron cot, was able to stroke my hands and assure me that I was his finest creation, in recognition of which he pressed upon me a gold wristwatch, a present to him from Imelda whom God preserve, entreating me to keep it wound at all times as a symbol of our bond beyond the grave.

*   *   *

Never mistake, please, your mere translator for your top interpreter. An interpreter is a translator, true, but not the other way round. A translator can be anyone with half a language skill and a dictionary and a desk to sit at while he burns the midnight oil: pensioned-off Polish cavalry officers, underpaid overseas students, minicab drivers, part-time waiters and supply teachers, and anyone else who is prepared to sell his soul for seventy quid a thousand. He has nothing in common with the simultaneous interpreter sweating it out through six hours of complex negotiations. Your top interpreter has to think as fast as a numbers boy in a coloured jacket buying financial futures. Better sometimes if he doesn't think at all, but orders the spinning cogs on both sides of his head to mesh together, then sits back and waits to see what pours out of his mouth.

People come up to me sometimes during conferences, usually at the teasy end of the day between close of business and the cocktail frenzy. 'Hey, Salvo, settle an argument for us, will you? What's your mother tongue?' And if I consider they're being a bit uppity, which they usually are because they have by now convinced themselves they're the most important people on the planet, I'll turn the question round on them. 'Depends who my mother was, doesn't it?' I reply, with this enigmatic smile I've got. And after that, they leave me with my book.

But I like them to wonder. It shows me that I've got my voice right. My English voice, I mean. It isn't upper, middle or coach. It isn't *faux royale*, neither is it the Received Pronunciation derided by the British Left. It is, if anything at all, aggressively neuter, pitched at the extreme centre of Anglophone society. It's not the sort of English where people say, 'Ah, that's where he was dragged up, that's who he's trying to be, that's who his parents were, poor chap, and that's where he went to school.' It does not—unlike my French which, strive as I may, will never totally rid itself of its African burden— betray my mixed origins. It's not regional, it's not your Blairite wannabe-classless slur or your high-Tory curdled cockney or your Caribbean melody. And it hasn't so much as a trace of the gone-away vowels of my dear late father's Irish brogue. I loved his voice, and love it still, but it was his and never mine.

No. My spoken English is blank, scrubbed clean and unbranded, except for an occasional beauty spot: a deliberate sub-Saharan lilt, which I refer to sportingly as my drop of milk in the coffee. I like it, clients like it. It gives them the feeling I'm comfortable with myself. I'm not in their camp but I'm not in the other fellow's either. I'm stuck out there in mid-ocean and being what Brother Michael always said I should be: the bridge, the indispensable link between God's striving souls. Each man has his vanity and mine is about being the one person in the room nobody can do without.

And that's the person I wanted to be for my ravish- ing wife Penelope as I half killed myself racing up two flights of stone steps in my desperate effort not to be late for the festivities being held in her honour in the upstairs rooms of a fashionable winery in London's Canary Wharf, capital of our great British newspaper industry, prior to a formal dinner for the selected few at the exclusive Kensington home of her paper's newest billionaire proprietor.

*   *   *

Only twelve minutes late by Aunt Imelda's gold watch, you may say, and to all outward appearances salon fresh, which in bomb-scared London with half the tube stations on the blink might be regarded as an achievement, but to Salvo the hyper-conscientious husband it could as well have been twelve hours. Penelope's big night, the biggest of her meteoric career to date, and me her husband rolling up after all the guests have walked over from her paper's offices across the road. From the North London District Hospital where I had been unavoidably detained since the previous evening by circumstances outside my control, I had splashed out on a cab all the way home to Battersea, and made it wait while I quick-changed into my brand-new dinner jacket, this being *de rigueur* at the proprietor's table, with no chance to shave or shower or brush my teeth. By the time I arrived at the due destination and in the appropriate costume, I was in a muck sweat, but somehow I had made it and here I was; and here *they* were, a hundred or more of Penelope's assorted colleagues, the upper few in dinner jackets and long dresses, the rest smart-casual, and all of them crowded into a first-floor function room with low beams and plastic suits of armour on the wall, drinking warm white wine with their elbows out, and me the latecomer stuck at the edge with the waiters, mostly black.

I couldn't see her to begin with. I thought she'd gone AWOL like her husband. Then I had a moment hoping she'd decided to stage a late entry, until I spotted her squashed up at the far end of the room engaged in animated conversation with her paper's top brass and wearing the latest thing in flowing satin trouser-suits that she must have bought herself as a present and changed into at her office or wherever she'd last been. Why, oh why—cried one side of my head—had I not bought it for her? Why hadn't I said to her a week ago over breakfast or in bed, assuming she was there to say it to: Penelope my darling, I've had this great idea, let's go to Knightsbridge together and choose ourselves a new outfit for your big night, all on me? Shopping is what she likes best. I could have made an occasion of it, played her gentleman admirer, dined her at one of her favourite restaurants, never mind she's earning twice the money I am, plus perks you wouldn't believe.

On the other hand, for reasons to be addressed in a more reposeful moment, there was another side of my head that was very pleased I hadn't made any such proposal, which has nothing to do with the money, but says much for the contrary currents of the human mind under stress.

An unknown hand pinched my bottom. I swung round to meet the beatific gaze of Jellicoe, alias Jelly, the paper's latest Young White Hope, recently poached from a rival newspaper. Lank, drunk and whimsical as usual, he was tendering a hand-rolled cigarette between his slender finger and thumb.

'Penelope, it's me, I made it!' I yelled, ignoring him. 'Tough time at the hospital. Terribly sorry!'

Sorry for what? For the tough time? A couple of heads turned. *Oh him. Salvo. Penelope's spearman.* I tried louder, deploying wit. 'Hey, Penelope! Remember me? It's me, your late husband,' and I got myself all geared up to launch into an over-elaborate cover story about how one of my hospitals—I would not for security reasons have mentioned which—had summoned me to the bedside of a dying Rwandan man with a criminal history who kept going in and out of consciousness, requiring me to interpret not only for the nursing staff but for two Scotland Yard detectives as well, which I hoped was a predicament she would take to heart: poor Salvo. I saw a creamy smile come over her face, and I thought I'd got through to her till I realised it was beamed upwards at the thick-necked male who was standing on a chair in his dinner jacket shouting, '*Quiet, damn you! Will you shut the fuck up, all of you!*' in a Scottish brogue.

At once his unruly audience fell silent, gathering to him with sheepish obedience. For this was none other than Penelope's all-powerful editor-in-chief Fergus Thorne, known in press circles as Thorne the Horn, announcing that he proposed to make a facetious speech about my wife. I hopped about, I did my utmost to make eye contact with her, but the face from which I craved absolution was lifted to her boss like a flower to the sun's life-giving rays.

'Now we all *know* Penelope,' Thorne the Horn was saying, to jeers of sycophantic laughter which annoyed me, 'and we all *love* Penelope'—a significant pause— 'from our respective positions.'

I was trying to squeeze my way through to her but the ranks had closed and Penelope was being handed forward like the blushing bride till she was stationed obediently at Mr Thorne's feet, incidentally providing him with a bird's-eye view down the front of her highly revealing outfit. And it was beginning to enter my mind that she might not have registered my absence, let alone my presence, when my attention was diverted by what I diagnosed as God's judgment upon me in the form of a force twelve heart attack. My chest was trembling, I could feel a numbness spreading in rhythmic waves from my left nipple, and I thought my time had come and serve me right. It was only when I clapped my hand to the afflicted area that I realised that my cellphone was summoning me in its unfamiliar vibrator mode which was how I had set it prior to departure from the hospital one hour and thirty-five minutes previously.

My exclusion from the throng now turned to my advantage. While Mr Thorne developed his double-edged remarks about my wife, I was able to tiptoe gratefully towards a door marked TOILETS. Making good my exit, I glanced back one more time to see Penelope's newly coiffed head lifted to her employer, her lips parted in pleasurable surprise and her breasts on full parade inside the skimpy upper section of her trouser-suit. I let my phone go on trembling till I was down three steps into a quiet corridor, pressed green and held my breath. But instead of the voice I feared and longed to hear above all others, I got the avuncular north country burr of Mr Anderson of the Ministry of Defence, wanting to know whether I was free to take on a bit of rather vital interpreting for my country at short notice, which he sincerely hoped I was.

That Mr Anderson should be calling a mere part-timer such as myself in person indicated the magnitude of the crisis at hand. My normal contact was Barney, his flamboyant floor manager. Twice in the last ten days Barney had put me on standby for what he called a hot one, only to tell me I could stand down again.

'*Now*, Mr Anderson?'

'This minute. Preferably sooner, if that's convenient. Sorry to break up your drinks party and all that, but we need you fast,' he continued, and I suppose I should have been surprised that he knew about Penelope's party but I wasn't. Mr Anderson was a man who made it his business to know things denied to humbler mortals. 'It's your home territory, Salvo, your heartland.'

'But Mr Anderson.'

'What is it, son?'

'It isn't just her drinks party. There's the new proprietor's dinner afterwards. Black tie,' I added, to impress. 'It's unprecedented. For a *proprietor*, I mean. Editor-in-Chief, yes. But *proprietor*—' Call it guilt, call it sentiment, I owed it to Penelope to put up a show of resistance.

A silence followed as if I had caught him on the back foot, but nobody does that to Mr Anderson, he's the rock on which his own church is built.

'Is that what you're wearing, is it, son? A dinner jacket?'

'It is indeed, Mr Anderson.'

'Now? As we speak? You've got it on?'

'Yes.' What did he suppose? That I was attending a Bacchanalia? 'How long's it for anyway?' I asked in the ensuing silence, made deeper, I suspected, by the fact that he had put his massive hand over the mouthpiece.

'How long's what, son?'—as if he'd lost the thread.

'The assignment, sir. The urgent job you need me for. How long?'

'Two days. Call it three for safety. They'll pay good money, they expect to. Five K American would not be considered excessive.' And after further off-air consultation, in a tone of evident relief: 'Clothing can be found, Salvo. Clothing I am told is not a problem.'

Alerted by his use of the Passive Voice, I would have liked to enquire who *they* were who were offering me this totally unprecedented bonus instead of the modest retainer plus hours which normally is all you get for the honour of protecting your country, but a natural deference restrained me, which with Mr Anderson it usually did.

'I'm due in the High Court on Monday, Mr Anderson. It's a big case,' I pleaded. And donning my uxorial hat for the third and final time, 'I mean, what do I tell my wife?'

'A replacement has already been found for you, Salvo, and the High Court is comfortable with the new arrangements, thank you.' He paused, and when Mr Anderson pauses, you pause too. 'Regarding your wife, you may say that a long-standing corporate client requires your services as a matter of urgency, and you cannot afford to disappoint them.'

'Right, sir. Understood.'

'Further explanations will tie you in knots, so do not on any account attempt one. That's the whole caboosh you're wearing, is it? Shiny shoes, dress shirt, the lot?'

Through the swirling mists of my perplexity I admitted that it was indeed the whole caboosh.

'Why am I not hearing inane party chatter in the background?'

I explained that I had removed myself to a corridor in order to take his call.

'Do you have a separate exit within your reach?'

A descending staircase lay open at my feet, and amid my confusion I must have said as much.

'Then do not return to the party. When you emerge onto the street, look to your left and you will see a blue Mondeo parked outside a betting shop. Last three letters of the registration LTU, white driver name of Fred. What size shoes do you take?'

No man on earth forgets his own shoe size, yet I had to reach deep into my memory to retrieve it. Nine.

'Would that be a wide fitting or slim?'

Wide, sir, I said. I might have added that Brother Michael used to say I had an African's feet, but I didn't. My mind was not with Brother Michael or my feet, African or other. Neither was it with Mr Anderson's mission of vital national importance, keen though I was, as ever, to be of service to my Queen and country. It was telling me that out of a clear Heaven I was being offered the key to my escape, plus a much needed decompression chamber providing two days of remunerative work and two nights of solitary meditation in a de luxe hotel while I pieced together my displaced universe. In the process of extricating my cellphone from the inner pocket of my dinner jacket and placing it against my ear, I had inhaled the reheated body odours of a black African hospital nurse named Hannah with whom I had been making unbridled love commencing shortly after 11 p.m. British Summer Time of the night before, and continuing up to the moment of my departure one hour and thirty-five minutes ago, which in my haste to arrive at Penelope's party on time I had failed to wash off.

2

I am not one to believe in portents, auguries, fetishes, or magic white or black, although you can bet your bottom dollar it's in there somewhere with my mother's blood. The fact remains that my path to Hannah was flagged all the way, if I'd only had eyes to see it, which I didn't.

The first recorded signal occurred on the Monday evening preceding the fatal Friday in question, at the Trattoria Bella Vista in Battersea Park Road, our local greasy spoon, where I was not enjoying a solitary meal of recycled cannelloni and Giancarlo's weapons-grade Chianti. For self-improvement I had brought along with me a paperback copy of Antonia Fraser's *Cromwell, Our Chief of Men*, English history being a weak spot in my armoury, which I was endeavouring to repair under the gracious guidance of Mr Anderson, himself a keen student of our island story. The trattoria was empty but for two other tables: the big one in the bay which was occupied by a vocal party of out-of-towners, plus a small one earmarked for lonely-hearts and this evening occupied by a dapper professional gentleman, perhaps retired, and diminutive in stature. I noted his shoes which were highly polished. Ever since the Sanctuary I have set store by polished shoes.

I had not intended to be eating recycled cannelloni. The day being the fifth anniversary of my marriage to Penelope, I had returned home early to prepare her favourite dinner, a *coq au vin* accompanied by a bottle of finest burgundy, plus a ripe Brie cut to size at our local deli. I should by now have become accustomed to the vagaries of the journalistic world, but when she called me *in flagrante*—it was me who was *in flagrante*, I had just flambé'd the chicken joints—to inform me that a crisis had arisen in the private life of a football star and she would not be home before midnight, I behaved in a manner that afterwards shocked me.

I did not scream, I am not the screaming kind. I'm a cool, assimilated, mid-brown Briton. I have reserve, often in greater measure than those with whom I have assimilated. I put the phone down gently. I then without further thought or premeditation consigned chicken, Brie and peeled potatoes to the waste-disposal unit, and put my finger on the GO button and kept it there, for how long I can't say, but for considerably longer than was technically necessary, given that it was a young chicken offering little resistance. I woke again, as it were, to find myself striding briskly westwards down Prince of Wales Drive with *Cromwell* stuffed into my jacket pocket.

There were six diners at the oval table of the Bella Vista, three stalwart men in blazers and their equally heavy wives, all clearly accustomed to life's good things. They hailed from Rickmansworth, I quickly learned, whether I wished to or not, and they called it Ricky. They had been attending an open-air matinée of *The Mikado* in Battersea Park. The dominant voice, a wife's, disapproved of the production. She had never cared for the Japanese—had she, darling?—and giving them songs to sing did not, in her view, make them any nicer. Her monologue did not separate the topics but rolled on at the same level. Sometimes, pausing for what passed for thought, she would haw before resuming, but she need not have bothered because nobody had the temerity to interrupt her. From *The Mikado* she advanced without a breath or change of tone to her recent medical operation. The gynaecologist had made a total balls, but never mind, he was a personal friend and she had decided not to sue. From there she passed seamlessly to her daughter's unsatisfactory artist husband, a layabout if ever she knew one. She had other opinions, all strong, all peculiarly familiar to me, and she was expressing them at full volume when the little gentleman of the polished shoes punched together the two halves of his *Daily Telegraph* and, having folded the result lengthways, hammered his table with it: slap, bang, *slap*, and one more for luck.

'I *will* speak,' he announced defiantly into the middle air. 'I owe it to myself. Therefore I shall'—a statement of personal principle, addressed to himself and no one else.

After which he set course for the largest of the three stalwart men. The Bella Vista, being Italian, has a terrazzo floor and no curtains. The plastered ceiling is low and sheer. If they hadn't heard his declaration of intent, at least they should have heard the *ping* of his polished shoes vibrating as he advanced, but the dominant wife was treating us to her views on modern sculpture which were not merciful. It took the little gentleman several loud *Sirs* to make his presence known.

'*Sir*,' he repeated, speaking as a matter of protocol strictly to the Head of the Table. 'I came here to enjoy my meal and read my newspaper'—holding up what was left of it, like a dog-chew, as court evidence. 'Instead of which, I find myself subjected to a veritable deluge of dialogue *so* loud, *so* trivial, *so* strident, that I am—*yes*'—the *yes* to acknowledge that he had obtained the attention of the table—'And there is *one* voice, sir, one voice above all the rest—I will not point the finger, I am a courteous man—sir, I entreat you to restrain it.'

But having thus spoken, the little gentleman did not by any means quit the field. Rather he stood his ground before them like a brave freedom-fighter facing the firing squad, chest out, polished shoes together, the dog-chew stowed neatly at his side, while the three stalwart men stared incredulously at him, and the offended woman stared at her husband.

'*Darling*,' she murmured. '*Do* something.'

Do what? And what will *I* do if they do it? The big men from Ricky were old athletes, it was plain. The crests on their blazers exuded an heraldic lustre. It was not hard to suppose they were sometime members of a policemen's rugby team. If they elected to beat the little gentleman to a pulp, what did one innocent brown bystander do, apart from get himself beaten into an even worse pulp, and arrested under the Anti-Terror laws into the bargain?

In the event, the men did nothing. Instead of beating him to a pulp and throwing what was left of him into the street and me after him, they fell to examining their brawny hands, and agreeing among themselves in loud asides that the poor fellow was obviously in need of help. Deranged. Could be a danger to the public. Or himself. Call an ambulance, someone.

As to the little gentleman, he returned to his table, laid a twenty-pound note on it and with a dignified 'I give you goodnight, sir' directed at the bay and nothing at all at me, strode like a miniature colossus into the street, leaving me to draw comparisons between a man who says, 'Yes, dear, I completely understand,' and puts his *coq au vin* into the waste disposal, and the man who braves the lions' den while I sit there pretending to read my *Cromwell, Our Chief of Men.*

* * *

The second recorded signal was transmitted next evening, the Tuesday. Returning to Battersea after a four-hour stint in the Chat Room protecting our great nation, I astonished myself by jumping from my moving bus three stops early and striking out at full running speed, not across the park towards Prince of Wales Drive which would have been the logical direction, but back over the bridge to Chelsea whence I had just come.

Why on earth? All right, I'm impulsive. But what was impelling me? The rush hour was at its height. I detest, at any time, walking alongside slow-moving traffic, especially these days. I don't need the faces in the cars giving me the looks. But running—flat out in my best town shoes with leather soles and heels and rubber quarters—running, if you're my colour, build and age, and carrying a briefcase—running at full pelt in bomb-shocked London and looking straight ahead of you, manically, not asking anyone for help and bumping into people in your haste—that kind of running, at any time of day, is frankly unhinged, and at rush hour, demented.

Did I need the exercise? I did not. Penelope has her personal trainer, I have my morning jog around the park. The only thing in the world that explained me to myself as I charged down the crowded pavement and across the bridge was the frozen child I had spotted from the top of the bus. He was six or seven years old and he was stuck halfway up a granite wall that separated the road from the river, his heels to the wall and his arms spread, and his head twisted sideways because he was too scared to look up or down. There was traffic hurtling below him, and above him a narrow parapet that could have been designed for older bully-boys who wanted to show off, and there were two of them up there now, jeering down at him, prancing and catcalling, daring him to come on up. But he can't, because he's even more terrified of heights than he is of traffic, and he knows that on the other side of the parapet, if he ever manages to reach it, there's a sixty-foot drop waiting for him, to the towpath and the river, and he can't do heights and he can't swim, which is why I'm running for all I'm worth.

Yet when I arrive, panting, drenched in sweat, what do I see? No child, frozen or unfrozen. And the topography has undergone a transformation. No granite parapet. No giddying walk with hurtling traffic one side and fast-flowing Thames the other. And on the central reservation, one benign policewoman directing traffic.

'You mustn't talk to me, darling,' she says as she semaphores.

'Did you see three kids fooling here just now? They could have died.'

'Not here, darling.'

'I saw them, I swear I did! There was a small kid stuck against the wall.'

'I'll have to book you in a minute, darling. Now bugger off.'

So I did. I walked back across the bridge I'd had no business crossing in the first place, and all night long while I waited for Penelope to come home I thought about that frozen child in his make-believe hell. And in the morning when I tiptoed to the bathroom so as not to wake her, he was still bothering me, the child who wasn't there. And throughout the day while I was interpreting for a Dutch diamond consortium, I kept him locked in my head where a lot was going on without my knowledge. And he was still in there the next evening, arms outstretched and knuckles jammed against the granite wall when, responding to an urgent request from the North London District Hospital, I presented myself at 7.45 p.m. at the tropical diseases ward, for the purpose of interpreting for a dying African man of unidentifiable age who is refusing to speak a word of any known language except his native-born Kinyarwanda.

* * *

Blue night-lights have pointed me down endless corridors. Fancy signposts have told me which way to turn. Certain beds are screened off, denoting the most critical cases. Ours is such a bed. On one side of it crouches Salvo, on the other side with only a pair of dying man's knees between us, this *degree nurse*. And this degree nurse, whom I deduce to be of Central African origin, has knowledge and responsibilities that exceed most doctors', although this is not how she comes over, being lissom and imposing in her gait, with the unlikely first name of HANNAH on her left bosom, and a gold cross displayed at her throat, not to mention a long, slender body buttoned sternly into a blue-white uniform, but when she gets up and moves around the ward, fluid as a dancer's, plus neatly braided hair receding from her brow in furrows to the point where it is permitted to grow naturally, though cut short for practicality.

And all we're doing, this degree nurse Hannah and myself, is we're catching each other's eye for exponentially long periods of time while she fires her questions at our patient with what I sense to be a protective severity and I duly render them into Kinyarwanda and we both wait—sometimes for minutes on end, it seems to me—for the poor man's answers delivered in the mumbled accents of the African childhood which he is determined will be his last memory of life.

But this is not to take account of other acts of mercy that degree nurse Hannah is performing for him with the assistance of a second nurse, Grace, whom I know from her cadences to be Jamaican, and who is standing at his head, mopping up his vomit, checking his drips and worse, and Grace is a good woman too and by their interaction and the looks they exchange a good comrade to Hannah.

And you should know that I'm a man who hates, really hates hospitals, and is by religion allergic to the health industry. Blood, needles, bedpans, trolleys with scissors on them, surgical smells, sick people, dead dogs and run-over badgers at the roadside, I only have to enter their presence and I'm freaking out, which is no more than any other normal man would do who has been relieved of his tonsils, appendix and foreskin in a succession of insanitary African hill clinics.

And I have met her before, this degree nurse. Once. Yet for the last three weeks, I now realise, she has been an unconscious imprint on my memory, and not just as the presiding angel in this unhappy place. I have spoken to her, although she probably doesn't remember. On my very first visit here, I asked her to sign my completion document certifying that I had performed to her satisfaction the duties I had been contracted for. She had smiled, put her head on one side as if deliberating whether in all honesty she could admit to being satisfied, then casually drawn a fibre-tipped pen from behind her ear. The gesture, though doubtless innocent on her part, had affected me. In my over-fertile imagination, it was a prelude to undressing.

But this evening I am entertaining no such improper fantasies. This evening it is all work, and we are sitting on a dying man's bed. And Hannah the health professional, who for all I know does this three times a day before lunchtime, has set her jaw against extraneous feeling, so I have done the same.

'Ask him his name, please,' she commands me, in French-scented English.

His name, he informs us after prolonged thought, is Jean-Pierre. And for good measure adds, with as much truculence as he can muster in his reduced circumstances, that he is a Tutsi and proud of it, a piece of gratuitous information that both Hannah and I tacitly agree to ignore, not least because we could have told as much, Jean-Pierre being despite his tubes of classical Tutsi appearance, with high cheekbones, protruding jaw and a long back to his head, exactly as Tutsis are supposed to look in the popular African imagination, although a lot don't.

'Jean-Pierre who?' she enquires with the same severity, and I again render her.

Can Jean-Pierre not hear me or does he prefer to have no surname? The delay while Degree Nurse Hannah and I wait for his answer is the occasion for the first long look that we exchange, or long in the sense that it was longer than a look needs to be if you're merely checking that the person you are rendering for is listening to what you're saying, because neither of us was saying anything, nor was he.

'Ask him where he lives, please,' she says, delicately clearing her throat of an obstruction similar to my own; except this time, to my surprise and delight, she is addressing me as a fellow African in Swahili. As if that wasn't enough, she is speaking in *the accents of a woman of the Eastern Congo*!

But I am here to work. The degree nurse has asked our patient another question so I must render it. I do. From Swahili into Kinyarwanda. I then render the answer to it, from Jean-Pierre's Kinyarwanda straight into her deep brown eyes, while I replicate, if not exactly mimic, her deliciously familiar accents.

'I live on the Heath,' I inform her, repeating Jean-Pierre's words as if they were our own, 'under a bush. And that's where I'm going back to when I get out of this'—pause—'place'—omitting for decency's sake the epithet he uses to describe it. 'Hannah,' I go on, speaking English, perhaps in order to relieve the pressure slightly. 'For goodness' sake. Who are you? Where do you come from?'

To which, without the smallest hesitation, she declares her nationhood to me: 'I am from the region of Goma in North Kivu, by tribe a Nande,' she murmurs. 'And this poor Rwandan man is the enemy of my people.'

And I will tell you as a matter of unadorned truth that her half-drawn breath, the widening of her eyes, her urgent appeal for my understanding as she says this, declared to me in a single moment the plight of her beloved Congo as she perceives it: the emaciated corpses of her relatives and loved ones, the unsown fields and dead cattle and burned-out townships that had been her home, until the Rwandans swarmed across the border and, by appointing the Eastern Congo the battlefield for their civil war, heaped unspeakable horrors on a land already dying of neglect.

At first the invaders wanted only to hunt down the *génocidaires* who had hand-killed a million of their citizens in a hundred days. But what began as hot pursuit quickly became a free-for-all for Kivu's mineral resources, with the result that a country on the brink of anarchy went totally over the edge, which is what I strove and struggled to explain to Penelope, who as a conscientious British corporate journalist preferred her information to be the same as everybody else's. Darling, I said, listen to me, I know you're busy. I know your paper likes to stick within family guidelines. But please, on my knees, just this once, print something, anything, to tell the world what's happening to the Eastern Congo. Four million dead, I told her. Just in the last five years. People are calling it Africa's first world war, and you're not calling it anything. It's not a bang-bang war, I grant you. It's not bullets and pangas and hand grenades that are doing the killing. It's cholera, malaria, diarrhoea, and good old-fashioned starvation, and most of the dead are less than five years old. And they're still dying *now*, as we speak, in their thousands, every month. So there must be a story in there somewhere, surely. And there was. On page twenty-nine, next to the quick crossword.

Where had I got my uncomfortable information from? Lying in bed in the small hours, waiting for her to come home. Listening to the World Service of the BBC and remote African radio stations while she met her late-night deadlines. Sitting alone in Internet cafés while she took her sources out to dinner. From African journals purchased on the sly. Standing at the back of outdoor rallies, clad in a bulky anorak and bobble cap while she attended a weekend refresher course on what-ever it was she needed to refresh.

But the languid Grace, suppressing an end-of-shift yawn, knows nothing of this, and why should she? She didn't do the quick crossword. She doesn't know that Hannah and I are participating in a symbolic act of human reconciliation. Before us lies a dying Rwandan man who calls himself Jean-Pierre. At his bedside sits a young Congolese woman called Hannah who has been brought up to regard Jean-Pierre and those like him as the sole perpetrators of her country's misery. Yet does she turn her back on him?—does she summon a colleague or consign him to the yawning Grace? She does not. She calls him *this poor Rwandan man* and holds his hand.

'Ask him where he *used* to live, please, Salvo,' she orders primly, in her Francophone English.

And again we wait, which is to say Hannah and I stare at each other in dazed, out-of-body disbelief, like two people sharing a celestial vision that nobody else can see because they haven't got the eyes. But Grace has seen. Grace is following the progress of our relationship with indulgent attention.

'Jean-Pierre, where did you live before you moved to Hampstead Heath?' I ask in a voice as determinedly dispassionate as Hannah's.

Prison.

And before prison?

It is an age before he provides me with an address and a London phone number, but eventually he does, and I translate them for Hannah who again gropes behind her ear before writing in her notebook with the fibre-tipped pen. She tears off a page and hands it to Grace, who sidles down the ward to a telephone—reluctantly, because by now she doesn't want to miss anything. And it is at this moment that our patient, as if roused from a bad dream, sits bolt upright with all his tubes in him and demands in the coarse and graphic manner of his native Kinyarwanda *fuck my mother what is wrong with me* and why did the police drag him here against his will?—which is when Hannah, in an English weakened by emotion, asks me to interpret the *precise words* she is about to say to him, not adding or subtracting anything, Salvo, please, however much you might wish to do so personally out of consideration for our patient—*our patient* being by now a paramount concept to both of us. And I, in a voice equally weakened, assure her I would not presume to embellish anything she ever said, regardless of how painful it might be to me.

'We have sent for the Registrar and he will come as soon as he can,' Hannah is pronouncing deliberately, while also pausing in a more intelligent manner than many of my clients to allow me time for my rendering. 'I have to inform you, Jean-Pierre, that you are suffering from an acute blood disorder which in my judgment is too advanced for us to cure. I am very sorry but we must accept the situation.'

Yet there is real hope in her eyes as she speaks, a clear and joyful focus on redemption. If Hannah can handle news as bad as this, you feel, then Jean-Pierre ought to be able to handle it too, and so should I. And when I have rendered her message as best I can—*precise words* being somewhat of a layman's delusion since few Rwandans of this poor man's standing are conversant with such concepts as acute blood disorder—she gets him to repeat back to her via me what she just said so that she knows he knows, and he knows he does too, and I know both of them know and there's no fudging of the lines.

And when Jean-Pierre has gruffly repeated her message, and I've again rendered it, she asks me: does Jean-Pierre have wishes while he waits for his relatives to arrive? Which is code as we both know for telling him he will very likely die before they get here. What she doesn't ask, so I don't, is why he's been sleeping rough on the Heath and not back at home with his wife and kids. But I sense that she regards such personal questions as an intrusion upon his privacy, just as I do. For why would a Rwandan man want to go and die on Hampstead Heath if he didn't want to be private?

Then I notice that not only is she holding our patient's hand but she's holding mine too. And Grace notices it and is impressed, though not in a prurient way, because Grace knows, as I know, that her friend Hannah is not given to holding hands with just any interpreter. Yet there they are, my calf-brown, half-Congolese hand and Hannah's authentic all-black version with its pinky-white palm, both of them entwined on an enemy Rwandan's bed. And it's not about sex—how can it be, with Jean-Pierre dying between us?—it's about discovered kinship and consoling each other while we're giving our all to our shared patient. It's because she's deeply moved, and so am I. She is moved by the poor dying man, even though she sees such men all day and every day of her week. She is moved that we are caring for our perceived enemy, and loving him according to the Gospel she's been brought up to, as I can tell by her gold cross. She is moved by my voice. Each time I interpret from Swahili to Kinyarwanda and back again, she lowers her eyes as if in prayer. She is moved because, as I am trying to tell her with my eyes if only she will listen, we are the people we have been looking for all our lives.

*   *   *

I won't say we held hands from then on because we didn't, but we kept our inner eyes on each other. She could have her long back to me, be stooping over him, lifting him, caressing his cheek or checking the machines that Grace had fixed to him. But every time she turned to look at me, I was there for her and I knew she was there for me. And everything that happened afterwards, with me waiting beside the neon-lit gateposts for her to finish duty, and her coming out to join me with her eyes down, and the two of us not embracing in our Mission children's shyness, but walking hand in hand like earnest students up the hill to her hostel, down a cramped passage that smelled of Asian food to a padlocked door to which she had the key, it all flowed from the looks we had exchanged in the presence of our dying Rwandan patient and from the responsibility we felt for each other while a shared human life was slipping out from under us.

Which was why, between passionate bouts of lovemaking, we were able to conduct discussions of a sort unavailable to me since the death of Brother Michael, no natural confidant having until now presented himself in my life with the exception of Mr Anderson, and certainly not in the form of a beautiful, laughing, desiring African woman whose sole calling is to the world's sufferers, and who asks nothing of you, in any language, that you're not prepared to give. To provide factual accounts of ourselves we spoke English. For our lovemaking French. And for our dreams of Africa, how could we not return to the Congolese-flavoured Swahili of our childhoods with its playful mix of joy and innuendo? In the space of twenty sleepless hours Hannah had become the sister, lover and good friend who had consistently failed to materialise throughout my peripatetic childhood.

Did we do guilt—we two good Christian children, brought up to godliness and now five-star adulterers? We did not. We did my marriage, and I declared it dead, which I knew for a certainty it was. We did Hannah's small son Noah, left behind with her aunt in Uganda, and we jointly longed for him. We did solemn promises, and politics, and swapped memories, and drank cranberry juice with sparkling water, and ate take-in pizza, and made love right up to the moment when she reluctantly puts on her uniform and, resisting my entreaties for one last embrace, skips down the hill to the hospital for an anaesthetics class she's attending before beginning night shift with her dying patients while I go hunting for a taxi because, due to the bombings, the Underground is part-operational at best, and the bus will take too long, and Heavens above, look at the time. Her parting words, spoken in Swahili, were nonetheless ringing in my ears. Holding my face between her hands, she was gently shaking her head in joyous marvel.

'Salvo,' she said. 'When your mother and father made you, they must have loved each other very much.'

3

'All right if I open a window?' I called out to Fred my white driver.

Snug in the rear cushions of the Mondeo as it wove expertly through the dense Friday-evening traffic, I was enjoying feelings of liberation bordering on euphoria.

'Please yourself, mate,' he responded lustily, but my needle-sharp ear immediately spotted beneath the collo-quialisms the trace of an English public school accent. Fred was my age and drove with aplomb. I liked him already. Lowering the window, I let the warm night air wash over me.

'Any idea where we're heading, Fred?'

'Bottom end of South Audley Street.' And assuming my concern to be directed at the speed of his driving, which it wasn't: 'Don't worry, we'll get you there in one piece.'

I wasn't worrying but I was taken aback. My encounters with Mr Anderson had until now occurred at his Ministry's headquarters in Whitehall in a richly carpeted dungeon set at the end of a labyrinth of green-painted brick corridors guarded by sallow janitors with walkie-talkies. On its walls hung tinted photographs of Mr Anderson's wife, daughters and spaniels, interspersed with gold-framed testimonials awarded to his other love, the Sevenoaks Choral Society. And it was in this dungeon, after I had been summoned by confidential letter to a series of 'test-interviews' conducted above ground by an enigmatic body calling itself the Linguistic Audit Committee, that he had unveiled to me the full majesty of the Official Secrets Act plus its many threat-ened punishments, first by reading me a homily which he must have delivered a hundred times already, then by presenting me with a printed form with my name and date and place of birth electronically pre-entered, and addressing me over his reading spectacles while I signed it.

'Now you won't go getting big ideas, will you, son?' he said, in a tone which irresistibly recalled Brother Michael's. 'You're a bright lad, the sharpest pencil in the box if all they tell me is true. You've a cluster of funny languages up your sleeve and a Grade A profes-sional reputation that no fine Service such as this one can ignore.'

I wasn't sure which fine Service he was alluding to but he had already informed me that he was a Senior Servant of the Crown, and this should be sufficient for me. Neither did I ask him which of my languages he considered funny, although I might have done if I hadn't been on such a cloud, because sometimes my respect for people flies out of the window of its own accord.

'That doesn't make you the centre of the universe, however, so kindly don't think it does,' he went on, still on the subject of my qualifications. 'You'll be a PTA, that's a Part-time Assistant, and you can't get lower than that. You're secret but you're fringe, and fringe is what you'll remain unless you're offered tenure. I'm not saying some of the best shows aren't fringe, because they are. Better plays and better actors in my wife Mary's view. Do you understand what I'm telling you, Salvo?'

'I think so, sir.'

I use 'sir' too much and am aware of it, just as I said *Mzee* too much when I was a child. But in the Sanctuary everyone who wasn't a Brother was a sir.

'Then repeat to me what I've just told you, please, so that we can both be clear in our minds,' he suggested, availing himself of a technique later employed by Hannah to break the bad news to Jean-Pierre.

'That I shouldn't be carried away. I shouldn't get too—' I was going to say 'excited' but checked myself in time. 'Enthusiastic.'

'I'm telling you to douse that eager gleam in your eye, son. Henceforth and for evermore. Because if I see it again, I'll worry about you. We're believers but we're not zealots. Your unusual talents aside, what we're offering you here is normal meat-and-potatoes drudgery, the same as you'd be doing for any client on any wet afternoon, except you're doing it with Queen and country in mind, which is what you and I both like.'

I assured him—while careful not to appear over-enthusiastic—that love of country ranked high on my list of personal favourites.

'There's a couple of other differences, I'll grant you,' he went on, contradicting an objection I hadn't made. 'One difference is, we'll not be giving you much in the way of a background briefing before you put on your headphones. You'll not know who's talking to who or where, or what they're talking about, or how we came by it. Or not if we can help it, you won't, because that wouldn't be secure. And if you *do* come up with any little suppositions of your own, I advise you to keep them to yourself. That's what you've signed up to, Salvo, that's what secret means, and if we catch you breaking the rules you'll be out on your ear with a black mark. And our black marks don't wash out like other people's,' he added with satisfaction, although I couldn't help wondering whether he was making an unconscious allusion to my skin. 'Do you want to tear up that piece of paper and forget you came here?— because this is your last chance.'

Upon which I swallowed and said, 'No, sir. I'm *in*— really,' with as much cool as I could muster, and he shook my hand and welcomed me to what he was pleased to call the honourable company of sound-thieves.

*   *   *

I will say at once that Mr Anderson's efforts to dampen my ardour were futile. Crouching in a soundproof cubicle, one of forty, in a secure underground bunker known as the Chat Room—with suave Barney our floor manager in his coloured waistcoats watching over us from his cantilevered balcony—and he calls it meat and potatoes? Girls in jeans to fetch and carry our tapes and transcriptions and, contrary to the known rules of political correctness in the workplace, our cups of tea as well, while one minute I'm listening to a top-ranking Acholi-speaking member of the Lord's Resistance Army in Uganda plotting by satellite phone to set up a base across the border in East Congo, and the next sweating it out in Dar-es-Salaam docks with the clatter of shipping in the background, and the cries of hawkers, and the in-out hum of a wonky table-fan that's keeping away the flies, as a murderous bunch of Islamist sympathisers conspire to import an arsenal of anti-aircraft missiles in the guise of heavy machinery? And the very same afternoon being sole ear-witness to a trio of corrupt Rwandan army officers haggling with a Chinese delegation over the sale of plundered Congolese minerals? Or bumping through the honking traffic of Nairobi in the chauffeured limousine of a Kenyan political mogul as he wangles himself a massive bribe for allowing an Indian building contractor to cover five hundred miles of new road with a single paper-thin surface of tarmac guaranteed to last at least two rainy seasons?

This isn't meat and potatoes, Mr Anderson. This is the Holy of Holies!

But I didn't let the gleam show, not even to Penelope. If only you knew! I would think to myself, whenever she slapped me down in front of her bosom friend Paula, or went off for one of her weekend conferences that nobody else seemed to attend except her, and came back very quiet and content from all the conferring she'd done. If only you knew that your stuck-in-the-rut, toy-boy husband was on the payroll of British Intelligence!

But I never weakened. Forget instant gratification. I was doing my duty for England.

* * *

Our Ford Mondeo had skirted Berkeley Square and entered Curzon Street. Passing the cinema, Fred pulled up at the kerbside and leaned over the back of his seat to address me, spy to spy.

'It's down there, mate,' he murmured, tipping his head but not pointing in case we were observed. 'Number 22B, green door hundred yards up on the left. The top bell is marked HARLOW like the town. When they answer, say you've got a parcel for Harry.'

'Will Barney be there?' I asked, momentarily nervous at the prospect of confronting Mr Anderson alone in an unfamiliar environment.

'Barney? Who's Barney?'

Chiding myself for asking unnecessary questions, I stepped onto the pavement. A wave of heat rose at me.

A swerving cyclist nearly knocked me over and cursed. Fred drove off, leaving me feeling I could have done with more of him. I crossed the road and entered South Audley Street. Number 22B was one of a row of red-brick mansions with steep steps leading up to their front doors. There were six bell buttons, dimly lit. The top one read HARLOW like the town in faded ink. About to press it I was assailed by two conflicting images. One was of Penelope's head six inches from Thorne the Horn's fly as she gazed dotingly up at him with her breasts peeping out of her new designer suit. The other was of Hannah's wide eyes not daring to blink, and her open mouth silently singing her joy as she squeezed the last drops of life out of me on the sofa-bed in her nun's cell.

'Parcel for Harry,' I intoned, and watched the magic door open.

* * *

I haven't described Mr Anderson's appearance beyond remarking on his similarity to Brother Michael. Like Michael he is a man complete, at once tall and bearish, the features as permanent as lava stone, every movement an event. Like Michael, he is a father to his men. He is somewhere in his late fifties, you assume, yet you have no sense that he was yesterday a dashing lad, or tomorrow will be on the shelf. He is rectitude personified, he is constabular, he is the oak of England. Just crossing a room he takes the moral justification for his actions with him. You can wait an eternity for his smile, but when it comes you're closer to God.

Yet for me the real man, as ever, is the voice: the singer's considered tempo, the timed pauses always for effect, the fireside north country cadences. In Sevenoaks, he has told me more than once, he is the leading baritone. In his younger years he sang tenor-contralto and had been tempted to go professional, but loved his Service more. And it was Mr Anderson's voice again that dominated all other impressions at the instant of my venturing through the doorway. I was aware, dimly, of other sounds and other bodies on the premises. I saw an open sash window and billowing net curtains, so evidently there was a breeze blowing up here which hadn't been the case at street level. But the focus of my interest was the upright silhouette of Mr Anderson against the window and his homey northern tones as he went on speaking on his cellphone.

'He'll be here any minute, Jack, thank you,' I heard him say, apparently oblivious that I was standing six feet from him. 'We'll turn him round just as fast as we can, Jack—no faster.' Pause. 'You are correct. *Sinclair*.' But Sinclair wasn't the name of whoever he was talking to. He was confirming that Sinclair was the man. 'He's fully aware of that, Jack. And I shall make him even more aware when he arrives'—by now looking straight at me yet still not admitting to my presence—'no, he's not a new boy. He's done a bit of this and that for us, and you can take it from me he's the man for the job.

All the languages you can eat, capable in the extreme, loyal to a fault.'

Could it really be *me* he was referring to—*capable in the extreme—loyal to a fault*? But I contained myself. I doused the eager gleam in my eye.

'And his insurance goes on your tab, not ours, you'll remember, Jack. All risks, please, plus sickness in the field and repatriation by fastest available. Nothing ends on this doorstep. We're here if you need us, Jack. Just remember, every time you call up, you slow the process. I do believe he's coming up the stairs now. Aren't you, Salvo?' He had rung off. 'Now pay close attention to me, son. We've a lot of growing up to do in a short space of time. Young Bridget here will provide you with your change of clothing. That's a fine dinner jacket you're wearing, it's a pity you've to take it off. They've come a long way, have dinner jackets, since my day. It was black or black at the Annual Songsters' Ball. Dark red like yours was bandleaders. So you told your wife all about it, did you? A top-secret assignment of national importance which has blown up overnight, I expect?'

'Not a single word, sir,' I replied firmly. 'You told me not to, so I didn't. I bought it specially for her night,' I added, because, Hannah or no Hannah, I had a need to preserve his faith in my connubial fidelity until it was time for him to be advised of my altered arrangements.

The woman he called young Bridget had positioned herself square to me and was looking me over while she held a varnished fingertip to her lips. She was wearing pearl earrings and designer jeans well above her pay-grade, and she was swaying her hips to the rhythm of her cogitations.

'What waist have you got, Salv? We reckoned thirty-two.'

'Thirty, actually.' Hannah had said I was too thin.

'Know your inside leg?'

'Thirty-two, last time I looked,' I riposted, matching her jokey style.

'Collar?'

'Fifteen.'

She disappeared down a corridor, surprising me with a wildfire desire for her until I realised it was merely a resurgence of my desire for Hannah.

'We've a bit of live action for you, son,' Mr Anderson announced, with great portent, as he tucked his cell-phone back into his handkerchief pocket. 'No more sitting in a nice comfortable cubicle and listening to the world from a safe distance, I'm afraid. You're about to meet some of those ruffians in the flesh, and do a bit of good for your country while you're about it. You're not averse to changing your identity, I take it? Everybody wants to be somebody else at some point in their lives, they tell me.'

'Not averse at all, Mr Anderson. Not if you say it's necessary. Very willing indeed.' I'd already changed it once in the last twenty-four hours, so twice wasn't going to make a lot of difference. 'Who are we saving the world from this time?' I enquired, careful to conceal my excitement beneath a breezy manner. But to my surprise, Mr Anderson took my question to heart, mulling it over before putting one of his own.

'Salvo.'

'Mr Anderson?'

'How squeamish are you about getting your hands dirty in a good cause?'

'I thought I was doing that already—well, only in a *way*,' I corrected myself hastily.

I was too late. Mr Anderson's brow had clouded. He set great store by the moral integrity of the Chat Room, and did not care to have it impugned, least of all by me.

'Until now, Salvo, you have performed an entirely essential, but *defensive* rôle on behalf of our beleaguered nation. As of tonight, however, you will be taking the struggle to the enemy. You will cease to be *defensive*, and you will become'—he was hunting for the *mot juste*—'*proactive*. Do I sense a reluctance on your part to go that extra mile?'

'None at all, Mr Anderson. Not if it's a *good* cause, which you say it is. I'd be happy to. As long as it's just the two days,' I added, mindful of my life-decision regarding Hannah, which I was anxious to implement with all speed. 'Or three at the outside.'

'I do, however, have to warn you that from the moment you leave this building you will be *deniable* as far as HMG is concerned. If for any reason you are rumbled—*blown*, as we say—you will be abandoned without scruple to your fate. Did you hoist that aboard, son? You're looking somewhat other-worldly, if I may say so.'

With slender, well-groomed fingers, Bridget was coaxing my dinner jacket off me, unaware that, just a skull's width away from her, Hannah and I were nearly falling off her sofa-bed while we tore the remaining clothes off each other and made love a second time.

'Hoisted aboard and accepted, Mr Anderson,' I quipped gaily, if a little late. 'What languages do they need? Are we talking a specialised vocabulary here? Maybe I should pop back to Battersea while the coast is clear and grab some works of reference.'

My offer was clearly not to his liking, for he pursed his lips. 'That will be a matter for your temporary employers to determine, thank you, Salvo. We are not privy to their detailed plans, neither do we wish to be.'

Bridget marched me to a dingy bedroom but did not come in. Laid out on the unmade bed were two pairs of used grey flannels, three hand-me-down shirts, a selection of Prisoners' Aid underwear, socks and a leather belt with the chrome peeling off the buckle. And beneath them on the floor three pairs of shoes, part worn. A mangy sports coat dangled from a wire hanger on the door. Divesting myself of my evening wear, I was again rewarded with a waft of Hannah's body odour. Her tiny room had contained no washbasin. The bathrooms across the corridor were occupied by nurses about to go on duty.

Of the shoes, the least offensive were the worst fitting. In a mistaken victory of vanity over common sense, I nonetheless selected them. The sports jacket was of industrial-strength Harris Tweed with iron armpits: push my shoulders forwards and the collar sawed my neck. Backwards, it locked me in a citizen's arrest. An olive-green tie of knitted nylon completed the dismal ensemble.

And here, if only for a minute, my spirits plummeted, for I must own straight out to my love of sartorial finery, my relish for impact, colour and display that no doubt springs direct from my Congolese mother's genes. Peek into my briefcase any working day and what will you find tucked among the written depositions, briefings, background papers and deportation orders? Glossy give-away magazines of the world's most pricey menswear, items I could never in half a dozen lifetimes afford to buy. And now look at me.

Returning to the living room I found Bridget writing out an inventory of my possessions on a legal pad: one state-of-the-art cellphone—slimline brushed steel with flip camera—one bunch of house keys, one driving licence, one British passport which for reasons of pride or insecurity I always carry on my person, and one slender wallet of genuine calf containing forty-five pounds in notes plus credit cards. Obedient to my sense of duty, I handed her the last vestiges of my former glory: my dinner jacket trousers not yet run in, my Turnbull & Asser bow tie to match, my pleated dress shirt of best sea-island cotton, my onyx dress studs and cufflinks, silk socks, patent leather shoes. I was still undergoing this painful ordeal when Mr Anderson came back to life.

'Are you familiar with one *Brian Sinclair* by any chance, Salvo?' he demanded accusingly. 'Think hard, please. *Sinclair*? *Brian*? Yes or no?'

I assured him that, bar hearing him speak the name on his cellphone a few moments previously, I was not.

'Very well. From now on, and for the next two days and nights, *Brian Sinclair* is who you are. Note please the felicitous similarity of initials—B.S. In matters of cover, the golden rule is to remain as close to the reality as operational requirements permit. You are no longer Bruno Salvador, you are Brian Sinclair, a freelance interpreter raised in Central Africa, the son of a mining engineer, and you are temporarily employed by an internationally based syndicate registered in the Channel Islands and dedicated to bringing the latest agricultural techniques to the Third and Fourth Worlds. Kindly advise me whether you have any problems with that, of whatever nature.'

My heart didn't sink, but it didn't exactly rise either. His anxiety was getting to me. I was beginning to wonder whether I should be anxious too.

'Do I know them, Mr Anderson?'

'Know who, son?'

'The agricultural syndicate. If I'm Sinclair, who are they? Perhaps I've worked for them before.'

It was hard for me to see Mr Anderson's expression because he had his back to the light.

'We are talking, Salvo, of an *anonymous syndicate*. It would be illogical indeed for such a syndicate to have a name.'

'The directors have names, don't they?'

'Your temporary employer as such has no name, any more than the Syndicate does,' Mr Anderson rebuffed me. Then he appeared to relent. 'You will, however— and I suspect I am speaking out of turn—be given into the charge of one *Maxie*. Please do not on any account, at any future date, indicate that you have heard that name from me.'

'*Mr* Maxie?' I demanded. 'Maxie *Someone*? If I'm putting my head into a noose, Mr Anderson—'

'*Maxie* will be quite sufficient on its own, thank you, Salvo. In all matters of command and control you will, for the purposes of this exceptional operation, report to Maxie unless otherwise directed.'

'Should I trust him, Mr Anderson?'

His chin came up sharply and his first reaction, I am sure, was that anyone named by himself was by definition a person to be trusted. Then, seeing me, he softened.

'On the strength of such information as has reached me, you would indeed be justified in placing your confidence in Maxie. He is, I am told, a genius in his field. As you are, Salvo. As you are.'

'Thank you, Mr Anderson.' But the sound-thief in me had caught the note of reservation in his voice, which was why I pressed him further. 'Who does

Maxie report to? For the purposes of this exceptional operation? Unless otherwise directed?' Daunted by the severity of his glare, I hastened to modify my question in a manner more acceptable to him. 'I mean, we all report to someone, don't we, Mr Anderson? Even you.'

Pressed beyond bearing, Mr Anderson has a habit of breathing in deeply and lowering his head like a large animal on the point of charging.

'I understand there is a *Philip*,' he conceded with reluctance, 'or, I am told, *when* it serves him'—a sniff— '*Philippe*, in the French manner.' Despite his polyglot calling, Mr Anderson has always considered English enough for anybody. 'As you are in Maxie's hands, so Maxie is in Philip's. Does that satisfy you?'

'Does Philip have a rank, Mr Anderson?'

Given his previous hesitation, his answer came fast and hard:

'No, Philip does not. Philip is a consultant. He has no rank, he is a member of no official service. Bridget. Mr Sinclair's visiting cards, if you please, hot off the presses.'

With a facetious bob Bridget presented me with a plastic purse. Prising it open, I extracted a flimsy card introducing Brian S. Sinclair, Accredited Interpreter, resident at a post-office box in Brixton. The telephone, fax and e-mail numbers were unfamiliar to me. None of my diplomas was mentioned, none of my degrees.

'What does the S stand for?'

'Whatever you wish,' Mr Anderson replied magnanimously. 'You have only to select a name and stick to it.'

'What happens if someone tries to ring me?' I asked, as my thoughts went racing back to Hannah.

'A courteous recorded announcement will advise them that you will be back at your desk in a few days. Should somebody elect to e-mail you, which we consider improbable, that message will be received and dealt with in the appropriate manner.'

'But otherwise I'm the same person?'

My persistence was putting a strain on the last of Mr Anderson's patience.

'You are the same person, Salvo, recast in circumstances parallel to your own. If you are married, remain married. If you have a dear grandmother in Bournemouth, you may retain her with our blessing. Mr Sinclair himself will be untraceable, and when this operation is over, he will not have existed. I can't make myself plainer than that, can I?' And in a more emollient tone: 'It's a very normal type of situation in the world you are about to enter, son. Your only problem is, you're new to it.'

'What about my money? Why do you have to keep my money?'

'My instructions are that—'

He stopped. Meeting his stare, I realised that he was surveying not Salvo the sophisticated party-goer, but a coffee-coloured Mission boy in a Salvation Army sports coat, baggy flannels and increasingly tight shoes. The sight evidently touched a chord in him.

'Salvo.'

'Yes, Mr Anderson.'

'You're going to have to harden yourself up, son. You'll be living a lie out there.'

'You said. I don't mind. I'm ready. You warned me. I need to ring my wife, that's all.' For wife, read Hannah, but I didn't say so.

'You'll be mixing with others who are living lies. You understand that, don't you? They are not like us, these people. The truth is not an absolute to them. Not the Bible truth that you and I were brought up to, much as we might wish it was.'

I had never identified, and have not to this day, Mr Anderson's religious affiliations which I suspect were largely Masonic. But he had always made a point of reminding me that we were comrades in whatever faith we both adhered to. Having handed me my cell-phone for one last call, Bridget had removed herself to the bedroom no more than six feet from where I stood. Mr Anderson was anchored in the drawing room, and able to hear every word. Hunched in the little entrance hall, I underwent a crash course in the complexities of marital infidelity. My one desire was to tell Hannah of my undying love and warn her that, contrary to my assurances, I wouldn't be able to talk to her for two days. But with only a spindly door separating me from

my audience, I had no option but to ring my legal wife
and listen to her answerphone:

You have reached Penelope Randall's voicemail.
I'm away from my desk right now. If you'd care
to leave a message, do so after the tone. To talk to
my assistant, ask for Emma on 9124.

I took a breath. 'Hi, sweetie. It's me. Look, I'm
terribly sorry, but I've been called away on yet another
rather high-powered job. One of my oldest and best
corporate clients. They say it's a matter of life and
death. Could be two or three days. I'll try and ring you
but it's going to be tricky.'

Who was I sounding like? Nobody I'd met. Nobody
I'd listened to. Nobody I wanted to meet again. I tried
harder:

'Look, I'll call as soon as they give me a spot of
breathing space. I really am heartbroken, darling.
Oh, and your party looked just *great*. Repeat, *great*.
The outfit was fab. Everyone was talking about it.
I'm just *so* sorry I had to walk out on you all. Lots to
sort out when I come back, okay? See you, darling.
Bye.'

Bridget took back my cellphone, passed me my
night-bag and watched me while I checked its contents:
socks, handkerchiefs, shirts, underpants, a sponge-bag,
one grey pullover with V-neck.

'Using any medication at all, are we?' she murmured

suggestively. 'How about contact lenses? No lubricants, little boxes?'

I shook my head.

'Well, off you both go then,' Mr Anderson declared, and if he had raised his right hand and bestowed one of Brother Michael's floppy blessings on us, I would not have been surprised.

4

It is frankly a conundrum to me, observing these events from where I sit today, that as I followed Bridget down the stairs and back onto the pavement of South Audley Street, attired as I was in the garb of a secondary-school master up from the country, and with nothing to attach me to the world except a bunch of bogus business cards and the assurance that I was about to endure unfamiliar perils, I should have counted myself the most blessed fellow in London that night, if not the whole of England, the most intrepid patriot and secret servant, but such was indeed the case.

Fram is the name of the boat designed by the famous Norwegian explorer Nansen, a top member of Brother Michael's pantheon of men of action. *Fram* in the Norwegian language means *onwards*, and *Fram* was what inspired my dear late father to ride his heretic's bicycle across the Pyrenees. And *Fram* willy-nilly had been my mood ever since I had received what Brother Michael in a different context had dubbed the Great Call. *Onwards* while I gathered my fortitude for the decision that lay ahead of me, *Onwards* while I earned my wings in my country's silent war versus ruffians in the flesh, *Onwards*, and away from Penelope who had long been a stranger to me, *Onwards* while I mapped out my shining white path back to life with Hannah. *Onwards*, finally, to my mysterious new master, Maxie, and the even more mysterious consultant, Philip.

Given the extreme urgency of the operation and its importance, I expected to find Fred our white driver keenly revving his Mondeo at the kerbside, but what with a police cordon at Marble Arch and the traffic jams, Bridget assured me it was quicker to walk.

'You don't mind, do you, Salv?' she asked, taking a firm grip on my arm, either because she was thinking I might make a run for it, which could not have been further from my mind, or because she was one of the touchy-feely brigade who pat your cheek and roll the palm of their hand around your back and you never know, or I don't, whether they're distributing the milk of human kindness or inviting you to bed.

'Mind?' I echoed. 'It's a glorious evening! I couldn't borrow your phone a moment, could I? Penelope may not be picking up her messages.'

'Sorry, darling. Against the regs, I'm afraid.'

Did I know where we were headed? Did I ask? I did not. The life of a secret agent is nothing if not a journey into the unknown, the life of a secret lover no less so. Off we strode with Bridget setting the pace and me with my second-hand shoes hacking at my ankle bones. In the evening sunlight my spirits rose further, assisted perhaps unconsciously by Bridget, who had hoisted my right forearm so high against her that it was nestling under her left breast, which by the feel of its undercurve was self-supporting. When Hannah has lit your lamp for you, it's natural to see other women in its rays.

'You really love her, don't you?' she marvelled as she steered me through a bunch of Friday-night merrymakers. 'So many married couples I know, they just bitch at each other. It pisses me off. But you and Penelope aren't like that, are you? It must be great.'

Her ear was six inches from my mouth and she was wearing a scent called Je Reviens, which is the weapon of choice of Penelope's younger sister Gail. Gail, apple of her father's eye, had married a car-park owner from the lower branches of the aristocracy. Penelope, by way of retaliation, had married me. Yet even today it would take a board of top Jesuits to explain what I did next.

For why does a newly anointed adulterer, who hours earlier has abandoned himself body, soul and origins to another woman for the first time in his five-year marriage, feel an irresistible urge to put his deceived wife on a pedestal? Is he trying to re-create the image of her that he has defiled? Is he re-creating the image of himself before he fell? Was my ever-present Catholic guilt catching up with me in the midst of my euphoria? Was praising Penelope to the skies the nearest I could get to praising Hannah without blowing my cover?

It had been my firm intention to draw Bridget out regarding my new employers, and by means of artful questions learn more about the composition of the anonymous Syndicate and its relationship with the many secret organs of the British State that toil night and day for our protection, far removed from the sight of your average punter's eye. Yet as we threaded our way through near-stationary traffic I embarked upon a full-throated aria to my wife Penelope that proclaimed her the most attractive, exciting, sophisticated and faithful partner a top interpreter and secret soldier of the Crown could have, plus a brilliant journalist combining hard-nosed with compassionate, and this fantastic cook—which anyone would know verged upon the fanciful, seeing who did the cooking. Not everything that I said was totally positive, it couldn't be. If you're talking in the rush-hour to another woman about your wife, you can't help opening up a bit about her negative aspects or you wouldn't have an audience.

'But how the hell did Mr and Mrs Right ever find each other in the first place? That's what *I* want to know,' Bridget protested, in the aggrieved tones of one who has followed the instructions on the packet without success.

'Bridget,' an alien voice inside me answered, 'here is how.'

*   *   *

It is eight in the evening in Salvo's dingy bachelor bedsit in Ealing, I tell her as we wait arm-in-arm for the pedestrian lights to change. Mr Amadeus Osman of the WorldWide and Legal Translation Agency is calling me from his malodorous office in the Tottenham Court Road. I am to go directly to Canary Wharf where a Great National Newspaper is offering megabucks for my services. These are still my days of struggle, and Mr Osman owns half of me.

In an hour I am seated in the newspaper's luxurious offices with its editor one side of me and its shapely ace reporter—guess who?—the other. Before us squats her supergrass, a bearded Afro-Arab merchant seaman who for the price of what I'm earning in a year will dish the dirt on a ring of corrupt customs officers and policemen operating in Liverpool's dockland. He speaks only meagre English, his mother tongue being a classical Tanzanian-flavoured Swahili. Our ace crime reporter and her editor are caught in the muckraker's proverbial cleft stick: check out your source with the authorities and compromise the scoop; accept your source on trust and let the libel lawyers take you to the cleaners.

With Penelope's consent I assume command of the interrogation. As the questioning flies back and forth, our supergrass alters and refines his story, adds new elements, retracts old ones. I make the rascal repeat himself. I point out his many discrepancies until, under my persistent cross-examination, he admits all. He is a con-artist, a fabricator. For fifty quid he will go away.

The editor is jubilant in his gratitude. In one stroke, he says, I have spared their blushes and their bank account. Penelope, having overcome her humiliation, declares that she owes me a very large drink.

'People expect their interpreters to be small, studious and bespectacled,' I explained to Bridget modestly, laughing away Penelope's rapt and, in retrospect, somewhat blatant interest in me from the start. 'I suppose I just failed to come up to expectation.'

'Or she just totally freaked out,' Bridget suggested, tightening her grip on my hand.

Did I bubble out the rest to Bridget too? Appoint her my substitute confessor in Hannah's absence? Unveil to her how, until I met Penelope, I was a twenty-three-year-old closet virgin, a dandy in my personal appearance but, underneath my carefully constructed façade, saddled with enough hang-ups to fill a walk-in cupboard?—that Brother Michael's attentions and Père André's before him had left me in a sexual twilight from which I feared to emerge?—that my dear late father's guilt regarding his explosion of the senses had transferred itself wholesale and without deductions to his son?—and how as our taxi sped towards Penelope's flat I had dreaded the moment when she would literally uncover my inadequacy, such was my timidity regarding the female sex?—and that thanks to her knowhow and micro-management all ended well?—*extremely* well—more well than she could ever have imagined, she assured me, Salvo being her dream mustang—the best in her stable, she might have added—her starred Alpha Male Plus? Or, as she later put it to her friend Paula when they thought I wasn't listening, her *chocolate soldier* always standing to attention? And that one calendar week later, so blown away was he in all respects by his newfound and unquenchable prowess in the bedroom, so overwhelmed with gratitude and ready to confuse sexual accomplishment with great love, that Salvo with his customary impulsiveness and naivety proposed marriage to Penelope, only to be accepted on the spot? No. By a mercy, in that regard at least I managed to restrain myself. Neither did I get round to telling Bridget the price I had since paid, year by year, for this much needed therapy, but only because we had by then passed the Connaught Hotel and turned into the top end of Berkeley Square.

* * *

In my expansiveness of heart I was assuming, for no reason beyond the expectations we have of natural gravity, that our path would then take us down towards Piccadilly. But suddenly Bridget's grip on my arm tightened and she wheeled me left up some steps to a grand front door that I failed to get the number of. The door closed behind us and there we were, standing in a velvet-curtained lobby occupied by two identical blond boys in blazers. I don't remember her ringing a bell or knocking, so they must have been watching out for us on their closed-circuit screen. I remember they both wore grey flannels like mine, and their blazers had all three buttons fastened. And I remember wondering whether, in the world that they inhabited, this was regulation and I ought to be doing up the buttons of my Harris Tweed.

'Skipper's been delayed,' the seated boy told Bridget without lifting his eyes from the black-and-white image of the door we had just passed through. 'He's on his sweet way, right? Ten to fifteen. Want to leave *him* here with us or wait it out?'

'Wait,' said Bridget.

The boy stretched out his hand for my bag. On Bridget's nod I passed it to him.

The grand hall that we entered had a painted dome for a ceiling, with white nymphs, and white babies blowing trumpets, and a regal staircase that halfway up itself divided into two more staircases curving to a balcony with a row of doors, all closed. And at the foot of the staircase, on either side, two more doors, grand ones, capped by golden eagles with their wings spread. The right-hand door was closed off by a red silk rope with brass fittings. I never saw anyone go in or out of it. On the left-hand door a lighted red sign said SILENCE CONFERENCE IN PROGRESS without any punctuation, because I always notice punctuation. So if you wanted to be pedantic, you could interpret it as meaning that people were having a conference about silence: which only shows you how my personal state of mind was alternating between post-coital, skittish, out of it, and totally hyper. I've never done drugs, but if I had, this is how I imagine I would have been, which is why I needed to pin down everything around me before it transmogrified itself into something else.

Guarding the grand door stood a grey-headed bouncer who could have been Arab and must have been older than the two blond boys put together but was still very much a member of the pugilistic classes, having a flattened nose and dropped shoulders and hands cupped over his balls. I don't remember climbing the regal staircase. If Bridget had been ahead of me in her skin-tight jeans I would have remembered, so we must have climbed side by side. And Bridget had been in this house before. She knew the geography and she knew the boys. She knew the Arab bouncer too, because she smiled at him and he smiled back at her in a soft, adoring manner before resuming his pugilistic glower. She knew without being told where you waited, which was halfway up the staircase before it divided, something you could never have guessed from below.

There were two easy chairs, a leather sofa with no arms, and glossy magazines offering private islands in the Caribbean and charter yachts complete with crew and helicopter, price on application. Picking one up, Bridget leafed through it, inviting me to do the same. Yet even while fantasising about which *Fram* Hannah and I would sail away on, I was tuning my mind's ear to the boomy voices coming out of the conference room, because I'm a listener by nature and trained to it, not just by the Chat Room. No matter how confused I am, I listen and remember, it's my job. Plus the fact that secret children in far-flung Mission houses learn to keep their ears pinned back if they want to know what's likely to hit them next.

And as I listened I began to pick up the see-saw whine of fax machines working overtime in the rooms above us and the chirp of telephones too quickly smothered, and the fraught silences when nothing happened but the whole house held its breath. Each couple of minutes or less, a young female assistant came scuttling past us down our staircase to deliver a message to the bouncer, who opened his door six inches and slipped the message to someone inside before shutting it and putting his hands back over his balls.

Meanwhile the voices were still coming out of the conference room. They were male voices and each was *important* in the sense that this was a meeting of men who punched at their own weight, as opposed to one supremo talking to his underlings. I also noted that, although the *sound* of the words was English, the voices speaking them were of varying nationalities and cadences, now from the Indian subcontinent, now Euro-American or white African colonial, much in the manner of high-level conferences I am occasionally privileged to attend where platform speeches are delivered in English, but your off-stage discussions are conducted in the tongues of individual delegates, with the interpreters acting as the essential bridges between God's striving souls.

There was one voice, however, that seemed to be addressing me personally. It was native English, upper-class, and compelling in its tonal rise and fall. So finely were my antennae tuned that after a couple of minutes of what I call my third ear I had convinced myself it was the voice of a gentleman I was familiar with and respected, even if I hadn't caught a single word of what it was saying. And I was still hunting in my memory for its owner when my attention was diverted by a thunder-clap below me as the door to the lobby flew open to admit the cadaverous, breathless figure of Mr Julius Bogarde, alias Bogey, my late mathematics teacher and chief luminary of the Sanctuary's ill-fated Outward Bound Club. The fact that Bogey had perished ten years ago while leading a party of terrified schoolchildren up the wrong side of a mountain in the Cairngorms only compounded my surprise at his reincarnation.

'*Maxie*,' I heard Bridget breathe in reproachful awe as she sprang to her feet. 'You mad sod. Who's the lucky girl this time?'

And all right, he wasn't Bogey.

And I doubt whether Bogey's girls, if he had any, counted themselves lucky, rather the reverse. But he had Bogey's gangly wrists, and Bogey's manic stride and hellbent look about him, and Bogey's haywire mop of sandy hair blown to one side by a prevailing wind and stuck there, and rosy bursts of colour on his upper cheeks. And Bogey's sun-bleached khaki canvas bag, like a wartime gasmask case in old movies, swinging

from his shoulder. His spectacles, like Bogey's, doubled
the circumference of his faraway blue eyes, switching on
and off as he loped towards us under the chandelier.
And if Bogey had ever come to London, which was
against his principles, this was undoubtedly the outfit he
would have selected: a mangled go-anywhere, wash-it-
yourself, fawn-coloured tropical suit with a Fair Isle
sleeveless pullover and buckskin shoes with the nap
worn off. And if Bogey had ever had to storm the regal
staircase to our waiting area, this was how he would
have done it: three weightless bounds with his gasmask
case slapping at his side.

'My *fucking* pushbike,' he complained furiously,
giving Bridget a perfunctory kiss which seemed to mean
more to her than it did to him. 'Slap in the middle of
Hyde Park. Back tyre shot to pieces. Couple of tarts
laughed themselves sick. Are you the languages?'

He had swung suddenly round on me. I'm not used
to words of that strength from clients, nor to repeating
them in the presence of ladies, but I will say at once that
the man described by Mr Anderson as my fellow genius
in the field was like no client I'd ever met, which I knew
even before he fixed me with Bogey's diluted stare.

'He's Brian, darling,' Bridget said quickly, fearing
perhaps that I might say something different. 'Brian
Sinclair. Jack knows all about him.'

A man's voice was yelling up at us and it was the
same voice I had been relating to.

'Maxie! Hell are you, man? It's all hands to the pump.'

But Maxie paid the voice no attention and by the time I looked down, its owner had once more disappeared.

'Know what this caper's about, Sinclair?'

'Not yet, sir.'

'That old fart Anderson didn't tell you?'

'*Darling*,' Bridget protested.

'He said he didn't know either, sir.'

'And it's French, Lingala and Swahili-plus, right?'

'Correct, sir.'

'Bembe?'

'Is not a problem, sir.'

'Shi?'

'I also have Shi.'

'Kinyarwanda?'

'Ask him what he doesn't speak, darling,' Bridget advised. 'It's quicker.'

'I was interpreting Kinyarwanda only yesterday evening, sir,' I replied, sending messages of love to Hannah.

'Fucking marvellous,' he mused, continuing to peer at me as if I were some exciting new species. 'Where does it all come from?'

'My father was an African missionary,' I explained, remembering too late that Mr Anderson had told me I was the son of a mining engineer. It was on the tip of my tongue to add *Catholic* so that he would know the whole story, but Bridget was looking daggers at me so I decided to hold it back for later.

'And your French is a hundred per cent, right?'

Flattered as I was by the positive nature of his interrogation, I had to demur. 'I never claim a hundred per
cent, sir. I strive for perfection, but there's always room
for improvement'—which is what I say to all my clients,
from the mightiest to the humblest, but when I said it
to Maxie, it acquired a brave ring for me.

'Well, my French is failed O level,' he riposted. His
floating gaze had not left mine for an instant. 'And
you're game, right? You don't mind pushing the
envelope?'

'Not if it's good for the country, sir,' I replied,
echoing my response to Mr Anderson.

'Good for the country, good for Congo, good for
Africa,' he assured me.

And was gone, but not before I had notched up
other points of interest regarding my new employer. He
wore a diver's watch on his left wrist and on the other a
bracelet of gold links. His right hand, judging by its
texture, was bulletproof. A woman's lips brushed my
temple and for a moment I convinced myself they were
Hannah's but they were Bridget's, kissing me goodbye.
I don't know how long I waited after that. Or what I
found to think about that lasted more than two
seconds. Naturally I was pasturing on my newfound
leader and all that had passed between us in our brief
exchange. *Bembe*, I kept repeating to myself. Bembe
always made me smile. It was what we Mission school
kids yelled at each other, out on the red mud-patch,
playing splash-soccer in the teeming rain.

I also remember feeling piqued at being deserted by
Maxie and Bridget simultaneously, and there was a low
moment when I wished I was back at Penelope's party,
which was what made me jump to my feet, determined
to phone Hannah from the lobby, come what may. I
was already descending the staircase—it had a highly
polished brass handrail and I felt guilty putting my
sweaty palm on it—and I was bracing myself to cross
the hall under the eye of the grizzly bouncer, when the
doors to the conference room parted in slow motion,
and out poured its occupants in twos and threes until
some sixteen of them were assembled.

*   *   *

I must exercise caution here. When you walk in on a
large, buzzing group containing partly public faces,
you take your mental snapshots and you start fitting
names to them. But are they the right names? Of the
ten or eleven white men, I am able here and now
positively to identify two high-profile corporate chief-
tains from the City of London, one ex-Downing Street
spin-doctor turned freelance consultant, one septuagenarian corporate raider, knighted, and one evergreen
pop-star and intimate of the younger royals who had
recently been the target of drugs-and-sex allegations in
Penelope's great newspaper. The faces of these five
men are engraved in my memory for good. I recognised
them as soon as they emerged. They remained in a
bunch and talked in a bunch, not three yards from

where I was standing. I was privy to fragments of their conversation.

Neither of the two Indian men was known to me, although I have since identified the more boisterous of the two as the founder of a multi-billion-pound clothing empire with headquarters in Manchester and Madras. Of the three black Africans, the only one familiar to me was the exiled former finance minister of a West African republic which, given my present circumstances, I will refrain from naming further. Like his two companions, he appeared relaxed and Westernised in clothing and demeanour.

Delegates emerging from a conference tend in my experience to be in one of two moods: resentful, or ebullient. These were ebullient, but bellicose. They had extravagant hopes, but also enemies. One such enemy was *Tabby*, like Tabby the cat, spat out between the yellowed teeth of the seventy-something corporate raider. Tabby was a slimy bastard, even by the standards of his trade, he was telling his Indian audience; it would be a real pleasure to slip one past him when the opportunity arose. Such fleeting impressions were swept from my mind, however, by the belated emergence from the conference room of Maxie, and at his side, as tall as Maxie but more elegant in dress and deportment, the owner of the voice that had seemed to speak to me while I was waiting on the staircase: Lord Brinkley of the Sands, art lover, entrepreneur, socialite, former New Labour minister and—always his strong suit where I personally was concerned—long-time defender and champion of all things African.

And I will say at once that my impression of Lord Brinkley in the flesh amply confirmed my high regard for him as seen on television and heard on my preferred medium, radio. The clean-cut features with firm jaw and flying mane mirrored precisely the sense of high purpose I had always associated with him. How often had I not cheered him to the echo when he was berating the Western world for its want of an African conscience? If Maxie and Lord Brinkley were linking arms in a hush-hush pro-Congolese endeavour—and they were linking them now, literally, as they came towards me—then I was honoured indeed to be a part of it!

Lord Brinkley also enjoyed my esteem for a personal reason, namely Penelope. As I hovered deferentially at the edge of the gathering I remembered with relish how Sir Jack, as he then was, had hit her great newspaper for record damages arising out of baseless allegations regarding his financial dealings, and how his triumphant vindication had in turn imposed a strain on our domestic bliss, with Penelope as per usual defending the sacred liberty of the press to besmirch whomever it chose, and Salvo siding with Sir Jack in consideration of his outspoken sympathy for the continent of Africa, and his determination to free its peoples from the triple curse of exploitation, corruption and disease, thereby putting it back on the table economically where it belongs.

So great had been my indignation, indeed, that unbeknown to Penelope I had written a personal and private letter of support to Lord Brinkley, to which he was gracious enough to send a letter in reply. And it was this sense of personal kinship—mingled I will admit with a certain proprietorial pride as one of his loyal fans—that emboldened me to step forward from my place in the shadows and address him man to man.

'Excuse me, sir,' I said, having first reminded myself that this was a no-name operation, and therefore carefully *not* saying, which I might have done, 'Lord Brinkley' or 'My Lord' or 'Your Lordship'.

Upon which, he came to a smart halt, as did Maxie. From their puzzled demeanour I deduced they were unsure which *sir* I was addressing, so I shifted my stance until I was engaging Lord Brinkley directly. And I was pleased to note that, while Maxie appeared to be reserving judgment, Lord Brinkley was once more smiling graciously. With a certain kind of person, if you've got my skin colour, you get the double smile: first the token one, then the white liberal's overbright number. But Lord Brinkley's smile was a full-on application of spontaneous goodwill.

'I just wanted to say I'm very proud, sir,' I said.

I would have liked to add that Hannah would be equally proud if she only knew, but I contained myself.

'Proud? Proud what of, dear boy?'

'Being aboard, sir. Working for you in whatever capacity. My name's Sinclair, sir. The interpreter that

Mr Anderson sent. French, Swahili, Lingala, and minority African languages.'

The gracious smile did not waver.

'Anderson?' he repeated, searching his memory. 'Not a name to me. Sorry about that. Must be a chum of Maxie's here.'

This naturally surprised me, since I had wrongly assumed that the *Jack* of Mr Anderson's conversation was standing before me, but such was clearly not the case. Meanwhile, Lord Brinkley's fine leonine head had lifted, apparently in response to a summons from down the room, though I hadn't heard one.

'Be with you in just one jiffy, Marcel. Got a conference call booked for midnight and I want the three of you at my side. Dot the i's and cross the t's before that bugger Tabby does any more eleventh-hour cliff-hanging.'

He hurried off, leaving me with Maxie, who was regarding me in a quizzical manner. But my eyes remained fondly on Lord Brinkley. Arms gracefully outstretched, he was gathering the three Africans together in a single embrace: a regular persuader in any language, as I could tell by the radiant expressions on their faces.

'Something bothering you, old boy?' Maxie enquired, his Bogey-like eyes peering at me in veiled amusement.

'Nothing really, sir. I wondered whether I had spoken out of turn.'

At which he gave a raucous laugh and clapped a bulletproof hand on my shoulder.

'You were first rate. Scared the shit out of him. Got a bag? Where's your bag? Front desk. March.'

With barely a wave for the distinguished company he hurried me through the throng to the lobby, where a blond boy stood proffering my night-bag. A people-carrier with blackened windows and open doors was parked at the kerbside, a blue light turning on its roof, plainclothes driver at the wheel. A wiry man with a crew-cut hovered on the pavement. A giant with a grey ponytail and leather jacket was already seated in the rear corner of the car. The crew-cut bundled me into the back seat next to him and sprang after me, slamming the door shut behind him. Maxie plonked himself in the front beside the driver. As he did so, two police motor-cyclists came roaring into the square from the direction of Mount Street and our driver pulled out at speed behind them.

But I still managed to peer back over my shoulder. Under pressure, I'm like that. Tell me to look one way, I'll look the other. I turned, and through the rear window, which had a dusty translucence, I took a long look at the house we'd just left. I saw three steps or four leading to a dark blue, maybe black door, closed. I saw two CCTV cameras above it, big ones, high up. I saw a flat Georgian-style brick façade with white-painted sash windows and the blinds drawn. I looked for a number on the door and there wasn't one. The house was gone in a flash, but never tell me it wasn't there. It was there and I saw it. I had passed through its portals and shaken hands with my hero Jack Brinkley, and according to Maxie I had scared the shit out of him.

* * *

So was Salvo our neophyte secret agent not terrified out of his skin, you ask, to be hurtling at breakneck speed through the clogged Friday traffic of bombed London in the company of men he didn't know, destined for what perils he could only guess? He was not. He was off to serve his employers, do good for his country, the Congo, Mr Anderson and Hannah. I am again reminded of our neighbour Paula, confidante to Penelope and suspected wolverine, who studied psychology at a minor Canadian university. Being short on paying clients it is Paula's habit to practise her arts on anybody incautious enough to wander into her range, which is how she came to inform me, after imbibing the major part of a bottle of my Rioja, that what I lacked among my other deficiencies was *predator awareness*.

There were five of us inside that people-carrier as we tore off westward from Berkeley Square, chasing our police escort down bus lanes, shooting lights after them, circumnavigating traffic islands on the wrong side, yet the atmosphere inside was as calm as a day's outing on the river. Silhouetted against the windscreen our plainclothes driver was slipping so nimbly through the gears that he seemed scarcely to move at all. Next to him lounged Maxie without his seat belt. He had his gasmask case open on his lap and was consulting a mildewed notebook by the overhead light while he issued a string of casual orders over a cellphone:

'Where the fuck is Sven? Tell him to get off his elbows and take tonight's flight. I want sixty ready to go by the end of next week. If he's got to charter them up from Cape Town, tough shit. And fit, Harry. Seasoned but not over the hill, got it? Top dollar, full insurance. What else do you want? Free hookers?'

I was making the acquaintance of my disparate companions either side of me. The grey ponytail to my right was Benny, he told me over a crushing introductory handshake, and he had the spread body and pocked complexion of a boxer gone to seed. By his voice I guessed he was white Rhodesian. The crew-cut to my left was half Benny's size, and a root-and-bough cockney, although he called himself Anton. He wore a better sports coat than mine, sharply ironed gabardine trousers and brown shoes with boned toecaps. I have referred already to my respect for well-polished shoes.

'And that's all the luggage we've got, is it, governor?' Anton murmured, prodding with his toecap at my Rexine night-bag.

'Anton, that is all our luggage.'

'What's in it then?'—parting his lips so little that from any larger distance it would have been hard to tell he was speaking at all.

'Personal effects, officer,' I replied jauntily.

'How personal's that then, governor? Personal like tape recorder? Personal like a nine-millimetre automatic? Or personal like frothy knickers? You never know what's personal these days, do you, Benj?'

'Always a mystery, the personal aspect,' big Benny agreed from the other side of me.

Maxie's raunchy monologue continued unabated from the front seat:

'I don't care what time of night it is, Corky never slept in his life. If he can't be ready in five days from now, he'll miss the party. Well, have you got a fucking pencil, or have you lost that too?'

Knightsbridge sailed by, then Chelsea, where I was pleased to observe that no frozen child was clinging to the embankment wall. Our motorcycle escorts were heading west. Shooting another traffic light, they swerved left and swung due southward, causing an uncontrolled detonation inside my head. We were *crossing Battersea Bridge*! We were a thousand yards from number 17, Norfolk Mansions, Prince of Wales Drive, *my* apartment, *her* apartment, *our* apartment, and closing on it by the second! An idealised vision of our married life appeared before me, similar to the one I had forced on Bridget. To my left lay *our* park where any year soon I had planned to be taking *our* child to the funfair! Behind me lay *our* river! How many post-prandial, post-coital saunters had Penelope and I not shared along its towpath? Look, I could see our bedroom window! In my haste to get into my dinner jacket, I had left the lights on!

I steadied myself. Secret Servants of the Crown must not overreact, not even part-time ones, not even when struck by thunderbolts. Yet the sight of my own Battersea reaching out to her errant son had reduced me to a state of unreasoning terror familiar to all first-time adulterers: the terror of being turfed into the street with just the one suitcase; of losing the respect of the superb woman you remember too late that you cherish and desire above all others; of forfeiting your CD collection and your place on the property ladder, even if it's only a toehold; of dying a no-name death under a bush on Hampstead Heath.

We were over the bridge and within hailing distance of my front door when our police escorts peeled away leaving our driver to veer left yet again, this time down a ramp and through an open gateway before screeching to a halt. The doors of the people-carrier slammed open to admit the ear-splitting roar of engines, but in my confusion I did not locate the source. Then I saw, not thirty yards from us, glistening under a ring of sodium lights, a silver helicopter with its rotors turning.

'Where are we going?' I yelled after Anton as he leaped deftly onto the tarmac.

'For the ride of your life, governor! London by night! Get your arse out of the car, *now*!'

Maxie had not taken three strides towards the helicopter before he spun round, his gasmask case banging at his hip. Shoving Anton aside, he leaned in.

'Something amiss, old boy?'

'It's my home, sir. Up the road. Five hundred yards. It's where I live with my wife. It's her night,' I explained, forgetting once again in my perturbation that I was supposed to live in a post-office box.

'What do you mean, *her night*, old boy?'

'Her party, sir. She's been promoted. In her job. She's a top journalist.'

'All right. Which is it to be? Come with us, or go home to Mummy and dump us in the shit?'

The improbable figure of Thorne the Horn came galloping to my rescue, accompanied by all the other Thornes before him, plus all the chicken dinners I had metaphorically shoved down the waste-disposal unit, or failed to. In the kind of mood-swing that I was coming to expect of myself, I felt bathed in shame that in a moment of frailty my sense of high purpose had given way to such trivial considerations. With Maxie leading and Benny and Anton to either side of me, I scampered towards the waiting helicopter. Big Benny heaved me up the steps and through the open hatch, Anton pressed me into a window seat and sat himself firmly next to me, Maxie wedged himself beside the pilot and jammed on a pair of headphones.

Suddenly we were *Fram* come true. Battersea Power Station sank into the ground beneath us, taking Prince of Wales Drive with it. We were six hundred feet above reality and swinging north. Skimming over traffic crammed nose-to-tail in Park Lane, I took a glance at Lord's Cricket Ground but nobody was playing. Then to my heart's delight and pain, I saw the very hospital where, at a dying man's bedside, I had yesterday

evening been reborn. Craning my head, I watched it sail
into the far horizon. My eyes filled with tears, I closed
them and must have slept for a few minutes because
when I looked again, the lights of Luton airport were
rising to enfold us, and my one desire was to phone
Hannah come what may.

* * *

Every airport, I now know, has a light side and a dark side.
In the distance, normal planes were landing and taking
off, but the loudest sound as we hurried across the
fenced-off area came from the heels of my borrowed
shoes clattering on the concrete. A moist dusk was falling.
Ahead of us lay a green shed sunk amid banks of earth, its
doors open to receive us. The atmosphere inside was of an
army drill hall. Eight able-bodied white men in casual
wear stood about, kitbags at their feet. Maxie strolled
among them, a pat on the back here, an African's double
handshake there. I cast round for a public phone but saw
none. And anyway what was I going to use for change?

'Where's Spider, for fuck's sake?'

'Any minute, Skipper,' came Anton's respectful reply.
'Says his van is walking wounded.'

I spotted a door marked STAFF ONLY and stepped
inside. No phone on offer. I emerged to see Maxie in
conversation with a dyspeptic-looking man in a sloping
black beret and long raincoat standing in a corner of the
room, clutching a documents case. The two were
attempting to communicate in French. Maxie's, as he

had correctly informed me, was atrocious. Could the other man perhaps be the mysterious Philip or *Philippe*? I had neither time nor appetite to explore the question. A boy in a tracksuit was collecting cellphones, sticking labels on them, dropping them into a cardboard box and handing out cloakroom tickets as receipts. With each instrument that went into his box I saw my chances of talking to Hannah recede.

I appealed to Anton: 'I'm afraid I need to make a rather urgent phone call.'

'Who to then, governor?'

'My wife.'

'And why do we need to talk to our wife, if I may ask? I haven't talked to mine for eight years.'

'We're having a bit of a family crisis. A dear friend of ours is ill. She's at his bedside. My wife is. In the hospital. Tending him. He's dying.'

Maxie had abandoned his Frenchman in order to join our discussion. It seemed he missed nothing.

'Dying where, old boy?'

'Hospital, sir.'

'What of?'

'Acute blood disorder. Too advanced for them to cure.'

'Fucking awful way to go. Which one?'

'North London District.'

'Public or private?'

'Public. With private parts. Bits. It's got a special floor for blood disorders.'

'He'll want one more year. Dying chaps always think they want one more year. Does he want one more year?'

'He hasn't said so, sir. Well, not so far. Not that I've heard.'

'Can he swallow?'

I remembered the reek of methylated spirits on Jean-Pierre's breath. Yes, he could swallow.

'Slip him an overdose, my advice. Bottle of soluble aspirin, he can't miss. Make sure her fingerprints aren't on it, stash it under his pillow. Got your mobile, Anton?'

'Right here, Skipper.'

'He makes his call, then hand it to the boys. No mobiles on the op. And no bloody smoking,' he yelled to the whole room. 'That's your last fag, everybody. Fags out *now*!'

'I'd like to be private,' I told Anton, as soon as we were once more alone.

'Wouldn't we all, guv?' he replied, not budging from where he stood.

I pulled off my Harris Tweed jacket and rolled back my left shirtsleeve, exposing the telephone and extension number of Hannah's ward written in her own hand with the felt-tipped pen from behind her ear. I dialled, and a woman's voice sang, 'Tropical,' with a Jamaican lilt.

'Yes, hello, Grace,' I said brightly. 'I'm ringing regarding the patient Jean-Pierre. I believe Hannah is at his bedside. May I speak to her, please?'

'Salvo?' My heart leaped, but it was still Grace. 'Is that you, Salvo? The interpreter man?'

'Yes, it is, and I'd like to speak to Hannah, please'— keeping the phone pressed hard against my ear on account of Anton. 'It's personal and it's a tiny bit urgent. Could you kindly bring her to the phone? Just tell her it's'—I was about to say Salvo, but caught myself in the nick of time. 'Me,' I said, with a smile at Anton.

Grace, unlike Hannah, moved at African tempo. If something was worth doing, it was worth doing slowly. 'Hannah she's *busy*, Salvo,' she complained at last.

Busy? Busy with whom? Busy how? I adopted a military, Maxie-like tone.

'All the same, perhaps I could just speak to her for one minute, okay? It's important, Grace. She'll know *exactly* what it's about. If you don't mind, please.'

Another monumental delay, patiently shared by Anton.

'You farin' well, Salvo?'

'Fine, thank you. Is she there?'

'Hannah she's got some real heavy meetin' with Matron goin' on. They wouldn't appreciate at all to be disturbed. Better call another time, Salvo. Maybe tomorrow when she's off.'

With *Matron?* Like Matron who runs the world? *Real heavy?* About what? *Sleeping with married interpreters?* I must leave her a message, but what message?

'Salvo?' Grace again.

'What is it?'

'I got some real sad news for you.'

'What's that?'

'Jean-Pierre. The old bum who was sleepin' rough. We lost him, Salvo. Hannah was real cut up. Me too.'

I must have closed my eyes here. When I opened them Anton had removed the phone from my hand and given it to the tracksuit.

'That's our wife's name, is it?' he asked. 'Hannah?'

'Why shouldn't it be?'

'I wouldn't know, governor, would I? Depends who else you've got written on that arm of yours, doesn't it?'

Maxie's men were shouldering kitbags and stepping into the darkness. A no-name aeroplane loomed stubby and sinister in the twilight. Anton walked at my side while big Benny took care of the Frenchman in the beret.

5

It is a known fact that the thoughts of the most loyal raw recruit on the eve of battle stray in unforeseen directions, some of them downright mutinous. And I will not pretend that my own were in this regard exempt, given that the décor, ventilation and lighting system of our windowless flying machine would have been better suited to the transport of champion dogs, and that the howl of our twin engines, once you got hooked on it, was a composite of all the voices I didn't wish to hear, with Penelope's in pole position. In place of cushioned seats we had iron cages opening onto a central aisle, each equipped with a grimy prison mattress. Hammocks of orange webbing were slung from the ceiling, grab handles being provided for the convenience of those wishing to jump into the unknown. The one mitigating factor was the presence of Anton and Benny in the cells to either side of me, but Benny appeared to be doing his household accounts and Anton was ostentatiously absorbed in a pornographic magazine of great age.

Our flight deck, regarded by many as an aircraft's sanctum, was cordoned off with frayed ribbon. Our two pilots, middle-aged, overweight and unshaven, were so busy ignoring their passengers that you might well have asked whether they knew they had any. Add to that a chain of blue corridor lights evocative of a certain North London hospital and it was little wonder if my sense of high purpose should give way to the internal journeys I was making on the newly opened shuttle between Penelope and Hannah.

Within minutes of take-off our team, almost to a man, had fallen victim to African sleeping sickness, using their kitbags for pillows. Two exceptions were Maxie and his French friend who, huddled together at the aft end of the plane, were swapping sheets of paper like an anxious couple who have received a threatening communication from the mortgage company. The Frenchman had removed his beret, exposing an aquiline face, penetrating eyes and a tonsured pate fringed with straw-coloured hair. His name, which I extracted from the laconic Benny, was Monsieur Jasper. What Frenchman was ever called Jasper? I asked myself incredulously. But perhaps like me he was travelling under an alias.

'Do you think I should go over and offer them my services?' I asked Anton, suspecting that the two were having difficulty communicating.

'Governor, if the skipper wants your services, the skipper will take them,' he replied, without lifting his head from his magazine.

Of the remaining members of our team, save one, I can give no account. I remember them as a grim-jawed group in bulked-out anoraks and baseball caps who stopped talking whenever I drew close.

'Wife problems sorted, old boy? Chaps round here call me Skipper by the by.'

I must have been dozing, for when I looked up I found myself staring into the magnified blue eyes of Maxie as he squatted Arab-style at my elbow. My spirits instantly revived. How many times had I not listened to Brother Michael regaling me with the feats of arms performed by Colonel T. E. Lawrence and other great Englishmen at war? With the touch of a magician's wand the interior of our plane transformed itself into an Arab nomad's tent. The overhead webbing became our goatskin roof. In my imagination, desert stars were peeping through the gaps.

'Wife well and truly sorted, thank you, Skipper,' I replied, suiting my energetic manner to his. 'No further problems in that department, I'm pleased to say.'

'How about that ailing chum of yours?'

'Oh, well, he died actually,' I replied with equal casualness.

'Poor bugger. Still, no point in hanging around the back of the herd once your time's up. You a Napoleon buff?'

'Well, not exactly,' I replied, reluctant to admit that *Cromwell, Our Chief of Men* was as far as my historical researches had advanced.

'By the time he got to Borodino, he'd lost the plot. Sleepwalking at Smolensk, gaga by the time he got to Borodino, fucked at forty. Couldn't piss, couldn't think straight. Gives me three more years. How about you?'

'Well, twelve actually,' I replied, privately marvelling that a man with no French should appoint Napoleon his rôle model.

'It's a quickie. Anderson tell you that?' He ran on, not waiting for my answer. 'We tiptoe in, talk to a few Congolese chaps, cut a deal with 'em, get their signatures on a contract, tiptoe out. We've got 'em for six hours tops. Each of 'em has said yes separately, now we've got to get 'em to say yes to each other. Officially they're somewhere else, and that's where they've got to be by the time the clock chimes midnight. With me?'

'With you, Skipper.'

'This is your first gig, right?'

'I'm afraid it is. My baptism of fire, you might say,' I conceded, with a rueful smile to indicate that I was alive to my drawbacks. And, unable to restrain my curiosity: 'I don't suppose you'd like to tell me where we're going, would you, sir?'

'Little island up north where no one will disturb us. Less you know now, better you'll sleep later.' He allowed himself a slight softening of his features. 'Every time the same with these jobs. "Hurry up and wait", then "Where the fuck are you?" Next thing you know, there are ten other arseholes in the race, your chaps are scattered across the globe and your back tyre's got a puncture.'

His restless gaze lighted on a column of suitcase-style boxes, black-painted and of uniform size, tethered to a grid beside the cabin door. At their base, curled up on his mattress like a newborn calf, lay a gnomic man in a flat cloth cap and quilted waistcoat, to all appearances as sound asleep as his comrades.

'Any of that junk actually *work*, Spider?' Maxie demanded, raising his voice to carry across the width of the fuselage.

The gnome, no sooner addressed, vaulted to his feet acrobat-style, and stood comically to attention before us.

'Shouldn't think so, Skip. Load of old rubbish, by the looks of it,' he replied cheerfully, in what my top interpreter's ear instantly identified as a Welsh intonation. 'With twelve hours to cobble it together, what do you expect for your money?'

'What have we got to eat?'

'Well now, Skip, since you ask, an anonymous donor has very kindly sent this Fortnum's hamper, you see. Or I think he's anonymous, because search where you will regardless, there's not a sender's name to be found anywhere, not so much as a card.'

'Anything inside it?'

'Not a lot, frankly, no. A whole York ham, I suppose. About a kilo of foie gras. A couple of sides of smoked salmon, a fillet of cold roast beef, cheesy Cheddar biscuits, magnum of champagne. Nothing to whet the appetite, not really. I thought of sending it back.'

'Have it on the way home,' Maxie ordered, cutting him short. 'What else is on the menu?'

'Chow mein. Luton's best. Should be nice and cold by now.'

'Dish it up, Spider. And say hello to the languages here. Name of Brian. On loan from the Chat Room.'

'The Chat Room, eh? Well, that takes me back, I will say. Mr Anderson's sweat shop. He's still a baritone, is he? Not castrated or anything?'

Spider, as I now knew him, smiled down on me with his boot-button eyes and I smiled back at him in the confidence of having another friend in our great enterprise.

'And you can do military,' Maxie announced, extracting from his gasmask case an old tin flask clad in khaki cloth and a packet of Bath Oliver biscuits. The flask, I later learned, contained Malvern water.

'What military were we thinking of, Skipper?' I countered.

My chow mein was cold and gluey, but I was determined to make a good fist of it.

'Weaponry, ordnance, firepower, calibre, all that crap'—taking a bite of his Bath Oliver biscuit.

I assured him that, thanks to my experience of the Chat Room, I was familiar with a range of technical and military terms. 'But basically what happens, where there's no vernacular equivalent, is they filch it from the nearest colonial language,' I added, getting into my stride. 'Which, in the case of a Congolese, would naturally mean French.' And, unable to restrain myself, 'Unless of course they've been Rwandan or Ugandan trained, in which case you'll get some purloined English, such as *Mag*, or *Ambush*, or *RPG*.'

Maxie appeared no more than politely interested. 'So a Munyamulenge rabbiting away to a Bembe would talk about a *semi-automatique* so to speak?'

'Well, assuming they could talk to each other at all,' I replied, keen to show off my expertise.

'Meaning what, old boy?'

'Well, for instance, a Bembe might speak Kinyarwanda, but not be able to make the *total* bridge to Kinyamulenge.'

'So what do they do?'—wiping his wrist across his mouth.

'Well, basically, they'd have to muddle through on whatever they had in common. Each would understand the other—to a point, but not necessarily all the way.'

'So after that?'

'They might do a bit of Swahili, a bit of French. It depends what they've got, really.'

'Unless they happen to have you around, that it? You speak 'em all.'

'Well, in this case, yes,' I replied modestly. 'I wouldn't impose, naturally. I'd wait to see what was needed.'

'So whatever they speak, we speak it better. Right? Well done us,' he mused. But it was clear from his tone that he wasn't as satisfied as his words suggested. 'Question is, do we need to tell 'em all that? Maybe we should play it canny. Keep our hardware under wraps.'

Hardware? What hardware? Or was he still talking about my proficiency in military matters? I cautiously voiced my confusion.

'*Your* hardware, for Christ's sake. Your arsenal of languages. Every child knows a good soldier doesn't advertise his strength to the enemy. Same with your languages. Dig 'em in and keep the tarps over 'em till you need to wheel 'em out. Common sense.'

Maxie, I was beginning to discover, possessed a dangerous and beguiling magic. Part of this magic was making you feel that his most outlandish plan was the normal one, even if you had yet to discover what his plan entailed.

'Try this one for size,' he suggested, as if offering me a compromise that would satisfy my over-exacting standards. 'Suppose we put it out that you speak English, French and Swahili and call it a day? That's more than enough for anybody. And we keep your little ones to ourselves. How would that grab you? Different kind of challenge for you. New.'

If I had understood him correctly, it wouldn't grab me in the least, but that wasn't quite what I replied.

'In what *context* exactly, Skipper—in what *circumstances* might we be saying that? Or *not* saying it,' I added, affecting what I hoped was a wise smile. 'I don't mean to be pedantic, but who would we be saying it *to*?'

'To everyone. Whole room. In the interests of the

op. To help the conference along. Look.' He made one of those pauses that professionals make when they're trying to explain something to a simpleton. In my time, I'll admit, I have been guilty of the same presumption. 'We have two Sinclairs'—holding out his bulletproof palms, one for each of me—'Sinclair *above* the water-line'—raising the left palm—'and Sinclair *below* the waterline'—dropping the right palm into his lap. 'Above the line, tip of the iceberg, you speak French and variations of Swahili only. Plus English to your chums, obviously. Which is normal rations for any middle-of-the-list interpreter. With me?'

'With you thus far, Skipper,' I affirmed, striving to evince enthusiasm.

'And *below* it'—I was now staring downward at his right palm—'the remaining nine-tenths of the iceberg, which is all the other stuff you speak. You could play that one out, couldn't you? Not all that difficult, once you've got a grip on yourself.' Taking back his hands, he treated himself to another biscuit while he waited for me to see the light.

'I still don't think I'm *completely* there, all the same, Skipper,' I said.

'Don't be a tart, Sinclair, of course you are! It's dead simple. I walk into the conference room. I introduce you.' He did so, in excruciating French, while he masti-cated his biscuit: '"*Je vous présente Monsieur Sinclair, notre interprète distingué. Il parle anglais, français et Swahili.*" And Bob's your uncle. Anyone who looses off in another language within your hearing, you don't understand 'em.' My facial expression, despite my best efforts, was still not to his liking. 'For Christ's sake, man. It's not such a big deal, acting dumb. Chaps do it every day without even trying. That's because they *are* dumb. Well, you're not. You're fucking brilliant. Well, *be* brilliant. Young strong chap like you, it's a doddle.'

'So when do I get to use my *other* languages, Skipper? The ones you call below the waterline,' I persisted.

The languages I'm proudest of, I was thinking. The languages that separate me from the pack. The languages that in my book are not submerged at all, but triumphantly salvaged. The languages, if you're me, that should be paraded for all to hear.

'When you're told to and not before. You're under sealed orders. Part one today, part two in the morning, soon as we get final confirmation that the show's on the road.' Then to my relief his rare smile came up, the one you'd cross deserts for. 'You're our secret weapon, Sinclair. Star of the show and don't forget it. How many times in life does a fellow get a chance to give a shove to history?'

'Once if he's lucky,' I rejoined loyally.

'Luck's just another word for destiny,' Maxie corrected me, his Bogey-like eyes gleaming mystically. 'Either you make your own or you're screwed. This isn't some candy-arsed training caper. It's delivering democracy at the end of a gun barrel to the Eastern

Congo. Get the right groundswell going, give 'em the right leadership, and the whole of Kivu will come running.'

My head was swirling from this first glimpse of his great vision and his next words spoke straight into my heart—and Hannah's.

'Greatest sin committed by the big players in the Congo till now has been indifference, right?'

'Right,' I replied heartily.

'Intervene if you can make a fast buck, get the fuck out ahead of the next crisis. Right?'

'Right.'

'The country's in stasis. Useless government, chaps sitting around waiting for elections that may or may not happen. And if they *do* happen, will likely as not leave 'em worse off than before. So there's a vacuum. Right?'

'Right,' I echoed yet again.

'And we're filling it. Before any of the other buggers do. Because they're all at it, the Yanks, the Chinese, the French, the multinationals, the lot. Trying to get in before the elections. We're intervening, and we're *staying*. And this time, it's the Congo itself that's going to be the lucky winner.'

I attempted yet again to voice my appreciation of all that he had said, but he rode through me.

'Congo's been bleeding to death for five centuries,' he went on distractedly. 'Fucked by the Arab slavers, fucked by their fellow Africans, fucked by the United Nations, the CIA, the Christians, the Belgians, the

French, the Brits, the Rwandans, the diamond companies, the gold companies, the mineral companies, half
the world's carpetbaggers, their own government in
Kinshasa, and any minute now they're going to be
fucked by the oil companies. Time they had a break,
and we're the boys to give it to 'em.'

His restless eye had switched to Monsieur Jasper at
the other end of the fuselage, who was holding up his
arm in the manner of the checkout clerk at our Battersea
mini-market when she hasn't got enough pound coins.

'Part two of your sealed orders tomorrow,' he
announced and, grabbing his gasmask case, struck off
down the aisle.

* * *

When you're under Maxie's spell your brain gets
anaesthetised. Everything he had said was music to
my bi-cultural ear. But coming round, I began to hear
less compliant voices than my own making themselves
audible above the irregular throbbing of the plane's
engines.

I had said 'Right.' Had I said yes?

I hadn't said no, so presumably I had.

But yes to what, exactly?

Had Mr Anderson informed me, when handing me
my job description, that it involved turning myself into
a linguistic iceberg with nine-tenths of me below the
waterline? He had not. He had said he had a bit of live
action for me, and he was sending me into the field

where I would be living a lie and not the Bible truth that we had been brought up to. Of waterlines and controlled schizophrenia not one word.

Don't be a tart, Sinclair, it's dead simple. Simple how, please, Skipper? Pretending you've heard something when you haven't is relatively simple, I would concede that. People get away with it every day. Pretending you haven't heard something when you have, on the other hand, is in my perception the reverse of simple. Your top interpreter responds without premeditation. He is trained to leap in. He hears, he leaps, the art follows. All right, granted: he will in due course reflect. But the talent comes in the instant response, not in the rehash.

I was still meditating along these lines when one of our unshaven pilots yelled at us to hang on tight. As if hit by gunfire, the plane winced, winced again, and bounced ponderously to a halt. The cabin door banged open, a blast of chill air made me grateful for my Harris Tweed. Our skipper was first to vanish into the void; next went Benny with his kitbag, followed by Monsieur Jasper and his briefcase. At Anton's urging I clambered after them, my night-bag leading. Landing on soft earth I inhaled the smell of sea at low tide. Two sets of head-lights were bumping towards us over the field. First a half-truck pulled alongside, then a minibus. Anton shooed me aboard the minibus, Benny shoved Jasper after me. Behind us in the shadow of the plane, the anoraks were loading black boxes onto the half-truck. Our woman driver was a mature version of Bridget in a headscarf and fur-lined jacket. The pitted track possessed neither markings nor road signs. Were we driving right or left? By the meagre beam of our dipped headlights, stateless sheep gawped at us from the trackside. We mounted a crest and were starting our descent when, out of a starless sky, two granite gateposts lurched towards us. We rattled over a cattle grid, skirted a coppice of pine trees and came to rest in a cobbled courtyard with high walls.

Gables and roof lines were lost in darkness. In single file we followed our driver to a dimly lit stone porch twenty feet high. Rows of Wellington boots greeted us, their sizes written in white paint. The sevens had lines drawn through them in the continental manner. The ones began on the upstroke. Ancient snow-shoes like crossed tennis racquets were mounted on the wall. Had Scotsmen worn them? Swedes? Norsemen? Danes? Or was our host merely a collector of Nordic bric-à-brac? *Little island up north where no one will disturb us.* The less we knew, the better we would sleep. Our driver went ahead of us. A label on her fur collar said she was Gladys. We trooped into a raftered Great Hall. Corridors led in all directions. A tea urn and cold collation were on offer to those still peckish after their chow mein. A second woman, a smiler labelled Janet, was directing members of the team to wherever they needed to go. On Janet's orders I perched on an embroidered settle.

A bulbous grandfather clock was set at British time. Six hours since I had left Hannah. Five hours since I had left Penelope. Four hours since I had left Mr Anderson. Two hours since I had left Luton. Half an hour since Maxie had told me to keep my best languages below the waterline. Anton my good shepherd was shaking my shoulder. Traipsing after him up a spiral staircase, I convinced myself I was about to receive just punishment at the cleansing hands of the Sanctuary's Father Guardian.

'All right in here, are we, governor?' Anton enquired, pushing open a door. 'Not homesick for our wife and veg?'

'Not really, Anton. Just a bit—expectant,' I said stupidly.

'Well, that's a nice state of affairs, I will say. When's it due?'

Realising we had scarcely exchanged a word since my abortive phone call to Hannah, I thought it appropriate to bond. 'Are you really married, Anton?' I laughed, remembering the wife he claimed not to have spoken to for eight years.

'Now and then, governor. Off and on.'

'Between jobs, as it were?' I suggested.

'As it were, governor. As it might be. Given the way it is.'

I tried again. 'So what do you do with your spare time? When you're not doing this stuff, I mean?'

'All sorts really, governor. Bit of prison, when I've got the patience. Cape Town I like. Not the prison, the seaside. I fancy a girl here and there, well, we all do, don't we? Now you say your prayers nice, governor, because we've got a big day tomorrow, and if you screw up, we all screw up, which the Skipper wouldn't like, would he?'

'And you're his second-in-command,' I suggested admiringly. 'That must be quite a thing to handle.'

'Let's just say you can't be Mr Mercurial and not need a bit of looking after.'

'Am *I* mercurial, Anton?' I asked, surprising myself.

'Governor, if you want my humble opinion, with the height we've got, and those bedroom eyelashes we don't know what to do with, and all the ladies we've got up our sleeve, I would say we are a lot of people under one helmet, which is why we do the lingoes so nice.'

Closing the door on him, I sat down on the bed. A blissful exhaustion overcame me. Discarding my borrowed clothes I consigned myself to Hannah's waiting arms. But not before I had lifted the bedside telephone and rattled its cradle several times, only to confirm that it was not connected.

6

I woke abruptly in my underclothes at my usual early hour, and turned by force of habit onto my right side preparatory to adopting the 'spoons' position with Penelope, only to make the familiar discovery that she was not yet back from a nocturnal assignment. I woke a second time, and with greater circumspection, to the knowledge that I was lying in the bed of a deceased white relative whose bearded features, set in an ornate Victorian frame, frowned down on me from above the marble fireplace. Finally, to my pleasure, I woke a third time with Hannah curled up in my arms, enabling me to inform her, irrespective of the Official Secrets Act, that I was engaged on a clandestine mission to bring democracy to the Congo, which was the reason I hadn't phoned her.

Only then, with the morning sun peeping between the curtains, did I feel able to take stock of my well-appointed room, which harmoniously combined tradi-tional with modern, including a mirrored dressing table complete with old-style electric typewriter and A4 paper, chest of drawers and armoire, plus trouser-press and early-morning tea tray with plastic kettle and Shaker rocking chair. Venturing into my en suite bathroom, I was pleased to be welcomed by such luxuries as heated towel rail, bathrobe, shower facility, shampoo, bath oil, wipes and all the trimmings, but if I was searching for clues to my whereabouts, I searched in vain. The toiletries were by international makers, there were no fire instructions, laundry lists or complimentary matches, no messages of welcome from a foreign-sounding manager with a printed signature you can't read, and no Gideon Bible in any language.

Showered and wrapped in my bathrobe, I positioned myself at my bedroom window and, peering between its granite mullions, examined the view before me. The first thing I observed was a honey-coloured barn owl, wings outstretched and motionless except for the tips of its feathers. My heart swelled at the sight, but birds are of little help when it comes to national markings. To left and right of me rose hills of olive pastureland, and between them, the silver sea, on whose distant horizon I discerned the shadow of a container ship bound for I knew not where; and closer in to shore, a cluster of small fishing vessels pursued by gulls but, peer as I might, I could not make out their flags. No road was visible, save for the winding track that we had traversed the previous night. Our airfield was not in evidence, and I searched in vain for a telltale windsock or aerial. From the angle of the sun I deduced I was looking north and, from the foliage of the saplings at the water's edge, that the prevailing wind was westerly. Nearer at hand rose a grassy mound topped by a gazebo or summerhouse in the nineteenth-century manner, and to the east of it a ruined chapel and cemetery, in one corner of which stood what appeared to be a Celtic cross, but it could as well have been a war memorial or a monument to a departed grandee.

Returning my attention to the gazebo, I was surprised to observe the figure of a man perched on an elongated ladder. He had not been there a moment earlier, and must therefore have emerged from behind a pillar. On the ground beside him lay a black box similar to those that had flown with us on the plane. The lid being towards me, its contents were obscured. Was the man repairing something? Then what? And why, I wondered, at this early hour?

My curiosity aroused, I picked out two other men, also mysteriously engaged: the one on his knees beside a water main or access point of some nature, and the other in the act of shinning up a telegraph pole, a task for which he appeared to need neither rope nor ladder, thus incidentally putting Penelope's personal trainer, who fancies himself quite the Tarzan, in the shade where he belongs. And this second man, I instantly realised, was known to me not merely by sight but by name. He had scarcely reached the top of the pole before I had identified him as my voluble new Welsh friend Spider, team catering manager and veteran of the Chat Room.

My plan was instantly formed. Under the guise of a pre-breakfast stroll, I would engage Spider in casual conversation and afterwards peruse the inscriptions on the headstones in the cemetery with the aim of establishing the local language and hence my whereabouts. Donning my penitential grey flannels and Harris Tweed jacket and with my ill-fitting shoes in hand, I stole down the main staircase to the front porch. On trying the door, however, I found it locked against me, as were all adjacent doors and windows tested. But that was not all. Through the windows I glimpsed no fewer than three bulked-out anoraks standing guard around the house.

It is at this point that I must confess to a resurgence of anxiety regarding the professional demands Maxie proposed to make of me and which, despite my determination to be a player in our great venture, had plagued my sleep at intervals throughout the night, one dream in particular coming back to me. I was snorkelling out of my depth and the waterline was creeping steadily up my mask. If I didn't wake up, it would reach the top and I would drown. By way of distraction therefore, but also as a means of ridding myself of negative thoughts, I resolved on a fact-finding tour of the ground-floor rooms with the additional aim of acquainting myself with the scene of my approaching ordeal.

The house, true to what I believed to be its original function as a substantial family home, afforded on the garden side a connecting chain of reception rooms, each with French windows abutting onto a grass terrace which ascended by way of a broad stone staircase to the pillared gazebo at the summit. Keeping a weather eye for anoraks, I tentatively pushed open the door to the first of these rooms and found myself in a handsome library in Wedgwood blue with fitted mahogany bookcases and glass doors. In the hope that the books within might provide me with a clue to the identity of the owner, I placed my head to the glass and scrutinised the titles, but was disappointed to be confronted with uniform sets of the world's great writers, each in his original tongue: Dickens in English, Balzac in French, Goethe in German, and Dante in Italian. When I attempted to prise open the doors on the off-chance of a bookplate or inscription I found them locked against me, top and bottom.

After the library came a panelled billiards room. The table, which I estimated to be three-quarter size, possessed no pockets, thus placing it in the French or continental category, whereas the mahogany scoreboard was by Burroughes of London. The third room was a stately drawing room complete with gilt mirrors and an ormolu clock set neither to British nor continental time but stuck resolutely at the twelfth hour. A marble and brass sideboard offered an enticing spread of magazines which ranged from the French *Marie Claire* through the *Tatler* to the Swiss *Du*. It was while I was examining these that I heard the sound of a muffled French oath issuing from an adjoining, fourth room. The connecting door was ajar. Gliding silently across the polished floorboards, I stepped inside. I had entered a gaming room. At its centre stood an oval, green baize table. Eight card-player's chairs with broad wooden arms were arranged around it. At the furthest end, straight-backed behind a computer screen, sat a tonsured Monsieur Jasper without his black beret, typing with two fingers. A night's gingery growth adorned his long face, giving him the air of a great detective. For a while he examined me with an unrelenting stare.

'Why do you spy on me?' he demanded at last in French.

'I'm not spying on you.'

'Then why do you not wear your shoes?'

'Because they don't fit.'

'You have stolen them?'

'Borrowed.'

'You are Moroccan?'

'British.'

'Then why do you speak French like a *pied-noir*?'

'I was brought up in Equatorial Africa. My father was an engineer,' I retorted stiffly, not stooping to comment on his opinion of my French. 'Who are you, anyway?'

'I am from Besançon. I am a French provincial notary with a modest practice in certain technical spheres of international jurisprudence. I am qualified in

French and Swiss taxation law. I have an appointment at Besançon University where I lecture on the charms of offshore companies. I am engaged as the sole lawyer to a certain anonymous syndicate. Does that satisfy you?'

Disarmed by such expansiveness, I would gladly have corrected my earlier fictitious version of myself, but caution prevailed. 'But if your practice is so modest, how come you have landed such an important commission?' I enquired.

'Because I am pure, I am respectable, I am academic, I deal only in civil law. I do not represent drug-dealers or criminals. Interpol has never heard of me. I operate solely within the margins of my expertise. Do you wish to create a holding company in Martinique registered in Switzerland and owned by an anonymous Liechtenstein foundation which is owned by you?'

I laughed regretfully.

'Do you wish to suffer a painless bankruptcy at the expense of the French taxpayer?'

Again I shook my head.

'Then maybe you can at least explain to me how to operate this accursed Anglo-Saxon computer. First they forbid me to bring my laptop. Then they give me a laptop with no handbook, no accents, no logic, no—' The list of omissions becoming too lengthy, he gave a Gallic shrug of despair.

'But what are you working on that keeps you up all night?' I asked, noting the piles of paper and empty coffee cups strewn around him.

With a sigh, his long meagre body flopped back into his card-player's chair. 'Concessions. Cowardly concessions at different hours of·the night. "Why do you give way to these brigands?" I ask them. "Why do you not tell them to go to hell?"'

Ask *whom*? I marvelled silently. But I knew I must tread warily lest I interrupt the flow.

'"Jasper," they say to me. "We cannot afford to lose this vital contract. Time is precious. We are not the only horse in the race."'

'So you're drafting the *contract*,' I exclaimed, recalling that Maxie had declared a contract to be the purpose of the present exercise. 'My goodness. Well, that's quite a responsibility, I must say. Is it a complicated affair? I suppose it must be.'

My question, though designed to flatter, evinced a sneer of contempt.

'It is not complicated because I have drafted it with lucidity. It is academic and it is unenforceable.'

'How many parties are there?'

'Three. We do not know who they are, but the parties know. The contract is no-name, it is a contract of unspecified hypothetical eventualities. *If* something happens, then *maybe* something else will happen. If not—' Another Gallic shrug.

Cautiously, I ventured to challenge him.

'But if a contract is no-name, and the hypothetical eventualities aren't specified, and it is anyway unenforceable, how can it be a contract at all?'

A smirk of superiority suffused his skull-like features.

'Because this contract is not only hypothetical, it is agricultural.'

'*Hypothetically* agricultural?'

The smirk acknowledged that this was so.

'How can that be? A contract is either agricultural, surely, *or* it's hypothetical. You can't have a hypothetical *cow*—well, can you?'

Shooting bolt upright in his chair, Monsieur Jasper set his hands flat on the green baize and favoured me with the kind of contemptuous glower that lawyers preserve for their least wealthy clients.

'Then answer me this, please,' he suggested. 'If a contract concerns human beings—but refers to those human beings *not* as human beings but as *cows*—is the contract *hypothetical*, or is it *agricultural*?'

I was wise enough to concede his point. 'So what hypothesis are we actually talking about—in *this* case, for instance?'

'The hypothesis is an *event*.'

'What sort of event?'

'Unspecified. Maybe it is a death.' A bony forefinger warned me against precipitating the tragedy. 'Maybe it is a flood, or a marriage, or an act of God or man. Maybe it is the *compliance* or the *non-compliance* of another party. It is not depicted.' He had the floor and nobody, least of all myself, was going to take it from him. 'What is known is that, in the *event* of this unspecified event occurring, certain agricultural terms and conditions will become effective, certain agricultural materials will be bought and sold, certain agricultural rights will be assigned, and certain hypothetical percentages of certain agricultural profits will accrue to certain unnamed persons. But *only* in the event of that event.'

'But how did the anonymous Syndicate ever get to you?' I protested. 'There you are with this extraordinary expertise, tucked away in Besançon, hiding your light under a bushel—'

He needed no further encouragement. 'A year ago I negotiated many timeshare chalets in Valence. I performed superbly, the deal was the summit of my career. The chalets were not built, but delivery was not my responsibility. My client was an offshore property company, now bankrupt, registered in the Channel Islands.'

I made one of my lightning connections. *Timeshares in Valence*. Was this not the scandal that had projected Lord Brinkley onto the front pages of Penelope's newspaper? It was. PEER'S ELDORADO WAS PIE IN SKY.

'And this same company is back in business?' I asked.

'I personally had the honour of liquidating it. The company no longer exists.'

'But the company's directors exist.'

His expression of smug superiority, if it had ever left him, returned in full bloom. 'They do not exist, because they have *no name*. If they have names, they exist. If they have none, they are abstract concepts.' But either he had become bored with our conversa-

tion, or he had decided that we were overstepping the
bounds of legal propriety, for he passed a hand over his
unshaven face, then peered at me as if he had never set
eyes on me before. 'Who are you? What are you doing
in this shit-hole?'

'I'm the conference interpreter.'

'In which languages?'

'Swahili, French and English,' I replied reluctantly,
as the waterline once more engulfed my diving mask.

'How much are they paying you?'

'I don't think I'm supposed to tell you.' But vanity
got the better of me, which it sometimes does. The man
had been lording it over me long enough. It was time I
revealed my true worth. 'Five thousand dollars,' I said
casually.

His head, which had been temporarily resting in his
hands, lifted abruptly. '*Five?*'

'That's right. Five. Why?'

'Not pounds?'

'Dollars. I told you.' I did not at all like his
triumphant smile.

'To me they pay'—he enunciated the sum with
merciless   emphasis—'two—hundred—thousand—
Swiss—francs.' And to ram it home: 'Cash. In denomi-
nations of one hundred. No big ones.'

I was dumbfounded. Why should Salvo, master of
rare languages which he is forced to conceal, be receiving a fraction of the fee of a stuck-up French notary?
My indignation went further, all the way back to my

days of struggle when Mr Osman of the WorldWide and Legal Translation Agency took fifty per cent of my earnings at source. Yet I contained myself. I feigned admiration. He was the great legal expert, after all. I was just a run-of-the-mill interpreter.

'Do you happen to know where this accursed place is situated?' he demanded, as he resumed his labours.

I did not, accursed or otherwise.

'This was not part of the deal. I shall require a supplementary fee.'

The Sanctuary's gong was summoning us to prayer. By the time I reached the door Monsieur Jasper was back at his ponderous typing. Our discussion, it was plain from his attitude, had not taken place.

Directed by the smiling Janet to the Great Hall I sensed at once that all was not well with the team. Her de luxe buffet breakfast of British sausages, best back bacon and scrambled eggs had attracted few takers among our lads, who sat about in groups, bug-eyed and despondent. At one table Anton conversed in low tones with two equally gloomy anoraks; at another, Benny, vast chin in even vaster hand, glowered sightlessly into his cup. Adjusting my demeanour to the mood, I helped myself to a modest portion of smoked salmon and sat down in isolation to await events. I had barely consumed my first mouthful when the squeak of rubber soles approaching at speed down a flagstoned corridor signalled the arrival of our skipper Maxie in time-yellowed Oxford University rowing sweater, long shorts with frayed ends and old plimsolls without socks. His boyish cheeks were flushed with morning air, his bespectacled eyes radiant. Behind him lurked Spider.

'Panic's over,' Maxie announced, having first downed the glass of fresh orange juice that Gladys was holding out to him. 'Hundred per cent bull's-eye on all fronts'—ignoring the general expressions of relief—'rest of the op is on schedule. Philip and the Gang of Three will touch down two hours ten minutes from now.' Philip, at last! Philip, to whom Maxie answers! 'The time now is—'

Aunt Imelda's watch was running a minute fast. I quickly restrained it. Not in his wildest dreams could Brother Michael have imagined that his dying gift to me would be put to such use.

'Royal party will follow twenty minutes later. Conference kicks off eleven-thirty hours sharp, pee breaks to be determined *ad hoc* by Philip. Delegates' lunch buffet at fourteen-fifteen hours subject to Philip's say-so and assuming we've got the bulk of the work behind us, principals only. And we cultivate an atmosphere of leisure, please, not crisis. That's the way he wants it, and that's what we're going to give him. Met. reports are A1, so it looks good for the alfresco facilities. Absolute latest close-of-play, seventeen-thirty hours. Janet. No Smoking sign in the conference room please. A bloody big one. Sinclair, I need you. Where the fuck's Sinclair?'

I was about to receive part two of my sealed orders.

I will not deny that I was a touch nervous following Maxie down the cramped cellar steps, albeit the sight of Spider, Welsh eyes twinkling with honest mischief as he doffed his cap to us in humorous salutation, eased my apprehensions. I was further consoled to discover that, far from being on *terra incognita*, I had entered a Chat Room in miniature. From an unobtrusive service door not dissimilar to its Whitehall equivalent we proceeded along a soot-stained corridor festooned with overhead cables to a defunct boiler room turned audio centre. Technologically, it was true, we were a far cry from Mr Anderson's state-of-the-art wonderland, but with a lick of green paint, and a couple of his famous hortatory notices on the wall, I could well fancy myself back in the catacombs of Northumberland Avenue with the shadowy march of unindoctrinated feet crossing our cellar windows.

Watched intently by Maxie and Spider, I took stock of the somewhat antediluvian arrangements. The cables from the corridor fed into a Meccano grid with two banks of tape recorders, six to a bank and each recorder numbered and labelled according to its task.

'RA, Skipper?' I enquired.

'Royal apartments.'

'And GS?'

'Guest suite.'

I toured the labels: *RA/drawing room, RA/bedroom one, RA/bedroom two, RA/study, RA/hall, RA/bathroom & wc, GS/living room, GS/bedroom, GS/bathroom, verandah west, verandah east, stone steps upper, stone steps lower, walkway, gravel paths 1, 2 and 3, gazebo, porch, conservatory.*

'How's about it then, Brian?' Spider urged, unable to contain his pride any longer. 'We don't all have to be digital in the world, or we wouldn't have been born different, would we? Not unless we want a lot of foreign fishermen poking their noses into our business.'

I won't say I was shocked. In an undefined way I'd been expecting something like this. So probably it was stage fright that made the hairs rise on my spine, and Maxie wasn't helping matters by urging me to admire what he called my *hot-seat* at the centre of the room, which at first sight looked about as inviting as an electric chair, but on closer inspection turned out to be an ancient recliner with cables taped up the side of it, and a headset, and a kind of hospital bed-tray with shorthand pads laid out, and A4 paper, and pre-sharpened HB pencils, and a walkie-talkie cradled on the armrest; and on the other arm a console with numbers on it

which I was not slow to realise corresponded with the
numbers on the tape recorders.

'Soon as we recess, you hightail it down here,'
Maxie was saying in his pared-down voice of command.
'You listen to whatever you're told to listen to, you
interpret in fast order via your headset to Sam in the
ops room.'

'And *Sam* is, Skipper?'

'Your coordinator. All conversations are recorded
automatically. Sam will tell you which ones to listen to
live. Any spare time, you skim the secondary targets.
Sam will brief and debrief you and pass your material
out to the people who can use it.'

'And Sam would be in touch with Philip,' I
suggested, in my continuing efforts to draw nearer to
the fountainhead of our operation, but he declined to
rise to the bait.

'Soon as a recess is over, you whip upstairs, resume
your place at the conference table, act natural. The job
of Spider here is to service his system, make sure his
mikes aren't on the blink, log and store all tapes. He's
linked live to the surveillance team, so he tracks the
conference delegates' whereabouts, and puts 'em up in
lights on his map.'

It was less a map than a home-made version of the
London Underground plan, mounted on hardboard
and dotted with coloured light bulbs like a child's train
set. Cap askew, Spider placed himself before it with
proprietorial pride.

'Anton's in charge of surveillance,' Maxie went on. 'Watchers report to Anton, Anton tells Spider where the targets are located, Spider marks 'em up on his map, you listen to 'em, give Sam the low-down on what they're saying to each other. Every target is colour-coded. Surveillance is naked eye, static posts and inter-com. Show him.'

But first, for Spider's benefit, I had to provide what he called a for-instance. 'Name two colours, son,' he urged me. 'Your favourites. Any two.'

'Green and blue,' I ventured.

'The *where*, son, the *where*.'

'Stone steps upper,' I said, selecting a label at random.

Fingers flying, Spider pressed four buttons. Green and blue pinlights winked from the far left flank of the Underground plan. A tape recorder began silently turning.

'Like it, son? Like it?'

'Give him the master light,' Maxie ordered.

A brilliant purple light shone forth from the centre of the royal apartments, reminding me of the visiting bishops that the secret child had spied on from the Mission servants' quarters.

'Master light and royal apartments are out of bounds unless Philip personally tells you otherwise,' Maxie warned. 'Contingency mikes. Archival, not operational. We record but don't listen. Got that?'

'Got it, Skipper.' And—surprising myself with my

own temerity—'Who does Philip actually consult *for*, sir?' I asked.

Maxie stared at me as if suspecting insubordination. Spider was standing rock-still before his Underground plan. But I was not to be put off, which is something I never completely understand about myself: the streak of mulishness that asserts itself at inopportune moments.

'He's a consultant, right?' I blundered on. 'So who does he consult? I don't mean to be pushy, Skipper, but I've got a right to know who I'm working for, haven't I?'

Maxie opened his mouth to say something, then closed it. I had the impression he was genuinely confused: not by what he knew, but what I didn't.

'I thought Anderson had told you all that stuff.'

'All what stuff, Skipper? It's only background I'm asking for. If I'm not fully briefed I can't give of my best, can I?'

Another pause, in which Maxie fleetingly shared his bewilderment with Spider. 'Philip's *freelance*. Works for whoever pays him. He has *ties*.'

'Ties with the government? Ties with the Syndicate? Ties who with, Skipper?' If you're in a hole, don't dig, they say. But in this mood there's no pulling me back once I've started.

'*Ties*, man! Haven't you heard of *ties*? *I've* got ties. Spider here's got ties. We're not official, we're *para*, but we've got ties and we're arm's length. Way the world works, for Christ's sake.' Then he seemed to take pity on me. 'Philip's freelance, he's a consultant. He's under contract. His speciality is Africa, and he's boss of the op. That's good enough for me so it's good enough for you.'

'If you say so, Skipper.'

'Philip coralled the delegates, Philip set the terms of the deal and brought everyone to the table. Forty-eight hours ago there wasn't a cat's chance they would sit down in the same room with each other. So shut up and admire him for it.'

'I will, Skipper. I do. No problem.'

Maxie was loping angrily up the stone steps two at a time with me on his heels. Reaching the library, he flung himself into a chair and beckoned me to another, and there we sat like two gentlemen of leisure while we cooled down. Beyond the French windows, soothing lawns rose gently to the bugged gazebo.

'In a place not a thousand miles from here in Denmark, a seminar is in progress,' he resumed. 'With me?'

'With you, Skipper.'

'Calls itself the Great Lakes Forum. Heard of it?'

I hadn't.

'Bunch of long-haired Scandinavian academics masterminding off-the-record discussions to solve the problems of the Eastern Congo ahead of the elections. Grab hold of all the chaps who hate each other, invite 'em to let off steam, and something wonderful's bound to happen, long as you believe in fairies.'

I gave a knowing smile. We were back on course, comrades again.

'Today's their free day. They're supposed to be inspecting fish smokeries and sculpture parks but three of the delegates have begged off and they're coming here instead. For an off-the-record conference of their own.' He tossed a folder onto the table between us. 'That's the background you're after. Potted biographies, languages, ethnicity of players. Philip's labour of love. Three delegates, one unholy triangle,' he continued. 'Until a few months ago, they were cutting each other's balls off and butchering each other's wives and stealing each other's land, cattle and mineral deposits. With a little help they're now forming an alliance.'

'Who against this time, Skipper?' I asked in a suitably weary tone.

My scepticism spoke for itself, for what could be the purpose of any alliance in that benighted paradise unless it was against a common foe? I therefore took a moment to grasp the full, the momentous import of his reply.

'Not *who against* for once. *Under whose auspices.* Have you by any chance heard tell of this self-proclaimed Congolese saviour chap, an ex-professor of something, who's working the boards these days?—calls himself the *Mwangaza*—that's *light*, isn't it?'

'Or enlightenment,' I replied, which was pure interpreter's knee-jerk. 'Depends whether we're being figurative or literal, Skipper.'

'Well, the Mwangaza's our key man, figurative or my arse. If we can get him in place ahead of the elections, we're home free. If not, we're fucked. There's no second prize.'

To say my head was spinning would be a major understatement. Spiralling into orbit was more like it, while at the same time transmitting frantic signals to Hannah.

*   *   *

I have listened to him, Salvo, she is telling me, switching from French to English in a moment of rare repose during our lovemaking. *He is an apostle for truth and reconciliation. In Kivu he is everywhere on the local radio stations. Two weeks ago on my day off, my friends and I travelled all the way to Birmingham where he spoke to a great crowd of us. You could have heard a pin drop in that hall. His movement is called the Middle Path. It will do something no political party can do. That is because it is a movement of the heart, and not the purse. It will unite all the people of Kivu together, north and south. It will compel the fatcats of Kinshasa to pull out their corrupt soldiers from East Congo and leave us to manage ourselves. It will disarm the surrogate armies and genocidal militias and send them back over the border to Rwanda where they belong. Those who have a real right to remain may do so provided they truly desire to be Congolese. And do you know what is more, Salvo?*

What is more, Hannah?

*In 1964, in the great rebellion, the Mwangaza fought
for Patrice Lumumba and was wounded!*

But how can he have done that, Hannah? The CIA
assassinated Lumumba in 1961, with a little help from
the Belgians. That was three years before the great
rebellion began, surely.

*Salvo, you are being pedantic. The great rebellion was
Lumumbist. All who took part in it looked to Patrice
Lumumba for their inspiration. They were fighting for a
free Congo and for Patrice, whether he was alive or dead.*

So I'm making love to the revolution.

*Now you are being ridiculous as well. The Mwangaza
is not a revolutionary. He is for moderation and for discipline and justice, and for getting rid of all who steal from
our country but do not love it. He does not wish to be
known as a man of war, but as a bringer of peace and
harmony to all true patriots of Congo. He is l'oiseau rare:
the great hero who is come to cure all our ills. Am I boring
you, perhaps?*

Claiming to believe I am not taking her seriously, she
wilfully flings back the bedclothes and sits up. And you
have to know how beautiful she is, and how mischie-
vous in love, to imagine what that means. No, Hannah,
you are not boring me. I was temporarily distracted by
the night whisperings of my dear late father, who had a
dream very like yours.

*One Kivu, Salvo my son ... At peace with itself under
God and the Congolese flag ... Freed of the pest of foreign
exploitation but willing to absorb all who sincerely wish to*

share in the divine gift of its natural resources and the enlightenment of all its people ... Let us pray you live long enough to see that day dawn, Salvo my son.

* * *

Maxie was waiting for my answer. Well, had I heard of this Congolese saviour chap, or hadn't I? Like the Mwangaza, I opted for the Middle Path.

'Maybe I have at that,' I conceded, careful to inject just the right amount of disinterest into my voice. 'Isn't he some kind of recycled prophet of consensus?'

'Met him, have you then?'

'My goodness no!'—how could I have given him such an absurd impression?—'I make rather a point of steering clear of Congolese politics, to be frank, Skipper. I take the view I'm better off without.'

Which, pre-Hannah, was pretty much the truth. When you assimilate, you choose.

'Well, steel yourself, because you're about to meet him,' Maxie informed me, again glancing at his watch. 'The great man will be accompanied by a retinue of two: one faithful acolyte alias political advisor, and one semi-faithful Lebanese middleman named Felix Tabizi, Tabby for short. The Prof's a Shi, so's his acolyte.'

Tabby, I repeated to myself, as I was wafted back to the glittery house in Berkeley Square. Tabby the bastard, Tabby the eleventh-hour cliff-hanger. I was about to ask what a semi-faithful Lebanese middleman thought he was doing in the Mwangaza's entourage, only to discover that Maxie was already telling me.

'Tabby's the Prof's necessary evil. No African leader is complete without one. Ex far-out Muslim, used to run with Hamas, but recently converted to Christianity for his health. Helps manage the old boy's campaign, smoothes his passage, handles his finances, washes his socks.'

'And his languages, Skipper? Mr Tabizi's?'

'French, English, Arabic, and whatever he picked up free on his travels.'

'And Philip. What languages would he be speaking?'

'French, Lingala, bit of Swahili, not a lot.'

'English?'

'Of course he bloody does. He's an Englishman.'

'And the Professor speaks everything in the book, I take it. He's an educated man.' I didn't intend this as a dig at Maxie's lack of linguistic expertise, but from his frown of displeasure I feared he had taken it as such.

'So what's your point?' he demanded irritably.

'Well, you don't really need me, do you, Skipper? Not upstairs. Not as such. Not if the Mwangaza speaks French and Swahili. I'll just stay down in the boiler room with Spider and listen in.'

'Total and utter bullshit. You're star of the show, remember? Chaps who are in the business of changing the world don't expect to do their own interpreting. And I wouldn't trust Tabizi to tell me the time of day in any fucking language.' A moment of reflection.

'Apart from which, you're essential equipment. The Mwangaza insists on speaking Swahili because French is too colonial for him. We've got one chap who speaks perfect French and minimal Swahili, and another who speaks a bit of Swahili and minimal French.'

Flattered as I was by *star of the show*, I had one more question. More accurately, Hannah had.

'And the desired end-effect of the conference, Skipper? Our dream outcome? How would we define that?—which is a thing I always ask my clients.'

It wasn't, but my recalcitrance touched a nerve in him. 'We're *sorting* the place, Sinclair, for Christ's sake!' he expostulated in a pent-up voice. 'We're bringing *sanity* back to a fucking madhouse. We're giving piss-poor, downtrodden people their country back and forcing 'em to *tolerate* each other, make money, get a fucking *life*. Have you got a problem with that?'

The patent sincerity of his intentions, which to this day I have no cause to question, made me pause but not relent.

'No problems at all, Skipper. Only you did mention democracy at the end of a gun barrel, you see. And I was naturally wondering who exactly was in your sights when you said that. I mean, at the end of the gun barrel. Given there's an election coming up. Why get in ahead of it, if you follow me?'

Have I mentioned that Hannah had pacifistic tendencies, as Mr Anderson would have called them? That a breakaway group of nuns at her American-financed

Pentecostal Mission school had preached Quakerish non-violence at her with heavy emphasis on turning the other cheek?

'We're talking Congo, right?'

Right, Skipper.

'One of the world's worst graveyards. Right?'

Right. No question. Maybe *the* worst.

'Chaps dying like flies while we speak. Knee-jerk tribal killings, disease, starvation, ten-year-old soldiers and sheer fucking incompetence from the top down, rape and mayhem galore. Right?'

Right, Skipper.

'Elections won't bring democracy, they'll bring chaos. The winners will scoop the pool and tell the losers to go fuck themselves. The losers will say the game was fixed and take to the bush. And since everyone's voted on ethnic lines anyway, they'll be back where they started and worse. *Unless.*'

I waited.

'Unless you can put in your own moderate leader ahead of time, educate the electorate to his message, prove to 'em it works, and stop the vicious circle. With me?'

With you, Skipper.

'So that's the Syndicate's game plan, and it's the plan we're peddling today. Elections are a Western jerk-off. Preempt them, get your man in place, give the People a fair slice of the cake for once, and let peace break out. Your average multinational hates poor. Feeding starving millions isn't cost-effective. Privatising the buggers and letting them die is. Well, our little Syndicate doesn't think that way. Neither does the Mwangaza. They're thinking infrastructure, sharing, and long term.'

My thoughts sped back in pride to Lord Brinkley and his multinational group of fellow backers. *Little* Syndicate? Never before had I seen so many *big* people assembled in one room!

'Pot o' cash for the investors, that's a given, and why not?' Maxie was saying. 'Never grudge a chap his pound of flesh for taking a fair risk. But plenty left in the kitty for the home side when the shouting and shooting are over: schools, hospitals, roads, clean water. And light at the end of the tunnel for the next lot of kids coming up. Got a quarrel with that?'

How could I have? How could Hannah? How could Noah and his millions of fellows?

'So if a couple of hundred have to go down in the first couple of days—which they will—are we the good guys or the bad guys?' He was standing up, energetically rubbing his cyclist's hip. 'One more thing while we're on the subject.' He gave it another rub. 'No fraternising with the natives. You're not here to make enduring relationships, you're here to do a job. When lunch comes, it's down to the boiler room and a ship's biscuit with Spider. Any more questions?'

Apart from *Am* I *a native?*—none.

* * *

With Philip's folder clutched in my hand, I sit first on the edge of my bed, then on the Shaker rocking chair which rocks forward but not back. One second I am star of the show, the next I am scared witless, a one-man Great Lake with all the rivers of the world pouring into me and my banks overflowing. From my window everything remains deceptively serene. The gardens are awash with the sloping sunlight of Europe's African summer. Who would not wish to take a leisurely stroll in them, away from prying eyes and ears on such a day? Who could resist the tempting cluster of reclining sunchairs in the gazebo?

I open the folder. White paper, no hallmarks. No security classification top or bottom. No addressee, no author. Arm's length. My first page begins halfway down and is numbered seventeen. My first paragraph is number twelve, leading me to conclude that paras one to eleven are unsuitable for the tender gaze of a mere interpreter slogging his heart out for his country above and below the waterline. The heading of para twelve is WARLORDS.

Warlord the First is named Dieudonné, the Given One of God. Dieudonné is a Munyamulenge, and therefore racially indistinguishable from the Rwandans. I am instantly attracted to him. The Banyamulenge, as they are called in the plural version, were my dear late father's favourites among all the tribes. Ever the romantic, he dubbed them the Jews of Kivu in deference to their reclusion, their battle skills, and their direct communion with God on a day-to-day basis. Despised by their 'pure' Congolese brethren as Tutsi interlopers and therefore fair game at all times, the Banyamulenge have for the last hundred years and more installed themselves on the inaccessible Mulenge plateau in Kivu's Southern Highlands, where despite perpetual harassment they contrive to lead the pluralist life, tending their sheep and cattle and ignoring the precious minerals within their boundaries. Of this embattled people Dieudonné appears a prime example:

At thirty-two years of age a proven warrior. Part-educated in the bush by Scandinavian Pentecostal missionaries, until old enough to fight. No known interest in self-enrichment. Has brought with him the full empowerment of his elders to pursue the following aims:

a) inclusion of Banyamulenge in new provisional government of South Kivu ahead of the elections
b) resolution of land disputes on the High Plateau
c) right of return for the thousands of Banyamulenge driven out of the Congo, in particular those forced to flee after the 2004 troubles in Bukavu
d) integration of Banyamulenge in Congolese civil society and a formal negotiated end to the persecution of the last fifty years

Languages: Kinyamulenge and Kinyarwanda, Shi, Swahili, basic French (very).

I turn to Warlord the Second. He is Franco, named after the great African singer whose work is well known to me from Père André's cracked gramophone record in the Mission house. Franco is an old-style Bembe warrior from the Uvira region, aged around sixty-five. He has zero education but considerable cunning and is an impassioned Congolese patriot. But Philip should have put up a health warning before he went on:

Under Mobutu, served as an unofficial police thug in the Walungu hills. Imprisoned when war broke out in '96, escaped and fled to the bush and joined the Mai Mai as a means of escaping persecution for his former allegiance. Currently believed to hold the rank of colonel or above. Partially disabled by wound in left leg. One of his wives is daughter of Mai Mai General so-and-so. Has substantial landholdings and six wealthy brothers. Part literate. Speaks his native Bembe, Swahili, poor French, and somewhat surprisingly Kinyarwanda which he acquired in prison, as well as its close cousin Kinyamulenge.

It is hard to describe at this distance what grotesque images these few words conjured up in my secret child's mind. If the Mai Mai were not the dread

Simba of my father's day, they ran a close second to them in the barbarity stakes. And nobody should be fooled by 'colonel'. We're not talking cleaned-and-pressed uniforms, salute-your-officers, red flashes, medal ribbons and the like. We're talking feathered head-dresses, baseball caps, monkey-skin waistcoats, football shorts, tracksuits and eye make-up. Preferred footwear, sawn-off Wellington boots. For magical powers, an ability to change bullets into water, which the Mai Mai, like the Simba before them, can do any time they feel like it provided they've observed the necessary rituals. These variously include not allowing rain to enter your mouth, not eating from a plate with colour on it, and not touching any object that hasn't been sprinkled with magic potions, such powers being derived directly from the pure soil of the Congo which the Mai Mai are sworn to defend with their blood, et cetera. We are also talking random, feckless murder, rape galore, and a full range of atrocities under the influence of everything from leading-edge witchcraft to a gallon or two of Primus beer laced with palm wine.

How on earth these two groups—the Mai Mai and the Banyamulenge—are ever to become reconciled partners in a sovereign and inclusive Kivu under one enlightened leadership is therefore in my opinion somewhat of a major mystery. True, from time to time the Mai Mai have formed tactical alliances with the Banyamulenge, but this has not prevented them from sacking their villages, burning their crops, and stealing their cattle and women.

What does Franco hope to get out of today's conference?

a) regards Middle Path as potential fast route to money, power and guns for his militias

b) anticipates substantial Mai Mai representation in any new Kivu government: i.e. control of frontier crossings (revenue from bribes and customs) and mining concessions (Mai Mai sell mineral ore to Rwandans irrespective of their anti-Rwandan sentiments)

c) counts on Mai Mai influence in Kivu to raise its stock with federal government in Kinshasa

d) remains determined to cleanse all Congo of Rwandan influence provided Mai Mai can sell their mineral ore to other buyers

e) regards upcoming elections as threat to Mai Mai's existence and aims to preempt them

Warlord the Third is not a warlord at all, but the wealthy, French-educated heir to an East Congolese trading fortune. His full name is Honoré Amour-Joyeuse and he is known universally by its acronym of Haj. Ethnically he is a Shi like the Mwangaza, and therefore 'pure' Congolese. He recently returned to Congo from Paris, having attended business school at the Sorbonne where he passed with flying colours.

The source of his power, according to Philip, lies neither in the Banyamulenge's Southern Highlands nor in the Mai Mai's redoubts to north and south, but among the rising young entrepreneurs of Bukavu. I gaze out of the window. If my childhood has a paradise, it is the former colonial town of Bukavu, set at the southern tip of Lake Kivu amid rolling valleys and misted mountains.

Family interests include coffee and vegetable plantations, hotels, a brewery complete with fleet of trucks, a minerals *comptoir* trading in diamonds, gold, cassiterite and coltan and two newly-acquired discothèques which are Haj's pride. Most of these enterprises are dependent on trade with Rwandans from across the border.

So a warlord who is not a warlord, then, and is dependent on his enemies for his livelihood.

Haj is a skilled organiser who commands the respect of his workforce. Given the right motivation, he could instantly raise a militia of five hundred strong through his links with local headmen in the Kaziba and Burhinyi districts around Bukavu. Haj's father Luc, founder of the family empire, runs an equally impressive operation in the northern port of Goma.

I allow myself a quick smile. If Bukavu is my childhood paradise, Goma is Hannah's.

Luc is a veteran of the Great Revolution and long-standing comrade of the Mwangaza. He has the ear of other influential Goma traders who, like himself, are incensed by Rwanda's stranglehold on Kivu's commerce. It was Luc's intention to attend today's conference in person, but he is currently receiving specialised care at a heart hospital in Cape Town. Haj is therefore standing in for him.

So what precisely do they offer, this father-and-son duo of urban barons?

Given the moment and the man, Luc and his circle in North Kivu are ready to spark a popular uprising in Goma's streets and provide underhand military and political support to the Mwangaza. In return, they will demand power and influence in the new provincial government.

And Haj?

In Bukavu, Haj is in a position to persuade fellow intellectuals and traders to embrace the Middle Path as a means of venting their anger against Rwanda.

But perhaps there is a more prosaic reason for Haj's presence among us here today:

> As a token of his willingness to commit to the Middle Path, Luc has agreed to accept an advance commission of [DELETED] for which he has signed a formal receipt.

Haj speaks Shi, poor Swahili, and for trading purposes appears to have taught himself Kinyarwanda. By preference he speaks 'highly sophisticated' French.

So there we have it, I told Hannah, as I rose to answer the banging on my door: one Munyamulenge farmer-soldier, one crippled Mai Mai warhorse and one French-educated city slicker deputising for his father. What possible chance had a septuagenarian professor, however idealistic, of knocking this unlikely trio into a peace-loving alliance for democracy, whether or not it was at the end of a gun barrel?

'Skipper says here's the rest of your homework,' Anton advised me, shoving an office folder into my hand. 'And I'll take that item of obscene literature off you, while I'm about it. Don't want it lying around where the kids can get at it, do we?'

Or in plain language: here is a photocopy of Jasper's no-name contract in exchange for Philip's no-name briefing paper.

*   *   *

Restored to the Shaker rocking chair for my preparatory reading, I was amused to observe that the French accents had been added despairingly in ink. A preamble defined the unnamed parties to the agreement.

Party the First is a philanthropic offshore venture capital organisation providing low-cost agricultural equipment and services on a self-help basis to struggling or failed Central African states.

In other words, the anonymous Syndicate.

Party the Second, hereinafter called the Agriculturalist, is an academic in high standing, committed to the radical reorganisation of outdated methodologies to the greater advancement of all sections of the indigenous population.

Or in plain French, the Mwangaza.

Party the Third, hereinafter called the Alliance, is an honourable association of community leaders pledged to work together under the guidance of the Agriculturalist—see above ...

Their common aim will be to advance by all means at their disposal such reforms as are essential to the creation of a unified social structure embracing all Kivu, including a common fiscal policy and the repossession of Kivu's natural resources for the greater enrichment of all its people ...

In consideration of Syndicate's financial and technological assistance in the lead-up to these reforms, hereinafter called the Event, the Agriculturalist in consultation with his partners in the Alliance pledges to grant favoured status to Syndicate and such corporations or entities as Syndicate at its sole discretion sees fit from time to time to nominate ...

Syndicate for its part undertakes to provide specialised services, personnel and equipment to the value of fifty million Swiss francs by way of a one-time payment as per attached Annexe ...

Syndicate undertakes to provide out of its own purse all necessary experts, technicians, instructors and cadre personnel as may be necessary to the training of the local workforce in the use of such equipment, and to remain on site up to and including the formal consummation of the Event, and in all circumstances for a period of not less than six months from the date of commencement ...

For such an imprecise document, its Annexe is remarkably detailed. Basic items to be provided include shovels, trowels, pickaxes, scythes, heavy and light wheelbarrows. For use where, please? In the rain forests, what's left of them? I close my eyes and open them. We are bringing modernisation to Kivu with the aid of scythes and pickaxes and wheelbarrows?

The cost of any *second* tranche of equipment, should it be required, will not be borne by Syndicate but 'set against gross revenue generated by the Event prior to all deductions'. Syndicate's philanthropy, in other words, stops at fifty million Swiss francs.

A page of figures, terms and pay-out rates addresses a division of spoils in the wake of the Event. For the first six months, Syndicate requires solus rights on all extracted crops of whatever nature within the Designated Geographical Areas, defined by longitude and latitude. Without such solus rights, the deal is void. However, as a token of its goodwill, and subject always to the good faith of the Alliance, Syndicate will make a monthly ex-gratia payment to the Alliance of ten per cent of gross receipts.

In addition to its six-month free ride less ten per cent, Syndicate must be guaranteed 'exemption in perpetuity from all local levies, taxes and tariffs in the Designated Areas'. It must also be guaranteed a 'secure environment for the preparation, harvesting and transportation of all crops'. As 'sole backer and risk-taker', it would receive 'sixty-seven per cent of first dollar of gross receipts before deduction of overheads and administrative costs, but only with effect from commencement of the seventh month following the Event ...'

Yet just as I was beginning to feel that Syndicate was having things too much its own way, a final passage

triumphantly restored my hopes to the level they had
achieved after my discourse with Maxie:

> All remaining proceeds accruing after the termina-
> tion of the six-month period will be passed in their
> entirety to the Alliance to be distributed equally
> and fairly to all sections of the community accord-
> ing to accepted international principles of social
> advancement in the areas of health, education and
> welfare, with the sole aim of establishing harmony,
> unity and mutual tolerance under one flag.

Should factional divisiveness render a fair distribution unworkable, the Mwangaza would on his own
responsibility appoint a panel of trusted representatives
charged with allocating what was henceforth described
as 'the People's Portion'. Hallelujah! Here at last was
the source of money for schools, roads, hospitals, and
the next lot of kids coming on, just as Maxie had promised. Hannah could rest easy. So could I.

Settling to the antiquated electric typewriter on the
mirrored dressing table, I went briskly to work on my
Swahili rendering. My task completed, I stretched out
on the bed with the intention of talking myself into a
less excitable frame of mind. Half past eleven by Aunt
Imelda's watch. Hannah is back from night shift but she
can't sleep. She's lying on her bed, still in uniform,
staring at the dusty ceiling, the one we stared at
together while we traded our hopes and dreams. She's

thinking: where is he, why hasn't he rung, will I ever see him again, or is he a liar like the others? She is thinking of her son Noah, and of one day taking him back to Goma.

A small plane flew low over the gazebo. I sprang to the window to catch its markings but was too late. By the time the trusty Anton once more appeared at my door to collect my offering and command me downstairs, I had vowed to give the performance of my lifetime.

8

Breathlessly following Anton back into the gaming room where I had encountered Jasper earlier in the day, I was quick to observe that it had undergone a subtle scene-change. A lecturer's whiteboard and easel stood centre stage. The eight chairs round the table had become ten. A post-office clock had been installed above the brick fireplace, next to a No Smoking sign in French. Jasper, freshly shaved and brushed, and closely attended by Benny, lurked next to the door leading to the interior of the house.

I scanned the table. How do you put out name cards for a no-name conference? The Mwangaza was MZEE and had been placed at the centre on the inland side, the seat of honour. Flanking him were his faithful acolyte M. LE SÉCRETAIRE, and his less faithful M. LE CONSEILLER, alias Tabby, whom Maxie wouldn't trust to tell him the time of day. Across the table from them, their backs to the French windows, sat the Gang of Three, identified by MONSIEUR and initials only: D for DIEUDONNÉ, F for FRANCO and H for HONORÉ

AMOUR-JOYEUSE, the Mr Big of Bukavu, better known as Haj. Franco, as eldest, had centre position opposite the Mwangaza.

With the sides of the oval table thus occupied, it was left to the home team to divide itself between the two ends: at one, MONSIEUR LE COLONEL, whom I assumed to be Maxie, with MONSIEUR PHILIPPE next to him, and at the other Jasper and myself. And I could not help noticing that, whereas Jasper was awarded full honours as MONSIEUR L'AVOCAT, I was dismissed as INTERPRÈTE.

And in front of Philip's chair, a brass bell. It rings in my memory now. It had a black wooden handle and was a replica in miniature of the bell that had tyrannised the daily life out of us inmates of the Sanctuary. It had dragged us from our beds, told us when to pray, eat, go to the toilet, the gym, the classroom and the football field, pray again and go back to bed and wrestle with our demons. And as Anton was at pains to explain, it would shortly be sending me scurrying up and down to the boiler room like a human yo-yo:

'He'll ring it when he's calling a recess, and he'll ring it again when he wants you back at table because he's lonely. But some of us won't be recessing, will we, governor?' he added with a wink. 'We'll be down the apples-and-pears in the we-know-where having a quiet listen on the Spider's web.'

I winked back, grateful for his comradeship. A jeep was pulling up in the courtyard. Quick as an elf he darted through the French windows and was gone, I guessed to take command of his surveillance team. A second plane buzzed overhead and again I missed it. More minutes passed during which my gaze, seemingly of its own volition, abandoned the gaming room and sought respite in the stately grounds beyond the French windows. Which was how I came to observe an immaculate white gentleman in a Panama hat, fawn trousers, pink shirt, red tie and a tailored navy-blue blazer of the type known to Guards officers as a boating jacket, picking his way along the skyline of the grassy mound before coming to rest at the gazebo, where he posed himself between two pillars in the manner of a British Egyptologist of bygone times, smiling back in the direction from which he had just arrived. And I will say here and now, with that first glimpse of the man, I was conscious of a new presence in my life, which was why I never doubted that I was taking my first covert reading of our freelance Africa consultant and—Maxie's words again—*boss of the op*, Philip or *Philippe*, fluent in French, Lingala, but not Swahili, architect of our conference, befriender of the Mwangaza and our delegates.

Next, a slender, dignified black African man appeared on the skyline. He was bearded and clad in a sober Western suit, and so contemplative in his gait that he put me in mind of Brother Michael processing across the Sanctuary quad in Lent. It required accordingly no great insight on my part to appoint him our Pentecostal pasturalist, the warlord Dieudonné, empowered delegate of the despised Banyamulenge, so beloved of my dear late father.

He was followed by a second African who could have been designed as his deliberate opposite: a hairless giant in a glittery brown suit of which the jacket was scarcely able to encompass him as he limped along, dragging his left leg after him in ferocious heaves of his torso. Who else could this be then but Franco, our lame warhorse, former Mobutu thug and currently colonel-or-above of the Mai Mai, avowed adversary and occasional ally of the man who had just preceded him?

And finally, as a kind of lackadaisical concession to the rest of them, enter our third delegate, Haj, the egregious Sorbonne-educated, uncrowned merchant prince of Bukavu: but with such disdain, such foppery, and such determined distance from his fellows, that I was tempted to wonder whether he was having second thoughts about standing in for his father. He was neither skeletal like Dieudonné nor shiny-bald like Franco. He was an urban dandy. His head, close-shaven at the sides, had wavy lines engraved in the stubble. A lacquered forelock protruded from his brow. As to his clothes: well, Hannah's high-mindedness might have dulled my appetite for such vanities but, given the tat Mr Anderson had inflicted on me, his choice of suiting brought it rushing to the surface. What I was looking at here was the absolute latest thing in the Zegna summer collection: a three-piece, mushroom-coloured mohair for the man who has everything or wants it, set off by a pair of pointed slime-green Italian crocodile shoes which I would price, if real, at a good two hundred pounds a foot.

And I know now, if I didn't fully know it at the time, that what I was witnessing on the grassy mound was the closing moments of a guided tour in which Philip was showing off to his wards the facilities of the house, including the bugged suite where they could let their hair down between sessions, and the bugged grounds where they were free to enjoy that extra bit of privacy so essential to your full and frank exchange of views.

At Philip's behest the three delegates peer obediently out to sea, then at the cemetery. And as Haj turns with them, his Zegna suit jacket swings open to reveal a mustard silk lining and a flash of steel caught by the sunlight. What can it be? I wonder. A knife blade? A cellphone, and if so, should I warn Maxie?—unless, of course, I could borrow it and, in a surreptitious moment, call Hannah. And somebody, I suspect Philip again, must have made a joke at this point, perhaps a bawdy one, because they all four break out in laughter that rolls down the lawn and through the French windows of the gaming room, which are wide open on account of the heat. But this does not impress me as much as it should, life having taught me from an early age that Congolese people, who are sticklers for courtesy, don't always laugh at things for the right reasons, especially if they're Mai Mai or equivalent.

When the party has recovered from its mirth, it proceeds to the top of the ornamental stone staircase where, under Philip's lavish coaxing, Franco the lame giant slings an arm around the neck of the frail Dieudonné and, avowed adversaries though they may be, adopts him as his walking stick, but with such amiable spontaneity that my heart fills with optimism for the successful outcome of our venture. And it is in this manner that they commence their laborious descent, Philip tripping ahead of the bonded couple, and Haj trailing after them. And I remember how the northern sky above them was ice-blue, and how the enlaced Mai Mai warlord and his skinny prop were chaperoned down the hill by a cloud of small birds who high-jumped as they flew along. And how as Haj entered shadow, the mystery of his inside jacket pocket was resolved. He was the proud owner of a fleet of Parker pens.

What happened next was one of those cock-ups without which no self-respecting conference is complete. There was to be this greeting line. Anton had explained it to us in advance. Philip would march in with his Gang of Three from the garden side, Maxie would sweep in simultaneously from the house side with the Mwangaza's entourage, thus effecting the great historic coming-together of the parties to our conference. The rest of us would line up and either have our hands shaken or not, depending on the whim of our guests at the time.

Whereas what we got was a damp squib. Maybe Maxie and his party were that bit slow completing their own tour of the premises, or Philip and the delegates that bit premature. Maybe old Franco, with Dieudonné's bony frame to help him, was faster-footed than they'd given him credit for. The effect was the same: Philip and party swept in, bringing with them the sweet smells of my African childhood, but the only people on hand to greet them were one top interpreter with his minority languages missing, one French provincial notary, and big Benny with his ponytail— except that as soon as Benny spotted what was happening, he was out of the door to find Anton double quick.

At any other conference, I would have taken matters over at this point, because top interpreters must always be prepared to act as diplomats when called upon and I have done so on many an occasion. But this was Philip's op. And Philip's eyes, which were highly compelling inside the creaseless cushions of his fleshy countenance, summed up the situation in a trice. His two forefingers lifted in simultaneous delight, he emitted a cry of *ah, parfait, vous voilà!* and whisked off his Panama hat to me, thereby revealing a head of vigorous white hair, waved and flicked into little horns above each ear.

'Allow me to introduce myself,' he declared in finest Parisian French. 'I am Philippe, agricultural consultant and indomitable friend of the Congo. And you are, sir?' The perfectly groomed white head tilted towards me as if it had only the one good ear.

'My name is Sinclair, sir,' I responded with equal alacrity, also in French. 'My languages are French,

English and Swahili.' Philip's darting eyes inclined
towards Jasper, and I was quick to take the hint. 'And
allow me to present Monsieur Jasper Albin, our special-
ist lawyer from Besançon,' I went on. And for additional effect: 'And may I, on behalf of all of us here,
extend our very warmest greetings to our distinguished
African delegates?'

My spontaneous eloquence had consequences I had
not foreseen, and neither, I suspect, had Philip. Old
Franco had elbowed aside Dieudonné, his human
walking stick, and was grasping both my hands in his.
And I suppose that to your average unthinking
European he would have been just another enormous
African man in a glittery suit grappling with our
Western ways. But not to Salvo the secret child. To
Salvo he was our Mission's self-appointed and rascally
protector, known to the Brethren and servants alike as
Beau-Visage, lone marauder, father of numberless children, who would pad into our red-brick Mission house
at nightfall with the magic of the forest in his eyes and
an archaic Belgian rifle in his hand, and a case of beer
and a freshly killed buck sticking out of his game-bag,
having trekked twenty miles to warn us of impending
danger. And, come the dawn, would be found seated on
the threshold, smiling in his sleep with his rifle across
his knees. And the same afternoon, down at the town
market square, pressing his grisly souvenirs on the luckless safari tourists: an amputated gorilla's paw or the
dried and eyeless head of an impala.

'Bwana Sinclair,' announced this venerable gentleman, holding up a clenched fist for silence. 'I am Franco, a high officer of Mai Mai. My community is an authentic force created by our ancestors to defend our sacred country. When I was a child, Rwandan scum invaded our village and set fire to our crops and hacked three of our cows to pieces in their hatred. Our mother led us into the forest to hide. When we returned, they had hamstrung my father and two brothers and hacked them to pieces also.' He jabbed a curved thumb at Dieudonné behind him. 'When my mother was dying, Banyamulenge cockroaches refused to let her pass on her way to hospital. For sixteen hours she lay dying at the roadside before my eyes. Therefore I am not the friend of foreigners and invaders.' A huge breath, followed by a huge sigh. 'Under the Constitution, the Mai Mai is officially joined to the army of Kinshasa. But this joining is of an artificial nature. Kinshasa gives my general a fine uniform but no pay for his soldiers. They give him high rank, but no weapons. Therefore my general's spirits have counselled him to listen to the words of this Mwangaza. And since I respect my general and am guided by the same spirits, and since you have promised us good money and good weapons, I am here to do my general's bidding.'

Fired by such powerful sentiments, I had actually opened my mouth to render them into French when I was stopped dead in my tracks by another meaningful glance from Philip. Did Franco hear my heart beating?

Did Dieudonné, standing behind him? Did the popinjay Haj? All three were staring at me expectantly, as if encouraging me to render Franco's eloquent speech. But thanks to Philip the truth had dawned on me in the nick of time. Overwhelmed by the solemnity of the occasion, old Franco had lapsed into his native Bembe, a language I did not possess above the waterline.

Yet to believe his face Philip knew nothing of this. He was chuckling merrily, twigging the old man for his mistake. Haj behind him had exploded in hyena-like derision. But Franco himself, nothing daunted, launched upon a laborious repetition of his speech in Swahili. And he was still doing this, and I was still nodding my appreciation of his oratory, when to my intense relief the door to the interior of the house was banged open by Benny to admit a breathless Maxie and his three guests, with the Mwangaza at their centre.

*   *   *

The floor has not swallowed me up, nobody has pointed the finger and denounced me. Somehow we are gathered at the gaming table and I am rendering Philip's words of welcome into Swahili. The Swahili is freeing me, which it always does. Somehow I have survived the handshakes and introductions, and everyone is in his appointed place except Jasper who, having been presented to the Mwangaza and his advisors, has been escorted from the room by Benny, I presume for the greater safety of his professional conscience. Philip's speech is jocular and brief and his pauses fall where I would wish them.

For my audience I have selected a litre bottle of Perrier water twenty inches in front of me, eye contact in the early minutes of a session being your interpreter's deathtrap. You catch an eye, a spark of complicity flies, and the next thing you know, you're in that person's pocket for the duration. The most I permit myself, therefore, is a few furtive brushstrokes of my lowered gaze, in the course of which the Mwangaza remains a hypnotic, birdlike shadow perched between his two attendants: to one side of him, the pocked and formidable Tabizi, former Shiite and now Christian convert, clad head to toe in shades of designer charcoal; and to the other his glossy no-name acolyte and political advisor, whom I secretly christen the Dolphin on account of his hairlessness and the all-weather smile which, like the bootlace-thin pigtail sprouting from the nape of his shaven neck, seems to operate in detachment of its owner. Maxie sports a regimental-type tie. My orders are to render nothing into English for him unless he signals for it.

A word here regarding the psychology of your multilinguist. People who put on another European language, it is frequently observed, put on another personality with it. An Englishman breaking into German speaks more loudly. His mouth changes shape, his vocal cords open up, he abandons .self-irony in favour of dominance. An Englishwoman dropping into

French will soften herself and puff out her lips for pertness, while her male counterpart will veer towards the
pompous. I expect I do the same. But your African
languages do not impart these fine distinctions. They're
functional and they're robust, even when the language
of choice is colonial French. They're peasant languages
made for straight talk and good shouting in argument,
which Congolese people do a lot of. Subtleties and
evasion are achieved less by verbal gymnastics than by a
change of topic or, if you want to play safe, a proverb.
Sometimes I'll be aware, as I hop from one language to
another, that I have shifted my voice to the back of my
throat to achieve the extra breath and husky tone
required. Or I have a feeling, for instance when I am
speaking Kinyarwanda, that I'm juggling a hot stone
between my teeth. But the larger truth is, from the
moment I settle into my chair, I become what I render.

Philip has ended his speech of welcome. Seconds
later, so have I. He sits down and rewards himself with
a sip of water from his glass. I take a sip from mine,
not because I'm thirsty, but because I'm relating to
him. I steal another look at the mountainous Franco
and his neighbour the emaciated Dieudonné. Franco
boasts a single scar running from the top of the forehead to the end of the nose. Are his arms and legs
similarly marked as part of the initiation ritual that
protects him from flying bullets? Dieudonné's brow is
high and smooth as a girl's, and his dreamy gaze seems
fixed on the hills he has left behind. The dandy Haj,

lounging on Franco's other side, appears wilfully
unaware of either of them.

* * *

'Good morning, my friends! Are your eyes all turned
towards me?'

*He is so small, Salvo. Why is it that so many men of
small stature have more courage than men of size?* Small
as Cromwell Our Chief of Men was small, pushing out
double the energy per cubic inch of everyone around
him. Light cotton jacket, washable, as becomes your
travelling evangelist. Halo of grizzled hair the same
length all round: a black Albert Einstein without the
moustache. And at the throat where the tie should go,
the gold coin that Hannah has told me about, big as a
fifty-pence piece: *it is his slave collar, Salvo. It tells us he
is not for sale. He has been bought already, so bad luck. He
belongs to the people of all Kivu, and here is the coin that
purchased him. He is a slave to the Middle Path!*

Yes, all our eyes are turned to you, Mwangaza. My
own eyes also. I no longer need take refuge in my
Perrier bottle while I wait for him to speak. Our three
delegates, having afforded our Enlightener the African
courtesy of not staring at him, are now staring at him
for all they're worth. Who is he? Which spirits guide
him, what magic does he practise? Will he scold us? Will
he frighten us, pardon us, make us laugh, make us rich,
make us dance and embrace and tell each other all we
feel? Or will he scorn us and make us unhappy and

guilty and self-accusing, which is what we Congolese, and we half-Congolese, are threatened with all the time?—Congo the laughing stock of Africa, raped, plundered, screwed up, bankrupt, corrupt, murderous, duped and derided, renowned by every country on the continent for its incompetence, corruption and anarchy.

We are waiting for the rhythm of him, the arousal, but he keeps us waiting: waiting for our mouths to go dry and our groins to shrivel up—or that at least is what the secret child is waiting for, owing to the fact that our great Redeemer bears an unearthly likeness to our Mission's pulpit orator Père André. Like André, he must glower at each member of his congregation in turn, first at Franco, then Dieudonné, then Haj and finally at me, one long glower for each of us, with the difference that I feel not just his eyes on me, but his hands as well, if only in my hyperactive memory.

'Well, gentlemen! Since your eyes are now upon me, don't you think you have made a pretty big mistake coming here today? Maybe Monsieur Philippe's excellent pilot should have dropped you on a different island.'

His voice is too big for him, but true to my usual practice I render my French softly, almost as an aside.

'What are you searching for here, I am asking myself?' he thunders across the table at old Franco, causing him to grit his jaw in anger. 'You are not searching for *me*, surely? *I* am not your fellow at all! *I* am the Mwangaza, the messenger of harmonious coexistence and prosperity for all Kivu. I think with my head, not with my gun, or my panga, or my penis. I don't mess with cut-throat Mai Mai warlords like you, oh no!' He transfers his scorn to Dieudonné. 'And I don't mess around with second-class citizens like the Banyamulenge here either, oh no!'—a defiant lift of the jaw at Haj—'and I don't mix with rich young dandies from Bukavu, thank you very much'—an insider's smile nonetheless for the son of Luc his old comrade-in-arms and fellow Shi—'not even if they offer me free beer and a job at a Rwandan-run goldmine—oh no! I am the Mwangaza, the good heart of the Congo, and honest servant of a strong, united Kivu. If that is the person you have truly come to see—well, just possibly—but let me think about it—maybe you have landed on the right island after all.'

The oversized voice descends to the confiding depths. Mine clambers down after it in French.

'Are you by any chance a *Tutsi*, sir?' he enquires, peering into the bloodshot eyes of Dieudonné. He asks the same question of each delegate in turn, then of all of them at once. Are they Tutsi? Hutu? Bembe? Rega? Fulero? Nande? Or Shi, like himself?

'If so, will you please kindly leave the room now. Forthwith. Immediately. No hard feelings.' He points histrionically at the open French windows. 'Go! Good day to you, gentlemen! Thank you for your visit. And send me a bill, please, for your expenses.'

Nobody moves except the kinetic Haj, who rolls his eyes and peers comically from one to other of his incongruous comrades.

'What's stopping you, my friends? Don't be shy, now! Your pretty aeroplane is still out there. It has two reliable engines. It is waiting to take you back to Denmark at no charge. Away with you, go home, and nothing will be said!'

Suddenly he is smiling a radiant, five-star, all-African smile that splits his Einstein face in two, and our delegates are smiling and chuckling with him in relief, Haj the loudest. Père André knew how to play that trick too: switch off the heat when his congregation is least expecting it, and make you grateful to him, and want to be his friend. Even Maxie is smiling. So are Philip, the Dolphin and Tabizi.

'But if on the other hand you are from *Kivu*, from the north or the south or the middle'—the too-big voice reaches out to us in generous welcome—'if you are a true God-fearing Kivutian, who loves the Congo and wishes to remain a Congolese patriot under one decent and efficient government in Kinshasa—if you wish to drive the Rwandan butchers and exploiters back across their borders one and all—then kindly stay exactly where you are. Stay, please, and talk to me. And to one another. And let us, dear brothers, identify our common purpose, and decide together how we can best pursue it. Let us tread the Middle Path of unity and reconciliation and inclusiveness under God.'

He stops, considers his words, is reminded of something, starts again.

'Ah, but that Mwangaza is a dangerous separatist, you have been told. He has crazy personal ambitions. He wishes to break up our beloved Congo, and feed it piecemeal to the jackals across the border! My friends, I am more loyal to our capital city of Kinshasa than Kinshasa is to itself!' A high note now, but we shall go higher, wait and see. 'I am more loyal than Kinshasa's unpaid soldiers who pillage our towns and villages and violate our women! I am so loyal that I want to do Kinshasa's job better than Kinshasa ever did! I want to bring us peace, not war. I want to bring us manna, not starvation! To build us schools and roads and hospitals and give us proper administration instead of ruinous corruption! I want to keep all of Kinshasa's promises. I even want to keep Kinshasa!'

* * *

He gives us hope, Salvo.

She is kissing my eyelids, giving me hope. I have my hands round her sculptured head.

Can you not understand what hope *means to people of the Eastern Congo?*

I love you.

Those poor Congolese souls are so tired of pain they no longer believe in the cure. If the Mwangaza can inspire them with hope, everyone will support him. If not, the wars will go on and on and he will be one more bad prophet on their path to Hell.

Then let's hope he gets his message over to the electorate, I suggest piously.

Salvo, you are a complete romantic. For as long as the present government is in power, any elections will be incompetent and totally corrupt. People who are not bought will vote on ethnic lines, results will be falsified and tensions will increase. First let us have stability and honesty. Then we may have elections. If you had listened to the Mwangaza, you would agree.

I'd rather listen to you.

Her lips leave my eyelids and look for more substantial fare.

And I suppose you know that the Monster used to carry a magic stick around with him that was too heavy for any mortal man to lift, except the Monster himself?

No, Hannah, that gem of knowledge escaped me. She is referring to the late and pitiful General Mobutu, supreme ruler and destroyer of Zaire and her only known hate-figure to date.

Well, the Mwangaza also has a stick. It goes with him everywhere, just like the Monster's, but it is of a special wood chosen for its lightness. Anyone who believes in the Middle Path may pick it up and discover how easy is the journey to its ranks. And when the Mwangaza dies, do you know what will happen to this magic stick?

It will help him walk to Heaven, I suggest drowsily, my head upon her belly.

Don't be facetious, please, Salvo. It will be placed in a beautiful new Museum of Unity to be built on the banks of Lake Kivu, where all may visit it. It will commemorate the day when Kivu became the pride of Congo, united and free.

*   *   *

And here it is. The stick. The very one. It lies before us on the green baize table, a miniature House of Commons mace. The delegates have examined its magic markings, and tested it for lightness in their palms. For old Franco, it is an object of significance—but is the significance of the right kind? For Haj it is a piece of merchandise. What materials have they used? Does it work? And we can sell them cheaper. Dieudonné's response is less easily read. Will it bring peace and equality to my people? Will our prophets approve of its powers? If we make war for it, will it protect us from Franco and his kind?

Maxie has skewed his chair to the table so that he can stretch his legs. His eyes are closed, he leans back like an athlete waiting his turn, hands clasped behind his neck. My saviour Philip of the wavy white hair wears the quiet smile of an impresario. He has the eternal English actor's face, I have decided. He could be anything from thirty-five to sixty, and the audience would never know. If Tabizi and the Dolphin are listening to my rendering they show no sign of it. They know the Mwangaza's speeches the way I knew André's. By contrast I have acquired an unexpected audience in the three delegates. Having been harangued by the Mwangaza in Swahili, they have come to rely on my less emotive French replay for a second hearing. Haj the academic listens critically, Dieudonné thoughtfully, meditating upon each precious word. And Franco listens with his fists clenched, ready to strike down the first man who contradicts him.

*   *   *

The Mwangaza has ceased to play the demagogue and assumed the rôle of a lecturer in economics. I trim my interpreter's sails accordingly. Kivu is being robbed, he informs us sternly. He knows what Kivu is worth and what it isn't being paid. He has the figures at his professional fingertips and waits while I jot them on my notepad. I discreetly smile my thanks. He acknowledges my smile and reels off the names of Rwandan-backed mining companies that are plundering our natural resources. Since most have French names, I do not render them.

'Why do we let them do it?' he demands angrily, voice rising again. 'Why do we stand by and watch our enemies grow rich on our mineral wealth, when all we want to do is throw them out?'

He has a map of Kivu. The Dolphin has pegged it to the whiteboard and the Mwangaza is standing beside it, assailing it with his magic stick: clap, smack, as he rattles along, and I rattle along after him from my end of the table, but softly, tempering his words, defusing them a little—which in turn causes him to identify me if not as an active member of the resistance, at least as somebody who needs to be won over.

He stops speaking, so I do. He stares directly at me. He has the witch doctor's knack, when staring, of contracting his eye muscles to make himself more visionary and compelling. It's not my eyes he is looking at any more, it's my skin. He studies my face, then in case there's any change, my hands: mid to light tan.

'Mr Interpreter, sir!'

'Mwangaza.'

'Come up here, my boy!'

For a caning? To confess my shortcomings to the class? Watched by all, I walk down the table until I am standing before him, only to find that I am the taller by a head.

'So which are you, my boy?'—very jocular, stabbing a finger first at Maxie and Philip, then at the three black delegates—'Are you one of *us* or one of *them*?'

Under such pressure, I rise to his rhetorical heights. 'Mwangaza, I am one of both of you!' I cry back in Swahili.

He roars with laughter and renders my words into French for me. Clapping breaks out at both ends of the table, but the Mwangaza's booming voice effortlessly bestrides it.

'Gentlemen. This fine young fellow is the symbol of our Middle Path! Let us follow the example of his all-inclusiveness! No, no, no. Stay here, my boy, stay here one moment longer, please.'

He means it as an honour, even if it doesn't feel like one. He calls me fine young fellow and stands me beside him while he hammers the map with his magic stick and extols the Eastern Congo's mineral wealth, and I for my part clasp my hands behind my back and render teacher's lines without benefit of a notepad, thereby incidentally providing the conference with an example of my powers of memory.

'Here at Mwenga, *gold*, my friends! Here at Kamituga: gold, uranium, cassiterite, coltan and—don't tell anybody—diamonds too. Here at Kabambare, gold, cassiterite and coltan.' His repetitions are deliberate. 'Here coltan, cassiterite, and here'—the stick lifts, and drifts a little uncertainly in the direction of Lake Albert—'*oil*, my friends, unmeasured, and perhaps unmeasurable quantities of priceless *oil*. And you know something else? We have a little miracle that is hardly known about at all, though everybody wants it. It is so rare that diamonds are like pebbles in the street by comparison. It is called Kamitugaite, my friends, and it is 56.71 per cent uranium! Well, what on earth could anybody want *that* for, I wonder?'

He waits for the knowing laughter to rise and fade.

'But who will profit from all these riches, tell me?'

He waits again, smiling up at me while I ask the same question, so I smile too, in my newfound rôle as teacher's pet.

'Oh the fatcats in Kinshasa will get their pay-off, sure! They will not forgo their thirty pieces of Rwandan silver, oh no! But they won't be spending them on schools and roads and hospitals for Eastern Congo, oh no! In the fine stores of Johannesburg and Nairobi and Cape Town, maybe they will spend them. But not here in Kivu. Oh no!'

Pause again. Smile this time not at me, but at our delegates. Then ask another question.

'Do the people of Kivu get richer every time another truckload of coltan rolls across our borders?'

The magic stick moves inexorably eastward across Lake Kivu.

'When the oil begins to flow into Uganda, will the people of Kivu be better off? My friends, as the oil is drained away, they will grow poorer by the day. Yet these are *our mines*, my friends, *our oil, our wealth*, given to us by God to tend and enjoy in His name! These are not water wells that fill up again with the rains. What the thieves take from us today will not grow again tomorrow, or the day after.'

He shakes his head, muttering *Oh no* several times, as if recalling a grave injustice.

'And who, I wonder, sells these stolen goods at such vast profit, not one cent of which is restored to the rightful owners? The answer, my friends, is known to all of you! It is the racketeers of Rwanda! It is the carpetbaggers of Uganda and Burundi! It is our corrupt government of loquacious fatcats in Kinshasa who sell our birthright to the foreigners, and then tax us for our trouble! Thank you, my boy. Well done, sir. You can sit down now.'

I sit down and reflect upon coltan, not in real time for I am rendering the Mwangaza non-stop, but in the way a news flash rolls along the bottom of a television screen while the main action continues up above. What is coltan? It is a highly precious metal once found exclusively in the Eastern Congo, ask my commodity-dealing clients. If you were unwise enough to dismantle your cellphone, you would find an essential speck of it among the debris. For decades the United States has held strategic stockpiles of the stuff, a fact my clients learned to their cost when the Pentagon dumped tons of it on the world market.

Why else does coltan have place of honour in my head? Go back to Christmas in the Year of Our Lord 2000. Play Station 2, the must-have electronic toy for every rich British kid, is in desperately short supply. Middle-class parents are wringing their hands, and so is Penelope on the front page of her great newspaper: WE SET OUT TO NAME AND SHAME THE GRINCHES WHO STOLE OUR CHRISTMAS! But her anger is misplaced. The shortage is due not to the incompetence of the manufacturers, but to a tidal wave of genocide which has engulfed the Eastern Congo, thereby causing a temporary interruption in the supply of coltan.

Did you know that the Mwangaza is a professor of our Congolese history, Salvo? He knows every detail of our horror by heart. He knows who killed whom, how many, and on what date, and he is not afraid of the truth, which so many of our cowardly ones are.

And I am one of the cowardly ones, but at this bare green table where I am sitting there is no hiding place. Wherever the Mwangaza dares go, I must go too, conscious of every word I render. Two minutes ago he was talking production figures. Now he is talking genocide, and once again he has his figures off pat: how many villages razed, how many inhabitants crucified or hacked to death, suspected witches burned, the gang rapes, the endless back-and-forth of East Congo's internecine slaughter fomented from outside while the international community bickers and I turn off the television if Penelope hasn't turned it off already. And the dying continues even as the Mwangaza speaks, and I render. With every month that passes, another thirty-eight thousand Congolese die from the ravages of these forgotten wars:

'One thousand, two hundred deaths a day, my friends, including Saturdays and Sundays! That means today and tomorrow, and every day next week.'

I glance at the faces of my delegates. They are hangdog. Perhaps it is they for once who are on autopilot and I am not. Who can tell what they are thinking, if they have consented to think at all? They are three more Africans seated at the roadside in the midday heat and nobody on earth, perhaps not they themselves, can fathom what is in their heads. But why is the Mwangaza telling us all this with time so short? Is it to beat us down? No. It is to embolden us.

'Therefore we are *entitled*, my friends! We are *twice*,

three times entitled! No other nation on earth has suffered such disasters as our beloved Kivu. No other nation is in such desperate need of rebirth! No other nation has a greater right to seize its wealth and lay it at the feet of its afflicted ones, and say: "This is not *theirs* any more. This, my poor people—*nous misérables de Kivu!*—is *ours!*"'

His magisterial boom could have filled the Albert Hall, but the question in all our hearts is clear enough: if Kivu's wealth has fallen into the wrong hands, and the injustices of history entitle us to get it back, and Kinshasa is a broken reed, and everything from Kivu is exported eastwards anyway, what do we propose to do about it?

'Take a close look, my friends, at our great nation's politicians and protectors, and what do you see? New policies? Oh yes—*very* new policies, you are right. Quite pristine, I would say. And new political parties to go with them, too. With very poetic names'—*des noms très poétiques.* 'There is so much new democracy in the whore-city of Kinshasa that I am afraid to walk down Boulevard 30 Juin in my old shoes these days!'—*cette ville de putains!* 'So many new political platforms going up, and built of the very best timber too, at your expense. So many beautifully printed, twenty-page manifestos that will bring us peace, money, medicine and universal education by midnight next week at the latest. So many anti-corruption laws that you can't help asking yourself who has been bribed to draft them all.'

The laugh is led by the smooth-skinned Dolphin and the rugged Tabizi, and backed by Philip and Maxie. The Enlightener waits sternly while it fades. Where is he leading us? Does he know? With Père André there was never an agenda. With the Mwangaza, though I am too slow to sense it, there has been agenda all the way.

'But take a closer look, please, at these brand-new politicians of ours, my friends. Lift up the brims of their hats, please. Let a little good African sun into their hundred-thousand-dollar Mercedes limousines and tell me what you see. New faces full of optimism? Bright young graduates ready to offer up their careers in the service of our Republic? Oh no, my friends, you do not. You see the same old, old faces of the same old, old crooks!'

What has Kinshasa ever achieved for Kivu? he demands to know. Answer, nothing. Where is the peace they preach, the prosperity, the harmony? Where is their inclusive love of country, neighbour, community? He has travelled all Kivu, north and south, and failed to find the smallest evidence of it. He has listened to the People's tales of woe: Yes, we want the Middle Path, Mwangaza! We pray for it! We sing for it! We dance for it! But how, oh how, will we obtain it? How indeed? He mimics their pitiful cry. I mimic the Mwangaza: 'Who will defend us when our enemies send their troops against us, Mwangaza? You are a man of peace, Mwangaza! You are no longer the great warrior you used to be. Who will organise us and fight with us and teach us to be strong together?'

Am I truly the last person in the room to realise that the answer to the People's prayer was lounging at the head of the table with his scuffed suède boots stuck out in front of him? Evidently I am, for the Mwangaza's next words jolt me out of my reverie so fast that Haj swings round and peers at me with his comedian's bubbly eyes.

'*No name*, my friends?' the Mwangaza is yelling at us indignantly. 'This strange Syndicate that has dragged us here today has *no name*? Oh, this is very bad! Where can they have put it? This is all very fishy and mysterious! Maybe we should put on our spectacles and help them look for it! Why on earth should honest folk conceal their names? What have they to hide? Why don't they come out with it straight and say who they are and what they want?'

Start slow, Père André. Start low and slow. You have a long way to rise. But the Mwangaza is an old hand.

'Well now, my dear friends,' he confides, in a weary tone that makes you want to help him over the stile. 'I have spoken to these *no-name* gentlemen long and hard, I want to tell you.' He points at Philip without turning to look at him. 'Oh yes. We have had many tough talks together. From the going down of the sun and up again, I would say. Very tough talks indeed, and so they should be. Tell us what you want, Mwangaza, the no-names said to me. Tell it without adornment or evasion, please.

And then we will tell you what we want. And from this we shall establish whether we can do business, or whether we shall shake hands and say sorry and goodbye, which is normal commercial discourse. So I replied to them in the same coin'—absently fondling his gold slave collar, and thereby reminding us that he is not for sale—'"Gentlemen, it is very well known what I want. Peace, prosperity and inclusiveness for all Kivu. Free elections, but only when stability is established. But peace, gentlemen, it is also well known, does not come of its own accord, and neither does freedom. Peace has enemies. Peace must be won by the sword. For peace to be a reality, we must coordinate our forces, repossess our mines and cities, drive out the foreigners and install an interim government of all Kivu that will lay down the foundations of a true, enduring, democratic welfare state. But how can we do that for ourselves, gentlemen? We are crippled by discord. Our neighbours are more powerful than we are, and more cunning."'

He is glowering at Franco and Dieudonné, willing them to draw closer to each other while he continues his commercial discourse with the no-name gentlemen.

'"For our cause to prevail, we need your organisation, gentlemen. We need your equipment and your expertise. Without them, the peace of my beloved Kivu will forever be an illusion." That is what I said to the no-names. Those were my words. And the no-names, they listened to me carefully, as you would suppose. And finally one speaks for all, and I must not tell you his name even today, but I assure you he is not in this room although he is a proven lover of our nation. And this is what he says. "What you propose is well and good, Mwangaza. We may be men of commerce, but we are not without souls. The risk is high, the cost also. If we support your cause, how can we be sure that at the end of the day we shall not go away with empty pockets and a bloody nose?" And we on our side reply, "Those who join our great enterprise will join in its rewards."'

His voice drops even lower, but it can afford to. So does mine. I could whisper into my hand and they would hear me.

'The Devil, we are told, has many names, my friends, and by now we Congolese know most of them. But this Syndicate has none. It is not called the Belgian Empire, or the Spanish Empire, or the Portuguese Empire, or the British Empire, or the French Empire, or the Dutch Empire, or the American Empire, or even the Chinese Empire. This Syndicate is called *Nothing*. It is Nothing Incorporated. *No name* means no flag. *No name* will help to make us rich and united, but it will not own us or our people. With *no name*, Kivu will for the first time own itself. And when that day dawns, we shall go to the fatcats of Kinshasa and we shall say to them: "Good morning, fatcats. How are you today? You have all got hangovers as usual, I suppose!"'

Not a laugh or a smile. He has us.

'"Well, fatcats, we have some good news for you. Kivu has freed itself of foreign invaders and exploiters.

The good citizens of Bukavu and Goma have risen up against the oppressor and received us with open arms. The surrogate armies of Rwanda have fled and the *génocidaires* with them. Kivu has taken back its mines and put them into public ownership where they belong. Our means of production, distribution and supply are under one hat, and that is the hat of the people. We no longer export everything to the east. We have found alternative trade routes. But we are also patriots and we believe in the unity of one Congolese Democratic Republic within the legal borders of our Constitution. So here are our terms, fatcats—one, two, three, you can take them or leave them! Because *we* are not coming to *you*, fatcats. *You* are coming to *us*!"'

He sits down and closes his eyes. Père André used to do the same. It made the afterglow of his words last longer. My rendering complete, I permit myself a discreet poll of our delegates' reactions. Powerful speeches can bring resentment in their wake. The more an audience has been carried away, the harder it struggles to get back to shore. The fidgety Haj has ceased to fidget, contenting himself with a series of grimaces. The bone-thin Dieudonné has his fingertips pressed to his brow in distracted meditation. Beads of sweat have formed at the fringes of his beard. Old Franco next to him is consulting something on his lap, I suspect a fetish.

Philip breaks the spell. 'Well now, who will do us the honour of speaking first?' A meaningful glance at the post-office clock, because time is after all short.

All eyes on Franco, our senior member. He scowls at his great hands. He lifts his head.

'When Mobutu's power failed, the soldiers of the Mai Mai stood in the breach with pangas, arrows and lances to protect our blessed territory,' he asserts in slow Swahili. He glares round the table lest anyone should presume to challenge him. No one does. He continues, 'The Mai Mai has seen what has been. Now we shall see what comes. God will protect us.'

Next in class order comes Dieudonné.

'For the Banyamulenge to remain alive, we must be federalists,' he declares, speaking straight at his neighbour Franco. 'When you take our cattle, we die. When you kill our sheep, we die. When you take our women, we die. When you take our land, we die. Why can we not own the highlands where we live and toil and pray? Why can we not have our own chieftaincies? Why must our lives be administered by the chieftaincies of distant tribes who deny us our status and keep us captive to their will?' He turns to the Mwangaza. 'The Banyamulenge believe in peace as much as you do. But we will never renounce our land.'

The Mwangaza's eyes remain closed while the sleek-faced Dolphin fields the implied question.

'The Mwangaza is also a federalist,' he says softly. 'The Mwangaza does not insist on integration. Under his proposed Constitution, the rights of the Banyamulenge people to their lands and chieftaincies will be recognised.'

'And the Mulenge highlands will be declared a territory?'

'They will.'

'In the past, Kinshasa has refused to give us this just law.'

'The Mwangaza is not of the past, but of the future. You will have your just law,' the astute Dolphin replies: at which old Franco emits what sounds like a snort of derision, but perhaps he is clearing his throat. In the same moment, Haj jerks himself bolt upright like a jack-in-the-box and rakes the table with his wild, exophthalmic gaze:

'So it's a coup, right?' he demands, in the shrill, hectoring French of a Parisian sophisticate. 'Peace, prosperity, inclusiveness. But when you strip away the bullshit, we're grabbing power. Bukavu today, Goma tomorrow, Rwandans out, screw the UN, and Kinshasa can kiss our arses.'

A covert glance round the table confirms my suspicion that our conference is suffering from culture shock. It is as if the church elders had been sitting in solemn conclave when this urban heretic barges in from the street and demands to know what they're yacking about.

'I mean do we need all this?' Haj demands, dramatically spreading his open palms. 'Goma has its problems, ask my dad. Goma's got the goods, the Rwandans have got the money and the muscle. Tough. But Bukavu isn't Goma. Ever since the soldiers mutinied last year, our Rwandans have kept their heads down in Bukavu. And our town's administrators hate the Rwandans worse than anybody.' He flings out his hands, palms upward, in a Gallic gesture of disengagement. 'Just asking, that's all.'

But Haj is not asking the Mwangaza, he's asking *me*. His bubbly gaze may tour the table or settle respectfully on the great man, but no sooner do I begin to render him than it shoots back to me, and stays on me after the last echo of my voice has died in my ears. I'm expecting the Mwangaza to take up the challenge, or failing him, the Dolphin. But once more it's my saviour Philip who sidles in from the wings and gets them off the hook.

'That's today, Haj,' he explains, with the tolerance of his years. 'It's not *yesterday*. And if history is anything to go by, it won't be tomorrow, will it? Must the Middle Path wait for post-electoral chaos and the next Rwandan incursion before creating the conditions for a strong and lasting peace? Or does the Mwangaza do better to pick his time and place, which is your respected father's view?'

Haj shrugs, stretches out his arms, grins, shakes his head in disbelief. Philip grants him a moment to speak, but the moment is scarcely up before he lifts the hand-bell and gives it a little shake, announcing a brief recess while our delegates consider their positions.

9

I could never have imagined, as I stole down the cellar steps for the first time in my capacity as interpreter-below-the-waterline, that I would have the sensation of walking on air, but such was indeed the case. Haj's boorish intrusion aside, all was unfolding in the best possible manner. When, if ever, had such a voice of reason and moderation echoed across the lakes and jungles of our troubled Congo? When had two more capable professionals—Maxie the man of deeds, and Philip the rapier-witted negotiator—met together in the cause of an ailing people? What a *shove to history* we were giving! Even the case-hardened Spider, who on his own admission had not understood a syllable of what he was recording—nor, I suspected, the intricacies of our venture—was exhilarated by the positive atmosphere to date.

'Sounds like they're getting a real talking-to, if you ask me,' he declared in his Welsh singsong, as he clapped the earphones on me, checked my mouthpiece and practically tucked me into my hot-seat. 'Bang their heads together and maybe a bit of common sense will fall out, I say.'

But of course it was Sam I was waiting to hear: Sam my coordinator, Sam who would tell me which mikes to concentrate on, who would brief and debrief me on a running basis. Had I met Sam? Was he too perchance a sound-thief, another former denizen of the Chat Room, about to step out of the shadows and display his special skills? All the greater my surprise, therefore, when the voice that announced itself in my headphones turned out to be a woman's, and a motherly one at that.

Feeling good, Brian dear?

Never better, Sam. Yourself?

You did awfully well up there. Everyone's raving about you.

Did I detect the merest tingle of a Scottish accent amid these matronly words of comfort?

Where's home for you, Sam? I asked excitedly, because everything was still bright to me from upstairs.

If I said Wandsworth, would that shock you terribly?

Shock me? We're neighbours, for Heaven's sake! I do half my shopping in Wandsworth!

Awkward silence. Too late, I remember once again that I am supposed to live in a post-office box.

Then you and I will pass as trolleys in the night, Brian dear, Sam replies primly. *We'll kick off with all the sevens, if you don't mind. Subjects approaching now.*

The sevens are the guest suite. Eyes on Spider's Underground plan while I follow the delegates down the corridor and wait for one of them to delve for his key and unlock their front door—clever Philip to entrust them with keys to increase their sense of security! Next comes the cannon-fire of feet on floorboards and the deluge of lavatory cisterns and taps. *Vroom! Crash!* et cetera. Now they're in the living room, pouring themselves soft drinks, honking, clanking, stretching and emitting nervous yawns.

Their suite is as familiar to me today as the four dreary walls that presently enclose me, although I never saw it and never will, any more than I saw the inside of the Mwangaza's royal apartments, or Sam's ops room with its encrypted satellite phone for secure communications with the Syndicate and other persons unnamed—or so Spider informed me in one of our quick-fire opening exchanges, for Spider like many sound-thieves was garrulous, and Welsh with it. Asked what tasks he had performed during his days in the Chat Room, he replied that he was not an *earwig*—meaning linguist-transcriber—but a humble *bugger*, as the old joke runs, an installer of clandestine devices for the greater joy of Mr Anderson. But what he liked best was mayhem:

'Nothing like it in the world, Brian. Never happier than when I'm flat on my face in shit with ordnance coming in from all sides, and a nice piece of sixty-millimetre mortar up my arse.'

The stolen sound is coming over loud and clear, down to the ice cubes bursting into the tumblers, and a coffee machine that generates more bass-sound than a symphony orchestra. Spider, however many times he's been through this before, is as tense as I am, but there are no last-minute hitches, nothing has blown or fused or died on him, it's all systems go.

Except it isn't, because we are in the delegates' living room and nobody's speaking. We have background, but no foreground. Grunts and groans, but not a word spoken. A crash, a belch, a squeak. Then far away the sound of someone muttering, but who, in whose ear, is anybody's guess. But still no real voices, or none to overhear. Has the Mwangaza's oratory robbed them of their tongues?

I'm holding my breath. So's Spider. I'm lying mouse-still in Hannah's bed, pretending I'm not there while her friend Grace rattles the locked door, demanding to know why she didn't show up for tennis which Grace is teaching her, and Hannah who hates to deceive is pleading a headache.

Perhaps they're saying their prayers, Sam.

But who to, Brian?

Perhaps Sam doesn't know her Africa, for the answer could well be the obvious one: to the Christian God, or their versions of Him. The Banyamulenge so beloved of my dear late father are famous for talking to God at all times, directly or through their prophets. Dieudonné, I have no doubt, will be praying whenever he is moved to pray. And since the Mai Mai look to God for protection in battle and not a lot else, Franco's concerns are more likely to be fixed on how much is in it for him. A witch doctor will probably have provided him with leaves from a téké tree, squashed up and rubbed on his body so that he can ingest its power. Who Haj prays to is anyone's guess. Perhaps Luc, his ailing father.

Why has nobody spoken? And why—amid the creaks and shuffles and background clatter that I expect to hear—why do I sense a mounting tension in the room, as if somebody is holding a gun to our delegates' heads?

Speak, someone, for Heaven's sake!

I'm reasoning with them in my head, pleading with them. Look. All right. I understand. Back there in the conference room you felt overawed, patronised, resentful of the white faces round the table. The Mwangaza talked down to you, but that's who he is, he's a pulpit man, they're all the same. Plus you've got your responsibilities to consider, I accept that too. Wives, clans, tribes, spirits, augurs, soothsayers, witch doctors, stuff we can't know about. But please, for the Alliance's sake, for Hannah's, for all our sakes—speak!

Brian?

Sam.

I'm beginning to wonder whether we're *the ones who should be praying.*

The same awful thought has occurred to me: we're rumbled. One of our delegates—I'm suspecting Haj—has put a finger to his lips, and with his other hand the little smart-arse has pointed at the walls or the telephone or the TV set, or rolled his bulging eyes at the chandelier. And what he's telling them is: 'Fellows, I've been out there, I know the wicked world, and believe you me, we're bugged.' If so, one of several things will now happen, depending on who the Subjects are—or as Maxie had it, Targets—and whether they're feeling conspiratorial or conspired against today. The best scenario has them saying, 'To hell with it, let's go on talking anyway,' which is your average rational man's response, because like most of us he simply hasn't the time or patience to be bugged. But this isn't an average situation. And what is driving us both to the brink of dementia, me and Sam, is that our three delegates, if they would only have the wit to realise it, have a perfectly good remedy in their hands, which is why I'm sitting here waiting for them to use it.

Don't you wish you could just scream at them, Brian?

Yes, Sam, indeed I do, but a far worse fear is taking root in my mind. It's not Spider's microphones that have been rumbled: it's *me*, Salvo. My timely rescue by Philip didn't rescue me after all. By the time Franco fired his set speech at the wrong man in the wrong language, Haj had seen me do a double-take, which is what his long, goggle-eyed stares are all about. He saw me open my stupid mouth to reply, then shut it and try to look blank instead.

I am still mortifying my soul with these thoughts when, like a message of redemption, comes the bass voice of old Franco speaking, not Bembe, but his prison-acquired Kinyarwanda. And this time I'm allowed to understand him instead of doing a double-take!

* * *

The fruits of eavesdropping, Mr Anderson never tires of reminding his disciples, are by nature incoherent rubbish and endlessly frustrating. The patience of Job is not sufficient, in Mr Anderson's judgment, to separate the occasional nugget from the sea of dross in which it swims. In this regard, the opening exchanges of our three delegates in no way diverged from the norm, being the anticipated mix of scatological expressions of relief and, only rarely, sighting shots for the battles yet to be joined.

Franco: (*scathingly enunciating a Congolese proverb*) Fine words don't feed a cow.

Dieudonné: (*capping Franco's proverb with another*) The teeth are smiling, but is the heart?

Haj: Holy Shit! My dad warned me the old boy was heavy duty, but this is something else. *Aw, aw, aw.* Why does he talk Swahili like a Tanzanian with a pawpaw up his arse? I thought he was a home-grown Shi.

Nobody bothers to answer him, which is what happens every time you put three men in a room together. The biggest mouth takes over and the two people you want to listen to go mute.

Haj: (*continued*) Who's the pretty zebra anyway? (*Mystified silence, echoing my own*) The interpreter guy in the linoleum jacket? Who the fuck is he?

Haj is calling me a *zebra*? I've been called most
things in my time. At Mission school I was a *métis*, a
café au lait, a shaven pig. At the Sanctuary I was
anything from a fuzzipeg to a golliwog. But *zebra* was
a brand-new insult to me, and I could only suppose that
it was of Haj's personal manufacture.   •

Haj: (*continued*) I knew a guy like him once. Maybe
    they're related. A book-keeper. Fiddled the accounts
    for my dad. Screwed every girl in town till some
    angry husband shot his arse off. *Vump!* Wasn't me
    though. I'm not married and I don't kill guys. We've
    killed enough of ourselves. Fuck us. Never again.
    Cigarette?

Haj has a gold cigarette case. In the conference
room, I saw it peeking from the mustard silk lining of
his Zegna. Now I hear its clunk as he snaps it open.
Franco lights up and is seized by a gravedigger's cough.
    What on earth was that about, Brian?
    They're speculating about my ethnicity.
    Is that normal?
    Pretty much.
    Dieudonné, having first declined, mutters a fatalistic
'Why not?' and lights up also.

Haj: You sick or something?
Dieudonné: Something.

Are they sitting or standing? Listen carefully, you get the uneven squeak of lame Franco's track shoes while Haj prances around the hard floor in his slime-green crocs. Keep listening, you hear a grunt of pain and the puff of a foam cushion as Dieudonné eases himself into an armchair. That's how good we sound-thieves become under Mr Anderson's tutelage.

Haj: Tell you one thing for openers, pal.
Dieudonné: (*wary at being addressed so warmly*) What?
Haj: People in Kivu are a whole lot more interested in peace and reconciliation than those pricks in Kinshasa. (*affects a rabble-rouser's voice*) Kill 'em all. Gouge their Rwandan eyes out. We're right behind you, man. Like two thousand kilometres behind you, mostly jungle. (*Waits, I suspect for a reaction, but gets none. Slap of crocs resumes*) And this old boy he goes along with all that shit (*mimicking the Mwangaza, quite well*): Let us cleanse our fine green land of these pestilential cockroaches, my friends. Oh yes. Let us restore our homeland to our beloved countrymen! I agree with that. Don't we all? (*Waits. No response*) Motion carried unanimously. Chuck 'em out, I say. *Vump! Pow!* Fuck off! (*No response*) Just non-violently. (*rattle of crocs*) Problem is, where do you stop? I mean, what about the poor bastards who came over in '94? Do we sling them out too? Do we sling out Dieudonné here? Take your kids with you but leave your cows behind?

Haj is turning out to be the wrecker I feared when he was upstairs. In a casual yet subversive manner he has contrived to bring the conversation round within minutes to the most divisive issue before us: the unresolved status of the Banyamulenge people and Dieudonné's eligibility as an ally in our enterprise.

Franco: (*yet another proverb, this time spat out in challenge*) A log may remain ten years in the water. It will *never* become a crocodile!
    (*Long, tense pause*)
Dieudonné: *Franco!*

The screech in my headphones has nearly pitched me out of my hot-seat. In his fury, Dieudonné has shoved his chair across the stone floor. I imagine his hands clawing at its arms, and his sweated head lifting to Franco in passionate appeal.

Dieudonné: When is this ever going to end, Franco? You and us? The Banyamulenge may be Tutsis, but we are *not* Rwandans! (*His breathing gets him, but he keeps fighting*) We are *Congolese*, Franco, as Congolese as the Mai Mai! Yes! (*shouting down Franco's derision*) The Mwangaza understands that and sometimes so do you! (*and in French, to ram it home*): *Nous sommes tous Zaïrois!* Remember what they taught us to sing at school in Mobutu's time? So why can't we sing it now? *Nous sommes tous Congolais!*

No, Dieudonné, not *all* of us, I mentally correct him. I too was taught to sing those words at school in proud unison with my classmates, until the day they poked their fingers at the secret child and screamed: *Pas Salvo, pas le métis! Pas le cochon rasé!*

Dieudonné: (*continuing his tirade*) In the '64 rebellion, my father, a Munyamulenge, fought alongside your father, a Simba (*rasp as he reaches for breath*) and you as a young man fought alongside both of them. Did that make you our *allies*? (*rasp*) Our *friends*? (*rasp*) No, it did not. (*he breaks angrily into French*) *C'était une alliance contre la nature!* The Simba continued to kill us and steal *our* cattle for *their* troops, just as the Mai Mai kills us and steals our cattle today. When we retaliate, you call us Banyamulenge scum. When we restrain ourselves, you call us Banyamulenge cowards—(*drowning gulps now*). But if we can join together under this— (*rasp*)—stop the killing, and the hating (*rasp*)—stop avenging our dead ones and our mutilated ones—if we can stop *ourselves*—and unite—under this leader or any other ...

He breaks off. His wheezing is so bad it reminds me of Jean-Pierre in the hospital, minus tubes. I wait on the edge of my hot-seat for Franco's rejoinder, but must once more listen impotently to Haj.

Haj: Allies in *what*, for fuck's sake? To achieve *what*? A
united Kivu? North and south? *My friends. Let us
seize hold of our resources and thereby control our
destiny. Humph humph.* They've *been* seized, arsehole! By a bunch of Rwandan crazies who are armed
to the eyeballs and raping our women in their spare
time! Those interahamwe guys up there are so well
dug in, the fucking UN doesn't dare to fly over them
without asking their permission first.

Dieudonné: (*contemptuous laugh*) The UN? If we
wait for the UN to bring us peace we shall wait
until our children are dead, and our grandchildren
too.

Franco: Then maybe you should take your children and
grandchildren back to Rwanda now and leave us in
peace.

Haj: (*interceding fast in French, presumably to head off
the argument*) Us? I heard *us*? (*veritable fusillade of
croc-slapping, followed by dead silence*) You seriously
think this is about *us*? This old guy doesn't want *us*,
he wants *power*. He wants his place in history before
he croaks, and to get it he's prepared to sell us out
to this weirdo syndicate and bring the whole fucking
roof down on us.

I have barely finished rendering these heresies before
Philip's handbell summons us to round two.

*   *   *

And here I must recount an incident that at the time of its occurrence made little impact on my overburdened mind, but in the light of later events merits closer examination. Philip's bell sounds, I detach my headset. I rise to my feet and, with a wink at Spider in reply to his, ascend the cellar staircase. Reaching the top, I give the pre-arranged signal: three short taps to the iron door, which Anton opens part-way and closes behind me, unfortunately with a loud clang. Without a word passing between us Anton steers me round the corner of the house to the eastern end of the covered walkway, leaving me only a short distance to the gaming room, all again according to plan. But with one difference: neither of us had reckoned with the sunlight, which is shining straight into my eyes and temporarily unsighting me.

As I begin my walk, with my eyes directed downward in order to avoid the glare of the sun, I hear approaching footsteps and hoots of African laughter from the delegates coming at me from the opposite end of the covered way. We are about to encounter each other head-on. It is therefore apparent to me that I must be in possession of a convincing cover story to explain my emergence from the wrong side of the house. Did they glimpse Anton shooing me round the corner? Did they hear the clang of the iron door?

Fortunately I am trained to think on my feet, thanks to the One-Day Courses in Personal Security which all part-timers are obliged to attend. How had I been spending my precious leisure minutes while our delegates recessed for their private discussions? Answer, doing what I always do in breaks between proceedings—enjoying a bit of peace and quiet in some out-of-the-way corner until the bell rings. Thus mentally prepared, I continue my advance on the gaming-room door. I arrive, I stop. They arrive, they stop. Or rather Haj stops. Haj, being the most agile, is out front, whereas Franco and Dieudonné are following at a few paces' distance. They have still not caught up when Haj, who minutes earlier had dubbed me *zebra*, addresses me with exaggerated courtesy:

'So, Mr Interpreter, you are well refreshed? You are ready for our next battle?'

It was a harmless enough question and harmlessly put. The only problem was, he was speaking Kinyarwanda. This time, however, I needed no Philip to flash warning signals at me. I gave a puzzled smile, subtly tinged with regret. When that didn't do the trick, I shrugged my shoulders and shook my head, indicating my continuing incomprehension. Haj woke to his error, or appeared to, emitted a bark of apologetic laughter and slapped me on the upper arm. Had he been trying to trick me? He had not. Or so I persuaded myself at the time. He had merely fallen into the trap that awaits any multilinguist worth his salt. After speaking Kinyarwanda nineteen-to-the-dozen in the guest suite, he had neglected to change track. Happens to the best of us. Forget it.

10

'Gentlemen. I give you Monsieur le Colonel!'

The light of battle gleams in Maxie's washy blue eyes as he towers before the easel, hands on hips: three years to go before his Borodino. He has thrown aside his jacket but left his tie in place. Probably he wears one so seldom that he's forgotten about it. Our numbers have shrunk. The Mwangaza, once a veteran of the barricades but now a Prophet of Peace, has withdrawn to the seclusion of his royal apartments, taking his pigtailed acolyte with him. Only Tabizi—boxer's shoulders hunched, gaze lidded, dyed black hair scrupulously swept back to camouflage a bald crown—has stayed behind to see fair play.

But it's not Maxie I'm staring at, not Tabizi, not the delegates. It's my childhood. It's the large-scale military map of the town of Bukavu, jewel of Central Africa and some say all of Africa, set at the southern tip of Africa's highest and therefore coolest lake. And this lake, swathed in mist and cradled by smouldering hills, is magical, ask my dear late father. Ask the fishermen he gossiped with at the dockside while they picked the *sambaza* from their nets and tossed them into yellow plastic buckets, where they flipped for hours on end, hoping someone like me will put them back. Ask them about mamba mutu, the half crocodile, half woman; and the bad people who creep down to the shore at night and, by means of witchcraft, trade the living souls of innocent friends in exchange for favours in this world and retribution in the next. Which is why Lake Kivu is whispered to be cursed, and why fishermen disappear, dragged down by mamba mutu, who likes to eat their brains. Or so the fishermen assured my dear late father, who knew better than to mock their beliefs.

The main avenue is lined with classic colonial houses with rounded corners and oblong windows overhung with tulip trees, jacaranda and bougainvillea. The hills around bulge with banana groves and tea plantations like so many green mattresses. From their slopes you can count the town's five peninsulas. The grandest is called La Botte, and there it is, on Maxie's map: a boot of Italy with fine houses and pampered gardens descending to the lake's edge—le Maréchal Mobutu himself had deigned to have a villa there. To begin with, the boot shoots boldly into the lake, then just when you think it's headed straight for Goma, it crooks its foot sharp right and lashes out at Rwanda on the eastern shore.

Maxie's paper arrows are of strategic practicality. They point to the Governor's house, the radio and tele-vision stations, the United Nations headquarters and the army barracks. But none to the roadside market where we ate goat brochettes when my father brought me into town for my birthday treats; none to the green-roofed cathedral, built like two washed-up ships turned upside down, where we prayed for my immortal soul. None for the grim-stoned Catholic university where one day, if I worked hard, I might get to study. And none for the White Sisters' Mission where they fed sugar biscuits to the secret child and told him what a dear kind uncle he had.

Maxie stands with his back to us. Philip sits at his side, his features so fluid that you have to be quick to catch a particular expression. You think you see one, but when you look again, it's gone. Our three delegates sit where they sat before, Franco at their centre. Dieudonné has acquired a harder face. The muscles of Franco's neck are braced. Haj alone displays a provocative disdain for our proceedings. Zegna-clad elbows on the baize, he appears more interested in the window than in his own fiefdom on the easel. Does he care? Does he love Bukavu as much as I do in my memory? It is hard to believe so.

Enter Anton, bearing billiards cue. His appearance confuses me. Why isn't he out there with his watchers where he belongs? Then it dawns on me that, for as long as our delegates are in the conference room, there's nobody left for him to watch, which only goes to show that when you're geared up to peak performance with your nerve-ends out and your interpreter's third ear on red alert you can still be thick-headed when it comes to common sense.

'Bit of soldier talk coming up, old boy,' Maxie warns me in a murmur. 'That going to be all right for you?'

All right, Skipper? You asked, can I do military, and I can. Anton passes Maxie the billiards cue as a replacement weapon for the Mwangaza's magic stick. A drill movement, man to officer. Maxie grasps it at its point of equilibrium. Clipped, clear voice. Plain words and good pauses. Now hear this. I hear it and render it with everything I've got.

'First things first, gentlemen. There will be no, repeat, no armed intervention by non-Congolese forces in the province of Kivu. Make sure they've got that loud and clear, will you, old boy?'

Surprised though I am, I do as I am asked. Haj lets out a yip of delight, giggles and shakes his head in disbelief. Franco's gnarled face stirs in perplexity. Dieudonné lowers his eyes in contemplation.

'Any uprising will be a spontaneous, brushfire outbreak of traditionally opposed tribal groups,' Maxie goes on, undeterred. 'It will occur without, repeat, *without* involvement of non-Congolese forces—or none that are visible—whether in Goma, Bukavu, or wherever. Make sure Haj gets that. It's what his father signed up to. Tell him that.'

I do. Haj returns his gaze to the world outside the window where an air battle is raging between rival squadrons of crows and gulls.

'A delicate *domestic* balance of power will have been *temporarily* disturbed,' Maxie resumes. 'No outside agency, national, mercenary or otherwise, will have fanned the flames. As far as the international community is concerned, it will be Congolese business as usual. Ram that home for me, will you, old boy?'

I ram it home for the skipper. Haj's crows are in retreat, outnumbered by the gulls.

'UN headquarters in Bukavu is a pig's breakfast,' Maxie declares with mounting emphasis, though I am careful to use a less emotive term. 'One mechanised infantry company with mine-protected armoured personnel carriers, one Uruguayan guard company, one Chinese engineering unit, Rwandan and Mai Mai representatives bumping into each other in the corridors, one Nepali half-colonel soon to be retired running the shop. Smallest thing happens, they're on the satcom yelling at headquarters to tell 'em what to do. We know. Philip's been listening to their conversations, right?'

Philip takes a bow in response to the merriment occasioned by my rendering. A freelance *consultant* who eavesdrops on UN headquarters? I am secretly flabbergasted, but decline to let it show.

'If the fighting is reckoned to be Congolese on Congolese, the only thing the UN in Bukavu or Goma or anywhere else will do is bellyache, evacuate the civilians, withdraw to their installations, and leave it to the hellraisers to slog it out. *But*—and make it a bloody *big* but, will you, old boy?—if the UN or anybody else get the idea we're coming from outside, we're fucked.'

Swahili possessing a rich store of equivalents, I do not presume to water down the skipper's raunchy language. Yet if my rendering wins more approving laughter from Franco, and a wan smile from Dieudonné, the best Haj can offer is a war-whoop of derision.

'What the hell does he mean by that?' Maxie snaps out of the corner of his mouth, as if I, not Haj, had offended.

'Just high spirits, Skipper.'

'I'm asking him, not you.'

I pass the question to Haj, or more accurately to the back of his Zegna.

'Maybe nobody feels like rioting that day,' he replies with a lazy shrug. 'Maybe it's raining.'

On cue as ever, Philip glides into the breach.

'All the colonel is talking about here, Haj, is a few smashed shop fronts. A *little* looting and shooting, I grant you. A burning car here or there, but nobody's asking you to set your own town alight. Your father is quite determined there should be an absolute minimum of destruction in Goma, and I'm sure you feel the same about Bukavu. All we're looking for is enough fireworks—enough disturbance generally—to create a situation where a charismatic and popular leader with a message to impart—in this case, your father's old comrade the Mwangaza—can emerge triumphantly as the peacemaker. Luc had the rather *good* idea, for Goma, of kicking off with a protest rally that goes mildly wrong, and letting the beer do the work thereafter. You might consider taking a leaf out of his book for Bukavu.'

But not even Philip's diplomatic skills can put an end to Haj's tantrums. In fact they have the opposite effect, prompting him to wave his floppy hands above his head in a kind of universal dismissal of everything that is being said. And this in turn provokes Felix Tabizi to erupt in guttural, Arabic-flavoured French.

'*It will be as follows*,' he thunders all on one note as if to an erring servant. 'At the propitious moment, the Mwangaza and his advisors will quit his secret location outside the country's borders and arrive at Bukavu airport. A tumultuous crowd provided by your father and yourself will receive him and bear him into town in triumph. Got that? On his entry into Bukavu, all fighting will cease immediately. Your people down arms, stop looting and shooting, and celebrate. Those who have assisted the Mwangaza in his great cause will be rewarded, starting with your father. Those who haven't, won't be so lucky. Pity he's not here today. I hope he gets better soon. He loves the Mwangaza. For twenty years they've owed each other. Now they're going to collect. You too.'

Haj has abandoned the window and is leaning on the table, fingering a large gold cufflink.

'So it's a small war,' he ruminates at last.

'Oh come, Haj. Scarcely a war at all,' Philip reasons. 'A war in name only. And peace just round the corner.'

'Where it always is,' Haj suggests, and seems at first to accept the logic of Philip's argument. 'And who gives a shit about a *small* war anyway?' he continues, developing his theme in French. 'I mean what's a small death? *Pfui*. Nothing. Like being a little bit pregnant.' In support of which assertion, he treats us to a rendering of war-sounds similar to the ones I have already endured below the waterline: '*Pow! Vrump! Ratta-ratta!*'—then drops dead on the table with his arms out, before bouncing up again, leaving nobody the wiser.

*　*　*

Maxie is going to take Bukavu airport and to hell with anyone who wants to stop him. Kavumu, as it is named, lies thirty-five kilometres north of the town and is the key to our success. An aerial photograph of it has appeared on the easel. Did Bukavu have an airport twenty years ago? I have a memory of a bumpy grass field with goats grazing, and a silver-ribbed biplane piloted by a bearded Polish priest called Father Jan.

'Commandeer the airport, you've got South Kivu on a plate. Two thousand metres of tarmac. You can bring in *what* you like, *who* you like, *when* you like. And you've blocked the only airport where Kinshasa can land serious reinforcements.' The billiards cue smacks out the message: 'From Kavumu you can export *east* to Nairobi'—smack—'*south* to Johannesburg'—smack—

'*north* to Cairo and beyond. Or you can forget sub-Saharan Africa altogether and hightail it straight for the markets of Europe. A Boeing 767 can take forty tons and do the job non-stop. You can give two fingers to the Rwandans, the Tanzanians and Ugandans. Think about it.'

I render and we think about it, Haj deeply. Head sandwiched between his long hands, his bubbly gaze fixed on Maxie, he is the unconscious twin to Dieudonné, who broods beside him in a similar attitude.

'No middlemen, no bandits, no protection money, no customs or troops to pay off,' Maxie is assuring us, so I am too. 'Service your mines from base, shuttle your ore direct to purchaser, no slice of the cake for Kinshasa. Spell it out for 'em loud and clear, old boy.'

I spell it out for 'em and they are duly impressed—except for Haj, who jumps in with another maddening objection.

'Goma's runway is longer,' he insists, striking out an arm.

'And one end of it is coated in lava,' Maxie retorts, as his billiards cue taps a tattoo on a cluster of volcanoes.

'It's got two ends, hasn't it? It's a runway.'

Franco emits a bark of laughter, Dieudonné allows himself a rare smile. Maxie takes a breath, and so do I. I wish I could have five minutes alone with Haj in his native Shi, man to man. Then I could explain to him how near he is to snarling up the operation with his petty objections.

Maxie resolutely continues: 'We stick with Kavumu. Period.' He drags a fist roughly across his mouth and starts again. Haj, I fear, is really getting to him. 'I want to hear it from 'em, one by one. Are they all aboard, or not? Do we kick off by taking Kavumu or do we fuck around with half-measures, give the game to the competition, and lose the best opportunity for real progress the Eastern Congo has had in bloody years? Start with Franco.'

I start with Franco. As usual he takes his time. Glowers at me, at the map, then at Maxie. But his longest glower is reserved for the despised Dieudonné next to him.

'It is my general's judgment that Monsieur le Colonel is talking sense,' he grinds out.

'I want it straighter than that. And I'm talking to all of them. Do we take the airport—Kavumu airport— before advancing on the cities and mines? It's a clear question, needs a clear answer. Ask him again.'

I do. Franco unclasps his fist, glowers at something in his palm, closes it. 'My general is determined. We will first take the airport and afterwards the mines and cities.'

'As an alliance?' Maxie persists. 'Alongside the Banyamulenge? As comrades, forgetting your traditional differences?'

I stare at my Perrier bottle, conscious of Haj's manic gaze switching from one man to the other, and then to me.

'It is agreed,' Franco intones.

Dieudonné seems unable to believe what he is hearing.

'With *us?*' he asks softly. 'You accept the Banyamulenge as *equal partners* in this enterprise?'

'If we must, we will.'

'And afterwards, when we have won? Shall we jointly maintain the peace? Is that truly what is agreed here?'

'My general says with you, so with you,' Franco growls. And to clinch matters, hauls yet another proverb from his seemingly inexhaustible store. '"The friends of my friends are my friends."'

It's Dieudonné's turn. He looks only at Franco while he reaches for breath in painful gasps. 'If your general will keep his word. And you will keep yours. And the Mwangaza will keep his. Then the Banyamulenge will collaborate in this undertaking,' he pronounces.

All eyes turn to Haj, my own included. Conscious that he is the centre of attention, he plunges a hand into the mustard lining of his Zegna and half withdraws his gold cigarette case. Spotting the No Smoking sign, he pulls a face, lets it fall back into his pocket and shrugs. And for Maxie, it's a shrug too far.

'Mind telling Haj something for me, old boy?'

At your service, Skipper.

'Not terribly in love with this on-the-one-hand-and-on-the-other-hand shit. We're here to form an alliance, not sit around with the fence halfway up our arses. If he's standing in for his father, why can't he do his father's bidding instead of rocking the fucking boat? Think you can get that across without sounding offensive?'

There is a limit to how much the most dexterous interpreter can soften a blow, particularly when it is delivered by a client of Maxie's outspokenness. I do my best, and being by now conversant both above and below the waterline with Haj's undisciplined outbursts, I ready myself for the onslaught that is sure to come. Picture my surprise therefore when I find myself rendering the closely reasoned arguments of a starred graduate of the Sorbonne business school. His speech must have taken a good five minutes, yet I do not recall a single hesitation or repetition. It is challenging, it is dispassionate. It contains no hint that he's discussing the fate of his beloved home town, and mine. What follows is a digest:

Exploitation of the mines cannot take place without the compliance of the local population.

Military muscle by itself is not enough. What is needed for any long-term solution is a period without war, more commonly known as peace.

The issue before the delegates therefore is not whether the colonel's plan offers the best method of extracting and shipping ore, but whether the Mwangaza and his Middle Path can deliver on their promise to achieve a social consensus.

Access. Haj is referring not merely to physical access to the mines, but legal access. Clearly the proposed new government of Kivu under the Mwangaza will grant the Syndicate all necessary concessions, rights and permissions as required by local law.

But what about Congolese law? Kinshasa may be two thousand kilometres away, but it is still the capital city. At international level, it speaks for the Democratic Republic of Congo *in toto*, and its jurisdiction over the eastern regions is enshrined in the Constitution. In the long view, Kinshasa remains the key.

Haj turns his exophthalmic gaze on Philip:

'So my question is, Mzee Philip, how does your Syndicate propose to circumvent the authority of Kinshasa? The Mwangaza speaks of Kinshasa with derision. The colonel tells us Kinshasa will receive no financial benefit from the coup. But when the dust has settled, it will be Kinshasa, not the Mwangaza, who will have the last word.'

Philip has listened intently to Haj's discourse and, if his admiring smile is anything to go by, relished it. He passes a cupped hand lightly over his waved white hair, while managing not to touch it.

'It will require strong nerves and strong men, Haj,' he explains through his smile. 'The Mwangaza for one, your esteemed father for another. It will take time, and so it should. There are stages in the negotiating process that we can only deal with when we reach them. I suggest this is one of them.'

Haj acts amazed: to my eye, a little too amazed, but why? 'You mean no side agreements with the Kinshasa fatcats in advance? You're sure of that?'

'Absolutely.'

'You didn't think to buy them now while they're going cheap?'

'Certainly not!'—virtuous laughter.

'You're crazy, man. If you wait till you need them, they'll screw you.'

But Philip stands fast, for which I admire him. 'No prior talks with Kinshasa whatsoever, Haj, I'm afraid, no side deals, no backhanders, no slice of the cake. It may cost us down the line but it would be contrary to everything we stand for.'

Maxie bounds to his feet as if renewed, the tip of his billiards cue settles first on Goma, then follows the road southward down the western shore of Lake Kivu.

'Mzee Franco. I've heard that from time to time groups of your distinguished militia mount ambushes along this road.'

'So it is said,' Franco replies warily.

'Starting at first light on the day in question, we ask that their ambushes be intensified, closing the road to transport in both directions.'

Haj lets out a squeal of protest. 'You mean my dad's trucks? Our beer trucks, going north?'

'Your customers will have to go thirsty for a couple of days,' Maxie retorts, and returns to Franco. 'I have also heard that your revered general is in contact with significant groups of Mai Mai militia stationed *here*— between Fizi and Baraka.'

'What you have heard is possible,' Franco grudgingly concedes.

'And in the north around Walikale, the Mai Mai is also strong.'

'These are military secrets.'

'On the day in question, I ask that the Mai Mai converge on Bukavu. You also have groups of men around Uvira. They should come up in support.'

Once again, Haj must interrupt. Does he intend to sabotage Maxie's flow, or is it only chance? I fear the first.

'I would like to know, please, the colonel's precise plans for taking Kavumu airport. Okay, the troops are stoned. They're unhappy and they're not paid. But they've got guns and they like shooting people.'

Maxie replies on one note, all inflection gone. 'I plan a small, casually dressed squad of crack mercenaries with enough experience and discipline to bluff their way in without a shot being fired. All right so far?'

Haj gives a nod of his lacquered forelock. Chin in hand, he is leaning forward in an exaggerated pose of attention.

'Either they go in with the maintenance workers first thing in the morning, or they roll up on a Saturday

evening looking like a football squad in search of a
game. There are two soccer pitches, beer's on free flow
and girls come from the villages, so it's pretty informal.
Still with me?'

Another nod.

'Once inside they don't run, they walk. They stay
easy. They keep their guns out of sight, smile, wave. In
ten minutes we own the control tower, the runway and
the ammunition dump. We spread cigarettes and beer
around, money, pat everybody on the back, talk to the
head-boys, cut a deal. All we're doing, far as they're
concerned, we're informally renting the airport while
we fly in a few loads of mining equipment without
troubling customs.'

Haj's tone becomes unnaturally servile. 'With all
due respect for the colonel's military distinction, what
will be the precise composition of this squad of crack
mercenaries?'

'Top-rank professionals. South African, Special
Forces trained, hand-picked.'

'*Black*, Monsieur le Colonel? If I may enquire?'

'Zulus and Ovambos, brought in from Angola.
Veterans, no mavericks. Best fighters in the world.'

'How many, please, Monsieur le Colonel?'

'No more than fifty, no less than forty on present
count.'

'And who will lead these fine men into battle, please?'

'I will. In person. Me myself, who d'you think?'—
cutting his sentences shorter and shorter—'Plus

Anton here. Plus a couple of close comrades of my acquaintance.'

'But forgive me. Monsieur le Colonel is *white*.'

Maxie rolls back his right sleeve and for a moment I really do believe we have a situation. But he is only examining the underside of his forearm. 'Damn me, so I am!' he exclaims, to a relieved burst of merriment round the table in which Haj himself takes ostentatious part.

'And your colleagues, Monsieur le Colonel? They are also white?'—when the laughter has sufficiently subsided.

'As snow.'

'Then can you explain to us, please, how a small group of strangers, white as snow, can pull off a surprise attack on Bukavu airport without attracting a certain amount of attention from those who are not so fortunate?'

This time no one laughs. This time, all we hear is the gulls and crows and the rustle of warm wind coming down the grass rise.

'Very easily. On the Day in Question'—Maxie's term, we are learning, for the day on which the coup will be launched—'a Swiss manufacturing company specialising in air traffic control systems will be conducting an on-site survey of the airport's facilities as a prelude to making an unsolicited bid.'

Silence, broken only by my rendering.

'Their charter plane, which will contain technical equipment of an unspecified nature'—heavy emphasis which I am careful to reproduce—'will be parked close to the control tower. The Swiss company's technicians will be European. They will include myself, Anton here and Benny whom you briefly met. On a signal from me, my select band of mercenaries, who by now have entered the airport via the main gate, will board the plane. Inside it they will find heavy machine-guns, shoulder-held rocket-launchers, grenades, illuminated armbands, rations and a plentiful supply of ammunition. If anybody shoots at them, they will shoot back with the minimum of force.'

I totally understand why Philip did what he did next. Whose side was Haj on anyway? How much longer were we going to have to put up with his nitpicking? The man wasn't even an invited guest! He was his father's proxy, parachuted in at the last minute. Time to cut him down to size, get him to put his backside squarely on the line.

'Monsieur Haj,' Philip begins, silkily echoing Haj's own Monsieur le Colonel—'Haj, dear boy. With all due respect to your dear father, whom we sorely miss. We've all been very reticent so far, perhaps *too* reticent, about the vital part you personally will be playing in support of the Mwangaza's campaign. How will you be preparing for the great Coming? In Bukavu specifically, which is your manor, as it were? I wondered whether this might be a good moment for you to enlighten us.'

At first, Haj seems not to have heard Philip's question, or my rendering. Then he whispers a few words of

Shi which, though coarser, are oddly reminiscent of those spoken by the little gentleman at the trattoria in Battersea: *God give me strength to address this son of an arsehole, et cetera*—and of course I give no indication whatever of understanding this, preferring to make a few innocent doodles on my notepad.

After which he proceeds to go crazy. He leaps to his feet, pirouettes, snaps his fingers and flings his head about. And bit by bit he begins to compose a rhythmic response to Philip's question. And since words are my only music, and as far as Congolese bands are concerned I am a complete ignoramus, I couldn't tell you even today which great artiste, or which band, or which genus of music, he is mimicking.

But almost everyone else in the room could. For everyone but me and Maxie, whom I know by osmosis to be similarly devoid of musical appreciation, it is a virtuoso performance, instantly recognisable and very funny. The austere Dieudonné is laughing his head off and clapping his hands rhythmically in delight. Franco's great bulk too is rocking with pleasure, while your top interpreter, trained to function under all weather conditions, continues his renderings, now into French and now—on a hard glance from Maxie—into English, of which the following is a worked-up version, based on my frenetic jottings at the time:

We're going to *buy* the soldiers
We're going to *buy* the teachers and the doctors

We're going to *buy* the Garrison Commander of
Bukavu Town and the head of the police and the
second head of the police

We're going to bust open the prison and put a
truckload of fucking beer on the corner of every
fucking street in *Town*—and a couple of pounds
of Semtex to wash it *down*

And we're going to rally all the anti-Rwandan
Rwandans and give them fine new guns out of
our trucks, anybody not got a gun, just step this
way!

And all the bums and crazies and the guys who
shoot at you because they've seen the Devil in
you somewhere—we're going to give them beer
and guns *too*

And all the good Roman Catholics of Bukavu, and
all the priests and nuns, who love Jesus and
don't want any trouble, and aren't going to
make any because they know just how scarce
good Christians are—

We're going to tell them that the Prince of Poverty
Himself is riding into the new Jerusalem on his
fucking *ass*!

So have yourself another beer, baby, and make yourself another Molotov cocktail, and smash yourself
a few more fine windows and settle yourself a
few old scores—

Because the People's Paradise is sure as hell coming
to get *you*!

Now Philip too is laughing and shaking his head in wonder as he rings his handbell for the next recess. But it's Tabizi who commands my surreptitious attention. His face is a mask of ill-concealed fury. His pitch-black eyes, peering from the cover of heavy eyelids, are targeted like twin gun barrels at Haj's forehead, reminding me that there is a class of Arab who holds his sub-Saharan brother in unalterable contempt.

11

Where the hell are they, Sam? I'm getting a loud silence.

I'm checking, dear. Be patient.

I try to be patient. Unintelligible garble while Sam's voice consults Anton's, then Philip's.

We've found Franco.

Where?

In the royal apartments. Having a knees-up with the Mwangaza.

Go there? I enquire too eagerly.

On no account thank you, Brian. They'll do very nicely without you.

Over my headset I pick up Haj's crocs slapping down the walkway, accompanied by a second pair of footsteps which I tentatively assign to Dieudonné. Sam immediately confirms the identification: watchers report that Haj has grabbed Dieudonné by the elbow and is literally leading him up the garden path. Better still, Haj has put a finger to his lips, commanding Dieudonné's silence until they are clear of the house. My spirits soar. There is no finer music to your part-time sound-thief's ear than: 'Let's go somewhere where we can't be over-heard,' or 'Wait where you are while I get to a public phone box.'

Yet even in my excitement I feel a surge of sympathy for Dieudonné who, having been tugged in one direc-tion by Maxie's grand design, is now being tugged in the other by the recalcitrant Haj.

The two men have reached the gazebo steps and started climbing. As they climb Haj starts to dance. And as he dances he begins speaking in bursts: a rap of the crocs, a rap of speech. Sound-thieves hear like the blind. But sometimes they also see like the blind, which is what I'm doing now: bright and clear as day in my blind man's eye. I see Haj's slime-green crocs skimming the stone steps, slappety-whack, slappety-whack. I see his lacquered forelock bucking, his slender body arched backwards, hands trailing like silk scarves against the clear blue sky while he keeps his voice below the level of his slapping crocs. If his body is a wild man's, his voice is a steady man's, and the more quietly he talks, the more din he makes with his feet, and the more he flings his head around in the course of a single sentence as he feeds the mikes, one garbled morsel down each little throat.

What language is he speaking? His native Shi which Dieudonné also happens to speak. So what he's doing—or thinks he's doing—with a little improvisation, and a dash of French where he needs it—he's using a language that nobody overhearing them could possibly understand—except I can.

So I'm coming after him. I'm right in there with them. I'm coming after him so hard that when I press my eyes tight shut I can see him with my virtual eye. When Haj skips away, and Dieudonné trudges after him, spluttering his half cough, Salvo the top interpreter is there beside them with his headphones and his notepad. When Haj skips back, Dieudonné stands motionless— and so do I. Up another step, and Haj leaps onto the grass, and so do I. And Haj knows I'm there. I know he knows. He's playing Grandmother's Footsteps with me, and I'm playing them with him. He's leading the *zebra* a proper dance, and the *zebra* is returning the compliment, up and down the steps and all around.

What he can't know is how primitive our sound system is. He's modern man and I don't mind betting he's a techno-freak into the bargain. He thinks we've got the whole range of the Chat Room's state-of-the-art toys: directional, laser, satellite, you name it, but we haven't. And this isn't the Chat Room, Haj. And Spider's mikes are static, even if you and I and Dieudonné aren't. And Spider's system is good old-fashioned closed cable with no spillage and this *zebra* loves it.

It's one on one. It's Haj versus Salvo, *mano a mano*, with Dieudonné as the innocent bystander. It's Haj's Shi and Haj's tap-dancing and Haj's lunging and ducking versus Salvo's thieving ears. Haj's crocs are rapping like clogs on cobble. He's pirouetting, his voice goes up and down and all around, a bit of Shi, a bit of Kinyarwanda, then a bit of French argot to complicate the mix. I'm stealing sound from three separate mikes and three separate languages in one sentence and reception is as chaotic as the man. I'm dancing too, if only in my head. I'm up there on the stone steps duelling sabre to sabre with Haj, and every time he lets me catch my breath I'm passing hastily compressed renderings up the wire to Sam while my left hand pins down my notepad and the pencil in my right hand skips across the page to Haj's tune.

No need to shout, Brian dear. We're hearing you very nicely.

The take is nine minutes long, which is two-thirds of the recess. The *zebra* will never steal better sound in his life.

* * *

Haj: How sick are you anyway? (*staccato of crocs, up a couple of steps, down three, stop. Abrupt silence*) Very sick? (*No answer. Another staccato. Returns*) Wives too? Kids? (*Is Dieudonné nodding? Apparently yes*) Holy shit. How long have you got? (*No answer*) Know where you picked it up?

Dieudonné: From a girl. What do you think?

Haj: When?

Dieudonné: Ninety-eight.

Haj: The *war* of ninety-eight?

Dieudonné: What else?

Haj: Fighting against the *Rwandans?* (*another apparent nod*) You were fighting *Rwandans* and fucking for the one true Democratic Republic of Congo? Holy Jesus! Has anyone thanked you yet?

Dieudonné: For catching the plague?

Haj: For fighting another useless war, man. (*dancing up and down the steps*) Shit. Damn. (*more low-key expletives*) This no-name Syndicate wants your arse, know that? (*garbled*) The Banyamulenge have got the best warriors, discipline, motivation, the best minerals ... gold and coltan on the plateau ... and you don't even mine them, you love your fucking cows too much! ...

Dieudonné: (*through his coughs, dead calm*) Then we shall dictate terms. We shall go to the Mwangaza and say: first you must give us all you have promised, or we will not fight for you. We will fight against you. We will say that.

Haj: The *Mwangaza*? You think the Mwangaza is running this thing? What a hero *he* is! What—a—world-class—enlightener! ... What a selfless friend of the *poor*! That guy owns the poorest ten-million-dollar villa in Spain you ever saw. Ask my dad ... plasma television screens in every toilet ... (*violent tattoo of crocs, speech very garbled, then clears. Softly, in counterpoint to din that preceded it*) Dieudonné. Pay attention to me. You're a good man. I love you.

Dieudonné: (*unintelligible*)

Haj: You will not die. I do *not* want you to die. Okay? Deal? Not you, not the Banyamulenge. Not again. Not of war, not of hunger, not of after-war, not of the plague. If you've got to die at all, die of beer. Promise?

Dieudonné: (*grim laugh*) Beer and anti-retrovirals.

Haj: I mean, I do not want *any* fucker to die *anywhere* in the Congo for a very long time, except quietly and peacefully, of *beer*. You're sweating like a whore. Sit down.

Reception improves. Anton reports via Sam that Dieudonné has settled on a stone bench under a beech tree beneath the gazebo. Haj is jiggling round him in a radius of eight to ten feet. But I am there beside them.

Haj: ... the Rwandans are stronger than we are, know that? ... stronger than the ... Banyamulenge, stronger than the Mai Mai knuckle-draggers (*making ape noises*) ... stronger than the whole of ... Kivu put together ... Okay? Admit it.

Dieudonné: It is possible.

Haj: It's a fucking certainty and you know it. Listen to me (*returns to Dieudonné and speaks intensely close to his ear—twenty-twenty reception, presumably from mike in overhead branches of beech tree*) ... I love my father. I'm an African. I honour him. You got a father still? ... Okay, so that means you honour his spirit. You talk to his spirit, you obey his spirit, you're guided by it. Mine's alive, okay? Three wives and all the hookers he can eat. Owns a slice of Goma and fifty-one per cent of me, and the Rwandans are stealing his business, or he thinks they are.

Anton reports via Sam that Haj keeps darting behind the beech tree and reappearing. The in-and-out reception confirms.

Haj: Couple of months ago he calls me in, okay? ... solemn occasion, *humph, humph* ... office, not home ... doesn't want his ... wives listening at the fucking keyhole ... tells me about this great New Deal for Kivu he's involved in, how his old pal the Mwangaza is going to get in ahead of elections which are a recipe for civil war, throw out everybody he doesn't like and make everybody he likes rich, and the People rich too, because he's got this fine philanthropic Syndicate behind him, and they've got all this money, and these good intentions, and the guns, and the ammunition. Sounds great, I tell him. Sounds just like King Leopold when *he* came to Congo. Which naturally drove him ape. So I wait till he cools down, which is next day ... (*breaks up, returns*) ... meantime something bad. Really bad ... I consult some very evil people I know ... in Kinshasa ... guys my dad would kill me for knowing, guys it pays to be polite to if you don't want to wake up dead in the morning ... (*very garbled now*) ... what they told me, these guys? ... under a pledge of total secrecy which I am now dishonouring? Kinshasa is part of the deal. Kinshasa has a piece of the action ... the absolute worst piece ...

Perfect sound. Sam advises that Haj and Dieudonné are sitting side by side on the bench with a mike six feet above them and no breeze to disturb it.

Haj: So I go back to my dad and I say to him: Father, I love you and I am grateful that you paid for me to grow a fucking brain, and I respect your good motives regarding the Mwangaza and the Eastern Congo. Therefore allow me to tell you that on the basis of my professional expertise as a problem-solver that you are a very serious arsehole on two counts. You and the Mwangaza have in my estimation undersold yourselves to this no-balls Syndicate by approximately one thousand per cent. Count Two, and forgive my impertinence, but who needs another fucking war? You and I are totally dependent on Rwanda for our trade. They send our goods out into the world for us. For everybody except the Congolese, this would be the basis of a profitable and friendly trading partnership. It would not be a reason for slaughtering each other's wives and children, or installing a geriatric, untried leader who, however much you love him, is pledged to kicking everything that smells of Rwanda out of Congo. Do I tell him about my bad friends in Kinshasa? Do I fuck. But I do tell him about my good friend Marius, a fat Dutch fucker I happened to study with in Paris.

Reception temporarily ceases. Sam's team reports the couple making slow progress over grass on the other side of the gazebo. Reception very poor.

Haj: ... forty years old ... (*two seconds garbled*) ... mountain of institutional money ... African[?] vice president of ... (*seven seconds garbled*) ... So I told my dad ... (*four seconds garbled*) listened to me ... told me I was the biggest failure of his life ... disgrace to our ancestors ... then asked me where could he find this Marius so that he could ... tell him how sealing the Rwandan border with Congo was the only sane solution to the world's problems, which is how my dad talks when he doesn't want you to know he's changing his mind.

Shriek of metal, sigh of foam cushions, clarity restored. Sam reports that the two men are seated in a wind shelter looking out to sea. Haj's voice is urgent, almost reckless.

Haj: So my dad gets in his plane and goes to see Marius in Nairobi. Luc likes Nairobi. Knows a great hooker there. And he likes Marius. Smokes a couple of cigars with him. And Marius likes Luc. And Marius tells him what an arsehole he is. 'You are everything your pissant of a son says you are. A wise, fine man. And you and your Mwangaza want to throw the Rwandans out of Kivu so that they can no longer exploit you, which is a great idea except for one thing. Are you seriously suggesting they won't come and kick the living *shit* out of you, pay back with interest what you took away from them? Isn't that what they do every time? So why not be *really* smart and do the unthinkable for once in your life? Instead of throwing the Rwandans out, look at yourself in the mirror, put on your biggest smile, and act like you love them? You're in business with them whether you like it or not, so try liking it. Then maybe my company will stake you or buy you out, and we'll get some bright young guys like your pissant son on board, make sweet with Kinshasa, and instead of three million people dying we'll get some peaceful coexistence going.'

Dieudonné: (*after long thought*) Is your father in alliance with this man?

Haj: He's Luc, for fuck's sake. Best poker player in Goma. But you know what? The fat Dutch fucker was right. Because when the Rwandans *do* come back, who are they going to bring with them? The whole fucking catastrophe. Like last time round, but worse. The Angolans, the Zimbabweans and anybody else who hates our guts and wants what we've got. And when that happens, forget the peace process, forget international pressure, forget the

elections, because you poor Banyamulenge bastards
are going to die like flies, which is what you do best.
But not me. I'll be back in Paris, laughing my head
off.

*Stay exactly where you are, Brian dear. Help is on its
way to you now.*

* * *

'That Pitman's, old boy? Looks more like a roll of
barbed wire to me.'

Maxie is leaning over me, Bogey-style, his hands on
the arms of my hot-seat as he peers at what Mr Anderson
likes to call my Babylonian cuneiform. Spider has
disappeared, sent packing by Maxie. Philip in pink shirt
and red braces is standing in the doorway leading to
the corridor. I feel dirty and don't know why. It's as if
I'd made love to Penelope after she's come back from
one of her weekend seminars.

'My home brew, Skipper,' I reply. 'A bit of speed-
writing, a bit of shorthand, and a large chunk of me'—
which is what I say to all my clients, because if there's
one thing I've learned, it's never let them think your
notebook is a document of record or you'll end up in
court or worse.

'Read it for us again, old boy, will you.'

I read it again to them as ordered. In English, from
my notes as before, omitting no detail however slight,
et cetera. Maxie and Philip are annoying me, although

I'm careful not to let it show. I've already told them that without Mr Anderson's sophisticated sound-enhancer we could go on all night, but that doesn't deter them, oh no. They need to listen to the *actual sound* on my headphones, which strikes me as rather irrational, given that neither of them speaks a word of my below-the-line languages. The passage they are obsessing about is the seven garbled seconds just after the first reference to the big cigar-smoking Dutchman, and if I can't make head or tail of it, why on earth should they suppose *they* can?

I hand Philip my headphones, thinking they might like an ear each, but Philip hogs them both. He hears it once, he hears it three times. And each time he hears it, he gives Maxie this knowing nod. Then he hands Maxie the headphones and orders me to play the passage yet again and finally Maxie gives him a knowing nod back, which only confirms what I've been suspecting all along: *they know what they're listening for and they haven't told me.* And there is nothing makes a top interpreter look sillier, and more *useless*, than not being fully briefed by his employers. Furthermore it's *my* tape, not theirs. It's *my* trophy. It was me who wrested it from Haj's grasp, not them. *I* fought Haj for it, it was *our* duel.

'Great stuff, old boy,' Maxie assures me.

'My pleasure, Skipper,' I reply, which is only polite. But what I'm thinking is: don't pat me on the back, thank you, I don't need it, not even from you.

'Totally brilliant,' Philip purrs.

Then both of them have gone, though I only hear the one pair of footsteps bounding up the cellar stairs because Philip is this soundless consultant, and I wouldn't be surprised if he had no shadow either.

* * *

For what seems a long time after their departure, I did nothing. I took off my headset, wiped my face with my handkerchief, put my headset back on and, having sat with my chin in my fist for a while, played myself the seven-second splurge for the nth time. What had Maxie and Philip heard that I wasn't to be trusted with? I slow-motioned, I fast-forwarded, and I was none the wiser: three to four beats with a *u* at the beginning, a three- or four-syllable word with -*ère* or -*aire* at the end, and I could think of a dozen words straight off with an ending that would fit: *débonnaire, légionnaire, militaire,* any *air* you liked to play. And after it, a splurge *ak*, such as *attaque.*

I removed my headset yet again, buried my face in my hands and whispered into the darkness. My actual words elude me to this day. To say I had feelings of actual betrayal is premature. The most I will admit to is a sense of dismay creeping over me, the origins of which I was determined not to examine. In the anticlimactic aftermath of my single combat with Haj, I was wiped out and flat on the deck. I even wondered whether our duel was a fantasy I had cooked up in my imagination, until I remembered how surveillance-conscious Haj had been from the moment he arrived in the guest suite. I was *not*, however—contrary to anything Penelope's bosom friend Paula would maintain—*in denial*. I hadn't even begun to work out what it was I was denying. If I had a sense of letting anyone down, it was turned inward. I had let *me* down, which is how I described my condition over the ether to Hannah, in what I now regard as the lowest point in my graph of that momentous day.

Sam? It's me. Brian. What's cooking?

Nothing is cooking. Sam is not at her post. I was counting on a bit of womanly sympathy, but all I'm hearing over my headset is background male chatter. She hasn't even bothered to switch her mike off, which I consider somewhat careless and insecure. I glance at Aunt Imelda's watch. The recess is running into over-time. Haj's inconclusive account of his father's flirtation with a rival outfit run by a fat Dutch fucker who smokes cigars seems to have put the cat among the pigeons in a big way. Serves him right for calling me *zebra*. Spider still hasn't come back from wherever he went. There's too much about the geography of this house that nobody tells me. Like where the ops room is. Or where Anton's surveillance team keeps its lookouts. Where Jasper is hiding away. Where Benny is. But I don't need to know, do I? I'm just the interpreter. Everybody needs to know except me.

I glance at the Underground plan. Haj and Dieudonné have split up. Poor Dieudonné, all alone in the guest suite. Probably having a quick pray. Haj has taken himself back to the gazebo, the scene of his supposed triumph. If only he knew! I imagine him staring out to sea with his goggle eyes, congratulating himself on having queered the Mwangaza's pitch for him. Franco's pinlight is out. Still closeted with the Mwangaza in the royal apartments, presumably. Out of bounds. Archive purposes only.

I need sound. I don't like the accusing voices that are starting to raise themselves inside my head, Hannah's foremost. I'm not here to be criticised. I did my best for my employers. What was I supposed to do? Pretend I hadn't heard Haj say what he said? Keep it to myself? I'm here to do a job and be paid for it. Cash. Even if it's a pittance compared with what they're paying Jasper. I'm an interpreter. They talk, I render. I don't stop rendering people when they say wrong things. I don't censor, edit, revise or invent, not the way certain of my colleagues do. I give it straight. If I didn't, I wouldn't be Mr Anderson's favourite son. I wouldn't be a genius in my field. Legal or commercial, civil or military: I render everybody equally and impartially, regardless of colour, race and creed. I'm the bridge, Amen and out.

I try Sam again. Still away from her post. The background male babble in the ops room has stopped. Instead, thanks to Sam's carelessness, I hear Philip. Moreover, he is talking clearly enough for me to hear what he's saying. Who he's talking to is anybody's guess, and his voice is coming off at least one wall before it reaches Sam's mike, but that doesn't affect my hearing. I'm on such a low-high after my duel with Haj that if a fly coughed into my headset I could tell you its age and sex. The surprise is that Philip's voice is so different from the high-gloss version I associate with him that for the opening bars I'm actually chary of identifying him. He is talking to *Mark*, and to judge by Philip's imperious tone, Mark is an underling:

Philip: I want who his doctor is, I want the diagnosis, what treatment the patient's getting if any, when they expect to discharge him if they do, who he's receiving at his bed of pain and who's with him apart from his wives, mistresses and bodyguards ... No, I *don't* know which bloody hospital he's in, Mark, that's your job, it's what you're paid for, you're the man on the spot. Well, how many heart hospitals are there in Cape Town, for Christ's sake?

End of phone call. Top freelance consultants are too important to say goodbye. Philip needs to talk to Pat. He has dialled a new number and Pat is who he asks for when he gets through.

Philip: The name is *Marius*, he's Dutch, fat, fortyish, smokes cigars. He was recently in Nairobi and for all I know he's there now. He attended business school in Paris and he represents our old friend the Union Minière des Grand Lacs. Who is he otherwise?

(*ninety seconds in which Philip intermittently indicates that yes he is listening and making notes, as I am. Finally:*) Thank you very much, Pat. Perfect. Exactly what I feared, but worse. Just what we didn't want to know. I'm very grateful. Goodbye.

So now we know. It wasn't *débonnaire* or *légionnaire* or *militaire*. It was Minière and it wasn't *attaque*, it was *Lacs*. Haj was talking about a mining consortium of which the fat Dutchman was the African representative. I catch sight of Spider standing the other side of his Meccano grid, checking his turntables, switching tapes and marking up new ones. I lift an earpiece and smile in order to be sociable.

'Looks like we're going to have a busy lunchtime, then, Brian, thanks to you,' says Spider with mysterious Welsh relish. 'Quite a lot of activity planned, one way and another.'

'What sort of activity?'

'Well that would be telling, now, wouldn't it? Never trade a secret, Mr Anderson advises, remember? You'll always get the short end of the bargain.'

I replace my headset and take a longer look at the Underground plan. The Mwangaza's mauve pinlight is taunting me like a brothel invitation. *Come on, Salvo. What's stopping you? School rules?* Out of bounds unless Philip personally tells you otherwise. Archival, not operational. We record but don't listen. Not if we're *zebra* interpreters. So if *I*'m not cleared to listen, who is? Mr Anderson, who doesn't speak a word of anything but north country English? Or how about the no-balls Syndicate, as Haj called them: do *they* listen? As a diversion perhaps. Over the port and Havanas in their Channel Island fastness.

Am I really thinking like this? Has Haj's sedition got under my skin without my noticing? Is my African heart beating more loudly than it's letting on? Is Hannah's? If not, why is my right hand moving with the same deliberation with which it fed Penelope's *coq au vin* into the waste-disposal unit? I hesitate, but not because of any last-minute pangs of conscience. If I press the switch, will sirens go off all over the house? Will the mauve pinlight on the Underground plan flash out a distress signal? Will Anton's anoraks come thundering down the cellar steps to get me?

I press it anyway, and enter the DRAWING ROOM of the forbidden royal apartments. Franco is speaking Swahili. Reception perfect, no echoes or noises off. I imagine thick carpets, curtains, soft furniture. Franco relaxed. Perhaps they've given him a whisky. Why do I think whisky? Franco is a whisky man. The conversation is between Franco and the Dolphin. There is no firm evidence as yet of the Mwangaza's presence, although something in their voices tells me he's not far away.

Franco: We have heard that in this war many aircraft will be used.
Dolphin: That is true.

Franco: I have a brother. I have many brothers.

Dolphin: You are blessed.

Franco: My best brother is a good fighter, but to his shame has only daughters. Four wives, five daughters.

Dolphin: (*a proverb*) No matter how long the night, the day is sure to come.

Franco: Of these daughters, the eldest has a cyst on her neck which hampers her prospects of marriage. (*Grunts of exertion confuse me until I realise that Franco is reaching for the same spot on his own lame body*) If the Mwangaza will fly my brother's daughter to Johannesburg for confidential treatment, my brother will have good feelings towards the Middle Path.

Dolphin: Our Enlightener is a devoted husband and the father of many children. Transport will be arranged.

A clinking of glass seals the promise. Mutual expressions of esteem.

Franco: This brother is a man of ability, popular among his men. When the Mwangaza is Governor of South Kivu, he will be well advised to select my brother as his Chief of Police for all the region.

Dolphin: In the new democracy, all appointments will be the result of transparent consultation.

Franco: My brother will pay one hundred cows and fifty thousand dollars cash for a three-year appointment.

Dolphin: The offer will be considered democratically.

From the other side of his Meccano grid, Spider is peering at me, hooped eyebrows raised. I lift an earpiece.

'Something wrong?' I enquire.

'Not that I know of, boy.'

'Then why are you staring at me?'

'Bell's gone, that's why. You were too busy listening to hear it.'

12

'Three bases, gentlemen! Each base open-cast, minimally exploited, and a vital key to Kivu's revival.'

Maxie, billiards cue in hand, is once more haranguing us from the head of the table. The airport is ours, the Mwangaza is installed. Soon the Syndicate will control all South Kivu's mines but in the meantime here are three to be getting along with. They are out-of-the-way, with no official concession-holders to be dealt with. Re-entering the conference room, I have the sensation that its occupants have undergone a theatrical transformation. Haj and Dieudonné, who minutes ago were partners to a highly seditious conversation, are behaving as if they had never set eyes on one another. Haj is humming tra-las to himself and smirking into the middle distance. Dieudonné is meditatively drawing out the strands of his beard with his bony fingertips. Looming between them sits Franco, his gnarled face a mask of righteousness. Who would have imagined that minutes previously he had been attempting to bribe the seraphic Dolphin? And surely Philip is not now and never has been the author of certain peremptory commands barked over the sat-phone? His plump hands are linked across his shirt-front in parsonical tranquillity. Does he comb his waved white hair between acts? Coax up the little curls behind the ears? Tabizi alone seems unable to contain whatever unruly thoughts are seething in him. He may have the rest of his body under control, but the vengeful glint in his oil-dark eyes is inextinguishable.

The map Maxie is addressing is so large that Anton has to spread it like a counterpane over one end of the table. Like his skipper he has taken off his jacket. His bared arms are tattooed from elbow to wrist: a buffalo's head, a two-headed eagle clutching a globe and a skull on a star to commemorate the Escuadrón de Helicópteros of Nicaragua. He bears a tray of little plastic toys: gunships with bent rotors, twin-engined aeroplanes with their propellers missing, howitzers hauling ammunition trailers, infantrymen charging with fixed bayonets or, more prudently, lying flat.

Maxie marches down the table, cue at the ready. I am trying to avoid Haj's eye. Every time Maxie points with his cue, I glance up from my notepad and there's Haj waiting for me with his goggly stare. What's he trying to tell me? I've betrayed him? We never duelled with each other? We're bosom pals?

'Little place called Lulingu,' Maxie is telling Franco, as the tip of his billiards cue affects to skewer it. 'Heart of your Mai Mai territory. *Le coeur du Maï Maï. Oui? D'accord?* Good man.' He wheels round to me:

'Suppose I asked him to put three hundred of his best chaps there, would he do that for me?'

While Franco is pondering my offer, Maxie swings back to Dieudonné. Is he about to advise him to swallow a bottle of aspirin?—not to hang around at the back of the herd now his time's up?

'Your area, right? Your people. Your pastures. Your cattle. Your plateau.'

The cue wheels down the southern shores of Lake Tanganyika, stops halfway, veers left and stops again.

'It is our area,' Dieudonné concedes.

'Can you maintain a fortified base for me—here?'

Dieudonné's face clouds. 'For *you*?'

'For the Banyamulenge. For a united Kivu. For peace, inclusiveness and prosperity for all the people.' The Mwangaza's mantras are evidently Maxie's own.

'Who will supply us?'

'We will. From the air. We'll drop you everything you need for as long as you need it.'

Dieudonné lifts his gaze to Haj as if to plead with him, then sinks his face into his long thin hands and keeps it there, and for a split second I join him in his darkness. Has Haj persuaded him? If so, has he persuaded *me*? Dieudonné's head lifts. His expression is resolute, but in what cause is anybody's guess. He begins reasoning aloud in short, decisive sentences while he stares into the distance.

'They invite us to join Kinshasa's army. But only in order to neutralise us. They offer us appointments that give the illusion of power. But in reality they are worth-less. If an election comes, Kinshasa will draw borders that give the Banyamulenge no voice in Parliament. If we are slaughtered, Kinshasa will not lift a finger to save us. But the Rwandans will come to our protection. And that will be another disaster for Congo.' From between splayed fingers, he announces his conclusion. 'My people cannot afford to reject this opportunity. We shall fight for the Mwangaza.'

Haj stares wide-eyed at him, and emits a girlish laugh of disbelief. Maxie raps the tip of his cue on the foothills south-west of Bukavu.

'And this very fine mine belongs to *you*, Haj? Is that correct? You and Luc?'

'Nominally,' Haj concedes with an irritating shrug.

'Well, if it's not yours, whose else is it?'—part joke and part challenge, which I do not attempt to moderate.

'Our company has subcontracted it.'

'Who to?'

'Some business acquaintances of my father,' Haj retorts, and I wonder who else has heard the rebellious edge to his voice.

'Rwandans?'

'Rwandans who love Congo. Such people exist.'

'And are loyal to him, presumably?'

'In many circumstances they are loyal to him. In others, they are loyal to themselves, which is normal.'

'If we tripled the mine's production and paid them a cut, would they be loyal to *us*?'

'Us?'

'The Syndicate. Assuming they are well armed and supplied against attack. Your father said they would fight for us to the last man.'

'If that is what my father said, then what my father says is true.'

In his frustration, Maxie rounds on Philip. 'I understood all this was agreed in advance.'

'But of *course* it's agreed, Maxie,' Philip replies soothingly. 'It's a done deal, sealed and delivered. Luc signed up to all of it *long* ago.'

The dispute being in English and of a private nature, I elect not to render it, which does not prevent Haj from rolling his head around and grinning like an imbecile, thereby incurring the silent rage of Felix Tabizi.

'Three leaders, three independent enclaves,' Maxie forges on, addressing the conference at large. 'Each with its own airstrip, disused, used or part used. Each supplied by heavy air transport out of Bukavu. Your whole problem of access, extraction and transportation solved in one throw. Unfindable and—without enemy air power—impregnable.'

Enemy air power? The *enemy* being who precisely? Is this what Haj is wondering, or am I?

'It's not every military operation where you can pay your men out of the ground you're camping on, for God's sake,' Maxie insists, in the tone of a man overcoming opposition. '*And* have the satisfaction of knowing you're doing your country a bit of good while you're at it. Tell 'em that too, will you, old boy. Hammer the social benefits. Each militia collaborating with local friendly chiefs, each chief making a buck, and why shouldn't he, provided he passes it on to his clan or tribe? Not a reason on earth, in the long term, why the bases shouldn't flourish as self-maintaining communities. Schools, shops, roads, medical centres, you name it.'

Distraction while Anton sets a plastic toy airliner on Franco's jungle base and everybody watches. It's an Antonov-12, Maxie explains. Carrying a cargo of diggers, dump trucks, forklifts and engineers. The airstrip can handle it with room to spare. Whatever anyone needs, the Antonov can deliver it with bells on. But once again, Haj stops him in his tracks, this time by shooting his right arm in the air and holding it there in the manner of an obedient student waiting his turn.

'Monsieur Philippe.'

'Haj.'

'Am I correct in assuming that under the proposed agreement the militias must occupy their bases for a minimum of six months?'

'Indeed you are.'

'And *after* six months?'

'After six months the Mwangaza will be installed as the People's choice and the creation of an inclusive Kivu will be under way.'

'But for those six months—before the mines pass into the People's hands—who controls them?'

'The Syndicate, who else?'

'The Syndicate will mine the ore?'

'I certainly hope so.' Joke.

'And ship it?'

'Naturally. We explained all that to Luc.'

'Will the Syndicate also be *selling* the ore?'

'Marketing it, if that's what you mean.'

'I said sell.'

'And I said market,' Philip rejoins, with the smile of a fellow who enjoys a good set-to.

'And keeping all profits to itself exclusively?'

On the other side of the table, Tabizi is about to erupt, but nimble Philip is once more ahead of him.

'The profits, Haj—*revenue* is a kinder word—will, as you rightly imply, for the first six months go towards defraying the Syndicate's up-front investment. This of course includes the high costs incurred by supporting the Mwangaza's accession to power.'

Watched by all the room, Haj mulls this over. 'And these mines, these three bases your Syndicate has selected—one for each of us—' he resumes.

'What about them?'

'Well, they're not just any old mines, selected at random, are they? They may not look it, but these are highly specialised sites.'

'I fear you're losing me, Haj. I am not a technical man at all.'

'They have gold and diamonds, right?'

'Oh, I sincerely hope so! Otherwise we've made a most terrible mistake.'

'These mines are also *dumps*.'

'Oh, really?'

'Yes, really. All round them there are hill-works of coltan ore. Ore extracted, stockpiled and abandoned while we were so busy dying we didn't get around to shifting it. All you have to do is crude-process it on site to reduce the weight, ship it out, and you've got a bonanza. You don't even need six months. Two will do fine.'

At the edge of my screen, Tabizi is tenderly exploring the pockmarks on his jaw with the tips of his jewelled fingers, but to me it is Haj's jaw that he is thinking about.

'Well, thank you for that information, Haj,' Philip replies, bland as cream. 'I can't imagine that our experts are unaware of what you've told us, but I'll make sure it's passed on. Coltan isn't quite the wonder mineral it used to be, alas, but I'm sure you know that.'

*   *   *

'*Roamer*, Skipper?'

My hand is up, requesting clarification. Maxie tetchily supplies it. Well, how was I to know that roamer radios move so fast from one frequency to another that there's not a listening device in all Africa, let alone Bukavu, that can touch them?

'*Mercs*, Skipper?'

'Mercenaries, man! Bloody hell. What did you think they were? Cars? Thought you could do military.'

'And *PMC*, Skipper?'—not two minutes later.

'Private Military Company—Jesus, Sinclair, where the hell have you been all your life?'

I apologise, a thing a top interpreter should never do.

'*Cordons*. Got that, old boy? French word, you should be all right with that. Soon as a base is secured, we throw a cordon round it. Fifteen-mile radius, nobody goes in or out without our say-so. The whole outfit air-supplied by helicopter. Our helicopter, our pilot, but your base.'

Anton pops a toy helicopter on each base. Moving to avoid Haj's stare, I discover that Philip has taken centre stage.

'And these helicopters, gentlemen'—never shy of the showman's touch, Philip waits for total silence, gets it, starts again—'these helicopters, which are so *vital* to our operation, will for ease of identification be painted *white*. And for ease of passage, we propose to take the precaution of painting UN markings on them,' he adds in a throwaway tone which I do my level best to emulate while keeping my eyes fixed on my Perrier bottle, and my ears deaf to Hannah's ever louder cries of outrage.

Maxie is back. He favours the sixty-mill mortar, essential to Spider's beloved mayhem. He has a kind word or two for the rocket-propelled grenade which goes nine hundred yards then self-destructs, making mincemeat of a platoon, but it's the sixty-mill that has his heart. Rendering him, it's as if I'm in a long tunnel, hearing my own voice coming at me out of the darkness:

- First we ferry in fuel, then ammunition.
- Each man to get his own Czech-made Kalashnikov. Find me a better semi anywhere in the world.
- Each base to receive three Russian 7.62 machine-guns, ten thousand rounds of ammunition, one white helicopter for transporting freight and troops.
- Each white helicopter to carry one Gatling machine-gun in its nose cone, capable of firing four thousand rounds per minute of 12.7 mm ammunition.
- Ample time to be allowed for training. Never knew a unit yet that wasn't the better for training.

Tell 'em that, old boy.

I do.

No bell has rung but the post-office clock ticks on and we soldiers are sticklers for time. The double doors to the library swing open. Our forgotten women, wearing gingham aprons, are posed before a royal buffet. In my out-of-body state I observe lobsters on packed ice, a salmon garnished with cucumber, a cold collation of meats, a cheeseboard that includes a soft Brie that has escaped the waste-disposal unit, white wine in frosted silver buckets, a pyramid of fresh fruits and, as the jewel in the crown, a two-tiered cake surmounted by the flags of Kivu and the Democratic Congolese Republic. Via the French windows, with perfect timing, enter in solemn order of precedence the Mwangaza, his pious secretary the Dolphin, and Anton bringing up the rear.

'Lunch break, gentlemen!' jocular Philip calls as we dutifully rise. 'Please do all the damage you can!'

White helicopters bearing UN markings, I repeat to myself. Firing Gatling machine-guns from their nose cones at four thousand rounds a minute in the interests of peace, inclusiveness and prosperity for all Kivu.

*   *   *

I will say at once that in all my years of interpreting I had never before been placed in a situation where my clients did not vigorously insist upon my personal attendance at whatever type of hospitality they were extending, be it your full-scale, black-tie banquet complete with toastmaster, or your end-of-day complimentary cocktail plus cold and hot finger-food. But the skipper's orders had been unequivocal. Besides which, the undefined forebodings that were by now stirring in me had banished all thought of sustenance, notwithstanding the sumptuous spread of open sandwiches which for all Maxie's talk of a ship's biscuit greeted me on my return to the boiler room.

'We're stood down, boy,' Spider informs me, stuffing a chunk of cheese and gherkin into his mouth while

with his other hand bestowing an airy wave on his tape
recorders. 'Take a skim around the tables now and then,
and put your feet up till further orders.'

'Who said?'

'Philip.'

Spider's complacency fails to put my mind at ease, far
from it. With the same knowing smirk with which he
had earlier informed me that we were in for a busy
lunchtime, he was now telling me we were becalmed. I
put on my headset only to discover I am tuned to a
vacuum. This time Sam has not forgotten to switch off
her microphone. Spider is studying a tattered military
magazine and chewing vigorously, but he may be
watching me. I select LIBRARY on my console and hear a
predictable crashing of plates and cutlery as the buffet
gets under way. I hear Gladys—or it is Janet?—asking,
'May I cut you a slice, sir?' in surprisingly good Swahili.
I have a mental photograph of the layout in the library-
turned-dining room. It's assisted self-service and separate tables, two of two and one of four, and each table,
according to my console, separately bugged. The
French windows are open to those wishing to take the
air. Garden tables, also bugged, await their pleasure.
Philip is playing maitre d'hôtel.

'Monsieur Dieudonné, why not *here*?—Mzee Franco,
where would that leg of yours be most comfortable?'

What am I listening for? Why am I so alert? I select
a table and hear Franco in conversation with the
Mwangaza and the Dolphin. He's describing a dream

he's had. As secret child and captive audience of the Mission servants, I've listened to a lot of African dreams in my time, so Franco's comes as no surprise, neither does the far-out interpretation he puts on it.

'I entered my neighbour's courtyard and saw a body lying face downwards in the mud. I turned it over and saw my own eyes looking up at me. I therefore knew it was time for me to respect my general's orders and obtain good terms for the Mai Mai in this great battle.'

The Dolphin simpers his approval. The Mwangaza is non-committal. But I have ears only for what I'm *not* hearing: the slap of green croc on slate floor, a whoop of derisive laughter. I switch to the first small table and get Philip and Dieudonné discussing pastoral practices in a mix of Swahili and French. I switch to the second and get nothing. Where's Maxie? Where's Tabizi? But I am not their keeper. I am Haj's, and where is he? I switch back to the big table in the unlikely hope that he has been keeping his thoughts to himself out of deference to the great man's friendship with his father. Instead, I get thumps and heavings, but no voices, not even the Mwangaza's. Bit by bit I sort out what's happening. Franco has extricated his fetish purse from the recesses of his huge brown suit and is confiding its contents to his new leader: the knuckle bone of a monkey, an ointment box once the property of his grandfather, a fragment of basalt from a vanished jungle city. The Mwangaza and the Dolphin are polite in their appreciation. If Tabizi is

present, he doesn't bother to signify. And still no Haj,
however hard I listen.

I return to Philip and Dieudonné, and discover that
Maxie has grafted himself onto their conversation and is
applying his frightful French to the pastoral practices of
the Banyamulenge. I do what I should have done five
minutes ago. I switch to the Mwangaza's DRAWING
ROOM and hear Haj scream.

*   *   *

All right, the attribution was at first tentative. The
scream contained none of the wide-ranging sounds I
had thus far heard from Haj, and many I hadn't, such
as terror, agony and abject supplication, dwindling by
degrees to a whimper of recognisable words which,
though faint, enabled me to confirm my identification.
I can offer approximations of these words but no verba-
tim. For once in my life, my pencil, though poised,
failed to make contact with the notepad beneath it. But
the words were in any case banalities, such as *please* or
for God's sake or *no more*. They invoked *Maria*, though
whether Haj was appealing to the Virgin or a mistress
or his mother was never clear.

The scream on first hearing also struck me as
extremely loud, although I was later obliged to qualify
this. It had the effect of a wire strung between the
earpieces of my headset, passing through my brain, and
turned to red hot. It was so loud that I couldn't believe
Spider hadn't heard it too. Yet when I ventured a covert

look at him, his demeanour hadn't altered one jot. He was seated in the same position, munching the same chunk of bread, cheese and gherkin, and reading or not reading the same military magazine, and exuding the same air of superior satisfaction that had previously got on my nerves.

I switched quickly back to the library while I recovered my wits. Ensconced at his lunch-table, the Mwangaza was proposing to publish a selection of his thoughts on African democracy. At another, Philip, Maxie and Dieudonné were thrashing out matters of land irrigation. For a few deranged seconds I tried to convince myself that the scream was a fantasy, but I can't have been very persuasive, because before I knew it I was back in the Mwangaza's drawing room.

And here I will permit myself the advantage of hindsight, since several more screams followed before I was able to identify the other *dramatis personae*. For instance: it struck me early on that, while there were indications of other feet at work—two pairs of highly active rubberised soles on hard floor, and one pair of light leather which I tentatively awarded to the catlike Tabizi—there was no slapping of crocs, thereby leading me to the conclusion that Haj was either suspended above the ground in some way, or shoeless, or both. But it took a succession of exchanges between Haj and his tormentors before I felt able to assume that he was bound and, from the waist down at least, naked.

The screams I was hearing, though close to the microphone, were softer and more piglike than I had at first thought, being muffled by a towel or similar which was removed if Haj signalled that he had something worthwhile to say, and jammed back in place when he hadn't. It was also apparent that, in the view of his tormentors, he was making use of this signal too often: which was how I came to identify, first Benny—'You try that once more, and I'll burn your balls off'—and immediately after him Anton, promising Haj 'a one-way journey up your arse with *this*'.

So what was *this*?

We hear so much about torture these days, argue about whether such practices as hooding, sound-deprivation and water-boarding amount to it, that not much remains to the imagination. *This* was electrically powered: so much was quickly evident. There is Anton's threat to turn up the power, and there is a moment when Benny coarsely rebukes Tabizi for tripping over the fucking flex. Was *this* a cattle prod, then? A pair of electrodes? If so, the question that follows is: how did they come by *this*? Had they brought *this* along with them as a standard piece of equipment just in case—much as another person might carry an umbrella to work on a cloudy day? Or had they improvised *this* on the spot from stuff lying around—a bit of cable here, a transformer there, a dimmer-switch, an old poker, and Bob's your uncle?

And if they had, who would they most naturally turn

to for technical assistance and knowhow?—which was why, even in the midst of my turmoil, I found time to revisit Spider's smile. There was more than a suggestion of the creator's pride about it. Was that what he had been up to when he was called away from his post? Cobbling together a makeshift cattle prod from his toolbox for the lads? Doing them one of his famous lash-ups, guaranteed to win the heart and mind of the most stubborn prisoner? If so, the task had not spoiled his appetite, for he was chewing heartily.

I will not attempt here to offer anything more than the plain path of Tabizi's questioning, and Haj's futile denials which with merciful swiftness deteriorated into confession. I will leave to the imagination the guttural threats and curses on the one side, and the screams, sobs and entreaties on the other. Tabizi was clearly no stranger to torture. His laconic menaces, histrionics and fits of wheedling testified to long practice. And Haj, after an opening display of defiance, was no stoic. I didn't see him lasting long at the whipping post.

It is also important to note that Tabizi made no effort to protect his source: me. He took his information straight from the duel on the gazebo steps, and went through none of the usual hoops to disguise its origin. There were no phrases such as 'a trusted inform-ant reports' or 'according to liaison material received' with which Mr Anderson's desk officers attempt to obfuscate the location of his bugs. Only an interrogator whose victims will never again see the light of day would be so careless. First, in his gravelly French, Tabizi asks Haj after the health of his father Luc.

Bad. Real bad. Dying.

Where?

Hospital.

Hospital where?

Cape Town.

Which one?

Haj speaks guardedly, and with reason. He is lying. They have given him a taste of the cattle prod, but not the full treatment. Tabizi asks again which hospital in Cape Town. His shoes have a restless tread. I have a picture of him circling Haj while he snarls his questions at him, perhaps occasionally lending a hand of his own, but in the main leaving matters to his two assistants.

Tabizi: Luc never went to any fucking hospital, did he? ... did he? ... did he? ... Okay. So it's a lie ... Whose lie? Luc's? ... your *own* fucking lie? ... so where's Luc now? ... where is he? ... where's Luc? ... I said, where's Luc? ... in Cape Town, right. Next time make it easier for yourself. Luc is in Cape Town but he's not in hospital. So what's he doing? Speak up! ... Golf ... I love it. Who's he playing golf with? The fat Dutch gentleman? ... He's playing golf with his *brother*! ... the fat Dutchman's brother or his own brother? ... his *own* brother ... nice ... and what's the name of this brother? ... Étienne ... your uncle Étienne ... elder or younger? ... younger ...

So now what's the name of the Dutchman? ... I said
the Dutchman ... I said the fat Dutchman ... I said the
fat Dutchman we just talked about ... the Dutchman
your father isn't playing golf with today ... the fat
Dutchman you studied with in Paris who smokes
cigars ... remember him? ... remember him? ... the
fat Dutchman your father met in Nairobi, thanks to
your good offices, you little shit ... you want some
more of that? ... you want the boys to go right up
the scale so you know what it feels like? ... Marius ...
His name is Marius ... Mr Marius, Marius who? ...
Give him a rest a minute ... let him speak ... okay,
don't give him a rest, give him the whole ... van
Tonge ... his name is Marius van Tonge. And what
does Marius van Tonge do for a profession? ...
venture capital ... one of five partners ... we're
talking nicely now, so let's keep it that way, just don't
shit me and we'll lower the heat a little bit ... not too
much or you'll forget why you're talking ... So this
Marius sent you to spy on us ... you're spying for
Marius ... you're spying for the fat Dutch fucker,
he's paying you a lot of money to tell him everything
we talk about ... yes? ... yes? ... yes? NO! It's no.
Assume it's no ... you're not spying for Marius,
you're spying for Luc, how's that? You're Luc's spy
and as soon as you get home you're going to tell it
all to Daddy so he can go back to Marius and get
himself a better deal ... not true ... not true ... not
true ... still not true? ... still not true? ... don't go

to sleep on me ... nobody's going to let you sleep here ... open your eyes ... if you don't open your eyes in just fifteen seconds we're going to wake you up like you've never been woken up before ... Better ... that's much better ... all right, you came here of your own free will ... you're freelance ... your dad agreed to play sick so that you could come here of your own free will ... you don't want *what?* ... *War!* ... You don't want another war ... you believe in reconciliation with Rwanda ... *you want a trade treaty* with Rwanda ... when? In the next millennium? (*laughter*) ... you want a common market of all the nations of the Great Lakes ... and Marius is the man to broker that ... that's what you sincerely believe ... well, congratulations. (*in English*) Give him some water ... now tell us some more about these evil friends of yours in Kinshasa who've been telling you shitty stories about the Mwangaza. You don't *have* any evil friends ... you don't have any friends in *Kinshasa* ... Nobody in Kinshasa has talked to you ... guys who could make you wake up dead ... well, WAKE UP NOW, you little ... (*again in fractured English*): Give it to him, Benny, all the way ... I hate this nigger ... I *hate* him ... I *hate* him ...

Until now Haj's responses have been scarcely audible, hence Tabizi's practice of repeating them at full volume, I assume for the benefit of the contingency microphones that I wasn't cleared for, and for anyone else who may be listening on a separate link—I'm thinking particularly of Philip. But with the mention of *Kinshasa*, the mood in the living room alters radically, and so does Haj. He perks up. As his pain and humiliation turn to anger, his voice acquires muscle, his diction clears, and the old, defiant Haj miraculously re-creates himself. No more whimpering confessions extracted under torture for him. Instead we get a furious, freewheeling indictment, a barrage of forensic, vituperative accusation.

Haj: You want to know who they are, these wise guys in Kinshasa I spoke to? Your fucking friends! The Mwangaza's fucking friends!—the fatcats he won't have anything to do with till he's built Jerusalem in Kivu! You know what they call themselves, this band of altruistic public servants when they're swilling beer and screwing whores and deciding which kind of Mercedes to buy?—the Thirty Per Cent Club. What's thirty per cent? Thirty per cent is the People's Portion that they propose to award themselves in exchange for favours they are granting to the Middle Path. It's the piece of this crappy operation that persuades arseholes like my father that they can build schools and roads and hospitals while they line their fucking pockets. What do these fatcats have to do to earn themselves the People's Portion? What they like to do best: nothing. Look the other way. Tell their troops to stay in their barracks and stop raping people for a few days.

Haj adopts the wheedling tones of a sly street-trader. If he were able to do the gestures too, he would be happier:

Haj: No problem, Mzee Mwangaza! You want to stage a couple of riots in Bukavu and Goma, take the place over ahead of the elections, kick out the Rwandans and start a little war? No problem! You want to grab Kavumu airport, play the minerals game, steal the stockpiles, take them to Europe and depress the world market with a short-sell? Do it! One small detail. We distribute the People's Portion, not you. And how we distribute it is our fucking business. You want your Mwangaza to be Governor of South Kivu? He has our total, selfless support. Because every fucking building contract he awards, every road he thinks he's going to build and every fucking flower he plants along the Avenue Patrice Lumumba, we take one-third. And if you shit on us, we'll throw the constitutional book at you, we'll run you out of the country in your fucking underwear. Thank you for your time.

Haj's diatribe is interrupted by, of all things, the ring of a telephone, which startles me twice over because the only functioning telephone I'm aware of is the satellite phone in the ops room. Anton takes the call, says, 'Right here,' and passes the phone to Tabizi, who listens, then protests volubly in atrocious English:

'I just broke the bastard. I got a right!'

But his protests are evidently to no avail for as soon
as he has rung off, he delivers a parting salutation to
Haj in French: 'Okay. I got to go now. But if ever I see
you again, I will personally kill you. Not at once. First I
kill your women, your kids, your sisters and brothers
and your fucking father and everybody who thinks they
love you. Then I kill *you*. Takes days. Weeks, if I'm
lucky. Cut the bastard down.'

The door closes with a slam as he departs. Anton's
voice is confiding and tender.

'You all right there, son? We have to do what we're
told in life, don't we, Benny? Simple soldiers, us.'

Benny is equally conciliatory. 'Here, let's clean you
up a bit. No hard feelings, right, mate? Be on the same
side next time round.'

Caution tells me to switch back to the library, but I
am unable to move for Haj's pain. My shoulders are
rigid, sweat is dribbling down my spine, and there are
red marks in my palms where my fingernails have driven
into the flesh. I check on Spider: wolfing lemon cheese-
cake with a plastic spoon while he reads his military
magazine, or pretends to. Will Anton and Benny
provide him with a user's report: great little cattle prod,
Spider, we had him sobbing his heart out in no time?

Hearing a distant crash of water from the bathroom
of the royal apartments, I switch from DRAWING ROOM
to BATHROOM and am in time to catch a bawdy male
duet from Benny and Anton as they sponge their victim

down. I am beginning to wonder whether I should reluctantly leave him to recuperate on his own when I hear a surreptitious double click as a distant door opens and closes. And I know, since I hear no footsteps, that silky Philip has arrived to take the place of the over-zestful Tabizi.

Philip: Thank you, boys.

He's not thanking them, he's telling them to go. The same door opens and closes, leaving Philip alone. I hear an ambient tinkle of glass. Philip has picked up a drinks tray and is placing it somewhere more to his liking. He tries a sofa or easy chair, moves to another. As he does so, I hear the slow slap of slime-green crocs on hard floor.

Philip: You all right to sit down?

Haj sits on soft chair or sofa, swears.

Philip: You missed out on lunch. I brought you some tuna salad. No? Pity. It's rather good. What about a thin Scotch? (*He pours one anyway: a dash, plenty of soda, two plops of ice*)

His tone is incurious. What happened just now was nothing to do with him.

Philip: Regarding *Marius*. Your brilliant friend and colleague from Paris days. Yes? One of eight bright young partners in a multinational venture-capital house called the Union Minière des Grands Lacs. Their number two in Johannesburg, no less, with a special eye for the Eastern Congo.

Crackle of paper being unfolded.

Haj: (*in English, probably one of the few phrases he possesses*) Go fuck yourself.

Philip: The Union Minière des Grands Lacs is a multinational corporation wholly owned by a Dutch conglomerate registered in the Antilles. With me so far? You are. And the conglomerate is called—yes?

Haj: (*indistinct growl*) Hogen[?]

Philip: And their policy?

Haj: Make business, not war.

Philip: But who *owns* Hogen? You haven't enquired. A foundation in Liechtenstein owns Hogen and by any normal standards that should be the end of the trail. However, by a stroke of fortune we are able to provide you with a cast list.

The names that he reads out mean nothing to me nor, I suspect, to Haj. It's only when Philip begins to recite their job descriptions that my stomach starts to churn.

Philip: Wall Street broker and former presidential aide ...
CEO of the PanAtlantic Oil Corporation of Denver,
Colorado ... ex-member National Security Council,
vice president of the Amermine Gold & Finance
Corporation of Dallas, Texas ... principal advisor
to the Pentagon on acquisition and stockpiling of
essential minerals ... vice president of the Grayson-
Halliburton Communications Enterprise ...

There are nine names on my notepad by the time he
ends: collectively, if Philip is to be believed, a Who's
Who of American corporate and political power, indistinguishable from government, a fact that he is pleased
to underline.

Philip: Bold, conceptual thinkers, every one of them.
A-list neo-conservatives, geo-politicians on the grand
scale. The sort of fellows who meet in ski resorts and
decide the fate of nations. Not for the first time their
thoughts have turned to the Eastern Congo and
what do they find? An election looming, and anarchy
the likely outcome. The Chinese on the hunt for
resources and baying at the door. So which way to
go? The Congolese don't like Americans and it's
reciprocated. The Rwandans despise the Congolese,
and run a tight ship. Best of all they're efficient. So
the American game plan is to build up Rwanda's
commercial and economic presence in the Eastern
Congo to the point where it's an irreversible fact.

They're looking for a *de facto* bloodless annexation, and counting on a helping hand from the CIA. Enter your friend Marius.

If my brain is racing too fast, Haj's must be spinning out of control.

Philip: All right, I grant you, the Mwangaza has cut a dirty deal with Kinshasa. He won't be the first Congolese politician to cover his backside, will he? (*chuckle*) But he's a better bet than a Rwandan takeover, that's for sure. (*Pause to allow what I fear is a nod of acquiescence*) And at least he's working towards an independent Kivu, not an American colony. And if Kinshasa gets its money, why should it interfere? And Kivu stays within the federal family where it belongs. (*Sounds of pouring and clinks of ice as Haj's glass is presumably replenished*) So the old boy's got a lot going for him, when you work it out. I think you're being a little hard on him, Haj, frankly. He's naive, but so are most idealists. And he does *mean* to do good things, even if he never quite brings them off. (*abrupt change of tone*) What are you trying to tell me? What do you want? Your jacket. Here's your jacket. You're feeling cold. You can't speak. You've got a pen. What else do you want? Paper. Here's a piece of paper. (*Tears a page out of something*)

What in Heaven's name has happened to Haj's hyperactive tongue? Has the whisky gone to his head? Has the cattle prod? Scratch, scribble, as he writes vigorously with one of his Parker pens. Who's he writing to? What about? It's another duel. We're back in the guest suite and Haj has put a warning finger to his lips. We're on the gazebo steps and Haj is trying to baffle the microphones and me. But this time he's thrusting handwritten notes at Philip.

Philip: Is this a bad joke?
Haj: (*very low volume*) A good joke.
Philip: Not to me.
Haj: (*still low*) For me and my dad, good.
Philip: You're mad.
Haj: Just fucking do it, okay? I don't want to talk about it.

In front of *me*? He doesn't want to talk *with me listening*? Is that what he's telling Philip? Shuffle of paper passing from hand to hand. Philip's voice freezes over:

Philip: I can very well see why you don't want to talk about it. Do you seriously think you can gouge another three million dollars out of us just by scribbling out an invoice?
Haj: (*sudden yell*) That's our price, you arsehole! Cash, hear me?

Philip: On the day Kinshasa appoints the Mwangaza
    Governor of South Kivu, obviously.

Haj: No! *Now!* This fucking day!

Philip: A Saturday.

Haj: By Monday night! Or it's no fucking deal! Into my
    dad's bank account in Bulgaria or wherever the fuck
    he keeps it! Hear me?

His voice drops. The enraged Congolese is replaced
by the scathing Sorbonne graduate.

Haj: My dad undersold the deal. He neglected to
    maximise his leverage and I propose to rectify that
    error. The revised price is an additional three million
    US dollars or it's no deal. One million for Bukavu,
    one million for Goma, and one million for strapping
    me up like a fucking monkey and torturing the shit
    out of me. So get on the phone to your no-balls
    Syndicate now and ask for the guy who says yes.

Philip haggles while striving to retain his dignity: in
the unlikely event of the Syndicate considering Haj's
offer, how about half-a-million down and the rest on
completion? For the second time, Haj tells Philip to go
fuck himself. And his mother, if he ever had one.

*Sorry to have neglected you, Brian dear. How was it for
you?*

Sam's intrusion comes from another world, but I
respond to it calmly.

Uneventful, basically, Sam. Lot of food, not a lot of talk. Aren't we about due upstairs?

Any minute, dear. Philip's answering a call of Nature.

The door closes, leaving Haj alone drifting round the room. What's he doing? Staring at himself in the mirror, fathoming how he looks now he's sold himself for three million dollars by Monday, if he has? He starts to hum. I don't do that. I'm not musical. My humming embarrasses me even when I'm alone. But Haj is musical, and he's humming to cheer himself up. Perhaps cheer both of us up. He's shuffling heavily round the room to the sound of his humming, slap, slap, slap. He's humming away his shame and mine. His choice of tune, unlike anything he has sung or hummed in my hearing, is Mission church jingle, evoking the dismal hours I spent in Sunday School. We stand in line in our blue uniforms. We clap our hands and stamp our feet, *bomp-bomp*, and we tell ourselves an uplifting story. This one is about a little girl who promised God she would protect her virtue against all comers, *bomp*. In return, God helped her. Every time she was tempted, He reached down His hands and put her back on the straight path, *bomp*. And when she chose death rather than succumb to her wicked uncle, God sent Choirs of Angels to greet her at the Gates of Heaven. *Bomp, bomp.*

Philip's handbell is ringing for the next session. Haj hears it. I hear it distantly over the mikes, but I do not reveal this to Spider. I stay seated with my headphones on, scribbling on my notepad and looking innocent.

Haj bomps to the door, shoves it open and sings his way into the sunlight. All along the covered path to the guest suite, the microphones pick up his treacly dirge about virtue's triumph.

13

Even today I am hard pressed to describe the many contradictory emotions sweeping through me as I emerged from my incarceration below ground and took my place among the little cluster of believers entering the gaming room for the final session of the conference. Back there in the cellar I had seen no hope for mankind, yet traversing the covered walkway I convinced myself that I was in a state of divine grace. I looked at the world and concluded that in my absence a summer storm had washed the air and put a sparkle on every leaf and blade of grass. In the afternoon sunlight, the gazebo looked like a Greek temple. I imagined that I was celebrating a miraculous survival: Haj's and mine equally.

My second delusion, no more praiseworthy than the first, was that my mental faculties, impaired by repeated immersions beneath the waterline, had yielded to fantasy: that the entire passage of events, commencing with Haj's scream and ending with his cheesy song, had been a psychic hallucination brought on by overstrain;

our audio duel on the stone steps was another, and the same went for any other sinister fantasies about notes being passed or bribes negotiated.

It was in the hope of verifying this convenient theory that, on resuming my seat at the green baize gaming table, I undertook a swift survey of the players in my illusory drama, commencing with Anton, who had armed himself with a pile of buff folders and, in the parade-ground manner dear to him, was laying one to each place. Neither his clothing nor his personal appearance bore signs of recent physical activity. His knuckles were a little red, otherwise no abrasions. Toecaps glistening, trouser creases razor sharp. Benny had not yet materialised, which enabled me to believe that he had passed the lunch break minding his ward Jasper.

Neither Philip nor Haj being yet among us, I transferred my attention to Tabizi who appeared distracted, certainly, but so he should be, given that the post-office clock stood at four-twenty and the hour of reckoning was upon us. Next to him sat his master the Mwangaza. With the sun glinting on his slave collar and making a halo of his white hair, our Enlightener was the embodiment of Hannah's dreams. Could he really be the same man who in my fantasy had traded the People's Portion for the tacit connivance of the Kinshasa fatcats? And on the Mwangaza's other side, the sleek Dolphin, smiling his cheery smile. As to Maxie, the mere sight of him, sprawled beside Philip's empty chair with his legs stretched out, was enough to convince me that it was

I who was the odd one out, and everyone around me was who he claimed to be.

As if to reinforce the point, enter by way of the interior door my saviour Philip. He bestows a wave on Dieudonné and Franco. Passing Tabizi, he stoops to murmur in his ear. Tabizi responds with an expressionless nod. Arriving at the place reserved for Haj, he conjures a sealed envelope from his jacket pocket and slips it like a tip inside the buff folder that awaits our missing delegate's arrival. Only then does he take his seat at the further end of the table, by which time I am, as Paula would say, out of denial. I know that Philip has spoken to London and asked for the man who says yes. I know from Tabizi's scowl that Haj accurately calculated the weakness of the Syndicate's position: namely that their preparations are too far advanced, the prize is too great for them to give up at this stage, they've put in so much already, they might as well put in a bit more, and if they pull out now they won't get a chance like this for a generation.

In the same grim light of reality I take a second look at the Mwangaza. Is his halo blow-dried? Have they shoved a poker down his back? Is he dead already, and strapped into his saddle like El Cid? Hannah saw him in the rosy haze of her idealism, but now that I am able to look at him clearly, the sad arc of his life is written all over his crunched-up face. Our Enlightener is a failed state of one. He has been brave—look at his record. He has been clever, diligent, loyal and resourceful throughout his life. He has done everything right, but the crown has always gone to the man next to him or the man below him. And that was because he wasn't ruthless enough, or corrupt enough, or two-faced enough. Well, now he will be. He will play their game, a thing he swore he'd never do. And the crown is within his grasp, except it isn't. Because if he ever gets to wear it, it will belong to the people he has sold himself to on the way up. Any dream he has is mortgaged ten times over. And that includes the dream that once he comes to power, he won't have to pay his debts.

Haj is only a couple of minutes overdue, but in my head he has kept me waiting several lifetimes. Everyone round the table has opened his buff folder, so I do the same. The document inside seems familiar, as well it might. In an earlier life I had translated it from French into Swahili. Both versions are on offer. So are a dozen pages of impressive-looking figures and accounts, all of them, so far as I can see, projected into the far future: estimated extraction rates, transportation costs, warehousing, gross sales, gross profits, gross deception.

Philip's groomed white head has lifted. I see it at the top of my frame as I work my way through my folder. He is smiling at somebody behind me, a warm, complicit smile of confidence, so look out. I hear the slap of approaching crocs on flagstone and feel sick. The slap-rate is below average speed. Haj saunters in, jacket open, flashes of mustard-coloured lining, Parker pens in place, lacquered forelock pretty much restored. At the

Sanctuary, when you rejoined your peers after a beating, ethic required you to appear carefree. Haj is guided by the same principle. His hands are thrust into his trouser pockets where they like to be and he is jiggling his hips. Yet I know that every movement is an agony to him. Halfway to his chair he pauses, catches my eye and grins at me. I have my folder before me and I have opened it, so in theory I could smile vaguely and return to my reading. But I don't. I meet his gaze full on.

Our eyes lock and they stay locked while we stare at each other. I have no idea how long our look actually lasted. I don't imagine the sweep hand of the post-office clock moved more than a second or two. But it was long enough for him to know that I knew, if either of us had ever doubted it. And long enough for me to know he knew I knew, and so back and forth. And long enough for any third party who chanced to be watching us to know we were either a pair of homosexuals sending out mating signals, or two men with a very large piece of illicit knowledge in common, and how did *that* come about? There wasn't much light in his bubbly eyes, but after what he'd been through, why should there be? Was he telling me, 'You bastard, you betrayed me'? Was *I* reproaching *him* for betraying himself, and Congo? Today, with more days and nights than I need to reflect on the moment, I see it as one of wary mutual recognition. We were both hybrids: I by birth, he by education. We had both taken too many steps away from the country that had borne us to belong anywhere with ease.

He sat down at his place, winced, spotted the white
envelope peeking out of his folder. He fished it out with
the tip of his finger and thumb, sniffed at it and, in full
view of whoever might be looking on, fiddled it open.
He unfolded a postcard-size piece of white paper, a
printout of some kind, and skim-read the two-line text
which I presume acknowledged, in suitably guarded
language, the deal he had just negotiated for himself
and his father. I thought he might tip a nod to Philip,
but he didn't bother. He screwed the bit of paper into
a pellet and lobbed it, with impressive accuracy given his
condition, into a porcelain urn that stood in a corner of
the room.

'Bull's-eye!' he exclaimed in French, swirling his
hands above his head, and won himself a tolerant laugh
from round the table.

I will pass over the laborious negotiations, the
endless trivialities by which delegates of every stamp
convince themselves they are being astute, protecting
the interests of their company or tribe, are smarter than
the delegate sitting next to them. Putting myself on
autopilot, I used the time to get my head and my
emotions under control and, by whatever means that
came to hand—such as manifesting total indifference
towards anything that Haj happened to say—dispel the
notion that he and I might in some way be—to employ
a phrase favoured by our One-Day Course instructors—
mutually conscious. Privately I was wrestling with the
notion that Haj might be suffering from internal

damage, such as bleeding, but I was reassured when the ticklish matter of the Mwangaza's official remuneration was raised.

'But, Mzee,' Haj objects, flinging up an arm in the old manner. 'With respect, Mzee. Hang on a minute!'—in French which, because it's Haj speaking, I render tonelessly to the Perrier bottle—'these figures are frankly ridiculous. I mean, fuck'—now energetically appealing to his two companions for support—'can you imagine *our Redeemer* living on this scale? I mean, how will you *eat*, Mzee? Who will pay your rent, your fuel bills, your travel, entertainment? All those necessary expenses should come out of the public purse, not your Swiss bank account.'

If Haj had drawn blood, it was appropriate that none be visible. Tabizi's face turned to stone, but it was pretty much stone already. Philip's smile didn't flinch, and the Dolphin, replying on behalf of his master, had his answer pat.

'For as long as our beloved Mwangaza is the People's choice, he will live as he has always lived, which is to say, on his salary as a simple teacher and the modest income from his books. He thanks you for your good question.'

Felix Tabizi is padding round the table like an ogre turned choirboy. But it isn't a hymn sheet he's handing round, it's what he calls *notre petite aide-mémoire*—a one-page conversion table setting out, for the comfort and convenience of our readers, what is understood in the real world by such lighthearted expressions as *shovel*, *trowel, pickaxe, heavy and light wheelbarrows* and the like. And since the information is provided in Swahili as well as French, I am able to remain as silent as everybody else in the room while philosophical comparisons are drawn between words and meaning.

And to this day, I couldn't tell you what was what. The best *light wheelbarrows* hailed from Bulgaria, but what on earth were they? Rockets to put in the nosecones of white helicopters? Ask me today what a *scythe* was, or a *tractor*, or a *combine harvester*, and I would be equally at a loss. Did it pass through my mind that this might be the moment for me to spring to my feet and cry foul?—act like the brave little gentleman in the trattoria? Roll up my buff folder, hammer it on the table: *I will speak, I owe it to myself. Therefore I shall?* If so, I was still debating the question as the interior doors opened to admit our distinguished notary Monsieur Jasper Albin, accompanied by Benny, his conscientious minder.

Jasper has acquired status. He didn't have it earlier in the day when he seemed proud that he had nothing to offer but his venality. I remember experiencing wonderment that an enterprise so audacious and richly funded should have placed its legal business in such hands. Yet here was a Jasper grown to the part, even if what followed was a piece of theatre—or more accurately mime, since much of my memory's soundtrack of the historic moment has mercifully gone missing. Afternoon sunlight continues to pour through the French windows. Specks of dust or evening dew float in its rays as, from his fat briefcase, Jasper draws two identical leather folders of regal appearance. On the covers is inscribed the one word CONTRAT. Using only his fingertips, he opens each folder in turn, then sits back, permitting us to behold the original, the sole, the ribbon-bound, unenforceable document, one version in Jasper's French and the other in my Swahili.

From his magician's bag he produces an antiquated hand-press of stippled grey metal which in my out-of-body state I identify as Aunt Imelda's orange squeezer. It is followed by a single A4-sized sheet of greaseproof paper on which are mounted eight peel-off, Soviet-style red stars with extra spikes. At Philip's beckoning I rise to my feet and position myself at Jasper's side while he addresses the delegates. His speech is not a rousing one. He has been advised, he tells us, that the parties to our contract are in accord. Since he has not been privy to our deliberations, and since complex matters of agriculture are outside the ambit of his professional expertise, he must absolve himself from responsibility for the technical wording of the contract which, in the event of a dispute, will be for a court to determine. Throughout my entire rendering, I have contrived to avoid Haj's eye.

Philip invites all signatories to rise. Like communicants at Mass they form a queue with Franco at its head. The Mwangaza, too important to stand in line, lurks to one side, flanked by his handlers. Haj, whom I continue to ignore, brings up the rear. Franco stoops over my

Swahili version, starts to sign, and recoils. Has he spotted an insult, a bad omen? And if not, why are his old eyes brimming with tears? He shuffles round, dragging his bad leg after him, until he is face to face with Dieudonné his many-times enemy and now, for however long, his brother-in-arms. His huge fists rise to shoulder height. Is he about to tear his new friend limb from limb?

'*Tu veux?*' he bellows in French—you want to do this?

'*Je veux bien, Franco,*' Dieudonné replies shyly, upon which the two men fall into each other's arms in an embrace so fierce that I fear for his ribcage. Horseplay follows. Franco, eyes streaming, signs. Dieudonné shoves him aside and tries to sign, but Franco has him by the arm: he must have one more embrace. Finally Dieudonné signs. Haj rejects the fountain pen offered him and whisks one from the pocket of his Zegna. With no pretence of reading, he scrawls a reckless signature twice, once for the Swahili, once for the French. The applause starts with Philip and spreads to the Mwangaza's camp. I clap with the best of us.

Our women appear with trays of champagne. We clink glasses, Philip speaks a few exquisitely chosen words on behalf of the Syndicate, the Mwangaza responds with dignity, I render both with gusto. I am thanked, though not lavishly. A jeep pulls up in the forecourt. The Mwangaza's handlers lead him away. Franco and Dieudonné are at the door, holding hands

African-style, kidding with each other as Philip tries to shoo them towards the jeep. Haj offers me his own hand to shake. I accept it cautiously, not wishing to hurt it, not knowing how the gesture is meant.

'You have a card?' he enquires. 'I'm thinking of opening an office in London. Maybe I shall use you.'

I delve in the pockets of my sweat-soaked Harris Tweed and fish out a card: Brian Sinclair, accredited interpreter, resident in a post-office box in Brixton. He examines it, then me. He laughs, but only softly, not the hyena cackle we are accustomed to. Too late, I realise he has yet again been addressing me in the Shi with which he assailed Dieudonné on the gazebo steps.

'If you ever think of coming to Bukavu, send me an e-mail,' he adds carelessly, this time in French, and extracts a platinum card-case from the recesses of his Zegna.

The card is before me as I write, not physically perhaps, but printed indelibly on my visual memory. It's a good three inches by two, with gilt edges. A second border inside the gilt portrays the romping animals of Kivu past and present: gorilla, lion, cheetah and elephant, an army of snakes locked in happy dance, but no zebras. For background we have scarlet hills with pink sky behind, and on the reverse side, the silhouette of a high-kicking chorus girl with a champagne glass in her hand. Haj's name and many qualifications are given with the flourish of a royal proclamation, first in French, then English, then Swahili. Below them come his business and home addresses in Paris and Bukavu, and after them a string of telephone numbers. And on the reverse side, next to the chorus girl, an e-mail address hastily hand-scrawled in ink.

* * *

Retracing my familiar path along the covered walkway, I was pleased to note that, in the haste traditional to the closing moments of all conferences, Spider and his helpers were already distributed about the grounds dismantling their handiwork. Spider in cap and quilted waistcoat stood feet astride on Haj's stone steps, reeling electric cable while he whistled. In the gazebo, two anoraks were mounted on ladders. A third was on his knees before the stone bench. In the boiler room, the Underground plan was propped with its face against the wall, wires coiled and bound. The tape decks were stowed in their black box.

A brown burn-bag, mouth gaping and half full, stood on top of Spider's desk. Empty drawers were pulled open in the best Chat Room tradition. Anyone who has passed through Mr Anderson's hands is a slave to his rules of Personal Security, which range from What You May or May Not Tell Your Significant Other to not placing apple cores in your personal burn-bag lest they inhibit the incineration of secret waste and Spider was no exception. His digital audio tapes were immaculately tagged and numbered and slotted into trays. Beside them lay the exercise book in which he kept his log.

Unused tapes, still in their boxes, were stacked on a shelf above them.

For my main selections I consulted the logbook. The handwritten list at the front comprised the tapes that were known to me: guest suite, royal apartments, et cetera. I selected five. But what was the list at the back, also handwritten? And who or what was S? Why, in the column where the location of the microphone should be entered, did we get instead the letter S? S for Spider? S for Syndicate? S for Sinclair? Or how about—here was a thought!—S for *satellite*? Was it conceivable that Philip or Maxie or Sam or Lord Brinkley, or one of his no-name partners, or all of them, had decided for reasons of self-protection, for the record, for the archive, to bug their own telephone conversations? I decided it was. There were three tapes marked S in ball-point. Grabbing three blanks, I scrawled the same S on their spines and helped myself to the originals.

My next task was to hide the tapes around my body. For the second time since I had been forced to put it on, I was grateful for my Harris Tweed. With its over-large interior pockets it could have been tailor-made for the job. The waistband of my grey flannels was equally accommodating, but my notepads were unyielding and ring-backed. I was deliberating what to do with them when I heard Philip's voice, the sleek one he used onstage.

'Brian, dear man. *Here* you are. I've been dying to congratulate you. Now I can.'

He was poised in the doorway, one pink-sleeved arm for the frame and his slip-on shoes comfortably crossed. My instinct was to be gracious, but in the nick of time I remembered that, after a peak performance such as the one I had given, I was more likely to feel drained and scratchy.

'Glad you liked it,' I said.

'Tidying up?'

'That's right.'

To prove it, I tossed one of my notepads into the burn-bag. I turned back to find Philip standing directly in front of me. Had he spotted the bulges round my midriff? He raised his hands and I thought he was going to make a grab for them, but instead he reached past me and retrieved my notepad from the burn-bag.

'Well, I *must* say,' he marvelled, licking his finger and flipping through my pencilled pages. 'No good complaining it's all Greek to me, is it? The Greeks couldn't make head nor tail of it either.'

'Mr Anderson calls it my Babylonian cuneiform,' I said.

'And these twiddly bits in the margin—they are what?'

'Notes to self.'

'And what do they *say* to self?'

'Style points. Innuendo. Things to pick up on when I'm rendering.'

'Such as?'

'Statements as questions. When something's meant as a joke and isn't. Sarcasm. You can't do much with sarcasm, not when you're rendering. It doesn't come over.'

'How perfectly fascinating. And you keep all that in your head.'

'Not really. That's why I write it down.'

He's the customs officer at Heathrow who pulls you out of the arrivals queue because you're a *zebra*. He doesn't ask you where you've stashed your cocaine, or whether you've been attending an Al Qaeda training course. He wants to hear where you spent your holiday, and was the hotel nice, while he reads your body language and blink rate, and waits for the tell-tale change in your voice-level.

'Well, I'm most impressed. You did it all so well. Upstairs, downstairs, everywhere,' he said, returning the notepad to the burn-bag. 'And you're married. To a popular journalist, I gather.'

'That's right.'

'And she's a beauty, I'm told.'

'People say so.'

'You must make a fine pair.'

'We do.'

'Well, just remember careless pillow-talk costs lives.'

He had gone. To make sure he had gone, I tiptoed to the top of the cellar staircase and was in time to see him disappear round the corner of the building. On the hillside Spider and his men were still hard at work. I returned to the boiler room, recovered the notepad and gathered up the other three. Helping myself to four new ones from a stack, I scuffed their covers, numbered them in the same manner as my used ones and dropped them into the burn-bag as replacements. My pockets and waistband were full to bursting. With two notepads in the small of my back and one in each pocket, I waded up the cellar steps and back along the covered walkway to the relative safety of my bedroom.

* * *

It's back to Blighty at last! We're three thousand feet above sea-level and there's a street fest in every cage and why not? We're ourselves again, the same band of brothers that set out from Luton in the same no-name aeroplane twenty-four hours earlier, coming home with our tails up and a contract in our pocket, everything to play for and the Cup within our grasp! Philip is not among us. Where he has gone, I neither know nor care. Perhaps to the Devil, and let's hope so. First down the plane's aisle minces Spider in an improvised chef's hat, passing out plastic plates, beakers, knives and forks. After him trots Anton with a hand-towel for an apron around his midriff, bearing our no-name donor's hamper from Messrs Fortnum & Mason of Piccadilly. Hot on his heels ambles big Benny our gentle giant with a magnum of nearly cold champagne. Not even the great lawyer Jasper, cloistered in the end cage that he occupied on the outward journey, can resist the festive spirit. True, at first he makes a show of refusing everything, but after a sharp word from Benny and a glance at the label on the bottle, he tucks in with a will, as I do, because a top interpreter who has played his part to the full must never be a killjoy. My imitation leather night-bag nestles above me in the overhead webbing.

'What did you make of 'em, old boy?' Maxie asks, doing his T. E. Lawrence act of dropping down beside me, beaker in hand. And it's really nice to see our skipper having a proper drink for a change, not just Malvern water. It's nice to see him so flushed and pumped up with success.

'The delegates, Skipper?' I ask judiciously. 'What did I *make* of them?'

'Think they'll come through? Haj wobbled a bit, I thought. The other two seemed pretty solid. But will they deliver two weeks from now?'

I put aside the question of Haj's wobbling and draw upon my father's repertoire of aphorisms. 'Skipper, I'll tell you frankly. The important thing with your Congolese is to know how much you *don't* know. I couldn't say that before, but now I will.'

'You haven't answered my question.'

'Skipper, it is my firm belief that two weeks from now, they will be at your side as promised,' I reply, unable to equivocate in my need to be of service to him.

'Chaps!' Maxie is yelling down the aisle. 'I want to hear it for Sinclair. We ran him ragged and he didn't blink.'

A cheer goes up, glasses are raised. I am lifted on a

wave of emotion combining guilt, pride, solidarity and gratitude. When my eyes clear, Maxie is proffering a white envelope similar to the one that was peeking out of Haj's buff folder.

'Five grand US, old boy. That what Anderson told you?'

It was, I admitted.

'I got 'em up to seven. Not enough in my view, but best I could do.'

I start to thank him but my head is down, so I'm not sure he hears me. The bulletproof hand thumps my shoulder for the last time, and when I look up Maxie is at the other end of the plane and Benny is shouting at us to watch our arses for landing. Obediently, I reach for my night-bag and prepare to watch my arse, but it was too late, we had landed.

I never saw them go. Perhaps I didn't want to. What more was there to say? I have an apocryphal image of them with their kitbags slung over their shoulders, whistling Colonel Bogey while they march out of the rear doors of the green shed, and up a small incline to a no-name bus.

A woman security guard escorts me down airport corridors. The night-bag is tapping at my hip. I am standing before a fat man who sits behind a desk. The night-bag is on the floor beside me. On the desk, a sports bag of red nylon.

'You're to check contents and identify your possessions,' says the fat man, not looking at me.

I unzip the sports bag and identify my possessions: one dinner jacket, dark red with matching trousers, one dress shirt, white, one cummerbund, silk, and the whole lot rolled into a tight ball round my patent leather shoes. One padded envelope containing passport, wallet, diary, miscellaneous personal effects. My black silk dress socks are wedged into my left patent leather dress shoe. I pull them out and reveal my cellphone.

I am in the rear of a black or midnight blue Volvo Estate on my way to gaol. My driver is the same woman security guard. She wears a peaked cap. I see her snub nose in the driving mirror. The night-bag is squashed between my knees. The nylon sports bag is on the seat beside me. My cellphone is against my heart.

Dusk is falling. We pass through a subtopia of hangars, machine workshops, brick offices. Floodlit iron gates festooned in razor wire spring at us. Bulked-out armed police in jockey hats loiter. My driver points the bonnet of the car straight at the closed gates and accelerates. They part. We cross a lake of tarmac and pull up beside a traffic island covered in red and yellow flowers.

The doors of the Volvo unlock themselves. I'm free after all. The time by the Arrivals hall clock is twenty past nine of a hot Saturday evening. I'm back in the England I never left, and I need to change some dollars.

'Have a great weekend,' I urge the driver, which, being interpreted, means thank you for helping me smuggle my tapes and notepads out of Luton airport.

The speed-coach to Victoria station stands empty and pitch dark. Drivers smoke and chat beside it. The escaped prisoner selects a corner at the back, places the night-bag between his feet and slings the red sports bag onto the rack above his head. He presses the power button on his cellphone. It lights up, then begins to tremble. He dials 121 and presses green. A severe woman warns him that he has FIVE new messages.

Penelope, Friday, 1915: Salvo. You mad bastard. Where the fuck are you? We've looked *everywhere*. You show up late and are seen by *several* witnesses sneaking out of a side door halfway through the party. Why? Fergus has tried the loos and the bars downstairs and sent people running up and down the road shouting for you—(*muffled 'yes, darling, I know'*)—we're in the limo, Salvo, and we're on our way to Sir Matthew's house for dinner. Fergus has the address in case you've lost it. *God*, Salvo!

Thorne the Horn, Friday, 1920: (*Scots brogue, London-weighted*) Salvo, listen, we're hellish worried for you, old man. If you've not signified that you're in the land of the living within the hour, I'm proposing to have my people drag the rivers. Now do you have a pencil handy at all? And a piece of paper? What?—(*garbled, roar of coarse laughter*)—Penelope says you write things on your arm! What else do you write them on, man? (*A Belgravia address follows. End of message*)

Penelope, Friday, 2030: I am in Sir Matthew's hall, Salvo. It's a very beautiful hall. I have received your message, thank you. I don't give a fuck who your oldest and best corporate client is, you have no right to humiliate me like this. In one minute, Fergus. You may not know this, Salvo, but Sir Matthew happens to be extremely superstitious. Thanks to you, we are *thirteen* at table on a *Friday*. So what is happening even as I speak is that Fergus is desperately phoning around for—ah, he's found one!—and whom have you found, Fergus?—(*a hand descends over the phone*)—he's found Jellicoe. Jelly will step into the breach. He possesses no dinner jacket but Fergus has ordered him to sober himself up and come as he is. So *don't* turn up here, whatever else you do, Salvo. Just go on doing whatever the fuck you're doing. Sir Matthew's table does *not* take fifteen and I have suffered enough *fucking* embarrassment for one night!

Penelope, Saturday, 0950: It's me, darling. Sorry if I was catty last night. I was just so terribly worried for you. I can't say I'm not still furious, but when you tell me all about it, I'll probably understand. The dinner party was actually rather fun, as pompous parties go. Jelly was feeling no pain, but Fergus made sure he didn't disgrace himself. You'll laugh when I tell you what else happened, though. I couldn't get inside our flat. I'd switched handbags at the office and left my keys behind, *rather* assuming my ever loving would be on hand to take me home and give me a good seeing to. Paula was out gallivanting, which meant I couldn't use *her* key, so I was reduced to staying at Brown's Hotel for the night—I *hope* at the paper's expense! And *today*—which is a *total* chore, but I thought I'd better do it, seeing as how you've gone AWOL on me—I've agreed to be a good scout and go and hear Fergus address a flock of high-flying advertisers at a posh country house in Sussex. There's a knees-up afterwards apparently, with some big names in the industry, so I thought it might do me a bit of good. To meet them in an informal setting, I mean. Sir Matt is coming, so I'll be properly chaperoned. Anyway I'm on my way to the office now. To pick up my stuff. And do another quick-change act. So see you soon, darling. Tomorrow if not tonight. I'm still in a total rage with you, naturally. So you'll have to make the most *marvellous* amends. And please don't blame yourself about last night: I do understand really. Even if I pretend not to. *Tschüss.* Oh, and I'll be off the air while I'm there—no mobiles, apparently. So if there's a crisis, ring Paula. Bye-ee.

Hannah, Saturday, 1014: SALVO? Salvo? (*power loss already evident*) Why haven't you … (*power fading fast as she shifts from English into desperate*

Swahili) ... you promised, Salvo! ... oh God ... oh no! (*power gone*)

If I were in the Chat Room or back in the boiler room I would say that either the mike was malfunctioning or that Subject was deliberately keeping her voice below the radar. But the line stays open. There's background noise, a bit of garble, passing footsteps, colliding voices in the corridor outside her room, but no foreground. I therefore conclude that Hannah has let the hand that is holding her cellphone flop to her side while she goes on sobbing her heart out for a further fifty-three seconds until she remembers to switch off. I dial her number and get her voicemail. I dial the hospital. An unfamiliar voice informs me that hospital staff are not permitted to take personal calls during night shift. The bus is filling up. Two women hikers look at me, then at the red nylon sports bag above me in the rack. They decide to sit up front where it's safe.

14

Out of consideration for my slumbering neighbours I ascended the communal staircase quietly, carrying the red nylon sports bag baby-style across my chest in order not to glance it against the bannisters in error. Midsummer Saturdays in Prince of Wales Drive, you never know. Some nights it's high-jinks till all hours, with Penelope, if she's in, bawling out the police on the telephone and threatening to run a story in her paper about too few coppers on the beat. Other nights, what with the schools on holiday and the bomb scares and everyone having second homes these days, all you hear as you approach the entrance to Norfolk Mansions is your own footfall on the pavement, plus the Apache-like hoot of owls in Battersea Park. For the moment, however, there was only the one sound that was of any concern to me, which was Hannah's heartbroken voice choking out its accusations.

As usual the front door lock rejected me, which I tonight considered symbolic. As usual I had to pull the key back, fidget it and try again. Once inside the hall, I felt like my own ghost. Nothing had changed since I died. The lights were on, well, they would be. I had left them on when I dropped by to fling on my dinner jacket, and Penelope hadn't been back since. Pulling off the hated shoes, I was drawn to a blotched engraving of Tintagel Castle that for five years had hung unremarked in the gloomiest recess. Penelope's sister had given it to us for a wedding present. The sisters hated each other. Neither had any connection with Tintagel. They had never been there, didn't want to go. Some gifts say it all.

In the marital bedroom as was, I threw off my pris-oner's garb and with sensations of distaste and liberation consigned it to the laundry basket. For good measure I tossed my rolled-up dinner jacket after it. Perhaps Thorne the Horn would think it worth going on a diet for. Fetching my shaving kit from the bathroom, I confirmed with perverse satisfaction that the blue sponge-bag with the teddy-bear in which Penelope kept what she archly called her Press Kit was still missing from its shelf: just what every girl needs for a weekend with a flock of high-flying advertisers in Sussex.

Back in the bedroom I emptied my stolen goods onto the bed, by which I mean the tapes and notepads and, obsessively tidy as I am, worried how best to dispose of Mr Anderson's plastic night-bag until I remembered the wastebin in the kitchen. I was about to chuck Brian Sinclair's visiting cards after it, but decided for no reason I remember to keep them for what Aunt Imelda called a rainy day. I then put on the clothes of a free man: jeans, trainers, and a pre-Penelope leather jacket I had bought for myself on my first graduation. As a crowning glory, I added my navy-blue, woollen bobble hat which she had banned as too Afro.

I recount these actions in linear detail because as I performed them I was conscious of ceremony. Each movement I made was another step towards Hannah in the rash hope that she would have me, which I considered open to doubt. Each item hand-selected from my chest of drawers was part of the going-away wardrobe that would accompany me into my new life. From the hall I fetched my Antler Tronic Medium Roller-Case with integrated combination lock and adjustable towing handle, once a treasured possession to adorn a meaningless existence. First into it went the tapes and notepads which I wrapped in an old shirt before stowing them in an interior compartment. Moving methodically round the flat, and cutting off at source all nostalgic tugs, I swept up my laptop and attachments, but no printer on account of space, my two tape recorders, the one pocket-sized, the other desk-sized, both in robust carrying cases, plus two sets of earphones and my little transistor radio. To these I added my father's life-stained missal, Brother Michael's hortatory letters from his deathbed, a gold locket containing a spray of Aunt Imelda's untameable mop of white hair, a folder of personal correspondence including Lord Brinkley's letter to me and his Christmas cards, and the sturdy cloth shoulder-bag that had carried home the ingredients for my *coq au vin*.

From the desk in the bay window I extracted a wax-sealed envelope marked BRUNO'S COPY containing the pre-nuptial agreement drafted by Penelope's far-sighted father to cover precisely this moment. I had always recognised that he had a more realistic view of our marriage than I did. As solemnly as if I was laying a wreath at the Cenotaph, I set the twice-signed agreement on Penelope's pillow, removed the wedding ring from the third finger of my left hand and positioned it plumb centre. With this ring I thee unwed. If I felt anything, it was neither bitterness nor anger but completion. An awakening that had begun long before the little gentleman's outburst in the trattoria had reached its only possible conclusion. I had married Penelope for the person she didn't want to be: a fearless champion of our great British press, my faithful and enduring lover forsaking all others, my lifestyle instructor and the mother of my future children and, in my lowest moments, my own white mother-substitute. Penelope for her part had married the exotic in me, only to discover the conformist, which must have been a major disappointment to her. In that regard she had my heartfelt sympathy. I left no note.

Snapping my Roller-Case shut and refusing to take a last look round, I set course down the passage towards the front door and freedom. As I did so I heard the lock turning without its usual impediment, and a pair of lightweight feet enter the hall. My immediate reaction was fear. Not of Penelope personally, because that was over. Fear of having to put into words what I had already put into action. Fear of delay, of loss of impetus, of precious time wasted in argument. Fear that Penelope's fling with Thorne had come to grief and she would be returning home in search of consolation, instead of which she was going to suffer another humiliating rejection, and from a quarter she regarded as incapable of credible resistance: me. I was therefore relieved to encounter not Penelope standing in front of me with her hand on her hip but our neighbour and psychological consultant Paula, wearing a raincoat and, as far as I could determine, nothing else.

'Hannibal *heard* you, Salvo,' she said.

Paula's voice is mid-Atlantic monotone, a kind of permanent mope. Hannibal is her rescue greyhound.

'When pretty boys go sneaking around trying to be quiet, Hannibal hears them,' she continued gloomily. 'Where are you going, for fuck's sake? You look wild.'

'Work,' I said. 'Late call. It's urgent. Sorry, Paula. Got to go.'

'In those clothes? Tell me another. You need a drink. Got a bottle?'

'Well, not *on* me, if you know what I mean'—joke.

'Maybe *I* have for once. Got a bed too, if that's what you're looking for. You never thought I fucked, did you? You thought I warmed my ass at your fires. Penelope doesn't live here any more, Salvo. The person who lives here is token Penelope.'

'Paula, please. I've got to go.'

'The real Penelope is an insecure, overcompensating bitch who does action for doubt. She's also psychopathic and delusional and my dearest friend. Why don't you attend my Inner Body Experience group? We talk a lot about women like Penelope. You could aspire to a higher level of thought. What's the job?'

'Hospital.'

'With that suitcase? Where's the hospital—Hong Kong?'

'Paula, please. I'm in a hurry.'

'How about fuck first, *then* go to hospital?'

'No. Sorry.'

'Hospital then fuck?'—still hopeful. 'Penelope says you do a great job.'

'Thanks but no.'

She stepped aside, and I slipped gratefully past her down the communal staircase. At any other time I would have marvelled that our in-house supplier of life's verities and recipient of countless bottles of my Rioja should so effortlessly have crossed the line from guru to nymphomaniac, but not tonight.

* * *

I took up my position on a park bench opposite the main doors of the hospital at approximately 0700 hours by Aunt Imelda's watch, aware though I was from my discreet enquiries of Reception that night staff did not stand down till 0830 earliest. A brutalist modern sculpture lay in my line of sight, enabling me to observe without being observed. To either side of the glass entrance stood a uniformed representative of one of Britain's ever-multiplying private militias. *Zulus and Ovambos*, I hear Maxie say proudly. *Best fighters in the world*. At a basement-level carport, a procession of white ambulances unloaded their wounded. Beside me on the bench lay the cloth bag to which I had transferred my tapes and notepads. Conscious of my fragile grasp on life, I had looped the shoulder strap round my wrist.

I was super-awake and half asleep. Finding a bed at midnight in the bombing season when you are a *zebra* and lugging a large suitcase is no easy task. I therefore considered myself fortunate indeed when a friendly police officer, having pulled alongside to take a closer look at me, directed me to a floodlit mock-Tudor boarding house off Kilburn High Road that in the words of its cricket-loving owner Mr Hakim was open to all skins at all hours provided they played the game. For cash up front—Maxie's dollars, converted into sterling—I had become the instant tenant of the Executive Suite, a commodious double bedroom at the rear of the house plus kitchenette and bay window overlooking a pocket-sized vegetable garden.

It was by now past three in the morning but sleep does not come naturally to a man determined to reconnect with the woman of his life. Mr Hakim's ample wife had scarcely closed the door on me than I was prowling the room with earphones on, tape recorder in hand.

And S did indeed stand for *satellite*. And Philip had made copious use of it. He had talked to the voice that was empowered to say yes. And the voice that said yes, to my chagrin, belonged to none other than my long-time hero and scourge of Penelope's great newspaper, Lord Brinkley of the Sands, although his tone of righteous indignation gave me grounds for hope. At first he was incredulous:

'Philip, I am simply not hearing you. If I didn't know you better I'd say you were pulling one of Tabby's tricks.'

And when Philip advises him that the deal will otherwise be scuppered:

'It's the most immoral thing I've heard in my life. What's a handshake for, for God's sake? And you say he won't even settle for part now, the rest afterwards? Well he must. Reason with him.'

And when Philip insists they have done all the reasoning they can think of, Brinkley's tone is, to my relief, the very model of injured innocence:

'The boy's off his head. I shall speak to his father. Very well, give him what he asks. It will be strictly on account of future earnings and we shall be actively seeking ways to recover it from day one. Tell him that, Philip, please. I'm disappointed in you, frankly. And in him. If I didn't know you better, I'd be wondering who's doing what to whom.'

* * *

At seventeen minutes past eight a young man in a white overall came fluttering down the hospital steps. He was followed by two grey-habited nuns. At twenty past came a posse of nurses, male and female, mostly black. But somehow I knew that Hannah, though gregarious, wasn't going to be part of a group today. At eight-thirty-three another batch came galloping out. They were a happy crowd and Hannah would have fitted well among them. But not today. At eight-forty she came out alone, walking the crippled walk that afflicts people listening to cellphones. She was in uniform but without her nurse's cap. Hitherto I had only ever seen her in uniform or naked. She was frowning in the studious way she frowned when she was taking Jean-Pierre's pulse, or making love to me. Reaching the bottom step, she stopped dead, ignoring those who were obliged to walk round her on their way up or down, which for a woman so considerate of others might have been surprising, but not to me.

She stood still, glowering in reproof at her cellphone. I half expected her to shake it or throw it away in disgust. Eventually she jammed it back to her ear, tilting her long neck to meet it, and I knew she was listening to the last of my eight messages transmitted through the small hours of today. As her head lifted, the hand holding the cellphone flopped to her side and I guessed that she had once again forgotten to switch it off. By the time I reached her she was starting to laugh, but as I grabbed hold of her the laughter turned to tears. And in the cab she did a bit more crying, then a bit of laughing, which was what I was doing too, all the way to Mr Hakim's boarding house. But there, as is the way of serious lovers, a mutual reserve overtook us, obliging us to release each other, and walk separately across the gravel forecourt. We both knew that explanations were owed, and that our journey into one another's arms should be a considered one. With due formality therefore, I drew back the door to the bedroom and stepped aside, inviting her to enter of her own free will rather than at my behest, which after a fractional hesitation she elected to do. I followed her in and dropped the latch, but seeing that her arms remained firmly at her side I resisted the impulse to embrace her.

I will however add that her eyes had not for one second left mine. There was nothing of accusation or hostility in them. It was more a prolonged study-visit they were paying, which made me wonder how much she saw of the turmoil buried in them, because this was a woman who spent her days tending men in dire straits, and therefore knew her way round our faces. Her inspection of me complete, she took my hand and led me on a tour of the room, the apparent purpose of which was to link me to my possessions: Aunt Imelda's locket, my father's missal, et cetera and—because a degree nurse doesn't miss a trick where her patient is concerned—the vacant nearly-white mark on the third finger of my left hand. After which, by osmosis as it seemed to me, she picked up one of my four notepads—

number three, as it happened, devoted to Maxie's war plan—and, much as Philip had done only sixteen hours earlier, demanded explanations which I was hesitant to supply, given that my strategy for her indoctrination required sophisticated preparation, in accordance with the best principles of tradecraft.

'And *this*?' she insisted, pointing unerringly at one of my more intricate hieroglyphics.

'Kivu.'

'You have been talking about *Kivu*?'

'All weekend. Well, my clients have, put it that way.'

'Positively?'

'Well, creatively, put it that way.'

I had planted the seeds, if ineptly. After a silence, she gave a sad smile. 'Who can be creative about Kivu these days? Maybe nobody. But according to Baptiste, wounds are beginning to heal. If we can keep going that way, perhaps Congo will one day have children who don't know war. Kinshasa is even talking seriously about holding elections, at last.'

'Baptiste?'

She seemed at first not to hear me, so absorbed was she in my cuneiform. 'Baptiste is the Mwangaza's unofficial representative in London,' she replied, handing me back my notepad.

I was still pondering the existence of a Baptiste in her life when she let out a cry of alarm, the first and last I ever heard from her. She was holding up Maxie's envelope containing the six thousand dollars in bills that I had not yet changed into sterling, and the accusation in her face was clear to read.

'Hannah, it's not stolen. It's earned. By me. Honestly.'

'Honestly?'

'Well, legally, anyway. It's money given me by'—I was about to say 'the British Government' but for the sake of Mr Anderson changed my mind—'the clients I've been working for over the weekend.' If I had allayed her suspicions, they were reignited by the sight of Brian Sinclair's visiting cards which I had left lying on the mantelpiece. 'Brian's a friend of mine,' I assured her with mistaken guile. 'Somebody we both know, actually. I'll tell you all about him later.'

I saw at a glance that I was failing to persuade her and was half deciding to pour out the whole story to her then and there—Mr Anderson, the island, Philip, Maxie, Haj, Anton, Benny, Spider, and ten times Haj—but a pensive fatigue had overtaken her, as if she had heard all she could take of me for one session. So instead of plying me with questions, the weary night nurse stretched herself fully dressed along one side of the bed, and fell into a catnap which was the more surprising for the smile that refused to leave her face. Keen to follow her example, I too closed my eyes, wondering how on earth it was ever going to be possible to explain to her that I was the unwilling accomplice in an armed coup against her country. Baptiste, I repeated to myself. It had not occurred to me that her admiration for the Mwangaza might extend to members of his organisation. Yet despite my fraught condition Nature must have come to my aid, for when I woke, I was still wearing my jeans and shirt, and Hannah was lying naked in my arms.

* * *

I am not a friend of explicit, neither in that regard was Brother Michael. Acts of love, in his opinion, were as private as acts of prayer, and should remain so. Therefore I shall not dwell on the ecstasy of our physical rejoining, which took place in all the frankness of the morning sunlight streaming through the bay window onto the many-coloured counterpane of Mrs Hakim's bed. Hannah *listens* to you. I was not accustomed to people who did that. In my overwrought anticipation I had feared she would be caustic or even incredulous. But that was Penelope, not Hannah. Now and then, it's true—for instance when I was forced to disillusion her about the Mwangaza—a few tears rolled down her cheeks and made blobs on Mrs Hakim's sky-blue pillowcase, but not once did her sympathy or her concern for my predicament desert her. Two days ago, I had marvelled at the delicacy with which she had informed a man that he was dying, and I was determined to emulate it, but I lacked both the skill and the reserve. Once started I gave way to my need to tell her everything at once. The revelation that, albeit in a part-time capacity, I was an indoctrinated employee of the all-powerful British Secret Service took her breath away.

'And you are truly faithful to these people, Salvo?'

I was speaking English, so she was too.

'Hannah, I have always tried to be. And shall do my best to continue so,' I replied, and even this she seemed to understand.

Curled round me like a sleepy child, she thrilled to my magic journey from attic flat in South Audley Street to gilded palace in Berkeley Square, the helicopter ride and mystery flight to a no-name island in the north. Introducing her to our warlords, I watched her face pass through three seasons in as many minutes: dark anger at the rascally Franco with his lame leg and love of battle, followed by knowing sadness for the Aids-stricken Dieudonné. It was only when I presented my preliminary sketch of the outrageous Haj, our French-trained Bukavu wide-boy and nightclub owner, that I encountered Pentecostal Mission girl, and was suitably redressed.

'Nightclub owners are crooks, Salvo. Haj will be no different. He sells beer and minerals, so probably he sells drugs and women also. That is how the young élite of Kivu behave today. They wear dark glasses and drive flashy four-tracks and watch pornographic movies with their friends. His father Luc has quite a bad name in Goma, I don't mind telling you. A big man who plays politics for personal gain, not at all for the People.' But then her brow puckered as she reluctantly modified her verdict. 'However, one must also accept that today in Congo it is not possible to make money without being a crook. One must admire his acumen at least.'

Observing my expression, she broke off, and again studied me thoughtfully. And when Hannah does that, it is not easy to preserve one's Personal Security. 'You have a special voice for this Haj. Do you also have special feelings for him?'

'I had special feelings for them all,' I replied evasively.

'Then why is Haj different? Because he is Westernised?'

'I let him down.'

'How, Salvo? I don't believe you. Maybe you let yourself down. That's not the same.'

'They tortured him.'

'Haj?'

'With an electric prod. He screamed. Then he told them everything they wanted to know. Then he sold himself.'

She closed her eyes and opened them. 'And you listened?'

'I wasn't meant to. I just did.'

'And you recorded him?'

'They did.'

'While he was being tortured?'

'It was archive tape. Archival, not operational.'

'And we have it?' She jumped from the bed and marched to the table in the window bay. 'This one?'

'No.'

'This one?' Seeing my face, she quietly laid the tape back on the table, returned to the bed and sat beside me. 'We need food. When we have eaten, we'll play the tape. Okay?'

Okay, I said.

But before food, she needed normal day clothes, which she would have to fetch from the hostel, so I lay alone with my thoughts for an hour. She'll never come back. She's decided I'm mad and she's right. She's gone to Baptiste. Those footsteps tripping up the stairs aren't Hannah's, they're Mrs Hakim's. But Mrs Hakim weighs a good thirteen stone, while Hannah is a sylph.

* * *

She is telling me about her son Noah. She is eating pizza with one hand and holding mine with the other while she talks to me in Swahili about Noah. The first time we were together she had spoken shyly of him. Now she must tell me everything, how he happened, what he means to her. Noah is her love-child—except, Salvo, believe me, there was no love, none at all.

'When my father sent me from Kivu to Uganda to be trained as a nurse, I fell for a medical student. When I became pregnant by him, he told me he was married. He told another girl he slept with that he was gay.'

She was sixteen years old and instead of her belly filling up with baby she lost a stone before she found the courage to take an HIV test. She tested negative. Today if she needs to do something unpleasant, she does it immediately in order to reduce the waiting time. She bore the baby and her aunt helped her look after it while she completed her training. All the medical students and young doctors wanted to sleep with her but she never slept with another man until me.

She breaks out laughing. 'And look at you, Salvo! You are married too!'

No longer, I say.

She laughs and shakes her head and takes a sip of the house red wine that, we have already agreed, is the lousiest wine we ever drank in our lives—worse than the stuff they force on us at the hospital's annual dance, she says, which is saying something, believe me, Salvo. But not as bad as Giancarlo's weapons-grade Chianti, I counter, and take time out to tell her about the brave little gentleman at the Trattoria Bella Vista in Battersea Park Road.

Two years after Noah's birth, Hannah completed her training. She rose to senior nurse, taught herself English and went to church three times a week. Do you still do that, Hannah? A little bit. The young doctors say God is not compatible with science, and in the wards, if she is frank, she sees little sign of Him. But this doesn't stop her praying for Noah, for her family and for Kivu, or helping out with her Sunday School kids, as she calls them, at the church in North London where, with the little faith remaining to her, she goes to worship.

Hannah is proud of being a Nande, and she has every right to be, since the Nande are celebrated for their enterprise. She came to England through an agency when she was twenty-three, she tells me over the coffee and another glass of the terrible red wine. She has told me this before, but in the game we are playing if you drop out you go back to the beginning. The English weren't bad but the agency treated her like shit, which was the first time I heard her use an obscenity. She had left Noah in Uganda with her aunt, which broke her heart, but with the help of a fortune-teller in Entebbe she had identified her life's destiny, which was to expand her knowledge of Western medical practices and technologies and send money home for Noah. When she has learned enough and saved enough, she will return with him to Kivu.

At first in England she dreamed every night of Noah. Telephoning him upset her until she rationed herself to once a week at cheap rates. The agency never told her she would have to attend adaptation school which took up all her savings, or that she would have to climb the nursing ladder all over again from the bottom up. The Nigerians with whom she was billeted failed to pay the rent, until one day the land-lord threw the whole lot of them onto the street, Hannah included. To gain promotion in the hospital she had to be twice as good as her white competitors, and work twice as hard. But with God's help, or, as I preferred it, by dint of her own heroic efforts, she had prevailed. Twice a week she attends a course on simple surgical procedures in poor countries. She should be there tonight but she will make it up. It is a qualifica-tion she has promised herself she will acquire before reclaiming Noah.

She has left the most important bit till last. She has persuaded Matron to let her take an extra unpaid week of leave, which would also allow her to accompany her Sunday School kids on their two-day outing to the seaside.

'Was it only on account of the Sunday School children that you asked for leave?' I enquire hopefully.

She pooh-poohs the very idea. Take a week's leave on the off-chance that some fly-by-night interpreter will keep his promises? Ridiculous.

We've done coffee and paid the bill out of Maxie's converted dollars. In a minute it will be time to go home to Mr Hakim's. Hannah has helped herself to one of my hands and is examining the palm, thoughtfully tracing its lines with her fingernail.

'Am I going to live for ever?' I ask.

She shakes her head dismissively and goes on examining my captive palm. There were five of them, she murmurs in Swahili. Not nieces really. Cousins. But she thinks of them as her nieces even now. Born to the same aunt who looked after her in Uganda and is currently looking after Noah. They were all the children the aunt had. No sons. They were aged six to sixteen. She recites their names, all Biblical. Her eyes are lowered and she is still talking to my hand and her voice has flattened to a single note. They were walking home along the road. My uncle and the girls, in their best clothes. They had been to church and their heads were full of prayer. My aunt was not well, she had stayed in bed. Some boys came up to them. Interahamwe from across the border in Rwanda, doped out of their minds and looking for entertainment. They accused my uncle of being a Tutsi spy, cut the girls' tendons, raped them, and tossed them into the river, chanting *butter! butter!* while they drowned. It was their way of saying they would make butter out of all Tutsis.

'What did they do to your uncle?' I ask of her averted head.

Tied him to a tree. Made him watch. Left him alive to tell the village.

In some kind of reciprocity, I tell her about my father and the whipping post. I have never told anybody but Brother Michael until now. We walk home and listen to Haj being tortured.

* * *

She sits upright across the room, as far away from me as she can be. She has put on her nurse's official face. Its expression is locked. Haj may scream, Tabizi may rant and taunt him, Benny and Anton do their worst with whatever Spider obligingly ran up for them from his toolbox, but Hannah remains as impassive as a judge with eyes for nobody, least of all for me. When Haj pleads for mercy, her expression is stoical. When he pours scorn on Tabizi and the Mwangaza for cutting their dirty deal with Kinshasa, it barely falters. When Anton and Benny wash him under the shower she emits a muted exclamation of disgust, but this in no way transmits itself to her face. When Philip appears on the scene and starts to talk Haj round with sweet reason, I realise she has been sharing every living second of Haj's agony, just as if she were ministering to him at his bedside. And when Haj demands three million dollars for selling out his country, I expect her to be at the very least indignant, but she merely lowers her eyes and shakes her head in sympathy.

'That poor show-off boy,' she murmurs. 'They killed his spirit.'

At which point, wishing to spare her the final mockery, I am about to switch off the tape, but she stays my hand.

'It's just singing from now on. Haj tries to make it better for himself. He can't,' I explain tenderly.

Nevertheless on her insistence I play the tape to the end, starting with Haj's tour of the Mwangaza's drawing room, and ending with the slap of crocs as he stomps defiantly along the covered way to the guest suite.

'Again,' she orders.

So I play it again, after which for a long time she sits motionless.

'He's dragging one foot, you heard that? Maybe they damaged his heart.'

No, Hannah, I hadn't noticed him dragging his foot. I switch off the tape but she doesn't stir.

'Do you know that song?' she demands.

'It's like all the songs we sang.'

'So why did he sing it?'

'To cheer himself up, I suppose.'

'Maybe it's you he's cheering up.'

'Maybe it is,' I concede.

* * *

Hannah is practical. When she has a problem to solve she makes for the root of it and works her way from there. I have Brother Michael, she has her Sister Imogène. At her Mission school Imogène taught her everything she knew. When she was pregnant in Uganda, Imogène sent her letters of comfort. Imogène's Law, never to be forgotten in Hannah's view, argues that since no problem exists in isolation, we must first reduce it to its basic components, then tackle each component in turn. Only when we have truly done this—and not until—will God point us the right way. Given that this was Hannah's *modus operandi*, both in her work and in her life at large, I could not object to the somewhat bald interrogation to which, with all due gentleness and occasional reassuring caresses, she now subjected me, using French as our language of clarity.

'How and when did you steal the tapes and notepads, Salvo?'

I describe my final descent to the boiler room, Philip's surprise appearance, and my narrow escape.

'During the flight back to Luton, did anybody look at you suspiciously or ask you what was in your night-bag?'

Nobody.

'You are sure?'

As sure as I can be.

'Who knows by now that you have stolen the tapes?'

I hesitate. If Philip decided to return to the boiler room after the team's departure and take a second look inside the burn-bag, they know. If Spider, on his arrival in England, checked his tapes before handing them over for archival purposes, they know. Or if whoever he handed them over to decided to check them for themselves, they know. I'm not sure why I adopted a patronising tone at this point, but it was probably in self-defence.

'However,' I insist, resorting to the style of the long-winded barristers I am occasionally obliged to render, 'whether or not they know, there is little doubt that *technically* I am in serious breach of the Official Secrets Act. Or am I? I mean how *official* are these secrets? If I myself am deniable, then so presumably are the secrets. How can an interpreter who doesn't exist be accused of stealing secrets that don't exist when he's acting on behalf of a no-name Syndicate which, by its own insistence, doesn't exist either?'

But Hannah, as I might have guessed, is less impressed than I am by my courtroom oratory.

'Salvo. You have robbed powerful employers of something that is precious to them. The question is whether they will find out, and if they catch you, what will they do to you? You said they will attack Bukavu in two weeks. How do you know this?'

'Maxie told me. On the plane home. It's about taking the airport. Saturday's a football day. The white mercenaries will arrive by Swiss charter, the black mercenaries will pretend to be a visiting football team.'

'So now we have not two weeks but thirteen days.'

'Yes.'

'And not certainly but possibly, you are a wanted man.'

'I suppose I am.'

'Then we must go to Baptiste.'

She takes me in her arms and for a time we forget everything but one another.

* * *

We are lying on our backs, both staring at the ceiling, and she is telling me about Baptiste. He is a Congolese nationalist who is passionate for a united Kivu and has recently returned from Washington where he was attending a study forum on African consciousness. The Rwandans have sent their thugs several times to track him down and kill him but he is so smart that he has always outwitted them. He knows all the Congolese groups including the bad ones. In Europe, in America, and in Kinshasa.

'Kinshasa where the fatcats come from,' I suggest.

'Yes, Salvo. Where the fatcats come from. Also many good and serious people like Baptiste who care about the Eastern Congo and are prepared to take risks to protect us from our enemies and exploiters.'

I want to agree unconditionally with everything she says. I want to be as Congolese as she is. But the rat of jealousy, as Brother Michael used to call it, is gnawing at my entrails.

'So even though we know that the Mwangaza has cut a dirty deal in Kinshasa,' I suggest, 'or Tabizi has, or his people have, you still think it's safe to go to the Mwangaza's representative here in London and blow the whole story to him? You trust him that much.'

She lifts herself onto her side and stares down at me.

'Yes, Salvo. I trust him that much. If Baptiste hears what we have heard and decides that the Mwangaza is corrupt, which I do not yet believe, then Baptiste, because he is honourable and dreams of peace for all Kivu as we do, will know who to warn and how to prevent the catastrophe that is round the corner.'

She flops back and we resume our study of Mrs Hakim's ceiling. I ask the inevitable question: how did she meet him?

'It was his group who organised the coach trip to Birmingham. He is Shi as the Mwangaza is, so it was natural that he saw the Mwangaza as the coming man. But that does not blind him to the Mwangaza's frailties.'

Of course not, I assure her.

'And at the last minute, just before our coach departed, completely unexpectedly he jumped aboard and gave an impressive address on the prospects of peace and inclusiveness for all Kivu.'

To you personally? I ask.

'Yes, Salvo. To me personally. Out of thirty-six people in the coach, he spoke only to me. And I was completely naked.'

* * *

Her first objection to my preferred champion, Lord Brinkley, was so absolute that it smacked to me of Sister Imogène's fundamentalism.

'But Salvo. If wicked people are dragging us into war and stealing our resources, how can there be grades of guilt among them? Surely each one is as evil as the next, since all are complicit in the same act?'

'But Brinkley's not like the others,' I replied patiently. 'He's a figurehead like the Mwangaza. He's the kind of man the others march behind when they want to do their thieving.'

'He is also the man who was able to say yes.'

'That's right. And he's the man who expressed his shock and moral outrage, if you remember. And practically accused Philip of double-dealing while he was about it.' And as a clincher: 'If he's the man who can pick up the phone and say yes, he can also pick it up and say no.'

Pressing my case harder, I drew on my wide experience of the corporate world. How often had I not observed, I said, that men at the helm were unaware of what was being done in their name, so preoccupied were they with raising funds and watching the market? And gradually she began nodding her acceptance, in the knowledge that there were after all areas of life where my grasp exceeded hers. Piling on the arguments, I reminded her of my exchange with Brinkley at the house in Berkeley Square: 'And what happened when I mentioned Mr Anderson's name to him? He hadn't even heard of him!' I ended, and then waited for her response, which I sincerely hoped would not include any further advocacy for Baptiste. Finally I showed her my letter, thanking me for my support: *Dear Bruno*, signed, *Yours ever, Jack*. Even then she didn't totally give up:

'If the Syndicate is so anonymous, how can they use Brinkley as a figurehead?' And because I had no good answer ready: 'If you must go to one of your own, at least go to Mr Anderson whom you trust. Tell him your story and place yourself at his mercy.'

But I was able once more to outmanoeuvre her, this time with my knowledge of the secret world. 'Anderson washed his hands of me before I ever left his safe flat. The operation was deniable, *I* was deniable. Do you think he's going to un-deny me when I walk in and tell him the whole thing was a scam?'

Side by side before my laptop, we went to work. Lord Brinkley's website was reticent about where he lived. Those who wished to write should do so care of the House of Lords. My Brinkley press cuttings came into their own. Jack was married to one Lady Kitty, an aristocratic heiress involved in good works on behalf of Britain's needy, which naturally commended her to

Hannah. And Lady Kitty had a website. On it were listed the charities that enjoyed her patronage, plus the address to which donors could send their cheques, plus a notification of her Thursday coffee morning *At Homes* to which benefactors were invited by prior arrangement only. *At Home* being Knightsbridge, the heart of London's golden triangle.

* * *

It is an hour later. I lie awake, my head super-clear. Hannah, trained to sleep whenever she is able, does not stir. Silently pulling on my shirt and trousers, I take my cellphone and descend to the guest lounge, where Mrs Hakim is clearing away breakfast. After the mandatory exchange of commonplaces, I escape to the little garden which lies in a canyon among tall brown buildings. Printed into me is a running awareness of what our One-Day trainers would term Penelope's *trade routes*. After her torrid weekend with Thorne, she will be putting in at Norfolk Mansions for a morning refit before embarking on the rigours of the week. Her best telephoning is done from taxis paid for by her paper. Like all good journalists, she has thought a lot about her opening line.

And fuck you too, Salvo darling! If you'd waited another week I could have spared you the bother! I won't enquire where you spent your weekend after making a laughing-stock of me in front of

the proprietor. I just hope she's worth it, Salvo.
Or should I be saying he? Fergus says he's afraid
to go into the same loo with you …

I returned to the bedroom. Hannah lay as I had left her.
In the summer's heat, the bed-sheet was draped like a
painter's veil across one breast and between her thighs.

'Where were you?'
'In the garden. Getting divorced.'

Hannah in her firm-minded way had convinced me that I should not take the tapes and notepads with me into the Brinkley house. And since she was equally determined to see me to the front door and wait outside till I emerged, we reached a compromise whereby she would sit with my stolen goods in a nearby corner café, and I would call her on my cellphone when I judged the moment right, whereupon she would drop them in unattributably at the front door and return to the café to wait for me.

It was five o'clock of the Monday evening before we emerged from Mr Hakim's emporium and with due circumspection boarded a bus to Finchley Road tube station. It was six before we were scanning the finely curved Knightsbridge terrace from the pavement across the road, and twenty past by the time I had settled Hannah at a window table in the café. On the bus journey she had undergone a loss of confidence, in contrast to my own mood, which was increasingly upbeat.

'A couple of hours from now, our troubles will be over,' I assured her, massaging her back in an effort to relax her, but her only response was to say she proposed to pray for me.

Approaching the target house, I was offered the choice of descending to a basement marked TRADE or mounting the steps to a pillared doorway boasting an old-style bell pull. I chose the latter. The door was opened by a plump-faced Latino woman in a black uniform, complete with white collar and pinny.

'I'd like to speak to Lord Brinkley, please,' I said, summoning the imperious tone of my more upmarket clients.

'He office.'

'How about Lady Kitty?' I asked, staying the door with one hand and with the other extracting the Brian Sinclair card. Beneath my alias, I had written BRUNO SALVADOR. And on the back, the words SYNDICATE INTERPRETER.

'No come,' the maid commanded me and, true to her intention, this time succeeded in slamming the door, only for it to be opened seconds later by Lady Kitty herself.

Ageless as such high-society ladies are, she wore a short skirt, Gucci belt and straight ash-blonde hair. Among the tiers of finest-quality jewellery on her wrists, I identified a tiny Cartier watch in two tones of gold. Her silk-white legs were tipped with Italian shoes of faultless elegance. Her blue eyes appeared permanently startled, as if from some horrific vision.

'You want Brinkley,' she informed me, her gaze flitting in nervous looks between my card and my face as if she was doing my portrait.

'I've been doing some rather important work for him over the weekend,' I explained, and broke off, uncertain how much she was cleared for.

'*This* weekend?'

'I need to talk to him. It's a personal matter.'

'Couldn't you have rung?' she enquired, eyes even more startled than before.

'I'm afraid not.' I fell back on the Official Secrets Act. 'It wouldn't have been prudent—*secure*,' I explained, with innuendo. 'Not on the telephone. We're not allowed to.'

'*We?*'

'The people who've been working for Lord Brinkley.'

We ascended to a long drawing room with high red walls and gilt mirrors and the smell of Aunt Imelda's Willowbrook: pot pourri and honey.

'I'll put you in here,' she announced, showing me a smaller room that was a replica of the first. 'He should be home by now. Can I fix you a drink? You *are* good. Then read his newspaper or something.'

Left alone, I made a discreet optical reconnaissance of my surroundings. One antique bombé desk, locked. Photographs of Etonian sons and Central African leaders. A resplendent Maréchal Mobutu in uniform: *Pour Jacques, mon ami fidèle, 1980*. The door opened. Lady Kitty strode to a sideboard and extracted a frosted silver cocktail shaker and one glass.

'That common little secretary of his,' she complained, mimicking a proletarian accent: '"Jack's in a meeting, *Kitty*." *God*, I hate them. What's the point of being a peer if everybody calls you Jack? You can't tell them or they take you to a tribunal.' She arranged herself carefully on the arm of a sofa and crossed her legs. 'I told her it's a crisis. Is it?'

'Not if we can catch it in time,' I replied consolingly.

'Oh we shall. Brinkley's frightfully good at all that. Catch anything any time. Who's Maxie?'

There are occasions in a part-time secret agent's life when only the lie direct will suffice.

'I've never heard of Maxie.'

'Of course you have, or you wouldn't be putting on that silly frown. Well, I've got my shirt riding on him, whether you've heard of him or not.' She plucked meditatively at the bosom of her designer blouse. 'Such as it is, poor thing. Are you married, Bruno?'

Go for another forthright denial? Or remain as close to the truth as security permits?

'I am indeed'—to Hannah, not Penelope.

'And have you simply oodles of marvellous babies?'

'I'm afraid not yet'—apart from Noah.

'But you will. In the fullness of time. You're trying day and night. Does the wife *work*?'

'She certainly does.'

'Hard?'

'Very.'

'Poor her. Did she manage to come with you this weekend, while you were devilling for Brinkley?'

'We weren't really having that sort of weekend,' I replied, forcing away images of Hannah seated naked beside me in the boiler room.

'Was Philip there?'

'Philip?'

'Yes, Philip. Don't be arch.'

'I'm afraid I don't know a Philip.'

'Of course you do. He's your Mr Big. Brinkley eats out of his hand.'

Which is precisely Brinkley's problem, I thought, grateful to have my expectations confirmed.

'And Philip *never* leaves telephone messages. None of you do. "Just say Philip rang," as if there was only one Philip in the whole world. *Now* tell me you don't know him.'

'I've already said I don't.'

'You have and you're blushing, which is sweet. He probably made a pass at you. Brinkley calls him the African Queen. What languages do you interpret?'

'I'm afraid that's something I'm not allowed to say.'

Her gaze had settled on the shoulder-bag that I had placed beside me on the floor.

'What are you toting in there, anyway? Brinkley says we're to search everybody who comes into the house. He's got a battery of CCTVs over the front door and brings his women through the back so that he doesn't catch himself napping.'

'Just my tape recorder,' I said, and held it up to show her.

'What for?'

'In case you haven't got one.'

'*We're in here, darling!*'

She had heard her husband before I had. Bounding to her feet she whisked her glass and the shaker into the sideboard, slammed it shut, squirted something into her mouth from an inhaler in her blouse pocket and, like a guilty schoolgirl, attained the door to the large drawing room in two wide strides.

'His name's *Bruno*,' she declaimed gaily to the approaching footsteps. 'He knows Maxie and Philip and pretends he doesn't, he's married to a hard-working woman and wants babies but not yet, and he's got a tape recorder in case we haven't.'

* * *

My moment of truth was at hand. Lady Kitty had vanished, her husband stood before me, attired in a sharp double-breasted navy pinstripe suit, waisted in the latest thirties fashion. Not a hundred yards away, Hannah was waiting for the summons. I had pre-typed the number of her cellphone into my own. In a matter of minutes, if all went to plan, I would be presenting Jack Brinkley with the evidence that, contrary to whatever he might think, he was about to undo all the good work he had done for Africa over the years. He looked first at me, then carefully round the room, then at me again.

'This yours?' He was holding my business card by one corner as if it was sopping wet.

'Yes, sir.'

'You're Mr *Who* exactly?'

'Sinclair, sir. But only officially. Sinclair was my alias for the weekend. You'll know me better by my real name, Bruno Salvador. We've corresponded.'

I had decided not to mention his Christmas cards because they weren't personalised, but I knew he'd remember my letter of support to him, and clearly he did, because his head lifted and, being a tall man, he did what judges on the bench do: peered down at me over the top of his horn-rimmed spectacles to see what he'd got.

'Well then, let's get rid of that thing first, shall we, Salvador?' he suggested and, having taken my recorder from me and made sure there was no tape in it, gave it back to me, which I remember was the nearest we got to a handshake.

He had unlocked his bombé desk and sat himself sideways to it. He was examining his own letter to me, with the handwritten PS saying how much he hoped we might meet one day, and—since he was at that time a Member of Parliament—what a pity I wasn't living in his constituency, with two exclamation marks, which always made me smile. From the jovial way he read it, it could have been a letter to himself, and one he was happy to receive. And when he'd finished, he didn't stop smiling, but laid it before him on the desk, implying he might need to dip into it later.

'So what's your problem exactly, Salvador?'

'Well, it's your problem, sir, actually, if you'll pardon me. I was just the interpreter.'

'Oh really? Interpreting what?'

'Well, everyone really, sir. Maxie obviously. He doesn't speak anything. Well, English. Philip doesn't speak much Swahili. So I was caught in the crossfire, so to speak. Juggling the whole thing. Above and below the waterline.'

I smiled deprecatingly to myself, because I rather hoped that by now he'd have received some word of my achievements on his behalf, which when you put them end to end were considerable, whether or not I'd ended up on the wrong side of the fence, which was what I wanted to explain to him as part of my personal rehabilitation in his eyes.

'*Waterline?* What waterline?'

'It was Maxie's expression, actually, sir. Not mine. For when I was in the boiler room. Listening in to the delegates' conversations while they recessed. Maxie had a man called Spider.' I paused in case the name rang a bell, but apparently it didn't. 'Spider was this professional eavesdropper. He had a lot of antiquated equipment he'd cobbled together at the last minute. A sort of DIY kit. But I don't expect you were aware of that either.'

'Aware of *what* exactly?'

I began again. There was no point in holding back. It was even worse than I feared. Philip hadn't told him a fraction of the story.

'The whole island was bugged, sir. Even the gazebo on the hilltop was bugged. Whenever Philip reckoned we'd reached a critical moment in negotiations, he'd call a recess, and I'd dive down to the boiler room and listen in, and relay the gist to Sam upstairs so that Philip and Maxie would be ahead of the game next time we convened. And take advice from the Syndicate and Philip's friends over the sat-phone when they needed it. Which was how we focussed on Haj. He did. Philip. Well, with Tabizi's help, I suppose. I was the unwitting instrument.'

'And who is *Haj*, if I may ask?'

It was shocking but true. Exactly as I had predicted, Lord Brinkley had no notion of what had been perpetrated under his aegis—not even in his rôle as the only man who could say *yes*.

'Haj was one of the delegates, sir,' I said, adopting a softer approach. 'There were three. Two militia chiefs—warlords, if you like—and Haj. He's the one who gouged you for an extra three million dollars,' I reminded him, with a rueful smile that he seemed to share: and so he should, given the moral outrage he had expressed so clearly over the satellite telephone.

'The other two chiefs being who?' he enquired, still puzzled.

'Franco, the Mai Mai man, and Dieudonné, who's a Munyamulenge. Haj doesn't have a militia as such, but he can always rustle one up any time he needs one, plus he's got a minerals *comptoir* in Bukavu, and a beer business, and a bunch of hotels and nightclubs, and his father Luc is a big player in Goma. Well, you know that, don't you?'

He was nodding, and smiling in a way that told me we were connecting. In any normal situation, I reckoned, he would by now be pressing a button on his desk and sending for the luckless executive responsible for the cock-up, but since he showed no sign of doing that, but to the contrary had folded his hands together under his chin in the manner of somebody settling down for a good long listen, I decided to take the story from the top, rather as I had done with Hannah, though in a much condensed form and with a lot less concern for the sensibilities of my distinguished audience, and perhaps *too* little, as I began to fear when we approached the devastating moment of truth regarding Haj's maltreatment.

'So where does all this lead us, in your opinion?' he asked, with the same confiding smile. 'What's your bottom line here, Salvador? Do we take it straight to the Prime Minister? The President of the United States? The African Union? Or all of them at once?'

I permitted myself a consoling laugh. 'Oh I don't think that's necessary, sir. I don't think we need take it that far at all, frankly.'

'I'm relieved.'

'I think it's just a case of calling a halt immediately, and making absolutely sure the halt happens. We've got twelve full days before they're due to go in, so there's plenty of time. Stop the war plan, stand the Mwangaza down until he can find proper, ethical supporters—well, like yourself, sir—tear up the contract—'

'There's a *contract*, is there?'

'Oh indeed there is! A really shady one, if I may say so, sir. Drafted by Monsieur Jasper Albin of Besançon—whom you have used in the past, and whom presumably your people decided to use again—and rendered into Swahili by none other than my humble self.'

I was getting a bit carried away by now. I suppose the notion that Hannah and I would any minute be emerging from the shadows and leading normal lives was going to my head.

'Do you happen to have a copy of this contract?'

'No, but I've seen it, obviously. And committed chunks of it to memory, which with me is—well, pretty much automatic, to be frank.'

'And what makes you think it's *shady*?'

'It's fake. Look, I've seen contracts. It's hypothetical. It pretends to be about agriculture but actually it's about supplying weapons and *matériel* to start a small war. But who ever heard of a small war in the Congo? You might as well be a little bit pregnant,' I ventured boldly, quoting Haj, and was encouraged by a knowing smile from my host. 'And the profits—from the minerals, I mean—the People's Portion, so-called—are a straight swindle,' I went on. 'A fraud, frankly. There's nothing in it for the People at all. No People's Portion, no profits for anyone except your Syndicate, the Mwangaza and his henchmen.'

'Terrible,' Lord Brinkley murmured, shaking his head in commiseration.

'I mean, don't get me wrong, sir. The Mwangaza is a great man in many respects. But he's old. Well, old for the job, forgive me. He's already looking like a puppet. And he's compromised himself so much that I just don't see how he can possibly cut free. I'm really sorry, but it's true, sir.'

'Oldest story in the game.'

After which we traded a few examples of African leaders who had shown signs of early greatness, only to go to the bad a few years later, although I privately doubted whether Mobutu, featured on the desk behind him, had ever qualified for this league. It did, however, pass through my mind that if, down the line, Lord Brinkley thought fit to reward me for my timely intervention, and incidentally keep me onside while he was about it, a job in his organisation might be the answer for both of us, because, my goodness, did they need somebody to sweep out that stable!

His next question therefore took me considerably aback.

'And you're quite sure you saw me that night.'

'What night is this, sir?'

'Whenever you say it was. Friday evening, am I right? I lost the thread for a moment. You saw me on Friday evening in Berkeley Square. In a house.'

'Yes.'

'Remember what I was wearing?'

'Smart casual. Fawn slacks, the soft suède jacket, loafers.'

'Remember anything about the house—apart from the number which you didn't get, or you've forgotten?'

'Yes. I do. Everything.'

'Describe it, will you? In your own words.'

I started to, but my head was reeling and I was having difficulty picking out salient features on demand. 'It had this big hall with a split staircase—'

'*Split?*'

'—and eagles over the doors—'

'*Live* eagles?'

'There were all sorts of people there apart from you. Please don't pretend you weren't there, sir. I spoke to you. I thanked you for your stand on Africa!'

'Can you name a few?'

I named them, if not with my usual aplomb. I was brewing up, and when I start to brew up, it's hard to get a grip on myself. The corporate raider known as Admiral Nelson on account of his eyepatch: I got him. The famous TV presenter from the world of pop: I got him too. The belted young nobleman who owns a chunk of the West End. The exiled African former finance minister. The Indian clothing billionaire. The supermarket tycoon who had recently acquired one of our great national dailies 'as a hobby'. I was breaking up but kept trying.

'The man you called *Marcel*, sir!' I shouted. 'The African man you wanted at your side when you made your conference call—'

'Was the Queen there?'

'You mean Philip? The man you call the African Queen? No, he wasn't! But Maxie was. Philip didn't show up till the island.'

I had not intended to raise my voice, but I had, and Lord Brinkley's reaction was to lower his own in counterpoint.

'You go on and on about *Philip* and *Maxie* as if they were these chums of mine,' he complained. 'I've never met them. I've never heard of them. I don't know who you're talking about.'

'Then why don't you ask your fucking wife about them?'

I'd lost it. You can't describe blind anger unless the person you're talking to has experienced it personally. There are physical symptoms. Pins and needles in the lips, giddiness, temporary astigmatism, nausea, and an inability to distinguish colours and objects in the immediate vicinity. Plus, I should add, an uncertainty regarding what you have actually said as opposed to what is boiling up in your mouth but you have failed to expel.

'Kitty!' He had flung open the door and was yelling. 'I've got something to ask my fucking wife. Would you mind joining us a minute?'

*   *   *

Lady Kitty stood sentinel-still. Her blue eyes, devoid of their sparkle, stared straight into her husband's.

'Kitty, darling. Two quickies. Names. I'm going to shoot them at you and I want you to answer straight away, instinctively, before you think. *Maxie.*'

'Never heard of him. Not in a thousand years. Last Max I knew died aeons ago. The only people who called him Maxie were the tradesmen.'

'*Philip.* Our friend here says I call him the African Queen, which I find rather insulting to both of us, frankly.'

She frowned, and ventured a forefinger to her lip. 'Sorry. Can't do a Philip either. There's Philippa Perry-Onslow but she's a girl, or says she is.'

'And while we have you, darling. Last Friday evening—what time was it, did you say?'

'Now,' I replied.

'So seventy-two hours ago if we're going to be precise—Friday, remember, when we normally go to the country, but forget that for a moment, I'm not trying to put thoughts into your head—*where were we?*' He glanced ostentatiously at his watch. 'Seven-ten p.m. Think very hard, please.'

'On our way to Marlborough, of course.'

'For what purpose?'

'For the weekend. What do you think?'

'And would you swear to that in a court of law if necessary? Because we have a young man here—very gifted, very charming, means well, I'm sure—who is under some very serious—some very *dangerous* for all of us—misapprehensions.'

'Of course I would, darling. Don't be silly.'

'And *how* did we go to Marlborough, darling? By what *means*?'

'By car, of course. Brinkley, what *are* you on about?'

'Did Henry drive?'

'You drove. Henry was off.'

'At what time did we leave, would you imagine?'

'Oh darling. You know very well. I had everything packed and ready by three, but you had a late lunch as usual so we hit the *worst* rush-hour traffic in the world, and didn't make the Hall till nine and sups was ruined.'

'And who spent the weekend with us?'

'Gus and Tara, of course. Freeloading, as usual. High time they took us to Wilton's. They always *say* they will, but they actually never *do*,' she explained, turning to me as if I would understand.

I had been cooling down till then, but meeting her expressionless gaze head-on was enough to bring the heat rushing back.

'You were *there*!' I blurted at him. I turned back to his wife: 'I shook his bloody hand, your husband's. Maxie was there too! He thinks he can do good in Kivu but he can't. He's not a schemer, he's a soldier. They were on the island and they planned a proxy war so that the Syndicate could hoover up the coltan market and short-sell it, and they tortured Haj! With a cattle prod that Spider made for them. I can prove it.'

I'd said it, and I couldn't unsay it, but at least I had the wisdom to stop.

'Prove it how?' Brinkley enquired.

'With my notes.'

'What notes?'

I was pulling back. I was remembering Hannah. 'As soon as I got back from the island, I made notes,' I lied. 'I've got perfect recall. Short term. If I'm quick enough, and I've got the verbatims in my head, I can write everything down, word for word. Which is what I did.'

'Where?'

'When I got home. Straight away.'

'Home being where?' His gaze dropped to the letter lying in front of him on his desk: *Dear Bruno.* 'Home being in Battersea. You sat down, and you wrote out everything you remembered, word for word. Marvellous.'

'Everything.'

'Starting when?'

'From Mr Anderson onwards.'

'Onwards to where?'

'Berkeley Square. Battersea Power Station. Luton airport. The island. Back.'

'So it's *your* account of what *you* saw and heard on *your* island, recalled in the tranquillity of *your* Battersea home, several hours later.'

'Yes.'

'I'm sure you're very clever but that is not, I'm afraid, what we would call either *proof* or *evidence*. I happen to be a lawyer. Do you have the notes with you?'

'No.'

'You left them at home perhaps.'

'Probably I did.'

'Probably. But you can put your hands on them, of course, should you ever take it into your head to blackmail me or sell your ridiculous story to the public prints.' He sighed, like a good man who has reached a sad conclusion. 'Well, there we have it, don't we? I'm very sorry for you. You're persuasive, and I'm sure you believe every word you say. But I would warn you to be circumspect before you repeat your allegations outside these four walls. Not everyone will be as lenient as we've been. Either you're a practised criminal of some sort or you need medical help. Probably both.'

'He's married, darling,' Lady Kitty put in helpfully from the wings.

'Have you told your wife?'

I believe I said no.

'Ask him why he brought a tape recorder.'

'Why did you?'

'I always carry one. Other people carry computers. I'm a top interpreter, so I carry a recorder.'

'Without any tapes,' Lady Kitty reminded us.

'I keep them separate,' I said.

There was a moment when I thought Brinkley might tell me to empty my pockets onto the table, in which case I would not have been accountable for my actions, but I believe now that he didn't have the nerve. Passing under Lady Kitty's battery of CCTVs, I would gladly have turned right instead of left, or for that matter hurled myself under the wheels of a convenient oncoming vehicle rather than confess the scale of my folly, anger and humiliation to my beloved Hannah, but fortunately my feet knew better than I did. I was about to enter the café, but she had seen me coming and met me on the doorstep. Even from a distance, my face must have told her all she needed to know. I took back the tapes and notepads. She held my arm in both her hands and steered me down the pavement the way she might have guided a casualty away from the scene of the accident.

*　　*　　*

From a supermarket somewhere we bought lasagne and a fish pie to cook in the Hakims' microwave, plus salad, fruit, bread, cheese, milk, six cans of sardines, tea, and two bottles of Rioja. Hailing a cab, I managed to recall the address of Mr Hakim's hostelry and even gave the driver a street number twenty houses short of our destination. My concern was not for myself but for Hannah. In a mistaken gesture of gallantry, I even went so far as to suggest she resume sleeping at her hostel.

'Good idea, Salvo. I take a beautiful young doctor and leave you to save Kivu.'

But by the time we sat down to our first home-cooked meal together, she had recovered her high spirits.

'You know something?'

'I doubt it.'

'That Lord Brinkley of yours. I think maybe he comes from a pretty bad tribe,' she said, shaking her head and laughing until I had no choice but to do the same.

* * *

It was four-fifteen by Aunt Imelda's watch when she woke me to tell me my cellphone was buzzing on the glass-topped table in the bay window. Having switched it on for my encounter with Lord Brinkley, I had neglected to switch it off when we got home. By the time I reached it, it had put the caller on record.

Penelope: My fucking *flat*, Salvo! The flat *you* deserted, not me. And you have the effrontery, you have the *arse* ... D'you know what I'm going to do? I'm going to have an ASBO served on you. My cupboards. Daddy's desk—*your* fucking desk—the one he gave you—locks smashed—your papers slung all over the room—(*breath*)—my clothes, you fucking pervert, all over my bedroom floor—(*breath*)—Okay. Fergus is on his way round here *now*. So look out. He's no locksmith but he's going to make sure you *never*, *ever*, get into this house again with *my* key. When he's done that, he's going to find out where you are. And if I were you, I'd run like hell. Because Fergus knows people, Salvo, not all of them very nice people. And if you think, for one minute ...

We lay on the bed, puzzling it out backwards. I had left Brinkley's house at seven-twenty. At seven-twenty

and a half or thereabouts he had made the call to Philip
or whoever he made the call to. By seven-thirty Philip
or similar had established that Penelope was launched
on the evening cocktail round. They had further
worked out, if they didn't already know, that there were
blank notepads in Spider's burn-bag purporting to be
mine, and blank tapes nestling in his archive collection
of stolen sound. Where better to look for them than in
the marital home?

* * *

'Salvo?'

An hour of semi-sleep has gone by without either of
us speaking.

'Why does a man who has been tortured sing a
childish song? My patients don't sing songs when
they're in pain.'

'Perhaps he's pleased to have got his confession off
his chest,' Salvo the good Catholic replies.

Unable to sleep, I tiptoe to the bathroom with my
transistor radio and listen through the headphones to the
BBC news on Radio 4. Car bombs in Iraq. Insurgents
kill dozens. But nothing yet about a top interpreter and
part-time British secret agent on the run.

16

'The whole afternoon to find *one man*?' I protest, playing the jealous husband in order to delay her departure. 'What are you going to do with him when you've found him?'

'Salvo, you are being ridiculous again. Baptiste isn't somebody you just call up. The Rwandans are very cunning. He must hide his tracks, even from his supporters. Now let me go, please. I have to be at the church in forty minutes.'

Church is the Bethany Pentecostal Mission church somewhere in the sticks of North London.

'Who are you meeting there?'

'You know very well. My friend Grace and the charity ladies who are paying for our coach and finding accommodation for our Sunday School kids. Now let me go, please.'

She is wearing a pretty pillbox hat with a long-skirted blue dress and bolero made of rough silk. I know its story without her telling me. For a special day like Christmas or her birthday, after she'd paid the rent and sent her aunt the monthly allowance for Noah, she treated herself to a new outfit. She's washed and ironed it a hundred times, and now it's on its last legs.

'And the beautiful young pastor?' I demand severely.

'Is fifty-five years old and married to a lady who never lets him out of her sight.'

I extract a last kiss, beg her forgiveness and extract another. Seconds later she is out of the house, hurrying down the pavement with her skirt swinging while I gaze after her from the window. All through the previous night we have held councils of love and councils of war. Other couples, I trust, do not experience in a lifetime the strains to which our relationship has been subjected in the course of four short days. My entreaties to her to run while there was time, to rid herself of the embarrassment of me, for her own sake, for Noah's, for the sake of her career, et cetera, had fallen on deaf ears. Her destiny was to remain at my side. It was ordained. By God, by a fortune-teller in Entebbe, and by Noah.

'By *Noah*?' I repeat, laughing.

'I have told him I have met his new father and he is very pleased.'

Sometimes I am too English for her, too indirect and withheld. Sometimes she is unreachable, an exiled African woman lost to her memories. My preferred strategy in the wake of the break-in at Norfolk Mansions was to change hiding places at once, get out, start afresh in a new part of town. Hannah did not agree, arguing that if the hue-and-cry was on, an abrupt change in our arrangements would draw attention to us. Better to stay put and act natural, she said. I bowed to her judgment and we had enjoyed a leisurely breakfast with our fellow guests rather than skulking like fugitives in our room. When we were done, she had shooed me upstairs, insisting she needed a private word with Mr Hakim, a shiny, self-admiring man, susceptible to female charms.

'What did you tell him?' I asked when she returned laughing.

'The truth, Salvo. Nothing but the truth. Just not all of it.'

I demanded a full confession. In English.

'I told him we are runaway lovers. Our angry relatives are pursuing us and telling lies about us. We must count on his protection or find another boarding house.'

'And he said?'

'We may stay another month at least, and he will protect us with his life.'

'And will he?'

'For another fifty pounds a week of your Judas money, he will be as brave as a lion. Then his wife came round the door and said she would protect us for nothing. If somebody had only offered her protection when she was young, she said, she would never have married Mr Hakim. They both found that very funny.'

We had discussed the tricky matter of communication, which I knew from the Chat Room to be the clandestine operator's weakest link. Mr Hakim's emporium boasted no public phone. The only house phone was in the kitchen. My cellphone was a deathtrap, I explained to Hannah, drawing on my insider's knowledge. With the technology these days, a live cellphone could reveal my whereabouts anywhere on the planet within seconds. I've seen it, Hannah, I've reaped the dividend, you should hear what I hear on my One-Day Courses. Warming to my subject, I allowed myself a digression into the arts of inserting a deadly missile into a cellphone's radio beam, thereby decapitating the subscriber.

'Well, *my* mobile will not blow you up,' she retorted, extracting a rainbow-coloured version from her compendious carry-bag.

At a stroke, our secret link was established. I would take possession of her cellphone and she would borrow Grace's. If I needed to call Hannah at the church, I could reach her through Grace.

'And *after* church?' I insisted. 'When you are out hunting for Baptiste, how will I contact you then?'

From her closed face I knew I had again encountered the cultural divide. Hannah might not be versed in the dark arts of the Chat Room, but what did Salvo know of London's Congolese community, or where its leading voices went to ground?

'Baptiste returned from the United States a week ago. He has a new address and perhaps a new name also. I shall talk first to Louis.'

Louis being Baptiste's unofficial deputy head of the Middle Path's European bureau, she explained. Also a close friend of Salomé who was a friend of Baptiste's sister Rose in Brussels. But Louis was currently in hiding, so it all depended whether Rose had returned from her nephew's wedding in Kinshasa. If not, it might be possible to talk to Bien-Aimé who was Rose's lover, but not if Bien-Aimé's wife was in town.

I accepted defeat.

*   *   *

I am alone, bereft until tonight. To operate my cell-phone requires, under the strict rules of tradecraft I have imposed on myself following the break-in at Norfolk Mansions, a mile-long walk away from Mr Hakim's house down a tree-lined road to a vacant bus shelter. I take the distance slowly, spreading it out. I sit on a lonely bench, press green and 121 and green again. My one message is from Barney, Mr Anderson's flamboyant adjutant and the Chat Room's in-house Don Juan. From his eagle's nest on the balcony, Barney sees into every audio cubicle, and down every eligible female's blouse. His call is routine. The surprise would be if he hadn't made it, but he has. I play it twice.

Hi, Salv: Where the fuck are you? I tried Battersea and got an earful from Penelope. We've got the usual dross for you. Nothing life-threatening, but give us a bell as soon as you get this message and let us know when you want to swing by. Tschüss.

With his seemingly innocent message, Barney has aroused my deepest suspicions. He is always relaxed, but this morning he is so relaxed I don't trust a word of him. *As soon as you get this message.* Why so soon, if we're talking the usual dross? Or is he, as I suspect, under orders to entice me to the Chat Room where Philip and his henchmen will be waiting to hand me the Haj treatment?

I'm walking again, but in a more sprightly manner. The desire to earn back my colours and hence Hannah's respect after the débâcle with Brinkley is acute. Out of humiliation comes an unexpected ray of inspiration.

Did Hannah herself not advise me to go to Anderson in preference to his Lordship? Well now I will! But on my terms, not Anderson's or Barney's. I, not they, will choose the time, the venue, and the weapon. And when everything is in place, but not until, I will admit Hannah to my plan!

Practical things first. At a mini-market I purchase a copy of the *Guardian* in order to obtain small change. I walk until an isolated phone box beckons. It is constructed of toughened glass, affording the caller all-round surveillance, and it accepts coins. I settle my shoulder-bag between my feet. I clear my throat, shuffle my shoulders to unlock them, and return Barney's call as requested.

'Salv! Get my message? Good man! How about this afternoon's shift and we do a beer afterwards?'

Barney has never in his life proposed a beer, before or afterwards, but I let this go. I am as relaxed as he is.

'Today's a bit tricky for me actually, Barnes. Heavy legal stuff. Boring but they pay a bomb. I could do you something tomorrow, if that's any good. Preferably evening, kind of four till eight.'

I'm fishing, which is what my brilliant plan demands. Barney is fishing and I am fishing. The difference is, he doesn't know I am. This time he is a little slow to answer. Perhaps someone is standing at his shoulder.

'Look, why not now, for fuck's sake?' he demands, abandoning the soft approach which is not his style at the best of times. 'Put the buggers off. A couple of hours won't make any difference to them. We pay you first refusal, don't we? Where are you, anyway?'

He knows very well where I am. It's on his screen, so why does he ask? Is he buying time while he takes more advice?

'In a phone box,' I complain cheerfully. 'My cell-phone's sick.'

We wait again. This is Barney in slow motion.

'Well, get a cab. Put it on expenses. The Boss wants to press you to his bosom. Claims you saved the nation over the weekend, but won't say how.'

My heart does a double somersault. Barney has played into my hands! But I remain calm. I am not impulsive. Mr Anderson would be proud of me.

'The earliest I can make it is tomorrow evening,

Barney,' I say calmly. 'The Boss can press me to his bosom then.'

This time there is no delayed action.

'Are you fucking mad? It's a *Wednesday*, man. Holy Night!'

My heart performs more antics, but I allow no triumphalist note to enter my voice.

'Then it's Thursday or nothing, Barnes. Best I can do for you unless you tell me it's dead urgent, which you say it isn't. Sorry, but there we are.'

I ring off. Sorry for nothing. Tomorrow is Holy Night and legend records that Mr Anderson hasn't missed a Holy Night in twenty years. Philip and his people may be beating on his door, vital notepads have escaped the flames, audio tapes have gone missing. But Wednesday night is Holy Night and Mr Anderson is singing baritone in the Sevenoaks Choral Society.

I am halfway. Repressing the desire to call Hannah immediately on Grace's phone and acquaint her with my stroke of genius, I dial Directory Enquiries and in a matter of seconds am connected with the Arts Correspondent of the *Sevenoaks Argus*. I have this uncle, I explain artfully. He is a leading baritone in the local choral society. Tomorrow is his birthday. Could she very kindly tell me where, and at what time, the Sevenoaks Choral Society meets of a Wednesday evening?

Ah. Well now. She can and she can't. Do I have *any* idea at *all* whether my uncle is *authorised* or *unauthorised*?

I confess I have none.

This pleases her. In Sevenoaks, she explains, we are unusual in having *two* choral societies. The UK-wide SingFest in the Albert Hall is only three weeks off. Both societies are entered, both hotly tipped for a prize.

Perhaps if she could explain the difference between them, I suggest.

She can, but don't quote her. *Authorised* means linked to a respectable church, *preferably* C of E but it doesn't *have* to be. It means having *experienced* teachers *and* conductors, but *not* professionals because you haven't got the money. It means using local talent *only* and *no* invited singers from outside.

And unauthorised?

*Un*authorised, but again don't quote her, means *no* church, or none that any of us has heard of, it means *new* money, it means buy, borrow or steal whoever you can get hold of from outside never mind *what* it costs, it means *no* residential qualifications and *practically* treating a choir like a professional football team. Has she made herself clear?

She has indeed. Mr Anderson has never done anything unauthorised in his life.

Returning to Mr Hakim's boarding house in what Maxie would call tactical bounds, I wasted no time in calling Hannah with every intention of acquainting her with my achievements to date. My call was taken by Grace, who had troublesome news.

'Hannah's real low, Salvo. Those charity folk, they got so many problems, you wonder where they get their charity from.'

When Hannah came on, I barely recognised her voice. She was speaking English.

'If we were just a *little* bit less black, Salvo. If we had some white excuse in our blood somewhere. Not you, you're okay. But we are *shocking*. We are black-black. There's no way round us.' Her voice faltered and recovered. 'We had three kids lodging with a Mrs Lemon. They never met kind Mrs Lemon but they love her, okay?'

'Okay.'

'Two nights in her boarding house at the seaside, that's a dream for them.'

'Of course it is.'

Another pause while she collects herself. 'Mrs Lemon is a *Christian* so she wasn't going to charge. Amelia, she's one of my Sunday School kids. Amelia made a painting of the sun shining on the sea, and the sun was a big smiling lemon, okay?'

'Okay.'

'Well, now Mrs Lemon isn't feeling very well.' Her voice rose in anger as she mimicked Mrs Lemon's voice. ' "It's my heart, dear. I mustn't get upset. Only I didn't know, you see. We thought the children were just deprived." '

Grace takes back her phone, and her voice is as scathing as Hannah's. 'There's a fine café halfway down the road to Bognor. Coaches Welcome. Me and Hannah, we did a deal with this fine café. Thirty chicken nuggets, complimentary meals for the carers and the driver. One soft drink per person. One hundred pounds. Is that fair?'

'Very fair, Grace. Very reasonable, by the sound of it.'

'The driver, he's been takin' groups to that fine café for like fifteen years. School kids, all kinds of kids. Except they're white. When the proprietor realised ours were goin' to be black, he remembered he had a new policy. "It's the pensioners," he tells us. "They come for the quiet, see. That's why we don't take no kids except white ones." '

'You know what, Salvo?' Hannah is back, this time in fighting mood.

'What do I know, my love?'

'Maybe Congo should invade Bognor.'

I laugh, she laughs. Should I tell her of my brilliant plan and risk causing her more anxiety, or keep it for later? Keep it, I tell myself. With Baptiste to worry about, she has enough on her plate already.

My brilliant plan requires paperwork.

For five hours, with no more to sustain me than a chunk of cold lasagne, I go to work on my laptop. Assisted by choice passages from my tapes and notepads which I render where necessary into English, plus an assortment of Philip's verbatims over the satphone, I assemble a damning exposé of the plot that Mr Anderson assured me was in the best interests of our country. Rejecting the traditional *Dear Mr Anderson*,

I open my attack with: *Knowing you as I do to be a man of honour and integrity*. Knowing him also to be a slow reader as well as a meticulous one, with views on plain English, I confine myself to twenty carefully compiled pages, which include as a tailpiece an account of the illegal break-in at Norfolk Mansions. In a final flourish I entitle my completed opus *J'Accuse!* after Émile Zola's spirited defence of Colonel Dreyfus, a saga of moral tenacity beloved of Brother Michael. I make a floppy and hasten downstairs to Mrs Hakim, a computer buff. With the stolen tapes and notepads returned to their hiding place behind our flimsy wardrobe, and my copy of *J'Accuse!* with them, and the floppy for security reasons discreetly smashed and consigned to Mrs Hakim's kitchen bin, I turn on the six o'clock news and am pleased to establish that there are still no unsettling reports of a mad *zebra* on the run.

* * *

I was not impressed by the operational arrangements for our rendezvous with Baptiste, but then neither did I expect to be. Since he refused to reveal his current address, he and Hannah had agreed over my head that she would bring me to Rico's Coffee Parlour in Fleet Street at ten-thirty that night. From there, a no-name comrade-in-arms would conduct us to a no-name meeting-point. My first thought was for the tapes and notepads. To take them with me or leave them in their hiding place? I could not envisage handing them to Baptiste on first acquaintance, but out of loyalty to Hannah I knew I must take them with me.

Given her morning's setback and her afternoon's exertions, I expected to find her in sombre mood but such, to my relief, was not the case. The immediate cause of her good spirits was Noah, with whom she had conducted a lengthy conversation only an hour previously. As usual she had first spoken to her aunt in case there was worrying news ahead, but her aunt had said, 'Let him tell you himself, Hannah,' and put him on the line.

'He is third boy in his class, Salvo, imagine,' she explained, all aglow. 'We spoke English together and his English is really coming on, I was amazed. And yesterday his school football team won the Kampala under-tens and Noah nearly scored a goal.'

I was sharing her euphoria when a mauve BMW with rap music pouring out of every open window screeched to a halt in the street outside. The driver wore dark glasses and a pointed beard like Dieudonné's. The burly African man beside him reminded me of Franco. We jumped aboard, the driver slammed his foot down. With erratic twists, we raced southward with precious little regard to traffic lights or bus lanes. We bumped across a pot-holed industrial wasteland of tyre dumps, and swerved to avoid a trio of kids stacked on a wheel-chair who came careering out of a side turning with their arms out like acrobats. We pulled up and the driver shouted, '*Now.*' The BMW made a three-point turn and roared away, leaving us standing in a reeking cobbled alley. Above the Victorian chimneys, giant cranes like giraffes peered down at us from the orange night sky. Two African men sauntered towards us. The taller wore a silky frock-coat and a lot of gold.

'This the guy with no name?' he demanded of Hannah in Congolese Swahili.

You speak English only, Salvo, she had warned me. *Anyone who speaks our languages is too interesting.* In return, I had extracted an agreement from her that, for the purposes of our interview, we were acquaintances not lovers. Her involvement in these events was of my own making. I was determined to keep her distant from them wherever possible.

'What's in the bag?' the shorter man asked, also in Swahili.

'It's private for Baptiste,' Hannah retorted.

The taller man advanced on me and with slender fingers sampled the weight and contents of my shoulder-bag, but didn't open it. With his colleague bringing up the rear, we followed him up a stone staircase into the house, to be greeted by more rap music. In a neon-lit café, elderly Africans in hats were watching a Congolese band playing its heart out on an industrial-sized plasma television screen. The men were drinking beer, the women juice. At separate tables, boys in hoods talked head to head. We climbed a staircase and entered a parlour of chintz sofas, flock wallpaper and rugs of nylon leopard skin. On the wall hung a photograph of an African family in Sunday best. The mother and father stood at the centre, their seven children in descending sizes to either side of them. We sat down, Hannah on the sofa, I on a chair opposite her. The tall man hovered at the door, tapping his foot to the beat of the music from the café beneath.

'You want a soft drink or something? Coke or something?'

I shook my head.

'Her?'

A quiet car was pulling up in the street outside. We heard the double clunk of an expensive car door opening and closing, and footsteps coming up the stairs. Baptiste was a Haj without the grace. He was sleek, hollow-featured and long-limbed. He was designer-dressed in Ray-Ban sunglasses, buckskin jacket, gold necklaces and Texan boots embroidered with cowboy hats. There was an air of the unreal about him, as if not only the clothes but the body inside them had been newly bought. He wore a gold Rolex on his right wrist. On catching sight of him, Hannah leaped to her feet in joy and cried his name. Without answering, he pulled off his jacket, slung it over a chair, and murmured, 'Blow,' to our guide, who vanished down the stairs. He placed himself pelvis forward and feet astride and held out his hands, inviting Hannah to embrace him. Which after a moment's puzzlement she did, then broke out laughing.

'Whatever did America do to you, Baptiste?' she protested, in the English we had agreed upon. 'You are so—' she hunted for the word—'so *rich* suddenly!'

To which, still without a word, he kissed her in what I considered an excessively proprietorial manner, left cheek, right cheek, then her left cheek a second time while he took the measure of me.

*   *   *

Hannah had resumed her place on the sofa. I sat opposite her, my shoulder-bag at my side. Baptiste, more relaxed than either of us, had slumped himself in a brocade armchair with his knees spread towards Hannah, as if proposing to enfold her between them.

'So what's the headache?' he demanded, thumbs Blair–Bush style jammed into his Gucci belt.

I proceeded cautiously, fully conscious that my first duty was to prepare him for the shock I was about to inflict on him. As gently as I could—and in hindsight, I admit, with a touch of Anderson-like verbosity—I advised him that what I had to tell him was likely to upset certain loyalties he had, and certain expectations regarding a charismatic and respected political figure on the Congolese scene.

'You talking about the Mwangaza?'

'I'm afraid I am,' I agreed sadly.

I took no pleasure in bringing him bad news, I said, but I had made a promise to an unnamed person of my acquaintance, and must now discharge it. This was the fictional character that Hannah and I, after much debate, had agreed upon. I will add that there are few things I enjoy less than talking to dark glasses. In extreme cases, I have been known to request my clients to remove them on the grounds that they curtail my powers of communication. But for Hannah's sake I decided to grin and bear it.

'Man person? Woman person? What kind of fucking person?' he demanded.

'I'm afraid that's not something I'm prepared to divulge,' I retorted, grateful for this early opportunity to print my mark on the proceedings. 'Let's call him *he* for simplicity's sake,' I added, as a conciliatory afterthought. 'And this *friend* of mine, who is totally trustworthy and honourable in my opinion, is engaged in highly confidential government work.'

'*British* fucking government?'—with a sneer on *British* which coupled with the Ray-Bans and the American accent might have raised my hackles, were he not a valued friend of Hannah's.

'My friend's *duties*,' I resumed, 'provide him with regular access to signals and other forms of communication passing between African nations and the European entities that they are in touch with.'

'Who the fuck's entity? You mean governments or what?'

'Not *necessarily* a government, Baptiste. Not all entities are nations. Many are more powerful and less accountable than nations. Also wealthier.'

I glanced to Hannah for encouragement but she had closed her eyes as if praying.

'And what this friend of mine has told me—in total confidence, after much agonising,' I continued, deciding to come straight to the point, 'is that a secret meeting recently took place on an island somewhere in the North Sea'—I allowed a pause for this to sink in—'between your Mwangaza—I'm sorry to have to tell you this—and the representatives of certain East Congolese militias'—I was watching the lower half of his face for signs of dawning apprehension, but the most I got was a barely perceptible straightening of the lips—'and *other* representatives of an offshore anonymous syndicate of international investors. At this same conference it was agreed that they would jointly mount, with the assistance of Western and African mercenaries, a military coup against Kivu.' I again waited for some hint of a reaction, but in vain. 'A covert coup. Deniable. Using the local militias that they have done a deal with. Units of the Mai Mai forming one such militia, the Banyamulenge another.'

Instinct having advised me to keep Haj and Luc out of the equation, I once more glanced at Baptiste to see how he was taking it. His Ray-Bans, so far as I could determine, were beamed on Hannah's bosom.

'The *ostensible* purpose of the operation,' I pressed on more loudly, 'is to create an inclusive, united, democratic Kivu, north and south. However, the *actual* purpose is somewhat different. It's to milk the Eastern

Congo of all minerals the Syndicate can get its hands on, including large stockpiles of coltan, thereby notching up untold millions for the investors, and absolutely nothing for the people of Kivu.'

No movement of the head, no change in the direction of the Ray-Bans.

'The people will be robbed. Ripped off, as per usual,' I protested, feeling by now that I was talking to no one but myself. 'It's the oldest story. Carpetbagging by another name.' I had kept back my trump card till last. 'And Kinshasa is in on the plot. Kinshasa will turn a blind eye provided it gets a piece of the action, which in this case means the People's Portion. All of it.'

From upstairs a child screamed and was soothed. Hannah gave a remote smile, but it was for the child, not for me. Baptiste's blacked-out expression had not altered by a quaver and his impassivity was by now having a seriously retarding effect on my narrative powers.

'When is all this shit supposed to have happened?'

'You mean, when did I talk to my friend?'

'The meeting on the fucking island, man. When?'

'I said: recently.'

'I don't *know* recent. Recent *how*? Recent *when*?'

'Within the last week,' I replied, because when in doubt stay close to the truth.

'Did he attend the meeting, your unnamed guy? Was he sitting on the fucking island with them, listening while they did the deal?'

'He studied the papers. Reports. I told you.'

'He studied the papers. He thought, holy shit, and he came to *you*.'

'Yes.'

'Why?'

'He's got a conscience. He recognised the scale of the deceit. He cares about the Congo. He doesn't approve of people starting foreign wars for their own profit. Isn't that a good enough reason?'

Evidently it wasn't. 'Why *you*, man? He some kind of white liberal, and you're the nearest he can get to a black guy?'

'He came to me because he cares. That's all you need know. He's an old friend, I won't say how. He knew I had links to the Congo and that my heart was in the right place.'

'Fuck *you*, man. You're shitting me.'

Springing to his feet, he began pacing the room, Texan boots skidding on the deep-pile gold carpet. After a couple of lengths he came to a halt in front of Hannah.

'Maybe I believe this schmuck,' he told her, tilting his skull-like head at me. 'Maybe I just *think* I do. Maybe you were correct in bringing him to me. Is he by any chance half Rwandan? I think he is half Rwandan. I think this may be the clue to his position.'

'*Baptiste*,' Hannah whispered, but he ignored her.

'Okay, don't answer. Let's do facts. Here are the facts. Your friend here fucks you, right? Your friend's friend knows he fucks you, so he comes to your friend. And he tells your friend a story, which your friend repeats to you because he's fucking you. You are rightly incensed by this story, so you bring your friend who is fucking you to me, so that he can tell it all over again, which is what your friend's friend reckoned would happen all along. We call that *disinformation*. Rwandan people are very clever at *disinformation*. They have people who do nothing except plant *disinformation*. Allow me to explain how it works. Okay?'

Still standing before Hannah, he turns his blacked-out eyes to me, then back to Hannah.

'Here's how it works. A great man—a *truly* great man—I am referring to my Mwangaza—is offering a message of hope for my country. Peace, prosperity, inclusiveness, unity. But this great man is not a friend of Rwandans. He knows that his vision cannot be achieved while the Rwandans borrow our land to fight their fucking wars on, colonise our economy and our people and send teams of killers to wipe us out. So he hates the fuckers. And they hate him. And they hate *me*. Know how many times those bastards have tried to take me out? Well, now they're trying to take out the Mwangaza. How? By planting a lie inside his camp. What is the lie? You have just heard the lie. It was spoken by the friend you are fucking: *the Mwangaza has sold out to the white man! The Mwangaza has mortgaged our birthright to the Kinshasa fatcats!*'

Forsaking Hannah, he places himself in front of me. His voice has risen a scale, forced upward by the rap coming through the gold carpet.

'Do you happen to know by any chance how one little match in Kivu can send the whole fucking region up in flames? Is that information available to you, in your head?'

I must have nodded, yes I know.

'Well, you're the fucking match, man, even if you don't want to be, even if all your good thoughts are in the right place. And this unnamed person of yours who loves the Congo so much, and wants to protect it from the white invader, he's a fucking Rwandan cockroach. And don't think he's the only one either, because we've got the same story being fed to us from about twenty different directions, all telling us the Mwangaza is the biggest fucking anti-Christ of all time. Do you happen to play golf? The noble game of golf? Are you a fucking golfer, sir?'

I shook my head.

'No golf,' Hannah murmured on my behalf.

'You said this great meeting took place within the last week. Right?'

I nodded yes, right.

'Know where the Mwangaza has been this last week? Every fucking day without exception, morning and fucking afternoon? Check his green fees. In Marbella, south Spain, taking a golf vacation before returning to Congo and resuming his heroic campaign for peaceful power. Know where I've been, every fucking one of these last seven days right up to yesterday? Check my green fees. In Marbella, playing golf with the

Mwangaza and his devoted associates. So maybe, just maybe, you should tell your friend to shove his island up his ass, and his dirty lies with it.'

All the time he had been talking, Baptiste's Rolex watch with its eighteen-carat bracelet and phases of the moon had been winking at me. The more he talked, the chunkier and more intrusive it became.

'You want to go somewhere, be driven someplace? You want a cab?' he asked Hannah in Swahili.

'We're fine,' Hannah said.

'Has the man you fuck got something in that bag he wants to give me? Libellous writings? Coke?'

'No.'

'When you get tired of him, let me know.'

I followed her back through the café, into the street. A new black Mercedes limousine was double-parked, its driver at the wheel. From its rear window, a black girl in a low-cut dress and white fur stole stared at us like somebody in peril.

17

Hannah was not a woman who naturally wept. The sight of her seated on the edge of Mrs Hakim's bed in her Mission girl's nightdress at one o'clock in the morning, face buried in her hands and the tears rolling between her fingers, moved me to depths of compassion hitherto unplumbed.

'We can do nothing to save ourselves, Salvo,' she assured me between sobs when, after much coaxing, I persuaded her to sit upright. 'We have such a wonderful dream. Peace. Unity. Progress. But we are Congolese. Every time we have a dream, we go back to the beginning. So tomorrow never comes.'

When I had done what I could to console her, I set to work making scrambled eggs, toast and a pot of tea while I prattled to her about my day. Determined not to compound her grief with contentious propositions, I was once more careful to omit all mention of certain phone calls I had made, or a certain classified document entitled *J'Accuse!* that I had tucked behind the wardrobe. In twelve short hours she would be departing for Bognor.

Better by far to wait till she returned, by which time I would have put my plan into action and all would be resolved. Yet when I proposed sleep, she shook her head distractedly and said she needed to hear the song again.

'Haj's song. The one he sang after they tortured him.'

'Now?'

'Now.'

Wishing by all available means to humour her, I extracted the relevant tape from its hiding-place.

'You have the business card he gave you?'

I fetched it for her. She examined the front and managed a smile at the animals. She turned it over and, frowning, studied the back. She put on the earphones, switched on the recorder and sank into an inscrutable silence while I waited patiently for her to emerge.

'Did you respect your father, Salvo?' she enquired, when the tape had twice run its course.

'Of course I did. Hugely. So did you, I'm sure.'

'Haj also respects his father. He is Congolese. He respects his father and obeys him. Do you really believe that he can go to his father and say, "Father, your life-long friend and political ally the Mwangaza is a liar," without any proof to show him?—not even the marks on his body if his torturers did their work well?'

'Hannah, please. You're dead tired and you've had an awful day. Come to bed.' I put my hand on her shoulder but she gently removed it.

'He was singing to you, Salvo.'

I conceded that such was my impression.

'Then what do you think he was trying to tell you?'

'That he'd survived and to hell with all of us.'

'Then why did he write his e-mail address to you? It's in a shaky hand. He wrote it *after* he was tortured, not before. Why?'

I made a bad joke of it.

'Rustling up business for his nightclubs, most likely.'

'Haj is telling you to contact him, Salvo. He needs your help. He is saying: help me, send me your recordings, send me the evidence of what they did to me. He needs the proof. He wants you to provide it.'

Was I weak, or merely cunning? Haj was in my book a playboy, not a knight in armour. French pragmatism and the good living had corrupted him. Three million dollars by Monday night was clear evidence of this. Should I destroy her illusions?—or should I enter into a bargain with her that I was confident I would not be obliged to honour?

'You're right,' I told her. 'He wants the proof. We'll send him the tapes. It's the only way.'

'How?' she demanded suspiciously.

It's dead simple, I assured her. All you need is someone with the gear—a sound recordist, a music shop. They turn the tape into a sound file for you, and you e-mail it to Haj. Job done.

'No, Salvo, *not* done'—her face puckering as she struggled to reverse her rôle just as I this minute had reversed mine.

'Why not?'

'It's a big crime for you. Haj is Congolese and these are British secrets. At heart you are British. Better to leave it.'

I fetched a calendar. Maxie's planned coup was still eleven days off, I pointed out, kneeling at her side. So there's no vast hurry, is there?

Probably not, she agreed doubtfully. But the more warning Haj had, the better.

But we could still hold off for a few days, I countered artfully. Even a week would do no harm, I added—secretly remembering the ponderous pace at which Mr Anderson moved to perform his wonders.

'A *week*? Why must we wait a week?'—frowning again.

'Because by then we may not need to send it. Maybe they'll get cold feet. They know we're on the case. Maybe they'll call it off.'

'And how shall we know they have called it off?'

To this I had no answer ready, and we shared a somewhat awkward silence, while she rested her head pensively on my shoulder.

'In four weeks, Noah has his birthday,' she announced abruptly.

'Indeed he does, and we've promised to find him a present together.'

'He wishes more than anything to visit his cousins in Goma. I do not wish him to be visiting a war zone.'

'He won't be. Just give it a few more days. In case something happens.'

'Such as what, Salvo?'

'They're not all monsters. Maybe reason will prevail,' I insisted, to which she sat up and gave me the kind of look she might have bestowed on a patient she suspected of lying about his symptoms.

'Five days,' I pleaded. 'On the sixth, we send everything to Haj. That still gives him all the time he can possibly need.'

I recall only one conversation of later significance. We are lying in each other's arms, our cares seemingly forgotten, when suddenly Hannah is talking about Latzi, Grace's crazy Polish boyfriend.

'You know what he does for a living? Works at a Soho recording centre for rock bands. They record all night, he comes home in the morning completely stoned and they make love all day.'

'So?'

'So I can go to him and get a good price.'

Now it is my turn to sit up.

'Hannah. I do *not* want you complicit. If anybody has to send those tapes to Haj, it will be me.'

To which she says nothing at all, and I take her silence for submission. We wake late and are in a flurry of packing. At Hannah's bidding, I fly downstairs barefoot and beg Mr Hakim to get us one of his minicabs. When I return, I find her standing at the rickety wardrobe, holding my shoulder-bag which has evidently slipped from its hiding place in the rush—but not, thank Heaven, my precious copy of *J'Accuse!*

'Here, let me,' I say and, using my greater height, put the bag back where it came from.

'Oh Salvo,' she says, in what I take for gratitude.

She is still only half dressed, which is fatal.

* * *

The non-stop express service from Victoria coach station to Sevenoaks had laid on extra buses for train travellers who since the bombings prefer the open road. I approached the queue warily, conscious of my pulled-down bobble hat and shade of skin. I had made the journey partly on foot and partly by bus, twice alighting at the last moment in order to shake off my hypothetical pursuers. Counter-surveillance takes its toll. By the time the security guard at the coach station had patted me down, I was half wishing he would identify me and be done with it. But he could find no fault with the brown envelope marked *J'Accuse!* that I had folded into the inside pocket of my leather jacket. From a phone box in Sevenoaks I rang Grace's cellphone to find her in fits of laughter. The coach journey to Bognor had not been without its moments, apparently:

'That Amelia, she threw up you wouldn't believe, Salvo. All over the bus, all over her new frock and shoes. Me and Hannah, we're just standin' here with mops, *rationalisin'!*'

'Salvo?'

'I love you, Hannah.'

'I love you too, Salvo.'

I had my absolution, and could proceed.

* * *

St Roderic's School for Boys and Girls lay in the leafy fringes of old Sevenoaks. Amid expensive houses with new cars parked on weedless gravel drives stood a looka-like of the Sanctuary, complete with turrets, battlements and an ominous clock. The glass and brick Memorial Hall had been donated by grateful parents and former pupils. A fluorescent arrow pointed visitors up a tiled staircase. Following large ladies, I arrived at a wooden gallery and took my place next to an elderly clergyman with perfect white hair like Philip's. Below us, forming three sides of a military square, stood the sixty-strong members of the Sevenoaks Choral Society (authorised). Perched on a rostrum, a man in a velvet coat and bow tie was addressing his flock on the subject of outrage.

'It's all very well to *feel* it. It's another for us to *hear* it. Let's think it through for a moment. The money-lenders have set themselves up in God's house, and what could be worse than that? No wonder we're outraged. Who wouldn't be? So lots of outrage. And very careful with our S's, tenors particularly. Here we go again.'

We went again. And Mr Anderson in the full expression of his outrage puffed out his chest, opened his mouth and saw me: but so completely and directly that you would think I was the only person in the hall, let alone the gallery. Instead of singing, his mouth snapped shut. Everyone round him was singing and the man on the rostrum was flailing at them with his little velvet arms, oblivious to the fact that Mr Anderson, having broken ranks, was towering beside him, scarlet with embarrassment. But the choir was not oblivious, and the singing slowly wound down. What passed between Mr Anderson and his conductor I shall never know for I had by then descended the stairs and placed myself in front of the doors that led to the main hall. I was joined by a middle-aged woman wearing a kaftan, and a thick-set adolescent girl who, if you took away the green hair and eyebrow rings, was the spitting image of her distinguished father. Seconds later Mr Anderson himself squeezed his bulk round the door and, looking past me as if I wasn't there, addressed his womenfolk in tones of command.

'Mary, I'll trouble you both to go home and await my return. Ginette, don't look like that. Take the car, please, Mary. I shall find alternative transport as required.'

Her charcoaled eyes beseeching me to witness the injury being done to her, the girl Ginette allowed herself to be led away by her mother. Only then did Mr Anderson acknowledge my presence.

'Salvo. You have personally interrupted my choir practice.'

I had my speech ready. It invoked my esteem for him, my respect for his high principles, and it recalled the many times he had told me I should bring my worries to him rather than keep them bottled up inside me. But this was not the moment to deliver it.

'It's about the coup, sir. My assignment at the weekend. It's not in the national interest at all. It's about plundering the Congo.'

The green-tiled corridor was hung with student artwork. The first two doors were locked. The third opened. At the other end of the classroom two desks faced each other, with my worst subject, algebra, on the blackboard behind them.

*   *   *

Mr Anderson has heard me out.

I have made my story brief which, as a talking man himself, is what he likes. He has kept his elbows on his desk and his hands clasped beneath his formidable chin and has never taken his eyes off me, not even when I approached the prickly moral labyrinth that is his own preserve: Individual Conscience versus Higher Cause. My copy of *J'Accuse!* lies before him. He puts on his reading spectacles and reaches inside his jacket for his silver propelling pencil.

'And this is your own title, is it, Salvo? You're accusing me.'

'Not you, Mr Anderson. Them. Lord Brinkley, Philip, Tabizi, the Syndicate. The people who are using the Mwangaza for their personal enrichment and sparking a war in Kivu to do it.'

'And it's all in here, is it? Written down. By you.'

'For your eyes only, sir. There's no copy.'

The tip of the silver pencil began its ponderous overflight.

'They tortured Haj,' I added, needing to get this part off my chest straight away. 'They used a cattle prod. Spider made it.'

Without interrupting his reading, Mr Anderson felt constrained to correct me. 'Torture is a very emotive word, Salvo. I suggest you use it with caution. The word, I mean.'

After that, I willed myself to calm down while he read and frowned, or read and scribbled himself a marginal comment, or tut-tutted at an imprecision in my prose. Once he flipped back a few pages, comparing what he was reading with something that had gone before, and shook his head. And when he had reached the last page, he returned to the first one, starting with the title. Then, licking his thumb, he examined the end once more, as if making sure he hadn't missed anything out, or been unfair in some way, before awarding his examiner's mark.

'And what do you propose to do with this document, may I enquire, Salvo?'

'I've done it. It's for you, Mr Anderson.'

'And what do you propose *I* do with it?'

'You take it right to the top, sir. The Foreign Secretary, Number 10 if necessary. Everybody knows you're a man of conscience. Ethical borders are your speciality, you once told me.' And when he said nothing:

'All they have to do is *stop*. We're not asking for heads to roll. We're not pointing fingers. Just *stop*!'

'*We?*' he repeated. 'Who's *we* suddenly?'

'You and I, sir,' I replied, although I'd had a different 'we' in mind. 'And all of us who didn't realise that this project was rotten from top to bottom. We'll be saving lives, Mr Anderson. Hundreds, perhaps thousands. Children too.' Now it was Noah I was thinking of.

Mr Anderson spread his palms flat over *J'Accuse!* much as if he thought I might snatch it back from him, which was the last thing I had in mind. He took a deep breath, which for my taste sounded too much like a sigh.

'You've been very diligent, Salvo. Very conscientious, if I may say so, which is no less than I would have expected of you.'

'I felt I owed it to you, Mr Anderson.'

'You have an excellent memory, as all who know your work are well aware.'

'Thank you, Mr Anderson.'

'There are extensive verbatims here. Are they also from memory?'

'Well, not entirely.'

'Would you mind in that case advising me what other sources you are drawing upon for this—accusation?'

'The raw material, Mr Anderson.'

'And how raw would that be?'

'The tapes. Not all. Just the key ones.'

'Of what exactly?'

'The plot. The People's Portion. Haj being tortured. Haj indicting Kinshasa. Haj doing his dirty deal. Philip spilling the beans over the satcom to London.'

'So how many tapes would we be talking about here, Salvo? In the aggregate, please?'

'Well, they're not all full. Spider does Chat Room rules. It's one intercept one tape, basically.'

'Just say how many, please, Salvo.'

'Seven.'

'Are we also talking of documentary evidence?'

'Just my notepads.'

'And how many of your notepads would there be?'

'Four. Three full. One half full. In my Babylonian cuneiform,' I added, for shared humour.

'So where would they all *be*, Salvo, tell me. At this moment in time? Now?'

I pretended not to understand him. 'The mercenaries? Maxie's private army? Still sitting around, I suppose. Oiling their weapons, or whatever they do. The attack isn't due for another ten days, so they've got a bit of time to kill.'

But he was not to be diverted, which I might have guessed. 'I think you know what I'm talking about, Salvo. Those tapes and notepads and whatever else you have feloniously obtained. What have you done with them?'

'Hidden them.'

'Where?'

'In a safe place.'

'That's a rather silly answer, Salvo, thank you. Where

is the safe place in which they are hidden?'

My lips had closed, so I let them stay closed, not pressed tightly together in refusal but not activated either, apart from the electric current that was passing through them and making them tingle.

'Salvo.'

'Yes, Mr Anderson.'

'You were assigned to that mission on my personal recommendation. There's a lot wouldn't have taken you on, what with your temperament and irregular background. Not for work like ours. I did.'

'I know that, Mr Anderson. I appreciate it. That's why I've come to you.'

'So where are they?' He waited a moment, then went on as if he hadn't asked the question. 'I have protected you, Salvo.'

'I know, Mr Anderson.'

'From the day you came to me, I have been your shield and protector. There were people inside the Chat Room and out of it who did not approve of your part-time appointment, your talents notwithstanding.'

'I know.'

'There were those who thought you were too impressionable. People in vetting section for a start. Too generous-hearted for your own good, they said. Not manipulative enough. Your old school thought you could turn rebellious. There was also the question of your personal preferences which I won't go into.'

'They're all right now.'

'I stood up for you come rain or shine, I was your champion. I never wavered. "Young Salvo is the tops," I told them. "There's no better linguist in the game, provided he keeps his head, which he will, because I'll be there to make sure he does."'

'I realise that, Mr Anderson. I'm appreciative.'

'You want to be a father one day, don't you? You told me so yourself.'

'Yes.'

'Not all pleasure, by any means, children aren't. But you love them anyway however much they let you down. You stick by them, which is what I'm trying to do for you. Have you remembered where those tapes are yet?'

Fearing that by saying anything at all I might end up saying more than I meant to, I plucked for a while at my lower lip with my forefinger and thumb.

'Mr Anderson, you must tell them to stop,' I said finally.

Whereupon he picked up his silver propelling pencil in both hands and, having commiserated with it silently for a while, fed it back into the inside pocket where it lived. But his hand remained stuck inside his lapel, in the manner of Maxie's Napoleon.

'That's final, is it? That's your last word to me on the matter. No "thank you", no apology, no tapes or notepads. Just "tell them to stop".'

'I'll give you the tapes and notepads. But only after you've told them to stop.'

'And if that's not what I'm going to tell them? If I have neither the inclination nor the authority to stop them?'

'I'll give them to someone else.'

'Oh? And who would that be?'

It was on the tip of my tongue to tell him Haj, but prudence restrained me.

'My MP or someone,' I replied, which elicited a contemptuous silence from him, and nothing more.

'So what precisely, in your frank opinion, Salvo,' he resumed, 'is to be gained by *stopping*, as you call it?'

'Peace, Mr Anderson. God's peace.'

My hopeful mention of God had evidently touched the right nerve in him, for a look of piety at once suffused his homely features.

'And has it never occurred to you that it might be God's will that the world's resources, which are dwindling even as we speak, do better in the hands of civilised Christian souls with a cultured way of life than some of the most backward heathens on the planet?'

'I'm just not sure who the heathens are, Mr Anderson.'

'Well, I am,' he retorted, and stood up. As he did so, his hand emerged and it was holding a cellphone. He must have had to switch it off for his choir practice, because his large thumb was crooked over the top of it while he waited for the power to come up. His big body was moving to my left, I assumed in order to get between the door and myself. So I moved to the left too, on the way helping myself to the copy of *J'Accuse!*

'I am about to make a very crucial telephone call, Salvo.'

'I know that, Mr Anderson. I don't want you to.'

'Once made, it will have reverberations that neither you nor I can control. I would like you please to give me one reason, here and now, why that call should not take place.'

'There are millions of reasons, Mr Anderson. All over Kivu. The coup is a criminal act.'

'A rogue country, Salvo—a country that is incapable of settling to an orderly way of life—a country that abandons itself freely to genocide and cannibalism and worse, is *not*'—another step—'in my considered opinion, entitled to respect under international law'—my escape route now all but cut off—'any more than is a *rogue element* in our *own* society—such as *yourself*, Salvo— entitled to indulge his naivety at the expense of his adoptive country's best interests. Stay where you are, please, there's no need to come any nearer. You can hear what I have to say to you from where you are. I'll ask you one more time, and that's it. *Where are the illegally held materials?* The details can be attended to in a calm manner. In twenty seconds from now, I'm going to make my phone call, and at the same time or just before, I'm going to make a citizen's arrest. I'm going to put my hand on your shoulder as the law requires and say, "Bruno Salvador, I hereby arrest you in the name of the law." Salvo. I'll remind you that I am unwell. I am fifty- eight years of age and a late-onset diabetic.'

I had taken the phone from his unresisting hand. We were standing face to face and I was six inches taller than he was, which seemed to startle him more than it did me. Through the closed door, the Sevenoaks Choral Society was striving for greater outrage without the benefit of its leading baritone.

'Salvo. I will offer you a fair choice. If you will give me your word of honour, here and now, that you and I tomorrow morning—first thing—will go together to wherever these materials are hidden, and recover them—you can remain in Sevenoaks for the night as my guest, have a nice supper with us in the family, simple home cooking, nothing fancy, there's my elder daughter's bedroom, she's not living with us at present—and in return for the recovered articles I will make it my business to speak to certain people and assure them—take care, Salvo, none of that now—'

The hand that should have been arresting me was raised to ward me off. I reached for the doorhandle, slowly so as not to alarm him. I took the battery from his cellphone and dropped the case back in his pocket. Then I closed the door on him, because I didn't think it right for people to see my last mentor in his diminished state.

* * *

Of my movements and actions over the next hours I have little awareness, nor had I at the time. I know I walked, then walked faster, down the school drive, that

I stood at a bus stop and, when no bus came soon enough for me, crossed the road and caught one going in the opposite direction, which is no way to appear inconspicuous; and that thereafter I backtracked and zigzagged across country, as much to shake off the memory of Mr Anderson as my real or imaginary pursuers; and that from Bromley I caught a late train to Victoria, thence by one cab as far as Marble Arch and a second to Mr Hakim's, courtesy of Maxie's generosity. And from Bromley South railway station, with twenty minutes to wait before my train arrived, I had called Grace from a phone box.

'You want to hear somethin' totally *crazy*, Salvo?'

Politeness required that I did.

'I fell off of a donkey, that's what! Flat on my butt, with all the kids watchin' and screamin'! Amelia, she stayed on and I fell off. And that donkey, Salvo, it took Amelia all the way down the beach to the ice-cream stall, and Amelia bought the donkey a 99p cornet and a chocolate flake with her pocket money, and the donkey ate that whole cornet and it ate the chocolate, and it brought Amelia all the way back! I ain't fibbin' to you, Salvo! And you're never goin' to get to see 'em, but I've got bruises on my butt you wouldn't believe, both halves, and Latzi's goin' to laugh his crazy head off!'

Latzi, her Polish boyfriend in the music business, I remembered fleetingly. Latzi who would give Hannah a good price.

'You know somethin' else, Salvo?'

At what point did I sense she was stringing me along?

'There was this Punch and Judy show, okay?'

Okay, I agreed.

'And the kids, they died for it. I never saw so many happy kids so scared in all my life.'

Great. Kids love to be scared, I said.

'And that café on the way down, Salvo—the place we stopped at after the other place wouldn't have us because we were golliwogs?—they were just *dandy*. So we don't care about a single thing.'

Where is she, Grace?

'Hannah?'—as if she'd only now remembered her— 'Oh, Hannah, she's taken the big ones to a movie up the road, Salvo. She said to say, if Salvo calls, she's goin' to call you back right soon. Maybe tomorrow mornin', because of the time. Me and Hannah, we're with different families, see. And I've got to hang onto my mobile for Latzi.'

I see.

'Because if Latzi can't reach me, he goes apeshit. And Hannah's family, well, they got a house phone but it's complicated, so best not try to call her there. It's in there with the family and the TV. So she'll call you just as soon as she can. Anythin' particular on your mind, Salvo?'

Tell her I love her.

'Now have you passed that information to Hannah already, Salvo, or is this breakin' news that I'm hearin'?'

I should have asked what movie Hannah was seeing with the big ones, I thought when I had rung off.

* * *

I had not realised how swiftly our little back bedroom had become home, supplanting in a few days all my years at Norfolk Mansions. I entered it and smelled, as if she were still there, Hannah's body, no perfume but her own. I greeted in comradely acknowledgement our unmade bed with its battered air of triumph. No detail she had left behind escaped my guilt-ridden gaze: her Afro-comb, the bracelets abandoned in favour of a circle of elephant hair in the last minutes of her delayed departure, our half-empty teacups, the photograph of Noah on the flimsy bedside table, put there to keep me company in her absence, and her rainbow cellphone, entrusted to me to receive her messages of love and inform me of her estimated time of return. Why would I not carry it on my person? Because I wished for nothing that could incriminate her in the event of my summary arrest. When could I expect her to reclaim it? Parents had been told to be at the church at one o'clock lunchtime, but it only took one naughty kid like Amelia to hide, she had warned me, or a bomb scare, or a road-block, and she might not make it back till evening.

I listened to the ten o'clock news and cruised the Most Wanted list on the Internet, expecting to see my mugshot staring at me above a politically correct description of my ethnicity. I was logging off when

Hannah's cellphone trilled out its birdsong. Grace had given her my message, she said. She was in a phone box with too little change. Immediately, I called her back.

'Who've you been running away from?' I asked, struggling for a jocular tone.

She was surprised: why should I think she'd been running?

'It's just how you sound,' I said. 'Breathless.'

I was already hating this call. I wished we could stop it right now, and start again when I had some coherent thoughts in my head. How could I tell her that Mr Anderson had failed me exactly as Lord Brinkley had, but with greater sanctimony? That he was another Brinkley exactly as she had foreseen?

'How are the kids?' I asked.

'Fine.'

'Grace says they're having a really great time.'

'It's true. They are very happy.'

'Are you?'

'I am happy because I have you in my life, Salvo.'

Why so solemn? So terminal?

'And I'm happy too. To have you in mine. You're everything to me. Hannah, what's going on? Is there someone in the box with you? You sound ... unreal.'

'Oh, Salvo!'

And suddenly, as if on a signal, she was talking passionate love to me, vowing she never knew such happiness existed, and how she would never do anything in her life to harm me, however small or well meant, for as long as she lived.

'But of course you won't,' I cried, fighting to overcome my mystification. 'You could never harm me, nor I you. We'll protect each other always, through thick and thin. That's the deal.'

And again: 'Oh, Salvo!'

She had rung off. For a long time I stood staring at the rainbow cellphone in my palm. We Congolese love colour. Why else had God given us gold and diamonds and fruit and flowers, if not to please our love of colour? I drifted round the room; I was Haj after he had been tortured, peering at myself in mirrors, wondering what was left of me that was worth saving. I sat down on the edge of our bed and put my head in my hands. A good man knows when to sacrifice himself, Brother Michael liked to say. A bad man survives but loses his soul. There was still time, just. I had one last shot to play. And I must play it now, while Hannah was still safe in Bognor.

18

It was ten o'clock next morning. Calm in the knowledge that I had reached an irreversible decision, I strode my obligatory mile with near-reckless zest, my bobble hat pulled low and my shoulder-bag slapping gaily at my hip. In a secluded side street lined with cars stood a cheerful red phone box. I dialled the over-familiar number and got Megan, everybody's friend.

'Hello, Salvo darling, well how are we today?'

If you had the flu, Megan told you it was all around, dear. If you'd been on holiday, Megan hoped you'd had a nice one.

'They say her party was just *lovely*. Wherever did she buy that outfit from? You spoil her, that's your trouble. We're engaged speaking at the moment, I'm afraid. What can I do you for? Put you on hold, dear? Voicemail? What's our preference today?'

'It's not Penelope I'm after, actually, Megan. It's Fergus.'

'Oh *is* it! *Well*, then! We *are* coming up in the world!'

Waiting to be put through, I pictured the exchange

that was taking place between Thorne the Horn and his notoriously loyal assistant regarding the best tactic to be adopted for handling an incoming call from yet another irate husband. Should Fergus be cloistered with the proprietor? On a long-distance conference call? Or should he be his own frank and fearless self and come out fighting?

'Salvo, old chap! Jesus, where are *you*? Have you trashed any good flats recently?'

'I've got a story for you, Fergus.'

'Have you, by Heaven? Well, I'm not sure I want to hear that story, Salvo. Not if it's to the detriment of a certain young lady. Grown-up people make their own decisions in life. Some of us have to face up to that fact and move on.'

'It's not about Penelope.'

'I'm glad to hear that.'

'It's a news story. A hot one.'

'Salvo?'

'Yes?'

'Are you by any chance pulling my pisser?'

'It's about Jack Brinkley. It's your chance to nail him. Him and Crispin Mellows and—' I reeled off the names of the great and good I had seen assembled in Berkeley Square, but as expected he had ears only for Jack Brinkley who had cost the paper a fortune, and Thorne nearly his career.

'Nail the bastard *how* precisely? Not that I'm believing you, of course. That's a given.'

'I'm not telling you over the phone.'

'Salvo.'

'What?'

'Is it the money you're after?'

'No. You can have him for free.'

I had misjudged my man. If I'd said a hundred thousand pounds or no deal, he'd have felt more comfortable.

'Is it some stupid game of sabotage you think you're playing, by any chance? Dragging us back into the libel courts for another million? Because, believe me, Salvo, if you're into that—'

'You took us to some club once. In the Strand. A cellar. It must have been around the time that you and Penelope were—'

'What about it?'

'What's the address?'

He gave it to me.

'If you meet me there in an hour, you can have Brinkley's balls on a charger,' I assured him, using the language he understood.

*   *   *

The Casbah Club, though a stone's throw from the Savoy Hotel, was not a salubrious place at the best of times, but mid-morning was its low point. At its dungeon-like entrance, a despondent Asian man was plying a Boer War vacuum cleaner. The stone staircase reminded me of the descent to the boiler room. Amid pillars and embroidered cushions, Fergus Thorne was seated in the very alcove where, six months previously, at a cosy threesome dinner, Penelope had kicked off her shoe and worked his lower leg with her stockinged toes while he told me what an asset to the paper she was. This morning to my relief he was alone, with a tomato juice at his elbow, reading the early edition of his own newspaper. Two of his ace reporters sat a couple of tables away from him: the egregious Jellicoe, alias Jelly, who had pinched my bottom at Penelope's party, and an ageing virago named Sophie who had dared to put herself forward as Penelope's rival and paid the price. Uninvited, I sat myself at Thorne's side and wedged the shoulder-bag between my feet. He turned his mottled face to me, scowled, and went back to his newspaper. I drew the copy of *J'Accuse!* from my jacket and laid it on the table. He took a sideways glance at it, grabbed it, and disappeared again behind his paper. As he began to read it, I watched the shrewdness slowly drain from his face, to be replaced by a translucent greed.

'This is total and utter *bullshit*, Salvo'—avidly turning a page—'you know that, don't you? Fabrication of the most blatant kind. Who wrote it?'

'I did.'

'And all these people at—where is it?'

'Berkeley Square.'

'You saw them?'

'Yes.'

'Personally. With your own eyes? Be careful now.'

'Yes.'

'Had you been drinking?'

'No.'

'Substances?'

'I don't do them.'

'Jelly. Sophie. Over here with you, please. I'm talking to a man who thinks he can bring us Big Jack's balls on a charger and I don't believe a word he's telling me.'

We are head to head, the four of us. Whatever reservations I may have harboured regarding our great British press are temporarily suspended as Thorne disposes his troops.

'Jasper *Albin?*—*that* Albin? He's the same Frog bastard who lied in his teeth to our Appeal judges!— and Big Jack has the *arse* to bring him back for *this?*— that is *hubris* of the first water!—Jelly, I want you to drop everything, fly to Besançon and hold Albin's feet to the fire. If he needs buying, buy him.'

Jelly scribbles officiously on his notepad.

'Sophie. Flash your tits at the security firms. Who's *Maxie? Colonel* Maxie? Maxie who? If he's a mercenary, he's ex Special Forces. *How* ex? Who does he fuck? What schools did he go to? What dirty wars has he fought? And find me that house in Berkeley Square. Who does it belong to, who pays the heat and electricity, who hired it that evening, who from, how much for?'

Sophie writes this down, her tongue shrewdly protruding. Her notepad is identical to certain others nestling at my feet.

'And find me that island'—to both of them—'and who flew a helicopter from Battersea to Luton last Friday? Check non-commercial air traffic out of Luton, check any North Sea islands for hire. Look for one with a gazebo. And follow the Fortnum's hamper: who ordered it, paid for it, delivered it. Get me the invoice. SMOKED SALMON FOR CONGO INVADERS—I love it.'

'Me too,' Sophie murmurs.

'Poetry,' says Jelly.

'And steer clear of the big players. If Jackie boy gets wind of us, he'll slap an injunction on us faster than we can spit. The brazen hypocrisy of the fellow! One minute preaching debt relief for failed states, the next ripping off the suffering Congolese for every penny he can screw out of them. It's an outrage. It's beautiful.'

While Thorne's enthusiasm is music to my ears, I feel it incumbent on me to remind him of the larger purpose of the story.

'It isn't just Jack we're after, Fergus.'

'Don't you worry, man. We'll bring his chums tumbling down with him. If they blame him, all the better.'

'I meant, there's a war to stop. The coup has to be called off.'

Thorne's bloodshot eyes, always too small for his face, examined me in contemptuous disbelief. 'You mean stop the coup and don't run the story? MAN FAILS TO BITE DOG. Is that what you mean?'

'I mean that all the enquiries you're proposing—find the helicopter, the hamper, the island—they're going to take too long. We've only got nine more days.' I waxed bolder. 'You either go with the story straight away or not at all, Fergus. That's the deal. *After* the coup's too late. The Eastern Congo could be in free fall.'

'Impossible.' He shoved *J'Accuse!* across the table at me. 'We need cast-iron evidence. Legalled every inch of the way. What you are offering me here is a fucking précis. I want Jack Brinkley with his knickers round his ankles and his hands in the till. Anything less and *he* will have *me* on my fucking *knees* before their Lordships, offering craven apologies for my impertinence.'

The moment I had been waiting for, yet dreading, was upon me.

'And if I had that evidence with me? Proof positive? Here and now?'

He leaned forward, fists on the table. I leaned forward. So did Jelly and Sophie. I spoke in deliberate tones.

'If I had Brinkley's voice—loud and clear on digital tape—authorising a bribe of three million dollars to one of the Congolese delegates—over the satellite phone—on behalf of the no-name Syndicate—would you call that sufficient evidence?'

'Who's he talking to?'

'Philip. The independent consultant. Philip needs to talk to whichever member of the Syndicate is empowered to say yes to three million dollars. The empowered

member is Jack Brinkley. You can follow the dialogue all
the way through from where the delegate demands the
money to where Brinkley signs off on the bribe.'

'Fuck *you*, man!'

'It's the truth.'

'I need to see that tape. I need to hear that tape. I
need to have that tape verified by a board of fucking
bishops.'

'You will. You can. We can go back to your office
now and play it. You can interview me and I'll tell you
the whole story in my own words. You can photograph
me and plaster my picture across your front page alongside Brinkley's. On one condition.' I closed my eyes and
opened them. Was this really *me* talking? 'Will you, on
your word of honour, before these two witnesses, go
with the story on Sunday? Yes or no?'

In a silence that is with me to this day, I pulled the
shoulder-bag from between my feet, but for security
reasons kept it on my lap. The notepads were in the big
compartment, the seven tapes in the smaller one.
Clutching the bag against my stomach, I unzipped the
smaller compartment, then waited for his answer.

'Terms accepted,' he muttered.

'So yes?'

'So yes, damn you. We'll go on Sunday.'

I turned to Jelly and Sophie, looking each straight in
the eye. 'You heard that. He'll run the story on Sunday
as ever is. Yes?'

'Yes.'

'Yes.'

I put my hand inside and fished. One by one I picked my way through the tapes, looking for tape number five which contained the Haj interrogation, and tape number six which contained Lord Brinkley's voice saying yes to three million dollars. As I watched my fingertips going back and forth across the stack I began, with no particular sense of revelation, to recognise, firstly that there were only five tapes, not seven, then that tapes number five and six were missing. I unzipped the large compartment and felt around among the notepads. For form's sake, I tried the little compartment at the back, which isn't a compartment in any real sense, more a purse for travel tickets or a bar of chocolate. They weren't in there either, and why should they be? They were in Bognor.

By now my head was so busy reconstructing recent events that I wasn't really very interested in the reaction of my audience which, as I recall it, varied from the sceptical—Thorne—to the effusively concerned—Jelly. I made excuses—silly of me, must have left them at home, et cetera. I wrote down Sophie's cellphone number for when I found them. I ignored Thorne's scathing eye and his insinuations about wanting to make a fool of him. I said goodbye to them and see you later, but I don't think any of us believed me, and certainly I didn't. Then I hailed a cab and, without bothering to give the driver a cover destination, drove home to Mr Hakim's.

Did I blame Hannah? Quite the opposite. I felt such a surge of love for her that, even before I gained the privacy of our sanctum, I was marvelling at her courage in the face of adversity—me. Standing before the open wardrobe, I observed with pride, not indignation, that Haj's business card, with his e-mail address scrawled on the back, had gone the way of the tapes. She had known from the start that Brinkley was no good. She had no need of One-Day Courses in security to tell her that in Salvo she was dealing with the remnants of a misguided loyalty that was lodged like a virus in my system and needed to work itself out with time. She didn't want Noah spending his birthday in a war zone. She had gone her own way as I had gone mine. We had both veered from the same path, each in our separate directions, she to her people, I to mine. She had done nothing that required my forgiveness. Propped on the mantelpiece was a copy of the Sunday School kids' programme: 12 noon Picnic lunch and singalong at YMCA hostel ... 2.30 p.m. Matinée performance of *The Wind in the Willows* by the Bognor Dance and Drama Club ... 5.30 p.m. Families Evening. Five hours. Five hours before I could return her message of total and undeviating love.

I switched on the midday news. *Laws are being framed to prosecute Islamist firebrands. Special tribunals to hear terrorist cases in secret. Suspected Egyptian bomber seized by US snatch team in Pakistan. Manhunt continues for thirty-year-old man of Afro-Caribbean origin whom police wish to interview in connection with*—wait for it!—*the suspected murder of two under-age girls.*

Run a bath. Lie in it. Catch myself attempting to reproduce Haj's Mission school jingle. Why does a tortured man sing? she had asked me. Her patients didn't sing, so why did Haj? Why does a grown man chant a dirge about a little girl's virtue when he's been beaten up?

Get out of bath. Clutching my transistor radio, I stand obliquely at the window, clad in my bath towel. Through the net curtains, I contemplate a no-name green van parked close to Mr Hakim's front gate. *Exceptional rainfall in southern India. Reports of landslides. Many feared dead. Now for the cricket.*

Five o'clock. I walk my mile but contrary to One-Day instructors' advice I use the same phone box. I put in a pound and keep another ready, but the best I get is Grace's answering service. If I'm Latzi, I should ring her after 10 p.m. when she'll be in bed *alone*! Hoots of laughter. If I'm Salvo, I should be her welcome guest and leave a love-message for Hannah. I attempt to rise to her invitation:

'Hannah darling, I love you.' But I do not, for security reasons, add, as I might have done: I know what you've done and you were right to do it.

Using side roads I make my desultory way back to Mr Hakim's. Post-bombing bicycles tick past me like ghostly horsemen. The no-name green van is still parked in front of the gates. It displays no parking permit.

Listen to six o'clock news. The world remains where it was at two.

Food as diversion. In the postage-stamp-sized fridge, find half a two-day-old pizza, garlic sausage, pumpernickel bread, gherkins, Marmite for me. When Hannah first arrived in London from Uganda she shared digs with a German nurse and consequently assumed that all English people ate Knackwurst and sauerkraut and drank peppermint tea. Hence a silver packet of same in Mr Hakim's fridge. Like all nurses, Hannah puts everything in the fridge whether or not it is perishable. If you can't sterilise it freeze it, is her axiom. Warm up butter as prelude to spreading on pumpernickel bread. Spread Marmite. Eat slowly. Swallow with caution.

The seven o'clock news is identical to the six o'clock. Can the world really have done nothing for five whole hours? Careless of security considerations, I go online and scroll through the day's trivia. *Suicide bombers in Baghdad have killed forty and injured hundreds*—or is it the other way round? *The newly appointed US Ambassador to the United Nations has filed another fifty objections to proposed reforms. The French President is entering hospital*, or coming out. *His ailments are subject to France's Official Secrets Act*—but it sounds as though he's got a bad eye. *Unconfirmed reports from the Congolese capital Kinshasa speak of a spontaneous outbreak of fighting between rival militias in the eastern region of the country.*

Hannah's rainbow cellphone is ringing. I bound across the room, grab her phone and return to my computer.

'Salvo?'

'Hannah. Marvellous. Hi.'

Sources close to the Congolese government in Kinshasa blame 'imperialist elements in Rwanda'. Rwanda denies involvement.

'You okay, Salvo? I love you so much.' In French, the language of our love.

'Fine. Great. Just longing for you to come back. How about you?'

'I love you so much it's stupid, Salvo. Grace says she never saw anyone so normal go so lovesick.'

The border area with Rwanda is described as peaceful with no unusual traffic.

I'm fighting on three fronts at once, which Maxie would not approve of. I'm trying to listen and speak and decide whether to tell her what I'm seeing when I don't know whether it's our war or someone else's.

'You know what, Salvo?'

'What, my darling?'

'Since I met you I lost three pounds.'

I have to digest this, reason it out. 'Blame the unaccustomed exercise!' I cry. 'Blame *me*!'

'Salvo?'

'What, my love?'

'I did something bad, Salvo. Something I've got to tell you about.'

A British Embassy official in Kinshasa describes rumours of British-led mercenaries in the region as 'fanciful and absurd'.

Of course they are! They must be! The coup is nine days off! Or did Brinkley fire the starting pistol the moment I walked out of his house?

'Listen. You haven't. It's all right. Truly! Whatever it is! Nothing matters! I know all about it. Tell me when you come back!'

Shrill kiddie noises off.

'I've got to go back in there, Salvo.'

'I understand! Go! I love you!'

End of endearments. End of phone call.

Four Swiss aviation technicians who were caught in the crossfire have requested the protection of Bukavu's UN commander.

Seated in the wicker chair with the transistor radio on the table beside me, I embark on a study of Mrs Hakim's wallpaper while I listen to Gavin, our Central Africa correspondent, giving us the story so far:

According to the Congolese government in Kinshasa, a Rwandan-backed putsch has been nipped in the bud, thanks to a brilliantly executed security operation based on first-class intelligence.

Kinshasa suspects French and Belgian complicity, but does not rule out other unnamed Western powers.

Twenty-two members of a visiting African football club are being held for questioning following the discovery of a cache of small arms and heavy machine-guns at Bukavu airport.

No casualties reported. The footballers' country of origin has not yet been ascertained.

The Swiss Embassy in Kinshasa, asked about the four Swiss aviation experts, declines to comment at this stage. Enquiries regarding their travel documents have been passed to Berne.

Thank you, Gavin. End of bulletin. End of any last lingering doubt.

Mrs Hakim's guest lounge is a regal place with deep armchairs and an oil painting of a lakeside paradise with houris dancing on the shore. In one hour from now it will be the haunt of hard-smoking Asian salesmen watching Bollywood videos on a television set as big as a Cadillac, but for the time being it has the sweetened silence of an undertaker's parlour and I am watching the ten o'clock news. Men in shackles change size. Benny has shrunk. Anton is bulky. Spider has grown nine inches since he passed out the plates in his improvised chef's hat. But the star of the show is neither the UN's Pakistani Commandant in his blue helmet, nor the colonel of the Congolese army with his swagger cane, but our skipper Maxie in fawn slacks with no belt and a sweat-soaked shirt minus one sleeve.

The slacks are all that is left of the go-anywhere khaki suit last seen when he was pressing a white envelope on me containing the seven thousand dollars' fee that, in the gallantry of his heart, he prised out of the Syndicate.

His face, deprived of Bogey's enlarging spectacles, lacks the charisma that had cast its spell over me, but in other respects has grown into the part, being formed in an expression of gritty endurance that refuses to acknowledge defeat, no matter how many days it spends at the whipping post. The bulletproof hands are manacled in front of him and folded over one another like a dog's paws. He has one desert boot on, and one bare foot to match the bare shoulder. But it isn't the missing boot that's slowing him down, it's another set of shackles, short ones for a man of his height, and by the look of them too tight. He is staring straight at me and to judge by his vituperative jaw action he is telling me to go fuck myself, until it dawns on me that he must be telling this to the person who is filming him, not me personally.

On Maxie's uneven heels come Anton and Benny, chained to one another and their skipper. Anton has some bruising on the left side of his face which I suspect has been caused by impertinence. The reason Benny looks smaller than actual size is that his chains hunch him downward in a mincing shuffle. His grey ponytail has been cropped to stubble by a single sweep of someone's panga, giving the impression that they've got him ready for the guillotine. After Benny comes Spider, improviser of cattle prods and my fellow sound-thief, chained but upright. He has been allowed to keep his cap, which gives him a certain pertness. Being the acrobat he is, he doesn't have the same problem as his short-stepping mates. Together, the four of them resemble an incompetent conga-party, jerking back and forth to a beat they can't get the hang of.

After the white men come the footballers, some twenty of them in a receding line of miserable black shadows: *veterans, no mavericks, best fighters in the world*. But when I search nervously for a Dieudonné or a Franco, on the off-chance that somehow, in the mayhem of a failed operation, they have been caught up in the main affray, I'm relieved to see neither the hulk of the crippled old warrior nor the spectre of the haggard Banyamulenge leader among the prisoners. I didn't look for Haj because somehow I knew he wouldn't be there. A tidbit relished by commentators is that Maxie—known thus far only as 'the alleged ringleader'—contrived to swallow his Sim-card at the moment of arrest.

I return to our bedroom and resume my study of Mrs Hakim's wallpaper. On the radio, a junior minister of the Foreign Office is being interviewed:

'Our hands are clean as a whistle, thank you, Andrew,' she informs her inquisitor in the feisty language of New Labour at its most transparent. 'HMG is nowhere in this one, trust me. All right, so one or other of the men is British. Give me a break! I'd have thought you'd have had a bit more respect for us, frankly. All the signals *we're* getting say this was a botched, incompetent bit of private enterprise. It's no good saying, "Who by?" all the time because I don't *know* who by! What I *do* know is, it's got amateur written all over it, and whatever else you may think we are, we're not amateurs. And I believe in free speech too, Andrew. Goodnight!'

Maxie has acquired a name. One of his ex-wives spotted him on television. A sweet man who just wouldn't grow up, son of a parson. Sandhurst-trained, ran a mountaineering school in Patagonia, worked under contract to the United Arab Emirates, she says brightly. A Congolese academic calling himself the Enlightener is believed to be the mastermind behind the plot, but he has gone into hiding. Interpol is launching an enquiry. Of Lord Brinkley and his multinationally backed anonymous Syndicate and its designs on the Eastern Congo's resources, nothing. Of Lebanese crooks and independent consultants and their friends, nothing. They were all playing golf, presumably.

I lie on the bed, listening to Mrs Hakim's brass clock chiming out the halves and quarters. I think of Maxie chained to a whipping post. The morning dawns, the sun rises and I am still lying in my bed, unchained. Somehow it's seven o'clock, then eight o'clock. Somehow the quarters keep chiming. The rainbow phone is trilling.

'Salvo?'

Yes, Grace.

Why doesn't she speak? Is she handing the phone to Hannah? Then why doesn't Hannah take it? There's background garble. A man's name is being called by a commanding north country female voice. Who on earth is *Cyril Ainley*? I've never heard of a Cyril or an Ainley.

Where are we? In hospital? In a waiting room somewhere? It's only seconds I'm talking of. Milliseconds,
while I steal every scrap of sound I can get my ears on.

'Is that you, Salvo?'

Yes, Grace. This is Salvo. Her voice is damped right
down. Is she phoning from a place where phones are
forbidden? I can hear other people phoning. Her
mouth is crammed into the mouthpiece, distorting the
sound. She's got a hand cupped over it. Suddenly the
words are pouring out of her: a breathless, demented
monologue that she can't stop even if she wants to, and
neither can I.

'They've got her Salvo who they are God Himself
only knows I'm at the police station reportin' it but I
can't talk too much they took her clean off the pavement from beside me right outside the church we got
rid of the kids and Amelia pretendin' to have a fit and
her mum sayin' we spoiled her and Hannah and me
we're goin' down the hill real cross at the ingratitude
when this car stops and two fellows one black one white
ordinary-lookin' fellows Salvo and a white woman
driver who keeps lookin' straight out ahead of her
through the windscreen never once turns her head the
whole time they get out and the black one says Hi
Hannah and puts his arm round her waist like he's an
old friend and sweeps her into the car and they've gone
and now this nice police lady she's askin' me what kind
of car and showin' me pictures of cars hours it's taken
Hannah never said a word to me she didn't have time

and now the police are sayin' maybe she wanted to go
with those boys maybe this was some guy she was
already goin' with or thought she'd like to earn herself
a few quid on her back with the both of them as if
Hannah would do a thing like that they just snatched
her off the street and the nice police lady is sayin' well
maybe she's on the game and maybe you're the same
Grace there's such a thing as wastin' the time of a police
officer you know it's actually a crime Grace maybe you
should be aware of that I lost my rag why don't you put
a bloody notice up I told her no blacks taken seriously
so now she's talkin' to everybody except me.'

'Grace!'

I said it again. Grace. Three, four times. Then I
questioned her the way we question children, trying to
calm her instead of scaring her. What happened? I don't
mean now, I mean in Bognor, while you were together.
I mean the first night you were there, the night you told
me she was at the movies with the big kids. That night.

'It was a surprise for you, Salvo.'

What kind of surprise?

'She was recordin' somethin' for you, a sound file,
she called it, some piece of music she loved and wanted
to give you. It was a secret.'

So where did she go to do that, Grace?

'Some place Latzi told her, back up a hill somewhere,
no traffic. We called up Latzi at his studio. These music
freaks, they got friends like everywhere, Salvo. So Latzi
knew a guy who knew a guy in Bognor, and Hannah,

she went up to see him, while I kept it secret and that's the whole of it. Jesus Christ, Salvo, what in high Heaven's name is goin' on?'

I ring off. Of course, Grace. Thank you. And having made the sound file from tapes five and six, she popped it into a computer, no doubt Latzi's friend had one, and sent it to Haj's e-mail address for his greater edification, to help him reason with his father whom he respects so much, but as it happened she needn't have bothered, because by then the operation was going up in smoke, and the listeners and watchers and all the other people I had once mistaken for my friends were gathering round her for the kill.

* * *

To catch a sinner, Brother Michael used to say, you must find the sinner in yourself, and in the space of a few moments, that's what I had done. I walked to the wardrobe where my leather jacket was hanging. I fished out my own cellphone, the one I had forbidden myself to use except for messages, and I switched it on. And yes, as expected, I had one new message. But it wasn't from Penelope this time, or Barney, or Hannah. It was from Philip. And Philip was speaking not in his nice beguiling voice but in the iceberg version I was counting on:

I have a number for you to call, Salvo. It's night or day. I also have a deal to propose to you. The

sooner you ring, the more comfortable everyone
will be.

I rang the number and got Sam. She called me Brian,
just like old times. *Got a pencil, Brian dear? And a
notepad? Of course you have, bless you. Here's the address.*

19

I will confess at once that my actions over the next ten minutes were not fully rational, veering as they did between the manic and the administrative. I do not recall violent feelings of rage or anger, although there is later evidence that these and related emotions were simmering below the waterline. My first thought—one of many first thoughts—was for my host and hostess the Hakims, with whom Hannah and I had struck up a warm personal relationship which extended to their two children, a tearaway lad called Rashid who was the apple of Hannah's eye, and the more reticent Diana who spent much time hiding behind the kitchen door on the off-chance that I might pass. I therefore put together a sizeable wad of my ill-gotten wealth and handed it to the bemused Mrs Hakim.

My next first thought, based upon the assumption that I would not be setting foot in the house again for some while, if ever, was to make sure we had left every-thing as shipshape as possible in the circumstances. Being of an obsessively tidy disposition—Penelope under Paula's guidance had termed it *anal*—I stripped the bed of its sheets, removed the pillowcases, puffed up the bare pillows, added the towels from the bathroom and made a neat bundle of laundry in a corner of the room.

Of particular concern to me was what to wear. In this regard I had at the forefront of my mind the fate recently meted out to Maxie and his men, who were self-evidently obliged to make do with a single outfit for many years to come. I settled therefore on a pair of stout corduroy jeans, my faithful leather jacket which had a good few miles left in it, sneakers, my bobble hat, and as many spare shirts, socks and underpants as I could cram into my rucksack. To these I added my most treasured personal items, including the framed photograph of Noah.

As a final act I removed the fateful shoulder-bag from its hiding place behind the wardrobe and, having once more checked the contents and reconfirmed the absence of the two tapes—because sometimes in the passage of the last forty-eight hours fantasy and reality had developed a way of changing places behind my back—I closed the door on our short-lived corner of Paradise, mumbled my last farewells to the mystified Hakims and stepped into the minicab that was waiting to convey me to the address in Regent's Park whither I had been bidden by Sam.

My reconstruction of what follows is as faithful as memory permits, given the disadvantages under which my vision and other faculties were labouring at the time. Drawing up at an elegant house in Albany Crescent, NW1—a couple of million pounds would not have secured it—I was greeted by the sight of two young men in tracksuits tossing a medicine ball back and forth in the front garden. Upon my arrival, they stopped playing and turned to eye me. Undeterred by their interest, I paid off my driver—careful also to add a handsome tip and advanced on the front gate, at which point the nearer of the two boys enquired jauntily whether he could be of assistance.

'Well, perhaps you can,' I replied, equally jauntily. 'It so happens I have come to see Philip on a private matter.'

'Then you've come to the right place, mate,' he replied, and with elaborate courtesy took possession of my rucksack while the second boy helped himself to my shoulder-bag, thereby leaving me unencumbered. The first boy then proceeded down the gravel path to the front door and pushed it open to facilitate my passage, while the second boy, whistling a tune, fell in behind us. The levity of our exchanges is quickly explained. These were the same two blond boys who, attired in tightly buttoned blazers, had stood behind the reception desk of the house in Berkeley Square. Accordingly, they knew me as submissive. I was the meek man who had been delivered to them by Bridget. I had checked in my night-bag with them as ordered. I had sat up on the balcony where I was told to sit, I had been led away by

Maxie. In the psychology of their trade, they had me down as a toothless underdog. This gave me, as I now believe, the element of surprise that I required.

The leading boy was a good four feet ahead of me as we entered the living room, and he was hampered by my rucksack. As a naturally cocky fellow, he was light on his feet, not braced. One thump was enough to send him flying. The boy behind me was at that moment engaged in closing the front door. In Berkeley Square I had observed a surly reluctance in his attitude. It was evident now. Perhaps he knew that, in gulling my shoulder-bag from me, he had landed first prize. A well-aimed kick to the groin put an end to his complacency.

My line of access to Philip now stood wide open. I was across the room in one bound and my hands were instantly round his throat, wrestling with the baby-fat of his chins. What larger intention I had in mind I don't know, and didn't then. I recall the oatmeal-coloured brickwork of the fireplace behind him and thinking I might smash his handsome white head against it. He was wearing a grey suit, white cotton shirt and an expensive necktie of watered red silk which I attempted, unsuccessfully, to use as a garrotte.

Could I have strangled him? I certainly had the madness on me, as my dear late father would have said, plus the power to match, until one of the boys switched it off with whatever he carried: a blackjack or similar, I never saw it. Three months on, I've still got, amid other abrasions, the pullet's-egg on the rear left side of my head. When I came round, Philip was standing safe and sound in front of the same brickwork fireplace, next to a venerable grey-haired lady in tweeds and sensible shoes who even before she had said, 'Brian dear,' could never have been anyone but Sam. She was all the lady tennis umpires you ever saw sitting on the top of their ladders at Wimbledon, advising players six feet beneath them to watch their manners.

Such were my first impressions on waking. I was puzzled by the absence of the two blond boys at first, until by turning my head as far as it would go I located them through the open doorway, seated across the passage from us, watching television without the sound on. It was Test Match time and the Australians were losing. Turning it in the other direction, I was surprised to register the presence of a recording angel in the room, for as such I construed him, male. He was ensconced at a desk in the bay window, which I briefly confused with the bay window in our bedroom at Mr Hakim's. Sunlight was streaming over him, making him divine, despite his bald patch and spectacles. His desk was Uncle Henry's campaign table, with crossed legs you could fold up before hurrying to your next battle. Like Philip he wore a suit, but a shiny one like a chauffeur's, and he was crouching over his table in the manner of a Dickensian clerk afraid of being caught slacking.

'And that's Arthur from the Home Office, Brian dear,' Sam explained, observing my interest. 'Arthur's kindly agreed to sort things out for us at the official level, haven't you, Arthur?'

Arthur didn't presume to answer.

'Arthur has *executive powers*,' Philip elaborated. 'Sam and I haven't. We're purely advisory.'

'And Hannah is in excellent hands, in case you feared otherwise,' Sam went on, in her genial tone. 'She'll be in touch with you just as soon as she gets home.'

Home? What home? Mr Hakim's? The nurses' hostel? Norfolk Mansions? Home as a concept understandably confused me.

'We're very afraid Hannah overstepped the terms of her visa,' Sam explained. 'That's why Arthur's here. To confirm everything, aren't you, Arthur? Hannah came to England to *nurse*, and pass her exams, bless her. And be useful to her country when she gets back. She didn't come here to take part in political agitation. That was never in the job description, was it, Arthur?'

'No way,' Arthur confirmed, speaking in a nasal twang from his eyrie in the window bay. 'It was "nurse only". If she wants to agitate, do it at home.'

'Hannah *marched*, Salvo,' Sam explained, in a commiserating tone. 'More than once, I'm afraid.'

'Marched where?' I asked, through the fog swirling in my head.

'Against Iraq, which wasn't her business at all.'

'Straight infringement,' Arthur observed. '*And* Darfur, which wasn't her business either.'

'That's in addition to her trip to Birmingham, which was *totally* political,' said Sam. 'And now *this*, I'm afraid.'

'This?' I asked, aloud or silently, I'm not sure which.

'Restricted materials,' Arthur pronounced with satisfaction. 'Acquiring, possessing and passing to a foreign power. She's in as deep as she can get. Added to which, the recipient of said material was involved with nongovernmental militias, which makes it straight terrorism.'

I was slowly recovering my faculties. 'She was trying to stop an illegal war,' I shouted, to my surprise. 'We both were!'

Philip, ever the diplomat, stepped in to defuse the situation.

'The point is neither here nor there, surely,' he gently remonstrated. 'London can't be a haven for foreign activists. Least of all when they're over here on a nursing visa. Hannah fully accepted that, irrespective of the legal niceties, didn't she, Sam?'

'Once we'd explained the problem to her, she was fully cooperative,' Sam agreed. 'She was sad, naturally. But she didn't ask for a lawyer, she wasn't tiresome or obstreperous, and she signed her waivers without a murmur. That was because she knew what was best for her. And for you. And for her small boy, of course, her pride and joy. *Noah*. They choose such sweet names, don't they?'

'I demand to talk to her,' I said, or perhaps shouted.

'Yes, well, I'm afraid there are no facilities for talking just now. She's in a holding centre, and you're where you are. And in just a few hours from now she'll be making an entirely voluntary exit to Kampala where she'll be reunited with Noah. What could be nicer than that?'

It took Philip to point the moral:

'She went quietly, Salvo,' he said, looking down at me. 'We expect you to do the same.' He had put on his soft-as-butter voice, but with a dash of official seasoning. 'It has been brought to the attention of the Home Office—by way of Arthur here, who has been extraordinarily helpful in his researches, thank you, Arthur—that the man who calls himself Bruno Salvador is not now and never has been a British subject, loyal or otherwise. In short, he doesn't exist.'

He allowed a two-second silence in memory of the dead.

'Your UK citizenship, with all its rights and privileges, was obtained by subterfuge. Your birth certificate was a lie. You were not a foundling, and your father was never a passing seafarer with a spare baby to get rid of—well, was he?' he went on, appealing to my good sense. 'We can only assume therefore that the British Consul in Kampala at the time of your birth succumbed to the blandishments of the Holy See. The fact that you were not technically of an age to participate in the deception is not, I am afraid, an excuse in law. Am I right, Arthur?'

'What law?' Arthur rejoined in a sprightly tone from the bay. 'There isn't one. Not for him.'

'The hard truth is, Salvo, that as you very well know, or *should* know, you have been an illegal immigrant ever since your ten-year-old feet touched down on Southampton dockside, and in all that time you never once applied for asylum. You simply carried on as if you were one of *us*.'

And here by rights my fury, which was coming and going pretty much of its own accord, should have jerked me out of my armchair for another go at his neck or some other part of his flexible, ultra-reasonable anatomy. But when you are trussed up like a fucking monkey, to use Haj's term, with your hands and ankles taped together, and the whole of you is strapped into a kitchen chair, opportunities for body language are curtailed, as Philip was the first to appreciate, for why else would he be risking an airy smile, and assuring me there is a silver lining even to the darkest cloud?

'The long and the short of it is that the Congolese, we are reliably informed, will—in principle, allowing time obviously for administrative necessities'—indulgent smile—'and a word in the right ear from our Ambassador in Kinshasa, and a birth certificate more representative of the historical realities, shall we say?'—even more indulgent smile—'be delighted to welcome you as their citizen. Welcome you *back*, I should say, since technically you never left them. Only if that makes sense to you, of course. It's your life we're talking about, not ours. But it certainly makes admirable sense to *us*, doesn't it, Arthur?'

'Go where he likes, far as we're concerned,' Arthur confirms from the bay. 'Long as it's not here.'

Sam in her motherly way agrees wholeheartedly with both Philip and Arthur. 'It makes perfect sense to Hannah too, Salvo. And why should we hog all their best nurses, anyway? They're desperate. And frankly, Salvo, when you think about it, what has England without Hannah got to offer you? You're not thinking of going back to Penelope, I trust?'

Taking these matters as settled, Philip helps himself to my shoulder-bag, unzips it, and counts the notepads and tapes onto the table one by one.

'*Marvellous*,' he declares, like a conjuror delighted with his trick. 'And Hannah's two make the full seven. Unless of course you ran off duplicates. Then there *really* wouldn't be any saving of you. Did you?'

I'm suddenly so drowsy that he can't hear my reply, so he makes me repeat it, I suppose for the micro-phones.

'Wouldn't have been secure,' I say again, and try to go back to sleep.

'And that was your only copy of *J'Accuse!* I take it? The one you gave to Thorne?' he goes on, in the tone of somebody wrapping up the final details.

I must have nodded.

'Good. Then all we have left to do is smash your hard disk,' he says with relief, and beckons to the blond boys in the doorway, who untie me but leave me on the ground while I get my circulation back.

'So how's Maxie doing these days?' I enquire, hoping to bring a blush to his creaseless cheeks.

'Yes, well, poor Maxie, alas for him!' Philip sighs, as if reminded of an old friend. 'As good as they come in that business, they tell me, but oh so headstrong. And silly of him to have jumped the gun.'

'You mean silly of Brinkley,' I suggest, but the name is unfamiliar to him.

There is business, as they say in the theatre world, about hauling me to my feet. After the whack on the head, I am heavier than I was, and one boy is not enough. Once they've got me standing, Arthur places himself in front of me, officiously pulling down the skirts of his jacket. He reaches into his breast pocket, produces a brown envelope marked ON HER MAJESTY'S SERVICE and slaps it into my unresisting hand.

'You have accepted this notice in the presence of witnesses,' he announces to a larger room. 'Kindly read it. *Now.*'

The printed letter, when I am finally able to focus on it, tells me I am an unwanted person. Arthur gives me one of Haj's Parker pens. I make a few passes with it and scrawl a ragged version of my signature. Nobody shakes hands, we're too British, or we were. I fall in between the two boys. We step into the garden and they walk me to the gate. It's a sweltering day. What with the bomb scares and half the city on holiday, there's barely a soul about. A dark green van with no name and no windows has pulled up in front of the house. It's the twin of the van that sat outside the Hakims' boarding house, perhaps the same one. Four men in denims emerge from it and walk towards us. Their leader wears a policeman's cap.

'This one trouble?' he asks.

'Not now he isn't,' says a blond boy.

20

An interpreter, Noah, even a top one, when he has nothing to interpret except himself, is a man adrift. Which is how I've come to write all this down without quite knowing whom I was writing to, but now I know it's you. It will be a few years yet before you are called upon to decipher what Mr Anderson liked to call my Babylonian cuneiform, and when you do, I hope to be there beside you, showing you how it works, which won't be a problem provided you know your Swahili.

Watch out, my dearest adopted son, for anything in your life marked SPECIAL. It's a word with many meanings, none good. One day I will read you *The Count of Monte Cristo*, a favourite of my late Aunt Imelda's. It's about the most *special* prisoner of them all. There are quite a lot of Monte Cristos in England now, and I am one of them.

A *special* van has no windows but special facilities on the floor for special detainees who for their safety and comfort are strapped to it for the three-hour journey. Lest they have it in mind to disturb the public peace with screams of protest, a special leather gag is provided at no extra cost.

Special prisoners have numbers instead of names. Mine is Two Six.

A special hospitality block is a cluster of repainted Nissen huts, built for our gallant Canadian allies in 1940 and surrounded by enough barbed wire to keep out the entire Nazi army, which is all right for the many British who still believe they are fighting the Second World War, but less all right for the incarcerated inmates of Camp Mary.

Why our camp should be named after the Mother of Christ is officially unknown. Some say the first Canadian commandant was a devout Catholic. Mr J. P. Warner, formerly of the Royal Corps of Military Police and now Special Hospitality Officer, has a different story. According to him, Mary was a lady of the local town of Hastings who, in the darkest days of the war when Britain stood alone, favoured an entire platoon of Canadian pioneers between the hours of last parade and curfew the same evening.

My early brushes with Mr Warner gave no hint of the warm relationship that would develop between us, but from the day he felt able to partake of Maxie's munificence, the bond was formed. He has no quarrel with darkies, he assures me, his grandfather having served in the Sudan Defence Force, and his father with our distinguished colonial police in Kenya during the troubles.

Special inmates enjoy special rights:

- the right not to venture beyond the borders of our compound
- the right not to join the dawn trek into town with other inmates, not to sell unscented roses to motorists at traffic lights, not to clean the wind-screens of their BMWs in exchange for a few words of abuse
- the right to remain silent at all times, to make and receive no phone calls, to send no letters, and to receive only such incoming items as have been previously approved by Authority and thereafter handed to me as a personal favour by Mr J. P. Warner, whose responsibilities, he assures me, are awesome.

'I'm not listening to you, Two Six,' he likes to advise me, wagging his finger in my face. 'It's air I'm sitting with,' he will add, accepting another glass of my Rioja. 'Not flesh and bone at all.' Yet Mr Warner is a shrewd listener who has swum in all the oceans of life. He has managed military prisons in far outposts—and even, long ago, for misdemeanours he refuses to divulge, had a taste of his own medicine. 'Conspiracies, Two Six, are not a problem. Everybody conspires, nobody gets done. But if it's cover-up time, God help us all.'

There is comfort of a sort in knowing you are one of a kind.

* * *

Looking back, it was inevitable that my confinement at
Camp Mary should have got off to a bad start. I see that
now. Just arriving at Reception with SPECIAL stamped all
over me was enough to put hackles up. To have PV in
addition against my name—PV standing these days for
POTENTIALLY VIOLENT—well, you get whatever you
deserve, as I learned when, in a spirit of solidarity, I
joined a sit-in of Somalis on the roof of the old vicarage
that serves as Camp Mary's headquarters. Our message
to the world was peaceful. We had wives and Sunday
School kids in bright cottons. The bed-sheets that we
held out to the beam of the camp's searchlights were
daubed with conciliatory words: DON'T SEND US HOME
TO BE TORTURED, MR BLAIR! WE WANT TO BE TORTURED
HERE! In one very important sense I was however at
variance with my fellow demonstrators. While they
were on their knees begging for permission to stay, I
couldn't wait to be deported. But in confinement, team
spirit is all, as I discovered to my cost when a contingent
of no-name policemen in motorcycle helmets dispersed
us with the aid of baseball bats.

Yet nothing in life, Noah, even a few broken bones,
is without its reward. As I lay in that sick bay, manacled
to the four corners of the bed and thinking there was
little enough of life to live for, enter Mr J. P. Warner
with the first of the fifteen weekly letters I have received
from the hand of your beloved mother. As a condition
of going quietly, she had with typical bravura prised an
address out of her captors where she could write to me.

Much of what she wrote is not yet for your young eyes or ears. Your mother, though chaste, is a passionate woman and speaks freely of her desires. But one cool evening, when you are very old, and you have loved as I have, I hope you will light a fire and sit beside it and read how, with every page your mother wrote to me, she brought tears of joy and laughter running down my prisoner's cheeks, washing away all thoughts of self-pity or despair.

The strides she is making in life more than compensate for my immobility. No mere Degree Nurse Hannah any more, but Sister Hannah in a brand-new teaching ward in the absolute best hospital in Kampala! And still somehow finding time to continue her studies in simple surgical procedures! On Grace's advice, she tells me, she has bought herself a temporary wedding ring to keep the wolves at bay till the day I am able to equip her with the permanent variety. And when a young intern groped her in the operating theatre, she gave him such a talking-to that he apologised to her three days running, then invited her to spend the weekend at his cottage, so she gave him another.

My one anxiety is that she may not know I have forgiven her for removing tapes five and six from my shoulder-bag and transmitting them without my prior knowledge to Haj. If only she could understand that there was never anything to forgive in the first place! And if she can't, will she, as a good Mission girl, turn her back on me in favour of a man who has nothing to reproach her with? Such are the ingenious terrors which imprisoned lovers inflict upon themselves in the endless hours of the night.

And there was one letter, Noah, that for want of moral courage I at first declined to open at all. The envelope was thick, oily brown and faintly lined, a sure warning that Britain's secret overworld was about to make its presence felt. For reasons of security, it bore a normal first-class stamp instead of the printed logo declaring it to be On Her Majesty's Service. My name, number and the camp's address, accurate in every detail, were written in a hand as familiar to me as my own. For three days it stood staring at me from my window-sill. At length, fortified by an evening passed with J. P. Warner and a bottle of Rioja procured for me with Maxie's ill-gotten wealth, I grabbed a soft plastic knife that is designed to spare me self-harm and slit its throat. I read the covering letter first. Plain white A4 paper, no watermark, address LONDON and the date.

Dear Salvo,

I am not officially familiar with the writer of the enclosed, neither have I perused its contents, which are in French. Barney assures me they are of a personal nature and not obscene. As you know, I do not believe in intruding upon the private domain unless the interests of Our Nation are at stake. It is my sincere wish that you will one day remember our collaboration in a more favourable light, since it is essential that Man at all times be protected from himself.

Yours ever,
R. (Bob) Anderson.

By now of course my eye had lighted on the second envelope to which Mr Anderson's covering letter made such tantalising reference. It was bulky and addressed in electronic print to Monsieur l'interprète Brian Sinclair at his post-office box number in Brixton. The sender's name, embossed in sky blue on the back, was given as the Comptoir Joyeux de Bukavu: a play, I quickly deduced, on Haj's full name of Honoré Amour-Joyeuse. The contents were not so much a letter as a wad of random jottings done over a space of days and nights. When I closed my eyes and sniffed the pages, I swear I inhaled the whiff of a woman's scent, and J. P. Warner said the same. The text was in French, hand-written in a meticulous academic style that even in hurried circumstances did not desert him, any more than did his scatological vocabulary.

Dear Zebra,

Tapes weren't necessary. You screwed me, I screwed them.

Who the fuck's Hannah?

Why does she talk a lot of medical crap at me and tell me to get my arse checked by a urologist?

And why does she tell me to stand up to my revered father Luc, and here's the evidence to help me do it?

I didn't need any fucking evidence. As soon as I got home I told Luc that if he didn't want to end up dead and bankrupt the first thing he should do was pull the plug on the Mwangaza.

The second thing he should do was advise the Mai Mai and the Banyamulenge they were making horses' arses of themselves.

The third thing he should do was confess his soul to the nearest UN big cheese, and the fourth thing he should do was take an extended holiday in Alaska.

Hannah says you're in deep shit in England, which knowing you does not surprise me. She prays that one day you may make it to the Congo. Well, maybe if you do, I'll behave like all the best crooks and endow a teaching post at the university of Bukavu, currently a disaster zone. And I won't give a fuck whether you teach languages or beer-drinking.

And make haste, because not all God's little angels at the gates of Heaven will protect Hannah's virtue from her wicked Uncle Haj's clutches when she comes back to Kivu.

In Bukavu it's business as usual. It rains nine months a year and when the drains back up, Independence Square becomes Independence

Lake. Most weeks we can offer riots, demos and shoot-outs, although timings are unpredictable. A couple of months back, our home football team lost a big match, so the crowd lynched the referee and the police shot the only six guys who were doing absolutely nothing. None of this deters white Bible-thumping American evangelists with perfect hair telling us to love George Bush, and not fuck any more because God doesn't like it.

There's an old Belgian priest here who got shot in the arse a few years back. Now and then he drops in on one of my nightclubs to get a free drink and talk about the good old days. When he mentions your father, he smiles. When I ask him why, he smiles a bit more. My guess is, your father screwed for the whole Mission.

My house in the Muhumba district is a Belgian colonial bastard's palace at the lake's edge, but he must have been a decent sort of bastard because he built a Garden of Eden all the way down to the water, with every flower you heard of and some you didn't. Candle trees, bottlebrush trees, aloe trees, bougainvillea, hibiscus, jacaranda, agapanthus and arrowroot, but my orchids are a fuck-up. We've got spiders the size of mice, and mouse birds with fluffy heads and long tails, in case you've forgotten. Our weaver birds have a great technique for pulling girls. The male weaves a nest on spec, then talks the girl inside. If she likes what she sees, they fuck. Tell that to your evangelists.

I meant to say that this garden has a bungalow. I built it for my sainted wet-nurse who took one look at it and died. She was the only woman I loved and never fucked. It has a tin roof and a verandah and is presently occupied by about a million butterflies and mosquitoes. If you ever make it to Bukavu, have it. The Goma cheese is still okay, the lights go out for three hours a day, but nobody puts out the lights on the fishing boats at night. Our leaders are total arseholes who can't think beyond the level of five-year-olds. Not long ago, our masters in the World Bank conducted a lifestyle survey of the Congo. Question: If the State was a person, what would you do to it? Answer: We would kill him. We have Black Awareness but every street hawker in town is selling skin-lightener guaranteed to give you cancer. Young Congolese talk of Europe as the promised land. So be aware: if you make it here, you're going to look like a rejected zebra. The elections won't deliver solutions but they're ours. We have a constitution. We have kids with polio and kids with the plague who are feeling richer by three million dirty dollars. One day, we may even have a future.

HAJ

We are on the coast here too, Noah. Each morning my heart rises with the autumn sun. Each evening it sinks. But if I bring my chair to the window, and there's a good moon shining, I can just make out a sliver of sea a mile beyond the wire. And that's where their England ends and my Africa begins.

ACKNOWLEDGEMENTS

Sincere thanks to Stephen Carter, my indefatigable researcher; to Brigid and Bob Edwards for journalistic and spiritual counsel; and to Sonja and John Eustace for matters nursing and medical. I am deeply indebted also to Jason Stearns of the International Crisis Group for his unique expertise and guidance during my brief visit to the Eastern Congo; to Al Venter, renowned veteran and chronicler of mercenary warfare; and to Michela Wrong, author of the splendid *In the Footsteps of Mr Kurtz* and *I Didn't Do It For You*, for giving so generously of her wisdom and editorial creativity. It is a convention in these cases to protest that the opinions expressed in this novel are, like its errors, mine alone. Such, as Salvo would say, is indeed the case. It is equally true that without my wife, Jane, I would still be floundering around page sixteen and wondering how two years had flitted by unnoticed.

John le Carré
Cornwall, 2006

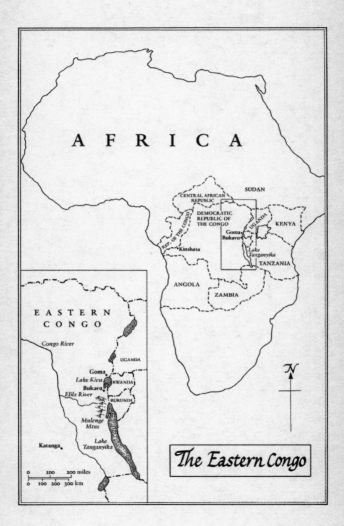

AFRICA

CENTRAL AFRICAN
REPUBLIC

SUDAN

REP. OF THE CONGO

DEMOCRATIC
REPUBLIC OF
THE CONGO

UGANDA

KENYA

Goma
Bukavu

Kinshasa

Lake
Tanganyika

TANZANIA

ANGOLA

ZAMBIA

EASTERN
CONGO

Congo River

UGANDA

Goma
Lake Kivu
Bukavu
Elila River

RWANDA

BURUNDI

Mulenge
Mtns

Katanga

Lake
Tanganyika

0   100   200 miles
0   100 200 300 km

The Eastern Congo